THE NIGHTMARE BRIDE

SHAYLIN GANDHI

ALSO BY SHAYLIN GANDHI

Contemporary Romance

When We Had Forever

Love Letters for Other People

Fantasy Romance

Once Charmed, Twice Cursed

Song of the Hundred-Year Summer

FOR MORE

For bonus content, ARC opportunities, and subscriber-only updates, please join my newsletter:

shaylingandhi.com/news

I.

The night before Amryssa's wedding, I readied her for bed as usual. Her groom hadn't yet arrived, but already, dread clamped my lungs in a vise. He would come. By this time tomorrow, another monster would stalk the halls of this old house, and I...

Well, I would have to do something about that. About *him*.

I tried to escape that awareness by bustling from one task to the next. I lowered the wick on Amryssa's bedside oil lamp. Draped her nightgown across the foot of her bed. My movements flowed with the ease of familiarity, but tonight, even the careworn rituals failed to soothe me.

This knot in my belly had been tightening for months, ever since Amryssa's father had agreed to marry her off to Elara's youngest prince. To worsen matters, Prince Kyven would stay with us after the wedding. He'd *live* here.

A wave of nausea swelled in my throat.

"Harlowe."

I yanked my gaze up. Over near the open window, Amryssa scanned the sky with pale eyes.

"What?" I said, unnerved by her tone. "What's wrong?"

"There's a nightmare," she murmured. "Heading this way."

I tensed, wanting to doubt her, but my best friend never joked. About anything. "*Another* one? But we just had one last week."

Amryssa didn't respond, but she didn't have to—a breeze billowed in, ruffling her skirts, drenching the room with the sticky brine of the sea. A whiff of fire, like burnt parchment, rode the edges of the gust. That distinctive smell turned a thousand screws inside my guts.

"Shit," I muttered.

"It's a bad one, too," Amryssa said.

My hand flew to the dagger sheathed at my waist. The weapon wouldn't protect me against a nightmare, but the feel of the antler hilt steadied me, anyway. "How far off?"

Amryssa studied the sky. Sickly violet light glinted on her cheekbones, hinting at what massed in the sky above the moss-draped trees. Long seconds passed without an answer.

"*Amryssa.*"

She blinked. "Hmm?"

I sighed. Her mind had clearly wandered. Again. "How much time do we have?"

"Oh. Twenty minutes, perhaps."

Twenty... Damn. So close, already? Why hadn't anyone sounded the bells?

I tossed her nightgown aside and arrowed toward the window. Against the cracked and weather-beaten frame, Amryssa looked almost ethereal tonight—a fragile, albino flower amidst this sea of faded finery. Her bone-white curls frothed on the breeze.

"Come on." I took her by the shoulders. "Let's get you ready."

Her gaze didn't stray from the sky. "But...I don't suppose you'd let me go outside?"

My mouth twisted. Always the same question, with her. "No, Am. You know how that'd end."

"Right. But...what about the prince? Has he arrived yet?"

I grimaced. Fuck the prince. More importantly, fuck the forest, with its twisted purple trees and their putrid purple glow and the bullshit purple weather they produced. I was sick of it, though more for Amryssa's sake than my own. Within the hour, she'd be screaming more loudly than I would, and gods help me, how I hated hearing her misery.

"No sign of your fiancé yet," I told her.

"Shouldn't we wait, then? Make sure he gets to safety?"

"And risk ourselves? For *him*? I'd rather chew on nails." I steered her from the window, then yanked the shutters closed without glancing out. No need to witness the coming carnage for myself. Already, fear coated my throat, thick and sour.

"But what if he gets caught out in the nightmare?" Amryssa said.

My fingers paused on the shutter-latch as a spark of hope flared beneath my ribs. "Then Zephyrine will have answered her first prayer in nine years."

That was the thing about living in the only territory in Elara whose patron deity had fallen asleep—no divine ears heard our pleas. No godly caretaker granted our most fervent wishes. Here in Oceansgate, we were on our own.

But since our slumbering goddess, Zephyrine, also dreamed these nightmares into existence, the prince getting overtaken by one might actually count as divine intervention. *Unintentional* divine intervention, but whatever.

I'd take what I could get.

"Whose prayer?" Amryssa's voice shrank. "You haven't wished my fiancé dead, have you?"

I snorted. "I've wished lots of people dead. *Especially* hateful princes who marry seneschal's daughters against their will." I rammed the shutter-bolt home, then locked it with the keyring from my skirt pocket. There. If Amryssa somehow got loose during the nightmare, she wouldn't be able to swan dive from the tower window.

When I turned, she regarded me with stricken eyes. Their color was so unearthly—not quite green, not quite gray, but some pale in-between, like tidepool water captured in two porcelain bowls. That look seemed to demand something of me—to be softer, maybe? Kinder, like other women?

Well, she'd have to hold her breath on that one.

"We don't *know* that Kyven's hateful," Amryssa said. "Not when we haven't met him."

A retort swelled in my throat, quickly smothered. *I* knew precisely how awful he was, though I hadn't shared that with her just yet. Maybe I'd never have to. With any luck, the nightmare would catch the prince on the road. He was coming from Elara's distant capital, miles and miles away, and had probably never been to our swampy, out-of-the-way backwater before. The tiny territory of Oceansgate dangled into the sea from the toe of the continent, so even if Prince Kyven had heard of our unique weather—discussed it from the safety of some palatial dining room in Hightower, maybe—he wouldn't understand the true power of a nightmare.

Or how to survive one.

Which might just spare me from having to sink my blade into his heart. For weeks, I'd sifted through options, only to circle back to one conclusion.

Amryssa's groom would have to die. The only question was when. Should I kill him before the vows? After, at the nuptial feast? Maybe in their chamber, before he coerced her in the marriage bed?

I hadn't decided yet, but now a new possibility massed in the sky outside. One that might save me from spending my remaining years in a dank prison cell.

"Come on," I said. "Let's get you to bed."

Amryssa blew out a breath, clearly having had her fill of my murderous intentions, and padded over to the four-poster. I freed her of her dress, then sheathed her insubstantial frame with the nightgown I'd laid out.

My attention snagged on a rip in the gown's collar, but mending would have to wait. I'd stitch it tomorrow, once I recovered.

As Amryssa laid atop her threadbare sheets, the nightmare boomed outside. I paused to breathe through the resulting dizziness, then hurried to her armoire, where the bottom drawer yielded at a touch—one of the only things in this rambling house that didn't squeak or stick, the hinges having been oiled to perfection. I dug for

Amryssa's manacles. Metal clanked as I carried the restraints to the bed.

She offered her arm, and I snapped a cuff around one dainty wrist. Outside, the nightmare growled again, rattling the walls, probing for cracks in my composure. Its bellowing reminded me of a dying animal, overlaid with a rustle of dark wings, like that last, futile warning before sharpened talons pierced your flesh and sank into your heart.

Amryssa whimpered. "Maybe if you'd let me go outside, I—"

"No." Steel girded my voice.

"But—"

"*No.*" I snapped a manacle around her other wrist.

She averted her face in defeat.

My stomach soured. Normally, I never denied her, but whatever screws had come loose in Amryssa's mind confused her. Unlike other people, she longed to flee *into* the arms of the approaching horror, not away.

As the house's resident keymistress, I made sure she didn't. That comprised my entire purpose here—a purpose that would soon fall to someone else, once the prince showed up. I only hoped Amryssa's father would find someone worthy to bequeath my dagger to once I committed regicide and got myself taken away in irons.

But even if he didn't, at least I'd go knowing Amryssa would never suffer Prince Kyven's punishing touch.

I hurried around the bed, restraining her ankles, then unwinding her bedpost chains and clipping each one to a manacle. Once I'd fastened everything tight, I turned the crank to take the slack out of the chains.

When I finished, Amryssa lay spread-eagled but secure. She gazed at the shutters with longing, as if the storm-tossed marsh outside might offer more safety than this tattered haven of mahogany and silk. "If the prince *is* out there, might he make it through?"

I laughed with savage humor. "Not a chance."

Moisture welled in Amryssa's eyes. Apparently, she couldn't stand the thought of anything suffering, even a creature as vile as Elara's youngest prince. "Surely there's a *chance*. What about the brigands in the woods? They endure the nightmares without—"

"That's a myth, Am. They chain up like everyone else. No one can withstand a nightmare's power."

"But Kyven could *die* out there." A tear slipped from between her lashes. "I might not want to marry him, but I'd never wish him harm."

"I know." I brushed at her tear, my fingertips lingering. Gods help me, she was so pure. So *noble*, and not because she'd someday succeed her father as seneschal, or because her family had governed Oceansgate for generations, or any of that nonsense.

Some people were just born better than the rest of us.

But I didn't have time to stand around thinking about it, so I dried my fingers on my skirts and arranged Amryssa's coverlet. The fabric tented weirdly over her chains, but it would have to do.

Still, I hung back before leaving. What if, once I scraped myself together tomorrow, I returned to find a dried-out husk in this bed? What if this frail, beautiful, scrap of a person couldn't weather the coming ordeal?

"Go." Anxiety thickened Amryssa's voice, though she didn't worry for herself, I knew. She only ever put others first, whether they deserved it or not. "Sound the alarm. Kyven might be close enough to hear."

I hesitated. Time already ran short, but...I couldn't abandon her like this.

"Hey." I sat, my body denting the mattress while Amryssa's merely floated atop it. "I'm sure your groom'll be fine. He's probably coming up the road as we speak."

Or not. I hoped he was miles away. I hoped he died screaming.

"In which case I'll have to marry him." Amryssa's voice quavered. "Tomorrow."

"Well...yes."

"Which frightens me, Harlowe. What husbands expect of their wives, it's..." A shudder rippled through her, one I knew had nothing to do with the nightmare bearing down on us. "I find it difficult to think about. Much less desire."

"I know." I brushed a white tendril back from her brow. "Which is why I'd spare you, if I could. I'd marry Kyven myself, if it meant you wouldn't have to."

She managed a watery smile. "Would you really?"

"In a heartbeat."

"Then I could be *your* keymistress. Wouldn't that be nice?"

I echoed her smile. Marrying the prince would be the exact opposite of nice, but it *would* get me close enough to slide my dagger between his ribs. Which I'd find a way to do, regardless. This bullshit arrangement Olivian had entered into on his daughter's behalf would never see fruition.

But I couldn't reassure Amryssa of that. She'd only try to stop me.

Precious seconds died one after the next. The nightmare rumbled, close enough now that its sinister energy leached in through the shutter-gaps. The candlelight took on a hissing quality.

"You have to go," Amryssa pleaded. "Sound the alarm. If not for the prince's sake, then for the townspeople's."

I sighed, not the least bit put out by risking hundreds of lives in order to caress her cheek one last time. The people of Oceansgate could look after themselves. Or perish, for all I cared, and take their dagger-sharp stares with them. Those, and the whispers of *witch, witch, witch*.

I really didn't give a shit.

But I *did* have to get myself to safety, so I rose and kissed Amryssa's forehead. "I'll be back when it's over. Once I can stand. All right?"

She nodded.

I made for the door. I would have just enough time to sound the bells at the house's far end before scuttling back to my chamber, which neighbored this one. By now, I could chain myself in a minute flat.

"Harlowe?"

I paused, my hand on the knob. "Yes?"

"The storm, it...calls to me." Amryssa closed her eyes, sealing herself into some private darkness. Her thin chest heaved under her thinner nightgown. "It tells me to go outside. To let it overtake me. Call me home."

Outside, thunder boomed. The chamber flexed and contracted; Amryssa's words seemed to stagger toward me from across a handful of miles.

Nausea threatened, but I willed it down. "That isn't real, Am. Nothing that's about to happen is. It's just the nightmare, twisting your mind. *Tricking* you."

"Right," she said faintly. "You're...right. Of course."

I hovered on the threshold, hating myself for doing this to her. I could have unlocked her restraints. Tossed them aside. I *wanted* to. But anyone who wandered out into a nightmare would never do it twice. The storm would invade their mind, showing them imagined horrors, turning their darkest fears against them. They'd be driven to end that misery any way they could—whether by jumping from a tower window or clawing out their own heart.

Not the kind of thing anyone came back from.

No, my job was to keep Amryssa safe, so my hand rose to the dagger at my waist, seeking its reassuring hum of magic. If I concentrated, I could make out its whispered words. *Protect, protect, protect. Guard her where she belongs.*

I squeezed the dagger in acknowledgment. I *would* protect. After all, Amryssa had done the same for me, once. She'd saved my life when not a single soul had cared if I'd lived or died. She'd risked herself and asked nothing in return.

Outside, thunder cracked. The buzz in my blood reached a fever pitch, spilling over into a tight smile.

"I love you," I said, knowing I'd do anything for her. Lie, cheat, steal. Lock her up. Whatever it took. "And I'll keep you safe, no matter what."

Her smile was tremulous. "I love you, too. Always."

"Then I'll see you when it's over, okay?"

"When it's over," she agreed.

At that, I turned away, and locked her door behind me.

2.

I'd made it halfway across the house and was hurrying down a hallway lined with tatty velvet wallpaper when I ran into a housemaid.

She stood motionless in the middle of the corridor. Broken white chunks littered the carpet at her feet—remnants of a plaster bust that had clearly taken a dive from its pedestal.

"I didn't mean to," she whispered in horror. "I was dusting, and heard the thunder, and..." Her throat worked as she aimed a helpless glance at me.

I surveyed the wreckage. The sculpture had been worthless, like everything else in this house, but Olivian would rage over its demise, regardless. Olivian raged over *everything*. But right now, that was the least of our concerns.

"Worry about it later," I said. "For now, just get to your room. Chain up."

As if in warning, thunder rumbled, making the wall-sconces flicker. Their anemic light did little to dispel the darkness—already, the nightmare permeated the house, driving the candleglow into retreat.

"But the seneschal," the housemaid warbled. "If he sees this, he'll

9

fire me. And then I won't be able to—" She bit her lip, cutting herself off.

I took her measure. We weren't friendly, exactly, but I was fairly sure her name was Althea. I also knew what she'd hesitated to say—that she had family in town, two young brothers she routinely snuck food to.

Yet another thing Olivian would've raged about, if he'd known. Here in the seneschal's house, we could barely feed ourselves. But the townspeople were no better off than we were, and Althea's brothers relied on her.

"I won't tell," I said. "He won't know it was you."

"But—"

"Harlowe," someone barked.

I startled. Down the hall, a hulking shape emerged from the shadows.

My stomach dropped—Olivian was coming, and if he saw this mess, he'd do as Althea had said. He'd dismiss her. Her brothers would starve, and while I didn't care for the people of Oceansgate, those boys were only innocent children.

"Go," I hissed. "Before he sees."

Althea's eyes widened. "But he'll think you did this."

"So let him."

She hesitated a moment longer, but when thunder boomed and the shadows clawed their way up the walls, she choked out a thank-you and fled.

And only just in time. The seneschal stopped before me, a bear of a man with bloodshot eyes and thick black hair that defied gravity. His morning coat was as rumpled as the rest of him, and spittle flecked his beard, as if he'd just concluded a screaming match with some unfortunate soul. "Harlowe."

"Olivian."

His gaze flicked to the wreckage at my feet. "What's the meaning of this?"

"It was an accident. I was on my way to sound the bells and bumped into a pedestal."

Anger blazed in his eyes, so I squared my shoulders and drew myself up to my full height. Olivian wouldn't fire me like he would Althea. At least, I *hoped* not.

"Did you secure my daughter, at least?" he snapped.

"Of course." As if I would be standing here, otherwise. As if I wouldn't die before risking Amryssa. "Her safety comes first. Always. You know that."

His jaw worked. "Fine. But I've sent Merron to sound the alarm, so you needn't bother."

The nightmare rumbled. I braced against a wave of vertigo while the seneschal did the same—his chest heaved as he swayed on his feet. Around us, shadows leapt, the darkness coming to life.

When reality finally stopped trembling, I gasped out, "But Merron should be chaining himself. Not dealing with the bells."

As if on cue, a clang rolled down the hallway, then another, gathering strength until the peals rode atop one another. I imagined Merron working the heavy ropes, his arms flexing while sweat beaded in his brown hair.

Goddess, he needed to get to his room. *Now.*

"Don't worry about him." Olivian's grizzled features hardened. "You have a different task, tonight. You'll go downstairs and await Amryssa's intended. Ensure the prince is safely secured."

"I'll...what?" Shit. Olivian might not be firing me, but I hadn't escaped punishment, apparently. "But there's no time. Kyven'll have to take care of himself."

Olivian glared. "I don't pay you to argue, girl."

"Pay me? You don't pay me at all."

"Don't I?" His reddened eyes strayed to the weapon at my belt. "You realize I could give that dagger to someone else, don't you?"

I flinched, though I knew what Olivian saw when he looked at me —no one special. No one of worth. Just a stubborn, foul-mouthed girl with a mean streak, who Amryssa had chosen as her protectress for some inexplicable reason.

In fairness, I couldn't argue. I knew I didn't deserve her. Or this house, shabby and faded as it was. Nor did I deserve the weapon at my waist, which granted me abilities I'd never earned.

But without those things, my life would amount to nothing, so I wouldn't relinquish the dagger unless I had to.

"Look," I said, reining in my frustration. "Why don't I go wait on my balcony? I'll call down, tell the prince how to chain up. But I won't go outside. Not even Amryssa could ask that of me."

"Kyven *must* survive this nightmare. He must marry my daughter."

"Right. So you've said. Without once asking Amryssa how she feels about it."

Olivian's eyes slitted. A feverish glint festered there, one that never guttered out, even between nightmares. "I don't need to. I'm her father. I decide what serves her best."

I ground my teeth, but again, I couldn't argue, if only because his reasons for this hare-brained match escaped me. I could guess the king's motives easily enough—a decaying estate on the southernmost fringes of civilization offered the perfect exile for the youngest and most sadistic of his sons. But what did Olivian stand to gain? Political favor? Money to revive Oceansgate's dwindling coffers? A means to shackle Amryssa to this place by looping yet another chain around her ankle?

I had no idea, and the seneschal refused to explain.

"Enough." Warning dripped from Olivian's words. "Go. Now. If the prince dies, I'll hold you responsible."

A feral smile worked its way across my lips. If the prince died, I'd welcome any punishment. "Fine. Works for me."

Olivian hesitated, thrown by my agreement. Around us, shadows coalesced to threatening dark pools. Ghostly shapes oozed at the periphery of my vision. Something with a dozen too many legs skittered along the baseboards.

My stomach quivered. We needed to chain up, but this toxic pissing contest seemed more important than the demonic energy piling in the hallway.

At least to me. Maybe not to Olivian—his focus jumped to something past my shoulder. Something I knew wasn't actually there.

"You again." He paled. "Haven't I told you to leave me be?"

I grinned. "Time to go," I said, sing-song.

Olivian turned to me with wild eyes, then rushed off.

My smile fell from my lips like it had dropped dead. I tried to hurry back the way I'd come, but thunder rippled, buckling my knees. I flung out a hand to steady myself, but the wallpaper turned sticky beneath my touch, sucking at my fingertips like a hungry mouth. I yanked myself away, my stomach roiling.

More thunder ruptured the air. This time, the sconce-lights ran together, and when they resolidified, the hallway curved downward instead of running straight.

I broke into a run, ignoring the illusory warp of physics long enough to reach my chamber and throw myself inside. I crossed the room with desperate strides. At a twitch of the latch, my balcony doors burst inward with such force they cracked against the wallpaper.

Salt-soaked wind poured in. I breathed deep and angled a shoulder into the gale.

Out on my balcony, the world heaved, a tornadic whirl of wind and darkness. To my left, the swamp pulsed like a glowing bruise. To my right, the road snaked toward town and the sea. But the storm eclipsed all that. I craned my head back, then back some more.

Indigo clouds hung in the sky like a gruesome planet on the verge of collision. Hellish lightning crackled within. The storm's stench singed my nostrils, like someone had blown out a match and shoved it up my nose, still sizzling.

My heart shriveled. A thousand times, I'd wished the prince dead, hoping Zephyrine might somehow hear me. I'd even whispered to my dagger, despite knowing its magic didn't work that way, but maybe my pleas had accomplished more than I'd realized. Maybe I'd called this behemoth to life without even meaning to.

Goddess, as much as I'd wanted Kyven gone, I hadn't meant for *this* to be the price.

No help for it now, though, so I wrenched my gaze downward. A sleek black carriage hurtled up the road, gravel churning beneath its wheels.

The prince.

My hands curled around the balcony railing as the storm intensified. Its roar burrowed into my brain, coaxing phantom whispers to life.

Amryssa will tire of you soon. She'll leave you. The only thing you're good for is walking away from.

I saluted the storm with a middle finger and forced the offending thoughts aside. Gripping my dagger, I whispered to the carriage. "Crash," I commanded. "Tip over. Just don't beat the storm."

Energy prickled against my hand, but fizzled out within moments. The carriage continued onward.

I bit back a curse. The prince was too far away. Even if he hadn't been, tipping his vehicle probably required more magic than my dagger housed.

My only hope lay with the purple maelstrom swallowing the sky.

Below, the carriage swerved, and my heart lifted. Maybe the horses wouldn't stop. Maybe they'd stampede against the house's walls and explode their cargo in a shower of wood and lacerated flesh.

But no. The vehicle skidded to a halt in the circular drive. A hulking coachman leapt down to yank open the doors. Two figures burst out, one diminutive—a woman?—the other medium-sized. The smaller helped the driver unload the luggage, then reached for the horses, but the panicked animals wheeled back the way they'd come, the now-empty vehicle jouncing behind them.

The storm's whine rose to a scream. From the darkness, a shadow swooped toward me—some mutant hybrid of bat and crow. It cawed harshly before exploding into wisps.

The shadowy tendrils hit my skin and burrowed through. It was an illusion, but I could no longer distinguish nightmare from reality, could only clutch the railing and swallow my horror while darkness writhed beneath my flesh.

Down in the drive, the largest and smallest figures darted into the manor. But the third paused to look up. Despite the fiery wind, a raised cloak hood shrouded his face. Sinister eyes glinted within.

My hands squeezed the rusted railing with such savagery that blood wetted my palms. This was the prince, clearly, but instead of hurrying inside, he just...stood there, as unyielding as a blade poised to fall.

Tingles sheeted through me at the audacity. How? How could he stay so still, anchored to the earth by nothing but his boots? How could he stand unmoving while the wind lashed his cloak into an inky frenzy?

Somewhere distant, Amryssa began to scream. A cry bubbled up my throat, too, but I sealed it behind pursed lips. The prince couldn't possibly reach safety now, and I wanted to see my triumph. I wanted to watch him fall apart.

But he only raised a hand in—what? Threat? Acknowledgment? Each finger narrowed to a point. Toxic violet light gleamed on wicked claws.

Another mirage, like the burrowing shadows, but this one mirrored the truth. Kyven was a monster. The letter in my armoire drawer proved it.

Pain ripped through my chest, and I glanced down to find my fingernails gouging furrows into my flesh. I forced the offending hand back to the railing. Time to go.

I leaned out. Hot blood seeped into my neckline while my hair thrashed around my face like cracking whips. "Die screaming," I shouted, then staggered inside and threw myself onto the bed. I fastened my chains with desperate urgency.

And not a moment too soon, because the storm broke over the manor. Double-jointed creatures streamed from the corners, their mouths and eyes in all the wrong places, their limbs too spindly to make sense. They snatched at my clothes while black thoughts billowed through my mind.

You are nothing. You are worthless.

I screamed. I didn't want to know. I wanted to rake the corrosive truths from my body with curled fingers, and I tried. Pain brightened in my wrists as I thrashed.

Anything to make it stop.

Only it went on. Shadows boiled in my bloodstream while the storm's vastness pressed me to a paper-thin shard. I was nobody. Nothing. Just a water droplet flung at a conflagration, so meaningless I exploded into vapor before even touching the flame.

The mutant creatures cackled and danced.

And I screamed, until my voice faded to a rasp and scalding tears coursed down my cheeks.

Then, when it still didn't end, I went right on screaming.

3.

In the morning, I awoke to silence.

A groan crept from my cracked lips as I pried my lashes apart. Across the room, my balcony doors hung askew, admitting sunlight so cheerful it threatened to make me retch.

I closed my eyes until the urge passed, then took inventory. My wrists and ankles burned where the manacles seared my rubbed-raw flesh. Meanwhile, someone had put my limbs through a sausage-grinder, and a throb had cemented itself to my bones.

But I'd lived, which meant I could go to Amryssa. That was all that mattered—her, and the fact that there would be no wedding today. Not when the prince was dead.

A grin pieced itself together on my aching face. Sweet Zephyrine, my prayers had actually been answered. Now the urge to kiss someone filled me. Maybe next time I passed Merron in the hall, I'd do just that. Months had passed since the last time, but today called for a celebration.

I just needed to unchain myself, first.

I raised my head. My keyring lay ten feet away, where I'd hurled it against a baseboard last night in a bid for survival.

I whispered to the dagger at my waist. I couldn't reach the hilt, but

I didn't need to—the dagger awoke, its energy curling in my mind like a question mark.

Yes?

"Keys," I rasped. "I need my keys."

The knife's energy flared. The keyring arced through the air, landing against my palm with an abrupt jangle. The dagger's sizzle subsided as whatever consciousness lived inside fell into slumber once more.

I thumbed through the keys with stiff fingers, then flung my chains away and stumbled out into the hall, where another key scraped in yet another lock. I shoved Amryssa's door open and lurched through.

The sight of her, wan and exhausted, shredded my heart, but at least she'd survived. I fumbled with her restraints. She watched with limpid eyes, too depleted to even greet me.

Which was probably was for the best. If I'd spoken, the truth of the prince's fate would've leapt from my swollen throat. But I refrained, knowing we'd have to feign surprise at breakfast. Someone would inevitably rush in, shrieking about the royal corpse in the drive—or the front hall, or whatever resting place Kyven had made it to in his final, ill-fated seconds—and Amryssa had zero capacity to lie.

Of course, I'd still tell her the truth, once I'd played dumb for Olivian. I wouldn't even protest the seneschal's punishment, as long as it didn't cleave me from Amryssa's side.

I helped my best friend from bed. While she clung to a bedpost, I exchanged her nightwear for a proper gown. My own dress—of burgundy cotton, its bodice stiff with dried sweat and blood—scraped at my skin, but I didn't have the stamina to change right now. No one would expect much of us this morning, anyway.

"Breakfast?" I managed.

Amryssa nodded.

We hobbled down the grand staircase together. In the breakfast room, sunlight stabbed through the windows, the air already verging on musty. By midday, the temperature would be unbearable in here, but we'd be in the rooftop cupola by then, seeking a reprieve in the meager breeze.

Apparently, Olivian had beaten us down. He sat at the head of the table, his black locks springing in every direction. He'd managed to don a waistcoat, though he'd neglected to fasten his topmost shirt buttons.

He didn't acknowledge us. He simply glared at the corner, which apparently he'd been doing for some time, because his chipped plate lay untouched. I followed his gaze to a brass torchier, then shrugged.

If he'd rather stare at the furnishings than interrogate me, fine. I just hoped the news of Kyven's untimely death would arrive *after* I'd had my coffee.

Amryssa collapsed in a high-backed chair. I went to the sideboard, where an array of platters and teapots awaited—Miss Quist's work, which never ceased to amaze me. No matter how brutal the nightmare, our cook always dragged herself from bed early and stocked the breakfast room with biscuits and eggs and a variety of other foods I couldn't have forced down my raw, stinging throat if I'd tried.

Amryssa shrank from the steaming tea I set before her. She looked so frail that she reminded me of the starling that had once crashed against these very windows. The bird had fallen to the gravel outside, and when I'd scooped it up, I'd found a creature of the poisoned bayou in my palm, with an extra eye in the middle of its forehead and seven toes on one foot. I'd tried to revive the poor thing with my dagger, but, when that had failed, I'd settled for hoping the bird had savored the wind in its last, explosive moments, and died with a song in its throat.

Because I didn't hate animals the way I hated people. Animals were innocent, only cruel when they had to be. Meanwhile, people injured each other for fun.

Not Amryssa, though. No, she'd saved me, back when I'd had nothing and no one.

Now I lowered myself beside her, taking the seat closest to Olivian. Once he tired of his staring contest with the torchier, he might start talking, and I liked to act as a buffer when I could.

"Last night was awful," Amryssa murmured. "I swear someone's turned my stomach inside-out."

"Tell me about it." I tipped milk into my coffee. Steam arose, pulling my attention up to the spotted mirror above the sideboard, which cast my reflection back at me.

The milk pitcher slipped from my hand and thunked against the table. Holy Zephyrine, I looked like shit.

My black hair hung in clumps. The skin of my face sagged as if dripping from my bones, and the melting-candlewax effect only served to sharpen my already severe nose. Dried blood crusted my chest, and my brows were little more than dark slashes over the haunted pits of my eyes.

I hunted for my napkin. A quick scrub cleared the rusty flakes from my chest, but the girl in the mirror was still haggard enough to look forty instead of twenty-seven. Beside me, Amryssa appeared almost untouched, as if the heavens had beamed down a bright ray of light.

Well...whatever. I wasn't here to impress anybody. I tossed the napkin aside.

Amryssa lifted her tea. She sipped tentatively while I rubbed soothing circles against her back. Her shoulder blades mapped out ridges and valleys beneath my palm.

Damn, but she'd gotten skinny. I really would have to coax her into eating more and staring out the window less.

Amryssa's cup clinked against its saucer. "And what of the prince?"

I glanced down the length of the table. Olivian stared blearily back, apparently invested enough in my answer to have abandoned his confrontation with the torchier.

"He got in last night," I said slowly. "I watched Kyven pull up from my balcony."

The seneschal grunted. "And you instructed him? Told him how to chain himself?"

I gnawed at my lip. "I told him everything he needed to know."

Not a lie, really. *Die screaming* had pretty much summed it up. But tossing in a few legitimate details to make things more convincing wouldn't hurt. "He sent his attendants inside, first. There were two of them—one tall, one short. I'm sure we'll be meeting them soon."

Or not. The nightmare had snuffed Kyven from existence like a beetle crushed beneath a bootheel, and the royal attendants—if they'd survived—would probably flee back to the capital at once. If I were them, I wouldn't have lingered in Oceansgate a moment longer than necessary.

Olivian nodded, seemingly satisfied, then frowned down at his plate, as if surprised to find it empty.

A rare sense of charity welled up. Normally, I steered clear of the seneschal's struggle with lucidity, but now I'd killed his plans. Stabbed them through the heart. The least I could do was offer him eggs. "Are you hungry?"

His gaze snapped up, as if he'd already forgotten me. In all likelihood, he had. "Hungry?"

"Yeah. You know...food? Coffee? Tea? What would you like?"

"I..." His eyes flicked back to the torchier and narrowed. "Anything."

I slurped more coffee and dragged myself to standing. "Amryssa?"

She stared down at the delicate creases spider-webbing her palms. "Do you ever wonder? What might come out if someone drew on you with a knife?"

I jolted. "What?"

"Everyone says it would be blood, but I think I'd spill brown earth and blades of grass, instead."

I surveyed Amryssa's place setting, then reached for the knife Miss Quist had included and whisked it out of reach. "Well, then. Why don't we use our forks to slice our sausage this morning?"

"Mmm-hmm."

I shook my head. Even in the best of times, Olivian and his daughter didn't boast the firmest grips on reality, but today, they'd ventured further afield than usual. But maybe food would speed their recovery. At the very least, it would help pad out Amryssa's pitiful frame.

I filled two plates with eggs, sausage, and biscuits, then deposited one in front of Olivian and the other before my best friend.

She eyed the offering without enthusiasm. "I hope you're eating, too, Harlowe. You must feel every bit as grim as I do."

My lips crooked. Her kindness never failed, but the more I ate, the less there'd be for her. "Don't worry about me."

"But I do. Of course I do."

"That's not your job," I said gently. "Just eat. Get your energy back."

She smiled up at me, and I hovered, hesitant to sit back down. Standing over her like this felt...right, somehow. Like I could shield her from her father's machinations, maybe even from the toxic marsh outside. Beyond the windows, the cypresses threw their noxious purple glow, visible even in the broad light of day.

"Take my biscuit, at least." Amryssa transferred a pastry from her plate to mine. "Please?"

The doors opened.

My battered body snapped to attention. I braced for a panicked housemaid, but a group of strangers sauntered in, instead. And there stood not one, not two, but *three* people I didn't recognize. All of them very much alive.

Fuck.

My stomach hollowed out. On the right stood last night's carriage driver, probably the largest man...well, ever. His size hinted at obscene strength, but a healthy layer of fat hid the specifics. His leather vest topped a white shirt that stretched against an impressive paunch, and his skin was as brown as Merron's. But his eyes were darker, like chips of coal set beneath protruding brows. A thick lower lip jutted out in an underbite so severe I wondered how he managed to eat.

On the left stood the smallest—not a woman, as I'd guessed, but a fox-faced man with an orange ponytail and a frame nearly as spare as Amryssa's. His attire mirrored the giant's, but with the addition of a shortsword at his side.

So Kyven's attendants had lived. And as for the prince...

My heartbeat spiked, bullying its way up my throat. The third man stood at ease, looking every inch the royal, his snowy shirtsleeves billowing from a green-and-gold waistcoat. Glossy red-brown hair swept over his forehead, setting off angular features and a narrow jaw. Blocky brows made a dramatic frame for his eyes, and...goddess, those eyes. I'd never seen anything like them. They were of the lightest possible blue, like the palest slice of sky in the coldest hour of dawn.

His gaze connected with mine.

My blood lurched, the feeling akin to taking an arrow in the chest. Prince Kyven was the most striking man I'd ever seen, and I hated him immediately.

"Is *this* where that delectable aroma is coming from?" His voice was smooth, his vowels round with the musicality of someone born and bred in the capital. Such pretty camouflage to hide the viper beneath. "It seems we've tracked down breakfast at last, boys."

"But you...died." The accusation plummeted from my lips. Over in the corner, a grandfather clock ticked, trying and failing to chip away at my disbelief. "Last night."

"Did I?" The prince rolled his shoulders, his expression distinctly amused. "In that case, I can't imagine why everyone makes such a fuss about this whole mortality business. I've never felt better."

The coffee in my belly curdled. "But... *How?* I *saw* you last night, in the drive. You never could've gotten inside in time." Shit, I shouldn't admit that in front of Olivian, but what did it matter now?

One corner of the prince's lips lifted. Goddess, what a stupid smile. Its lopsidedness made me want to hurl my dagger across the table. Tack up the other half of his mouth with my blade, just to make it match.

"It was an interesting night, I'll give you that. Yet here I am. Prince Kyven Windermere, of Hightower, at your service." He sketched a bow, then scanned the room with those sickeningly pale eyes, clearly expecting introductions.

Hot tears invaded my throat. This couldn't be happening. Kyven was dust. Amryssa was free. Just minutes ago, our future had looked so...*tolerable.* But now?

Bleak. Dark. Horrible.

Olivian roused from his stupor. Apparently, my confession had passed him by, because he stood without so much as glancing my way.

"Welcome to Oceansgate, Your Highness. I'm the Seneschal Olivian Marche. Allow me to introduce my daughter, Amryssa"—he waved a sausage-fingered hand in our direction—"and her keymistress, Harlowe."

Kyven took our measure, his attention so keen my heart kicked against my ribs. "Keymistress?" he said. "Dare I ask what that is? I can't say I've heard the term in Hightower."

"No, you wouldn't have. Consider it something like...an attendant, nothing more." Olivian sniffed, conveying his opinion of me with ruthless clarity. "It's Harlowe's job to look after Amryssa, primarily when we have incidents such as last night's. Which hopefully didn't tax you or your companions too greatly. At any rate, you can become acquainted with your bride over breakfast. I have some business to attend to, so I can't stay, but make yourselves comfortable. Eat as much as you like."

My jaw slackened. Where had Olivian unearthed *that* pretty speech? His pretentions might even have convinced me, if not for the way he kept glancing at the torchier as if it might spring to life and bite him.

"Very well, then." The prince stepped aside, allowing the seneschal to make his escape.

The doors banged shut. In the ensuing silence, Kyven's attention strayed to me, then the furrows I'd clawed into my flesh. "So. *You're* the one who advised me to die screaming last night. I hope you won't hold my continued existence against me. You might actually find me charming, if given half a chance."

My throat worked, but no sound came out. What was happening? How was he even standing here, alive and breathing and lauding his own virtues, no less? And how did he look so infuriatingly...healthy, his cheeks flush with color, his clothes as fresh as if he hadn't spent a night thrashing in physical and psychological agony? How could he possibly seem so *unconcerned*?

Something tugged at my hand. I broke from the prince's gaze to find wan fingers clutching mine.

"I'm not hungry." Amryssa spoke so faintly I had to strain to catch the words. "I think I'd rather go, if that's all right with you."

"Oh, don't leave on my account." The prince smirked, then sauntered to the sideboard and heaped food onto his plate as if this were just another morning. As if we had plenty to spare. His attendants followed suit, clearly more interested in the spread than us. "If you'll forgive my saying so, you both look a bit...piqued, and I'm a staunch believer in the power of bacon to cure all ills."

I curled a fist against the table and tried to tame the sting crowding my eyes. I needed strength. I needed to fix this.

I needed to kill this man.

Kyven claimed a seat at the table—the *head* of the table, the pompous ass—and slid Olivian's untouched plate aside. He attacked his spoils with the vigor of a teenage boy, though he had to have been pushing thirty.

"Mmmfffph." He groaned through a mouthful of eggs in an incredibly unprincely manner. "Heavenly."

I grimaced. His companions set upon their plates with equal enthusiasm, proving the giant did, indeed, have difficulty chewing. Flecks of biscuit showered the man's jerkin, which he made up for with the sheer volume of food he shoveled into his mouth.

Selfish jerks, the lot of them. Where did they think this all came from?

"Please," Amryssa whimpered. "I just...need a moment."

Kyven met my eyes. "Is our presence distressing her?" He nodded toward Amryssa, his smile softening into the sort one might direct at a child.

That show of tenderness wakened a billowing rage inside me. Did he think I was an idiot? I hadn't forgotten the icy glint of his eyes or the tortured warp of his claws, and now I recognized every word as fabricated, designed to project a humanity he didn't possess.

Amryssa's old tutor, Eliana, had warned me of this. She'd sent a letter weeks ago, telling me how Kyven mimicked a real person—he spoke the right words, followed the proper etiquette. Then he unleashed his malevolence in darkened rooms and dusty attics, where no one would hear the screaming.

"What was your name again?" Kyven asked Amryssa. "Harlowe, was it?"

Every cell in my body shrieked at me to shield my friend, to stop him from sullying her with a glance, but his question riveted me in place.

He'd just called her by *my* name. Which meant he thought I was... Amryssa?

My mind spun, but the mystery unraveled in moments. Of course —he'd walked in, noted my proximity to Olivian and our similar complexions, and assumed *I* was the seneschal's daughter. Not to mention Amryssa had been serving food onto *my* plate.

I held my breath, weighing the ways in which I could use this. The passing joke I'd shared with Amryssa last night—that tender jest about marrying the prince myself—became as functional and pointed as a blade in my hand.

Gods help me, I could do it. Actually do it. Rather than trussing up my friend like a lamb for the slaughter, I could give Kyven a bride who would go to the marriage bed with a dagger on her belt and hate in her heart.

I could spare Amryssa *all* of it—the screams, the blood, the gurgling. Maybe I could even spare myself. When the prince inevitably tried to hurt me, I'd be well within my rights to stab him. And self-defense didn't carry the same penalties as murder.

Heat crackled in my veins. Amryssa's biscuit still waited on my plate, so I crammed it into my mouth and chased it down with coffee. Strength bloomed in my belly, sharpening my focus.

"My keymistress is...delicate," I finally said. "She's still recovering from last night."

I glanced sidelong at Amryssa, a plea not to undermine my lie, but she only stared at the table. Goddess, we needed to escape this so-called breakfast, and quickly. I could sort out the details of bride-swapping later.

"I understand," Kyven said. "But you needn't fear Lunk, here." He jerked a thumb at the giant. "He's far more harmless than he looks."

The big man—Lunk, apparently, and what the hell kind of name was that for a royal attendant?—grinned, exposing yellowed, broken teeth. An unbridgeable chasm separated the bottom row from the top.

I fought back a grimace. He didn't look harmless. He looked like he could clobber me to death with one half-hearted punch.

"Vick is significantly less harmless, but he'll do as I tell him." Kyven smirked as if amused by that, then indicated Foxface. "For now, at least. Though you'll find he's allergic to things like small talk. And rules."

Vick sized me up with eyes as sharp as fresh-cut emeralds. His gaze seemed to take in...far too much.

A shiver skated down my spine. I escaped it by wrenching my attention back to Kyven.

"And you?" I couldn't keep the bite from my tone. "Should I fear *you*, my prince?"

His features slackened in what could only be feigned surprise. "Me? Oh, no, I'm perfectly safe. Unless you're threatened by a cunning wit and devastating good looks."

I only barely withheld my scoff. He was good, I'd give him that. Almost passable as a real, live human. I'd probably have been fooled, if not for Eliana's warnings. "Right," I said. "Well, this has been delightful, but I seem to have lost my appetite. If you'll excuse me."

We needed out. Screw the food, screw the prince, screw the crooked smile I wanted to slap right off his face. I tugged Amryssa to her feet, propelling her toward the door with barely restrained urgency, as if our lives depended on it.

Hers actually might, which was close enough for me.

"My Lady?"

I pretended not to hear. I yanked open the doors and steered Amryssa through, but the prince called after me again.

I closed my eyes for an overlong moment before turning. "What?"

"It was a pleasure making your acquaintance." Kyven winked. Actually fucking *winked* at me, the snake.

Revulsion swelled in my throat as my attention dropped to his hands. No claws, this time. Just normal, human hands, one clasped loosely around his breakfast knife.

Kill yourself, I commanded, my fingers clamped around my dagger. *Take that knife and stab yourself in the throat.*

Kyven's brow crinkled. He brought the blade haltingly toward his neck.

Sparks exploded in my bloodstream as I waited. Closer, closer... But no. The prince only itched his Adam's apple and lowered the knife again. My dagger went silent in my hand.

Well, shit. It had been worth a try.

Kyven offered me another one-sided smile. Goddess, didn't he know how to do anything else? "Marry you later, then?"

"Right." I summoned a blinding, artificial cheer. "Marry you later. Can't wait."

I turned and fled.

4.

On our way up the stairs, Amryssa stumbled, but I shored her up as best I could.

The tangled knot beneath my ribs only loosened once I locked us in my room. I sat Amryssa on my bed, stowed my castoff chains, and dug through the bottom drawer of my armoire, searching for the letter that had arrived weeks ago. My pulse blurred as I scanned the lines.

"What's that?" Amryssa said.

I swiveled to look at her. "A warning."

"A warning?" She frowned. "Against what?"

"Against letting you marry that...*thing* downstairs."

She chewed at her bottom lip. Her aura had dulled even further in the last few minutes, as if the prince had tarnished her merely by existing. "I don't see that I have much choice."

"No. To hell with that. I won't let it happen. I won't let him touch you."

"But...I thought he seemed kind enough. Didn't he?" Her eyes glazed over, as if only half of her occupied this room with me. "I'll just...lie back and close my eyes. Ask him to be gentle. I can endure gentle, I think."

My heart burst apart like a dropped globe of glass. Here she was, barely able to face this sanitized ideal she'd dreamed up, when meanwhile, the truth would destroy her.

"Kyven's not...what he seems." After a moment's hesitation, I offered Amryssa the letter. I hated to ambush her like this, but she needed to know the truth. "The prince isn't what he pretends to be."

She took the parchment, her gaze sharpening as she read. One snowy hand rose to circle her throat. "Oh my. This... No. This can't be right."

"It can. Eliana sent that letter. And you know she wouldn't lie."

Eliana—the articulate, well-bred woman who'd once served as Amryssa's tutor, then as her stand-in mother, after Amryssa's had died —had fled to the capital months ago to live with her sister. Before she'd gone, I'd begged her to unearth what she could about the prince, and so she had. She'd sent all the sordid details I could ever want, plus plenty more I didn't.

"We should show this to my father." Amryssa's voice wobbled. "He can't... He has to know about this."

I bowed my head, wishing the letter had the power to make the seneschal relent, but I might as well have tried to hope the nightmares out of existence. "Am, he won't listen. He agreed to this wedding months ago, for reasons that probably have nothing to do with you, and you know how he gets when he makes up his mind. What happens next is up to us."

The letter trembled in her grip. "What're you proposing, exactly?"

"A switch." My answer came out strong. Unhesitating. "Just now, at breakfast, Kyven mistook me for you. All I have to do now is put on your wedding dress and marry him myself. After that, he'll have no claim to you."

She recoiled. "But marrying Kyven is *my* duty. My fate."

"It doesn't have to be." I stood and went to her. The ruddy sunbeams streaming through the windows seemed to check themselves before reaching her. She looked oddly lifeless, all shades of white and boiled-down gray.

Her brow creased. "But my father would stop you. At the wedding. He'd object."

"Not if he isn't there. You could ask for a private ceremony. Make it a condition of your cooperation."

She paused. "He'd be furious, afterward."

"Let me deal with that."

"But you'd have a *husband*." Her words were a gossamer thread spun by pale lips, ready to snap. "You'd be tied to a brute."

My smile hardened to stone. *It's nothing a good stabbing can't cure.* "Until one of us dies, yes."

"No," Amryssa breathed, but there was no force in it. Only misery and an awful, bare-faced longing.

My throat constricted. My poor, sweet friend—so soft, so very gentle. How I wished that, just once, she would rail against the injustices that colored her existence. I wanted her to scream. Hurl something fragile against the wallpaper just to watch it explode. I wanted her to march downstairs, shake her finger in Olivian's face, and tell him she wouldn't marry filth like Kyven if her life depended on it.

But she wouldn't, of course. So I would do it for her.

"This is madness." Her voice quavered. "I *know* my father would see reason."

For all of two seconds, I wavered, but despite Olivian's tenuous grip on reality, he mostly behaved like an oak tree rooted in the earth. Once he made a decision, he pursued it, until he either bullied the world into changing shape or wore himself down to a nub. Usually the latter.

That was why we were still here, after all, in a dying territory that had lost its patron goddess years ago. Zephyrine had fallen asleep. Abandoned Oceansgate to rot and ruin and nightmares. Yet still we clung to this failing fiefdom, to this shell of a house, for one simple reason.

Olivian refused to admit defeat. And, for as long as the seneschal stayed, Amryssa would. And if Amryssa stayed, so did I.

She curled a slender fist against her skirts. "Why don't we go talk to him? Right now."

I cocked a brow. Maybe she'd scavenged some spirit from somewhere, after all. "Really?"

"Yes. He wouldn't subject me to this marriage if he knew Kyven's true nature. And I can't just let you sacrifice for me. I *won't*."

My chest ached at that, but if confronting Olivian would speed things along, fine. Maybe Amryssa would finally realize the truth—that her father didn't care about her. That he only cared about himself.

And maybe not even that. From what I could tell, the man had no sense of self-preservation. Only a steadfast obstinacy that would doom us all.

"Okay," I said. "But if...*when* he says no, we'll do this my way, all right?"

"It won't come to that. You'll see."

I smiled, dour. I hated that it would.

But if breaking Amryssa's heart would save her, so be it. At least this way, I'd still be here to pick up all the pieces, afterward.

We found Olivian on the second floor, holed up in his "study," which amounted to little more than an unused bedroom crammed with brass knick-knacks and dusty, half-filled ledgers.

The argument taking place inside reached my ears before I knocked. Olivian's baritone rose and fell, his words garbled by the thick slab of the door. I hesitated, wondering who had the misfortune of being trapped in there with him, then decided, *Fuck it*, and banged a demanding fist. Our current mission far eclipsed the importance of anything else in this house.

Olivian went silent within. Amryssa waited with me in the dingy hallway, her fingers twining like ashen snakes.

The door opened. The leftmost half of Olivian's hair stood at attention, as if he'd pulled at it in a fit of pique. "What?" he barked.

Amryssa flinched. The seneschal paused, forcing a smile through gritted teeth. "I mean... What can I do for you?"

"We have something to show you," I said. "Can your guest come back later?"

"My guest?"

I glanced past him, but the curtains were drawn. Shadows lay thick in the room. "Whoever it is you're talking to in there."

A long pause. "I was just...rehearsing my speech. For the wedding. Alone."

I took his measure, not buying that for a second. Yesterday's nightmare had clearly taken its toll, but maybe that would work to my advantage. If the seneschal was so out of sorts he'd resorted to arguing with shadows, he might not put up a fight when Amryssa requested a closed ceremony.

"Can we come in, then?" I said.

The narrowing of his eyes told me he wanted nothing less, but Amryssa ventured a thin plea.

"It's important, Father."

Olivian grumbled, but stepped aside to let us pass. Inside, the musk of aged paper filled my nose. I sat in an upholstered wingback chair with too many bald patches to count. In the corners, cobwebs glimmered, half translucent in the light of the lone candle. As Amryssa took a seat beside me, I imagined Olivian in here alone, ranting at no one, and almost succumbed to pity before abruptly coming to my senses.

"Well?" The seneschal arranged his bulk behind the desk. "What do you want?"

Amryssa slid Eliana's letter across his blotter.

He frowned. "What's this?"

"Read it," I said.

He did, though I couldn't imagine how, given the oily dimness. When he finished, he flung down the paper and fixed me with a baleful stare. "This letter's addressed to you."

"Yes."

"You asked Amryssa's tutor to investigate her betrothed?"

"I did."

He closed his eyes and stabbed at his lids with thick fingers.

"Zephyrine help me," he muttered. "I knew letting that woman abscond to Hightower would bite me in the ass."

I spluttered. "*Abscond?* A sweet old woman who's served you faithfully for years finally flees the nightmares, and you call that *absconding?*"

He dropped his hand and attempted to shear me in half with a glare.

I cleared my throat and folded my hands. *Play nice.* "I mean... I just needed to know what kind of man you were tying Amryssa to."

"It's none of your concern."

"It is." My tone turned strident, already escaping my control, and I clutched at my dagger. *For the love of all that's holy, grant me patience with this asshole.* "I've spent the past nine years keeping her safe. Of course I needed to know who you were saddling her with."

The seneschal glared. Silence coiled between us like a wound spring.

Amryssa leaned in, breaking our stand-off. "Father? You can't possibly intend to marry me to this man, can you? Not now?"

His fierceness softened, if only by half. "I have to, my sweet. This union is critical."

"But...you didn't know, did you? What he's really like?"

Olivian made a sound like stones grinding, then offered his hands over the desk for Amryssa to take. "I'd heard rumors, pet, but they're only that. Rumors. And I have ways of keeping you safe. Trust me when I say we need this marriage. *Oceansgate* needs this marriage."

Amryssa recoiled. I'd known this was coming, but still, the betrayal on her face gutted me. Filleted me open from neck to navel.

"But...what could possibly stand to gain?" she said.

Olivian hesitated. "Lawmen. For one."

I frowned. In the almost-decade since the nightmares had begun, the bulk of Oceansgate's populace had trickled away, including the entirety of the police force. Now, only our most reckless citizens remained, along with a group of lawbreakers who lived in the forest and apparently considered recurrent psychological torture a fair price to pay for lack of legal oversight. With our patron goddess lost to her divine slumber, Olivian's territory had devolved into chaos and anarchy, and without a police force at his disposal, there was very little he could do about that.

"But Oceansgate doesn't have any lawmen," I said. "Not anymore."

Olivian grunted. "Not at the *moment*."

A pause. Pieces clicked together in my head, and I gaped. *This* was what he'd sold his daughter for?

"So you intend to barter me?" Amryssa bleated, clearly having reached the same conclusion. "To buy lawmen off the king by joining me to his son, knowing full well what this man will do to me?"

"There's...so much you don't understand," Olivian said. "So much you *can't* understand, my sweet."

My molars grated, my palm itching for my dagger. Seven hells, if he started rhapsodizing about the deficits of the female intellect, I really would stab someone.

"As your father"—Olivian's fingers flexed, straining toward his daughter—"I'm asking you to trust me."

"I thought I *could*." Moisture pooled in Amryssa's eyes. "But perhaps I was mistaken."

Silence. The seneschal reclaimed his spurned hands with visible reluctance. He seemed not to know what to say.

My breath fled, but I would not, under any circumstances, say *I told you so*. "Private ceremony," I prompted Amryssa gently. "Remember? You said that's what you wanted."

"Right." She pinned her gaze to her lap, her voice leaden. "I'd like a closed wedding, Father. No guests apart from Harlowe. No other witnesses to this...forced union. You can grant me that, can't you? At the very least?"

Olivian shot me a thunderous look, as if to say, *This is your doing*. I shrugged, but my heart knocked against my ribs with such ferocity I swore the whole manor would hear.

If he refused...

"Very well," he spat, more at me than her. "So long as this wedding happens, I don't care what form it takes."

Warmth cascaded through me. Just minutes ago, I'd fantasized about imbuing Amryssa with some backbone, but now I blessed her for her lack of one.

Clearly, there was no room in Olivian's mind to suspect her of treachery. He simply assumed his daughter would obey, as she always had.

He sat back, swatting Eliana's letter to the floor. I dove after the fallen sheets and folded them into my skirt pocket.

"The officiant arrives at seven," Olivian grumbled. "You two will meet him in the library. I suppose this means you'd like to do away with the nuptial feast, as well?"

Amryssa nodded, not looking at him.

I leapt up and tugged her to her feet before facing the seneschal. "Well, that's settled. You can congratulate her tomorrow. Right now, I need to get her ready."

He lobbed me a look of pure loathing. "See that you do."

I responded with a smarmy, insincere smile and steered Amryssa away. She didn't resist. Her spirit seemed to have forsaken her body, leaving behind a hollow husk that moved when propelled, but had no will of its own.

Upstairs, I holed us up in her bedroom. Someone had apparently come and gone—Amryssa's wedding gown now hung from the armoire, a complex waterfall of rose satin and white lace.

A groan slipped from my throat. "Goddess, I'm never going to fit into that."

Amryssa gave no indication of having heard. She drifted toward the window, only stopping when her nose hovered an inch from the pane. She stared out, her expression vacant.

I sighed. "Are you okay?"

Her throat bobbed. "Would you be?"

"Well... No. Probably not."

Then again, I never would have wound up in her position. I didn't put faith in people. I didn't trust. I didn't *hope*.

I knew better.

But I couldn't hold Amryssa's innate goodness against her, so I went and gathered her into a hug. She felt birdlike in my arms, as if she might crumble to dust and float away on the wind. "I'm sorry," I said into her hair. "I wish I'd been wrong. But you agreed to do this my way, if I wasn't. So let's get you in the bath. Get you clean."

"Me? But why? When you're the one insisting on getting married?"

"Because. It's still my job to take care of you."

Her brow creased. "It shouldn't be, though. You ought to just let me go. Live your own life."

I stiffened. "Let you go? But...where?"

"Out there." Amryssa nodded toward the window. "Into the forest. The swamp."

I flinched, if only because I knew how deeply she longed for that. Every time she sat in the cupola and peered out like a butterfly pinned under glass, some broken thing was whispering its devilry inside her. She daydreamed of slipping among the poisoned cypresses, of crooning to the mutant animals and drinking the diseased water.

But if the brigands living out there didn't find her, what would happen when the next nightmare came through? Would Amryssa just...willingly join the goddess in her eternal sleep?

No, fuck that. I *needed* her. Maybe that made me selfish, but my mind couldn't hold a future that didn't include my best friend alive and breathing, in which she lightened this dreary house one caring word at a time.

"I can't let you do that," I said.

"Why not?" Something like despair rimmed her voice.

"Because," I said. "You saved me. You're the only person who's ever even given a shit, and I *need* you. Everyone does. You're the only bright spot in this entire messed-up place."

Her lips pressed together. "Is this really what you want, though? To just...save me from myself, over and over again? This is enough for you?"

I held her eyes. "Yes. It's enough."

Amryssa sighed, then turned back to the window. An age seemed to pass before she spoke again.

"Then I suppose I'll have that bath, now. If that's what truly makes you happy."

5.

After I'd cleaned Amryssa up and brushed the snarls from her hair, I put her to bed. She'd barely slept last night, and while a nap wouldn't restore her completely, it might ease the shadows beneath her eyes.

Once her breathing lengthened, I slid her wedding gown from its hanger and brought it next door to my room, where I spread it across my bed. The dress would never accommodate my average-sized torso and generous backside, and I didn't have the sewing skills to alter it. But I *did* have another means to solve the problem. I slid my dagger free and went to my vanity, where I plunked down before the splotched mirror.

My lip curled. I looked like lukewarm vomit. Zephyrine knew I would've liked to stay that way—to repel Kyven through sheer disgust —but I couldn't give him any reason to balk at this sham of a marriage.

Best reel him in with something at least halfway enticing.

I laid my dagger on the vanity. When I brushed the hilt, something quivered inside. I didn't know what, exactly—Olivian had never told me where he'd gotten this thing, and I'd never asked. But whatever witchery answered my summons felt...old. Primal, almost, though I'd never equated its single-mindedness with simplicity. I'd instead concluded that at some point, the dagger's inhabitant had gotten broken. Fragmented. Like a sheared-off piece of something that had once been whole.

"What are you?" I murmured.

The dagger's awareness pulsed beneath my skin. But it never answered *that* question, no matter how many times I asked.

With a wry laugh at myself, I set to work. Magic trickled from my fingertips, softening my flesh and turning it pliable. With careful strokes, I smoothed the hollows beneath my eyes, then sharpened the arch of my brows. I left my nose alone, but honed my cheekbones and chin. My skin warmed and reshaped, the magic seeping in like rainwater permeating soil.

When I finished, I looked different. Not so much that the prince would notice—he'd only assume I'd cleaned myself up, hopefully—but I'd accomplished what I wanted.

I looked...fiercer. Hawklike. Not beautiful, but striking enough to stand out in a crowd, and I wanted people to startle when they saw me. To sneak glances when I wasn't looking, to guess at whether the contours of my face divulged those of my soul. I wanted them to wonder whether I only looked like the sort of woman who'd slice them apart if crossed, or if I actually *was*.

I smiled, pleased to find an edge of menace there. Briefly, I tried to recall the face I'd been born with, but I hadn't glimpsed it in so long that my mind held only the vaguest impression of bland features, dishwater eyes, and a weak chin.

I didn't regret having shed that skin. Having forgotten.

Next, I smoothed a hand over my lank hair, infusing the locks with gloss and adding another inch of length. This was my one concession to vanity—this raven mass, so thick and black and slippery it shone even at night and resisted any efforts to constrain it in a braid.

That done, I went to work narrowing my waist. The result looked borderline absurd and squished my organs into places they didn't belong, but I would reverse this particular change the moment I wriggled free of Amryssa's dress tonight.

I rose to try on the gown, but a soft knock interrupted. Its distinct pattern shot a tiny smile across my lips. *Merron.*

I veered to the door and opened it. Our head steward waited in the hall, as solid and compact as if hewn from brown oak. Scruff clung to Merron's cheeks and last night's storm had carved new lines around his eyes, but somehow, he only looked handsomer for it.

He ran a hand through his dark hair. "Hi."

"Hi," I said, startled by the softness in that word. Somehow, Merron always relaxed my defenses.

"Sorry to show up unannounced. I just needed to know you were all right." His voice was husky, the usual byproduct of our nightmarish ordeals.

Not that I would ever point it out. Merron had never told me which truth the storms excised from his soul, honed to an edge, and used to lacerate his mind. But he always screamed sooner than the rest of us, so it had to be particularly bad.

"I'm fine," I said. "Just tired."

His gaze narrowed, sweeping my face. "Did you...change something?"

I glanced toward the vanity. "Yeah. A little of this, a little of that. Nothing I won't put back eventually."

"Oh. Well. It looks good on you."

My lips flirted with a smile. He always said that, no matter what I did. I could probably remold myself as a hag and Merron would react by singing her praises. "Thanks."

"No problem," he said. "Could I...come in, maybe?"

I paused, but I hadn't forgotten this morning's resolution. "Sure. Why not?"

Astonishment flitted across his features—unsurprising, given that I only occasionally said yes. Mostly I said no. But I was getting married tonight, and the urge to mark that transformation rushed through my veins. I wanted Merron to brand me. Not as his, but as...my own. As something uncaged that would now submit of its own accord.

I closed the door behind him and leaned against the wood.

He approached the bed and studied Amryssa's gown. "This is quite the dress. What's it doing in here?"

"It just needs some alterations." I crossed the room and ran my fingers up his spine to distract from the lie.

Merron gathered a breath, turning with it still trapped in his chest. He stared down, his pupils flowering to wide black pools.

"Harlowe," he rasped.

A smoky sound escaped me. "Merron."

"It's been so long."

It had, and there was a reason for that. "I don't want to talk. I just want everything *but* the talking. Do you think we could do that? Please?"

Hunger came alive in his eyes. "Of course. Whatever you want."

Oh, thank goddess.

He lowered his lips. I tilted my face up to meet him, palming the back of his head, sucking his tongue into my mouth. I wanted heat. I wanted sweat and pleasure and effort, the glorious mindlessness of skin on skin.

Merron's hands rose to circle my ribcage. I kissed him hard, fervently, and when he released my waist to spear his fingers into my hair, I pulled him down onto the bed atop me.

Amryssa's wedding dress rumpled beneath us. Merron half-straightened, propping himself on an elbow as he considered the crushed gown with alarm. "What, right here?"

"Yes, here." I tugged at his gray steward's jacket.

"Are you sure?"

"Very."

He searched my eyes, gauging my determination, but ultimately gave in. He dove for my mouth again, his hips slotting between my thighs as he fumbled with the fastenings of my dress.

I closed my eyes. This felt...right, somehow, desecrating the symbol of Amryssa's subjugation like this.

Soon, my red dress lay in a heap on the floor, joined shortly by Merron's livery, then my corset and underthings. I welcomed him, opening my arms, parting my legs, taking everything he could give.

His sweat mingled with mine as the sunshine cooked us to a simmer. I fell inward, into that endless warm ravine filled with sensation and half-formed whispers. My fingers roved over hot skin and shifting muscle. Merron's labored breaths scorched my ear as we moved together. Each minute melted into the next.

He finally spent himself with a guttural cry and collapsed on top of me.

I held him for long minutes. I didn't usually, but today, gratitude shone within me, spilling out in my embrace.

"I might not be able to do this again," I murmured. "Not for a while."

He raised his head, his brow pleated. "What? Why not?'

I bit my lip. I shouldn't have admitted that, but I cared for him. Not in the way he cared for me, exactly, but enough that I *wanted* to tell him the truth.

Which I couldn't, of course.

"Because," I hedged. "Amryssa needs me."

What would happen tomorrow, once Olivian discovered my treachery? Whatever my punishment, it probably wouldn't leave me free to couple with our head steward in the middle of the day. "She's losing weight, and her mind is getting worse. Which means I need to be with her. Now more than ever."

Merron twined my hair around his fist, his expression pained. "But you're always with her."

"Not *always*. Not right now."

"No, but..." His brows crooked. "She consumes you, Harlowe. I keep hoping you'll realize it. I wait for you every evening, you know, in my room. I fall asleep wondering if the door's about the crack open. If tonight'll be the night you finally come to me and say you've had enough."

My chest twinged. I eased out from under him and sat up. "I don't know why. I'm not worth dreaming about. And I thought we agreed to no talking."

"We did, but..." He trailed off, but apparently, he couldn't help himself. "You *are* worth dreaming about. You're the only person in this goddess-forsaken place that is."

I averted my face, an intolerable ache unfurling behind my breastbone.

"You understand that, right?" His tone grew imploring. "You must know you're the only reason I'm still here."

I stood and went toward my vanity. The walls bowed inward, crowding me, and I picked up the first thing my fingers touched, a dented metal hairbrush I turned over and over.

I remembered now why I hadn't slept with Merron in months. He always did this, no matter how many times he promised not to. "I don't think I can give you what you want. I'm sorry, Merron, but I can't."

An exhale punched out of him. "But I'm not asking for that much. Just for you to let me in, Harlowe. To stop running when I get close."

"I don't *run*." I thunked the brush down. "How can you even say that? I'm right here. I've *been* here. I suffer through these nightmares month after month, year after year. I never even complain."

"You know that's not what I mean." He yanked a hand through his hair, mussing it even more than my groping fingers already had. "You're so incredibly loyal, it's what I love about you, but it's all for Amryssa. Never for me, or even for yourself. It's like you don't care that I've asked you to leave. You don't trust that I'd take care of you, but I would. I'd build you a house somewhere. Get you out of Oceansgate, away from Olivian and this half-mad girl he's hung around your neck. I'd give you everything, if you'd just let me."

"Amryssa's not a chore," I snapped, ignoring the rest. "She's my friend."

He shook his head. "She isn't. She's never done a thing for you."

My teeth clamped together. Amryssa had done more for me than anyone else had, including my so-called parents. *Especially* my so-called parents. "You have no idea what you're talking about."

"Don't I?"

"No."

"Then tell me. Explain this hold she has over you. And why I can't break it, no matter what I do."

I stalked to an armchair and pulled a moth-eaten throw off the back, wrapping it around myself despite the sweat dampening my skin. "I don't owe you my story, Merron. I don't owe you anything."

He ground his jaw, visibly frustrated, and I relented.

"Look." I ventured over and stood between his knees. "You might think you want me, but you don't. Not really."

He hooked his hands behind my thighs, not seeming to care that he wore not a single stitch of clothing. Soulful chestnut eyes pleaded with mine. "How can you say that? How can you presume to know what I want better than I do?"

"Because." I sighed. "If I ran away with you, you'd regret it. Maybe not right away, or even in a year. But eventually, you'd meet some other woman who's more beautiful and kind-hearted than I am. Someone who's less work. Less trouble, less...everything. And then I'd become the stone around *your* neck. This is me doing you a favor, trust me."

He rested his forehead against my midsection and hugged my legs, nearly toppling me. "You have no idea what you are, do you? Or what we could be if you'd just...try."

I swallowed thickly and ran my hands through his hair. "You have no idea how misplaced your faith in me is."

His shoulders bunched as he squeezed me tighter, but nothing much remained for us to say. When he finally let go, I kissed him—a kind of farewell only I understood—and watched him dress. He moved stiffly, hurt rising off him in waves.

Sourness pummeled my stomach, but how could he not realize his devotion was simply bred by circumstance? We were trapped here, repeatedly pushed to the brink of sanity, and it was enough to confuse the best of men. To make anyone who could achieve a basic level of functioning look good.

But if I went with Merron, the adoration in his eyes would inevitably dim. Maybe he'd relish our life, at first. He'd build us a cottage where we would kiss and bicker and fuck like rabbits, but in time, he'd discover my sharp edges. He would come to know the real Harlowe, and his smiles would fade. He'd turn his back at night instead of cradling me in his arms.

He'd *leave* me. Even if he didn't go anywhere.

And I'd had more than enough of that.

So I knelt and helped him with his boots, then resisted when he tried to grab at my waist. This whole thing had been a mistake. I'd let my selfish desires overcome my good sense, and I hated myself for it.

"You should forget me," I said as he went to the door. "I'm no good for you, Merron. I never will be."

His jagged expression made it clear I'd just eviscerated him.

Still, I soldiered onward, for his sake, if not my own. "You should escape, like you said. Leave Oceansgate and don't look back. Go marry some woman who never gets angry and has birthing hips and wants nothing more than to make you armfuls of babies. Someone who actually deserves you."

He scowled. "*You* have birthing hips."

A downward glance confirmed my unsettling new narrowness. "Not at the moment."

"Well," he said. "Those, you should definitely put back."

"I will. But right now, you should go lie down. Get some sleep. You'll feel better afterward, I promise."

"I'm not giving up, you know," he said. "Not until you leave Oceansgate without me. Or marry someone else."

I masked my sudden bolt of unease by rewrapping the blanket. He had no idea how soon that day would come. That it already had. "You should go. And...I'm sorry. Really."

"Well, I'm not." He cast me a long look, then retreated. His boots thudded against the hallway carpet and faded.

I shut my door harder than necessary and rested my forehead against the carven whorls. What the hell had I just done? I'd gouged a canyon into him a mile wide, and I would do so much worse before the day ended.

I clenched my jaw until it ached, then whirled and plumbed the pocket of my crumpled dress until I found Eliana's letter. The sheets rasped as I unfolded them.

As ever, the words opened a cold black space inside me.

My dearest Harlowe,

I pray this letter reaches you ahead of its subject, though I regret not writing with better news.

I've arrived safely in the capital, which is as beautiful as everyone says. Hightower City is like nothing I've ever seen, full of bright white spires and marble avenues wide enough to get lost in. But I won't bore you with the particulars. They're not important, not in the face of what I've learned.

As you asked, I've devoted my time here to chasing news of Prince Kyven. I was even lucky enough to finagle a meeting with the man himself. My sister has a son who frequents the same gentleman's club as the prince, and she was kind enough to arrange a "chance" encounter in the street out front.

At first blush, Kyven impressed me. He kissed my hand, and I was immediately taken in by his impeccable manners and bright blue eyes. When he smiled, heads turned across the street. And I hoped, then. I wanted to believe Olivian had found a proper match for our Amryssa. Someone who might make her happy.

But my joy soon turned to horror. On his way into the club, the prince brushed shoulders with an emerging gentleman, and an unmistakable look of revulsion came over this stranger's face. Of course, I pursued the man and asked what he knew. At first, he tried to brush me off, but when I explained my purpose, he opened up, albeit reluctantly.

His story is too awful to relate in its entirety, but I'll paint it in broad strokes, because I know you need to know.

Prince Kyven is a monster. This man told me they'd been childhood friends, until the prince developed a...fascination, we'll call it, with pain. Namely with inflicting it. As Kyven grew, he left behind a trail of little deaths —defenseless creatures who met their ends at the point of a carving knife— and later, some not-so-little deaths.

The gentleman refused to go into detail about those. Forgive an old woman, but I'm grateful for it.

As he spoke, my heart slid out through a hole in the bottom of my stomach. Afterward, I wandered back to my sister's house in a daze, wondering if I'd unwittingly ensnared myself in some kind of gentleman's spat. But that evening, when I asked my nephew about the prince, his whole countenance changed, and I knew the accusations had merit.

Her son wouldn't go into specifics, except to say he'd once seen the prince leave a ball with a well-known seneschal's daughter. The girl went missing that same night. Days later, she turned up in an old, sealed-up boardinghouse across the city, with all manner of cuts and bruises she refused to explain.

No charges were filed.

No charges have ever been filed, despite the trail of crimes the prince has left across Hightower City.

You see, everyone is afraid. No one will risk saying anything about Kyven where royal ears might hear, so people turn a blind eye. As such, the prince has never answered for his crimes. Nor will he ever, I expect.

What unsettles me is how very charming he was. When I met Kyven in Burdock Street, he struck me as warm and charismatic. He looked so poised, wearing his beautiful clothes, dazzling me with that auburn hair and the twinkle in his eye. To think he could then commit such evils under the cover of darkness can only lead me to believe he has no soul.

So there you have it. The results of my investigation, such as they are. Be forewarned, Harlowe, and be careful. The prince will fool even you. But you must do whatever necessary to keep our sweet girl unharmed. If anyone can protect her, it's you.

I think you understand what I'm saying, do you not?

Give Amryssa my love, and I breathlessly await your reply,
Eliana Weatherby

I crushed the paper to my bosom. Wounding Merron had infused me with doubt, but now the letter crystallized my resolve once more.

I wouldn't let Kyven touch Amryssa. I wouldn't let him touch anyone, ever again.

Except me. And only once.

I dropped my blanket and went to the bathroom, then opened the taps to the hammered-copper tub. Steaming water cascaded into the basin. I stepped in, not caring that my skin pinked and sizzled in moments.

I washed my hair to gleaming, then scrubbed every inch of skin and soaked for so long that I grew waterlogged, my fingertips puckered.

When I emerged, I toweled dry, then went to go shove myself into Amryssa's wedding dress.

The same dress I would wear when I committed murder tonight.

6.

I couldn't breathe.

I tried to tell myself it was because Amryssa's wedding dress squeezed me so tightly my ribs knitted together, but the fact that Prince Kyven was coming definitely didn't help.

His bootheels clacked against the great hall's parquet, audible even through the library door. Each footfall stung my ears like a whipcrack. *Clack. Clack.*

This man—this monster—was about to become my husband.

I stole a glance at Amryssa. She waited, head bowed, her knuckles white around the loop of my keychain. After her nap, she'd fought my plan all over again, but I'd reminded her she'd agreed to this.

Now here we were.

Clack. Clack. My nerves sizzled like live coals. Across the library, the officiant contemplated his pocket watch, then cast a glance around.

I tried to calm my jittery nerves by imagining what he saw. Despite years of neglect, the library still commanded awe, a wonderland of crown molding and floor-to-ceiling windows. Gilt-trimmed books lined the walls, their spines gleaming with all the jewel tones of a beetle's carapace. Plush velvet armchairs dotted the room, their shabbiness softened by the lamplight.

Given that, this man probably assumed what everyone else in Oceansgate did—that Olivian was still rich. That the seneschal had abandoned them to the nightmares. That we'd shut ourselves up here willingly, with our full coffers and icy hearts for company.

But in truth, we simply had no means to help them anymore. We barely had the means to help ourselves. We were destitute.

Clack. Clack.

The doorknob turned. Shit. No matter what I'd told myself, I wasn't ready.

But there was no stopping what came next. Prince Kyven strode in, resplendent in shades of white and gold, and if I'd had trouble breathing before, now I was drowning.

In full, royal regalia, he overwhelmed me. I swore he glowed, his tailcoat as crisp as if the sartor had delivered it this morning, his russet hair threaded with fire by the lamplight. He came at me like an aimed javelin, his arctic eyes fastened on mine.

My lungs failed, but I couldn't blame it on the dress this time. Sweet Zephyrine, but he was beautiful. And absolutely poisonous. And really, how fucking dare he? Monsters like him should have the decency to wear their crimes on their faces, not show up looking like some unsuspecting woman's wet dream of an arranged husband.

Kyven's attendants strode in on his heels. Vick cataloged the library with methodical precision while Lunk gaped at the towering walls of books. I swore I caught a flash of appreciation in the giant's eyes.

"Why, my Lady Amryssa." Kyven's gaze swept over me. "I knew bacon had the power to restore you, but...just how much did you eat? You look ferocious."

"Ferocious?" My thready question barely put a dent in the quiet.

"Mmm. Like a dark lioness. Like you might tear me limb from limb, then pick your teeth with my bones, afterward."

My skin prickled. Was he telling me what he planned to do to me? Was this some kind of *game* to him?

"I like it," he purred. "Very much."

I shuddered, lamenting the way my skirts kept me from reaching for the dagger strapped to my thigh. Without access to my weapon, I felt naked, and stripped even barer by the malignant appreciation in Kyven's eyes.

He glanced around, granting my thrashing pulse a reprieve. "But what about your father? Where is he?"

"Not coming. He's sick," I said, then cursed myself. Amryssa would've said "taken ill." All those years spent under Eliana's tutelage had molded her diction into that worthy of a future seneschal.

But the prince didn't seem to notice my slip. He surveyed the waning grandeur, a smile playing around his mouth. "I can't say I pictured my wedding this way. I imagine you didn't, either."

"I..." I gave a weak cough. "What?"

"Well, neither of us chose this, did we? We're only here at the behest of other people. So I don't expect you to take this at all seriously. You can't possibly relish the prospect of tying your life to a stranger's."

I frowned, then reminded myself that for one of us, that life would prove very short, indeed. "It...probably won't be as bad as it sounds."

"One can certainly hope." Kyven smirked, then produced a bouquet of peonies seemingly from nowhere.

I frowned. "What's this?"

"I figured I ought to do *something* to brighten the occasion. An empty library seems a rather dismal stage for a royal wedding, does it not?"

A disbelieving laugh lodged in my throat. Some "royal wedding." This farce amounted to nothing more than Hightower tucking its cruelest monster into Elara's most forgotten pocket. No amount of offered flowers would change that.

"But you should know," Kyven continued, "that if you'd rather walk out that door than down this aisle, I won't stop you."

I paused. "You're...giving me an out?"

He shrugged. "Why not?"

I studied him. He looked earnest enough, but...why bother? Was he hoping to dodge this marriage and pin the blame on me? Or maybe he felt some shiver of foreboding when he looked at me. Did he gaze into my eyes and see his end reflected there?

Well, whatever the reason, it didn't matter. If I didn't marry this snake, Olivian would only repeat this blasphemy tomorrow night, with Amryssa in my place.

The thought steeled my spine, and I took the flowers from Kyven, my fingers grazing his. His warmth both repulsed and steadied me.

"Look." I raised my chin. "This match might've been Ol...er, my father's doing, but I'm here for my own reasons, now."

A slow smile claimed his face. "Oh?"

"Yes. I *want* this. You. So I choose aisle. Not door. But thanks."

The assurances slid from my tongue, smooth as oil, because I *did* want this. I needed this fiend to take me to the marriage bed, not my sweet, defenseless friend. *I* would be the one to see his fangs unveiled, to open his throat and watch him drown in his own blood.

He grinned. "Very well then, my lioness. Perhaps you're susceptible to my charms, after all."

I committed a series of mental gymnastics in order to keep from sneering. Wow. Arrogant, much?

"Shall we go get married, then?" he said.

Something fiery snapped inside me. "Let's."

The officiant pointedly cleared his throat, and Kyven broke from our tete-a-tete to face forward. I clasped the flowers, awaiting some kind of signal, but we wouldn't have any music, so after a beat of awkward silence, I simply started walking.

The prince matched my strides. "I can't imagine this matrimony business should be all that difficult, anyway," he said from the side of his mouth. "From what I've gathered, all it takes is trust, fidelity, and a healthy dose of selective hearing."

I cut him a startled glance.

"Oh, don't make that face, I'm only joking." He winked. "Fidelity is the last thing I'd expect."

I nearly stumbled. Goddess, if there was anything worse than marrying a gorgeous psychopath, it was marrying a gorgeous psychopath who thought he was clever.

"Glad to know you're taking your vows seriously," I choked out.

"I've never taken a vow seriously in my life," he said lightly. "I don't plan to start now."

Before I could respond, we reached the officiant, who instructed us to face each other. I obeyed, the peonies already limp in my grasp.

Thankfully, the man made short work of the ceremony. He clearly had somewhere more important to be, and our vows passed in a blur —something about growing alongside each other, our roots entwined like goddess-blessed oaks. It all felt ridiculously outdated, considering the swamp no longer served as anyone's temple and hadn't in years, but I forced myself to parrot the empty oaths. Kyven breezed through his with similar indifference. Not even his cultured Hightower lilt could lend the promises any weight.

The officiant clearly didn't care. With palpable disinterest, he crowned us with traditional marriage wreaths, both woven from the delicate moss that dripped from the trees—though I couldn't imagine where anyone had sourced the unruined silver stuff rather than the toxic purple kind that surrounded the manor. Then he bound our wrists with a length of cypress vine and pronounced us man and wife.

That was it. I squared my shoulders, bracing for some invisible weight to descend, but apparently being married—even to a monster —felt no different than *not* being married.

"You may kiss the bride," the officiant intoned.

That prompted a response. Every muscle in my body locked up, because I hadn't considered the kiss. *Why* had I not considered the kiss?

Kyven scanned my face. I swore he clocked the dread writhing in my stomach, because he smiled knowingly and turned to the officiant. "I think we'll save that for later. For when we don't have a pair of beady little eyes hungering for a free performance."

The man huffed. "Look, I don't care what you do, so long as I get my fee. I've done my bit, so Olivian'd better cough up some of those coins he's hoarding. Now, why don't you two run along and have yourselves a nice life? Shouldn't be hard, living here all comfy-like."

He stalked from the room before I could correct him.

Vick trailed the man as far as the doors. His vulpine features conveyed an impatience to get on with his evening, whatever that consisted of. Amryssa hovered at his elbow, silent.

"Well," Kyven said. "That was rather anticlimactic."

I hesitated. The doorway resembled the maw of some ravenous beast, ready to swallow me up.

Once I passed through, everything would change. Upstairs lay long halls and closed doors and privacy, and once I had the prince sequestered in my room, his mask would fall away. Then I'd find out just how deep the water I'd jumped into ran.

Many, many fathoms, I suspected.

Kyven—oh goddess, my *husband*, what the fuck?—offered his arm. I swallowed my revulsion and took it, then forced my feet to move, though it felt distinctly like being dragged.

Halfway to the door, Lunk astonished me by crushing Kyven into a hug.

I hung back, taking the opportunity to toss my peonies away beneath a chair. Kyven's attendant clung to him, and if I hadn't known better, I would've suspected true warmth existed between these men. Tears streaked the giant's face as he beamed a broken-toothed smile over Kyven's shoulder. I echoed the gesture, then wondered why I'd bothered, but Lunk seemed so overjoyed that I couldn't regret it too much.

When the big man finally let go, the vine at my wrist went taut, giving me no choice but to follow my new husband toward the door.

Vick nodded as we passed. "It's done, then. On to the next step."

The pronouncement gave me pause. What the hell did that mean, *the next step?* And why did Vick's Hightower accent sound so...different than Kyven's? It was stiffer, more hesitant. As if he'd pondered each syllable beforehand.

I squinted, but Vick's expression revealed nothing. I hurried onward, disconcerted.

In the great hall, Kyven mounted the staircase. Amryssa trailed after us, her eyes downcast. Apparently she'd taken my earlier warnings to heart.

Say nothing. Don't even look at anyone.

On the second floor, we threaded up the narrow staircase to the tower. While we climbed, Eliana's words spread like a stain on my mind, a black rot I couldn't scrape away.

As Kyven grew, he left behind a trail of little deaths, and later, some not-so-little deaths.

All too soon, we reached Amryssa's door. She finally met my gaze, abject terror in her eyes.

Oddly enough, her fear granted me courage like nothing else could. After all, I'd done this for her. Now only one last hurdle remained. Then she'd be free of this. Of *him.*

"Don't worry," I whispered, pulling her into a hug. "Just...try to ignore the screaming, all right?"

She stiffened. "Harlowe. No. What if he—"

I snatched my keyring from her grip, then shooed her into her bedroom and locked the door. Thankfully, she didn't scream. Didn't fight.

She never did.

That done, I drew a tattered breath and turned to the man I'd married.

Time to invite him in. Time for us to be alone.

7.

Kyven's brows arched as he crossed the threshold into my room. "You lock your keymistress in at night? Shouldn't it be the other way around?"

I closed the door and turned, my lips arranged in a smile. Zephyrine, my face would hurt by the end of this charade. "Usually, but tonight's different. I'd rather not have her...interrupting anything. If you know what I mean."

"Ah." The candlelight thawed his eyes to chilly flames. "Aren't you full of surprises, then?"

"Oh, just you wait." My tone played at seduction, but what I really meant was, *Your death will be swift and painful.*

"I must admit," he said, throaty, "I'm very much looking forward to this next part. I have been ever since I saw you at breakfast."

I nearly choked. I betted he had. He'd probably been dreaming about the many ways in which he could hurt me. Tattoo his ownership onto my flesh for everyone to see. Or maybe he didn't intend to let me live until morning at all. Maybe he planned to add to his list of not-so-little deaths before sunrise.

He ventured closer, and I backed away, my nerves coiling like cranked springs. Was this it? Would I meet the real Kyven now?

But he only plucked at the vine that bound our wrists, his face downturned. His hair slid over his forehead, sending a wave of his scent into my nose.

I stiffened. That *smell*. I recognized it. Knew it like I knew my own heartbeat.

Saltwater and cypresses and firesmoke.

Kyven yanked at the knots, but I barely felt it, because the vault of my past yawned wide, whisking me back to all those nights spent at the fireside under open stars, when I'd had no roof to call my own. When the wilderness had sprawled around me, endless and lightless and desolate, and I'd felt like the only person in existence. When loneliness had branded its name on my heart, each fall of the sun carving the word deeper.

Sweet Zephyrine, why did Kyven smell like the marsh?

But then I realized—he'd just made a month-long trek from the capital. Half that time would've been spent on the lonely Oceansgate road, which cut through miles of wild everglade, where he and his attendants would have bedded down on open ground.

I shook myself, blinking away the thoughts. When I forced my attention downward, Kyven had loosened his half of the vine and gone to work on mine.

"That's supposed to stay on until sunrise," I murmured, and couldn't have said why. I had no desire to honor the traditions, much less stay tied to him for another second. I wanted his evocative scent out of my nostrils, his shining hair far from my sight.

Preferably in a six-foot hole somewhere.

He released the vine and tossed it to the floor. "Don't worry. I've spent a lifetime skirting expectations and have somehow managed to survive. I doubt this will be any different." His mouth curled in a show of reassurance.

I searched his face. Why was he still talking this way, with such...warmth? He had no reason to maintain the charade any longer, so why not get down to the messy business of trying to hurt me?

Apparently, he had no immediate plans for that, because he turned and sauntered off. "I'll just go wash up. Be out in a minute."

The bathroom door closed. Once left to my own devices, I sagged against the wall. Goddess, I needed to get out of this gown. I hadn't taken a full breath in hours, which was clearly affecting my rationality. I ripped off my marital crown and hunted beneath my skirts for my dagger.

Get this stupid dress off, I told it.

The dagger awoke, and all along my spine, laces popped free. I shoved the gown to the floor, but that only solved half my problem. I pawed at my body next, reinflating my hips and waist, restoring their proper curves.

Oh, thank Zephyrine.

My stomach settled into its rightful place. My lungs lightened with sweet, sweet air. I gasped, then gasped some more, until the fuzzy shadows lining my vision faded.

By the time Kyven emerged from the bathroom, I'd mostly recovered. I lay on the bed in my nightgown, another aching smile pasted to my face. The dagger rested beneath my pillow, awaiting its moment.

Kyven stopped at the foot of the bed. He'd stripped to his shirt-sleeves and breeches. His hair had been wetted and combed back, freeing the planes of his face to glint in the candlelight.

I stared. My pulse throbbed in my throat, so thick and forceful I lost my breath all over again. Maybe because it finally sank in that I'd married this man, or maybe because, without all that wedding finery, I could trace my new husband's body right through his clothes. Broad shoulders tapered to a rangy waist while muscle cabled his arms and thighs. Despite his middling height, he radiated strength, but it was the hardened, hungry kind, the sort earned by days of hard labor that ended with too little on the table. Where he'd looked so refined in his formalwear, now the low light revealed a wild, starving edge. Prince or not, he looked nothing like a man who lounged around in gentleman's clubs and made polite noises over fine china.

Was this his predator's hunger shining through, then? Did the perverse appetites boiling inside him carve his body to hardness? Strip away the excesses of princehood?

"That bathroom has more mirrors than a carnival house," he said, breaking the grip of my thoughts. "I was beginning to think I'd never find my way out."

A grunt escaped me. I hadn't expected *that*.

But he wasn't wrong. Before this had been my chamber, it had been Eliana's, and the woman had apparently required thirty-six different viewing angles when choosing her wardrobe. Upon moving in, I'd left her mirror collection untouched, with the vague intention of finding out what Merron looked like from every perspective when he hoisted me onto the counter and ravished me.

Not that it would ever happen now, and not that Kyven needed to know that. "Are you sure you weren't getting lost in your own reflection?"

At my jibe, an appreciative spark flared in his eyes. "Tempting as that was, my wife was waiting for me. And I'm far more interested in admiring her than myself."

Wife. My breath hitched, but he said no more, only began a slow perusal of the room. At my vanity, he lifted a long-dry perfume bottle and sniffed at the nozzle with the entitled air of a man handling his own possessions. By the window, he ran a forefinger along the sill and inspected it for dust, then directed his attention outside.

He studied the forest's spectral purple glow, his face inscrutable.

I lay there, tension vibrating through me. What was he doing? Why this studied inventory of my life?

"This place is lavish," he murmured. "You're fortunate. Though I suppose you'd have no way to know that."

I frowned. I *was* fortunate, and absolutely knew it, but any prince of Hightower should see a long-faded bloom, a house whose glory days were so far past they'd flaked away to dust and collected beneath the baseboards.

Why did nothing about this man line up with expectations? Even Eliana's letter hadn't prepared me for...*this*.

Kyven took a seat on the empty side of the bed. He plucked a book from my nightstand and leafed through the pages, then swiveled to face me, brow raised.

"A romance?" His tone struck a balance between teasing and surprise. "You? I wouldn't have guessed."

I searched for my voice. "Why? Do I not seem like a reader?"

"Oh, I'd never cast doubts on your intellect. I just hadn't taken you for the love story type. You seem too...fiery for that."

My head spun. Now we were talking about...my reading habits?

"Lunk will like you, at any rate," he said.

"Lunk," I repeated dumbly.

"Mmm-hmm. He adores romances. Is this one any good? You'll have to recommend it to him, if so."

"Because Lunk...reads romances?"

"Oh, yes. Endlessly. He'll bend your ear in half, if you aren't careful." He made an elegant gesture in the air. "He's constantly trying to relate the plotline of his latest obsession to me. I can't tell you how many times I've had to remind him I prefer to *live* my love stories."

I couldn't help it—I scoffed.

"What?" Kyven looked at me askance. "I don't seem like a man who falls in love?"

I nearly bit through my tongue trying to keep from answering *that* question.

"Because I do," he said. "Oftentimes I fall in love in the evening, then out of it again by sunrise." He flipped a page and let out a hum of approval. Judging by his place in the book, I guessed he'd landed on the spiciest passage, the one I'd read so many times I'd lost count.

"I...see," he said as he scanned the lines. "Perhaps the love aspect isn't what interests you most?"

The tips of my ears burned. "There's more to romances than just the 'love aspect.'"

"Clearly." Kyven flicked the page, where I'd pressed in a dog-ear for easy reference. "It's enough to make me suspect you're no blushing maiden."

I should have denied that, because Amryssa was as virginal as a snowdrop in its first bloom. But I needed to do something—*anything*—to break this awful tension. To shock the smile off his face so we could get on with it. "I'm afraid not."

His expression melted into one of...appreciation? "Oh, thank Hyperion."

Hyperion. Hightower's bright, sunny patron god—a deity who probably dispensed blessings like candy, given that he hadn't spent the last decade sleeping. His name sounded so incongruous here, inside Zephyrine's crumbling walls. Like it had taken a wrong turn and lost its way.

But even the unfamiliar invocation couldn't dull my surprise. Here in Oceansgate, bridal purity had fallen from favor along with things like lawfulness and taxes, but last I'd checked, the notion had been alive and well in Hightower. Especially among the monarchy.

"That's...fine with you?" I ventured.

"Yes, it's *fine*," he said. "Of course it's fine. This next part won't be at all enjoyable for me unless it's enjoyable for you."

"The next part. Which is?"

But Kyven had already tossed the book aside. He crawled across the mattress and swung a leg over me, bracketing my hips with his knees, pinning me to the bed.

A cold thrill shivered through me. This was it, then. It had to be. I slid a hand beneath my pillow, curling my fingers around the hilt of my dagger.

"The *fun* part," he crooned. "The part that makes all this absurdity worthwhile."

My breathing accelerated. I would let him get close, I decided. As close as he liked. Then, the moment the pain began, he'd find a knife in his back for his trouble. "You mean the part where you make me scream?"

"If I do things properly, yes." He grinned. "May I?"

Sweat broke out on my palms. Was he really *asking permission* to hurt me? Whatever. I was done playing. "Go ahead." My voice rang with challenge. "Do your worst."

His eyes went hot and hooded. "How about my best?" He reached up and flicked his shirt buttons open, one by one.

An involuntary breath sliced from my lungs. I should have looked away. I really, really should have. Instead, I lay transfixed, like a snake beguiled by the charmer, or maybe a hapless rabbit, snared by the gaze of the lynx.

Kyven peeled off his shirt and tossed it aside. Fucking hell, but he was all lines and angles, sketched with an unforgiving sharpness that filtered straight into my bloodstream. And in that moment, I'd never envied Amryssa her imperviousness to temptation more, because this man had the kind of beauty that could make me forget myself. He was all chiseled savagery, flesh stripped to its barest essentials, malice gloved in the thinnest of satin.

Revulsion and excitement clashed in my belly. My dagger awoke, humming a question, but I couldn't bring myself to respond.

Kyven leaned down. When I didn't recoil, he angled his head to nuzzle at my neck, and the moment his mouth found my throat, my spine bowed. Everything in me rioted.

Gods among us, that didn't hurt. At all. It felt...fucking *divine*.

I closed my eyes and tried to think past the rush. Because this was all part of my plan, wasn't it? Yes, yes, the plan. Now I only had to decide where to sink my blade. Maybe into his kidney, or the back of his neck, or...

Or...

Oh *shit,* that made my toes curl.

Kyven's tongue painted languid strokes against my skin. One of his hands slid past my ear while he rucked up my nightgown with the other, his fingers trailing a caress along my thigh. The room shrank to an airless puddle, just heat and velvet and candlelight.

I whimpered. Seven hells, I should just stab this asshole and be done with it, but my willpower had receded. Probably because I'd never killed anyone before, and now the possibility immobilized me. Or maybe that was the russet-haired prince pinning me down.

The wet heat at my neck became insistent. Kyven sucked and teased and panted soft sounds against my ear. My stomach clenched, a million fluttering ribbons unspooling within.

Damn it. Maybe there *was* something worse than marrying a gorgeous psychopath who thought he was clever—marrying a gorgeous psychopath with whom I had blistering physical chemistry.

And who, for some inexplicable reason, had decided to be *passionate* with me.

Kyven's efforts increased. The dagger sizzled in my hand, but I rammed my eyes shut and blocked it out. As awful as it was, as horrific a person as it made me—and it did, it really did—no part of me wanted this to stop. That thing he was doing with his tongue was intoxicating. And the more I thought about it, didn't he owe me some kind of compensation for putting me to all this trouble of killing him?

Yes, I decided. Absolutely yes.

"Touch me, lioness." His breath was a lick of fire against my skin. "*Wife.*"

Heat flooded my cheeks. My free hand leapt to obey, skimming down hard planes of muscle before settling at the small of his back.

Kyven's hand roamed under my nightgown, dipping into the curve of my waist. His palm was unexpectedly rough, but that hardly mattered when it felt like someone had plunged me into a vat of my own yearning, then dumped me out on the bed again, flushed and slippery and panting.

An unchecked moan worked free of my throat. Kyven responded with a sound that made my thighs clench, and then he was pulling my legs apart, settling between them, rocking his hips into mine.

"I'm going to relish every moment of this," he said thickly. "There's something captivating about you. Like if I'm not careful, you'll bite."

Oh, he had no clue. "Maybe I will." I ground my hips upward, mirroring his movements.

"Mmm. Promise?"

When I didn't respond, he pulled away, taking that gift of a tongue with him. For long moments, he stared down. Only it wasn't *staring*, really. More like peering into my soul. His pupils were huge and black and bottomless, his irises little more than frosty haloes.

I stared back, my heart thudding a frantic rhythm. Had Merron ever looked at me like this? I didn't think so. He'd never kissed my neck that way, either, or sent me spinning through space with nothing to grab hold of. He'd never melted me to a red-hot glow. No, Merron was steady. Safe. He was...

Oh, goddess. *Merron.*

His name sliced through the haze. I'd had him on top of me mere hours ago, just like this. I'd had him *inside* me, for Zephyrine's sake. Right in this very spot.

What the hell was I doing?

Kyven bent, clearly aiming for a kiss this time. I managed to wrench my dagger free and angle it toward his throat. The blade stopped just short, the sharp edge kissing his skin, the flattened spine braced against my forearm.

Nothing moved. Harsh breaths invaded the quiet—mine? His?

Kyven's gaze flicked downward, then back up. "Is that a knife in your hand," he said slowly, "or are you just happy to see me?"

"Get off."

He jerked up into a sit, palms raised. I chased his retreat with my blade, never breaking contact with his skin.

"I'm...confused," he said.

"Really? What part of having a knife to your throat isn't clear?"

"That part's rather crystal. It's only...I thought you said you wanted this. That you wanted *me.*"

Dead, I told myself. That was how I wanted him. I eyed the soft, vulnerable flesh of his throat, where his pulse shimmered against the bright line of my dagger. Just a flick of my wrist, and his life would escape onto the floor.

Kyven studied me. "Lioness?"

I raised my eyes, searching his for some kind of tell. Surely a man who harbored horrors upon horrors couldn't contain them completely—some hint would *have* to leak through, like light from beneath a barred door.

But no matter how deeply I looked, I couldn't find an edge in him. Only confusion and the banked blue burn of desire.

A growl piled in my throat. Goddess, if only he'd hurt me, or let me peek beneath the facade, I wouldn't have hesitated. But he hadn't.

I lowered my blade, disgusted with both of us.

Kyven scooted away. He stretched out along the bed's far edge, his head propped on a hand, looking far more relaxed than a man who'd just rubbed elbows with death had any right to.

"Apologies," he said. "I thought... Well, when you said you wanted this, I took that to mean we'd both decided to enjoy ourselves."

"No." My voice sounded hollow. Ground down. As if he'd held a knife to *my* airway instead of the other way around. "This is about duty for me. That's all."

"Ah. My mistake, then." His tone was light, enough that I wondered if he was even capable of having a serious conversation. It didn't seem that way. "Though you didn't have to make your point *quite* so emphatically."

"Would you have stopped, if I hadn't?"

He scoffed. "If you're suggesting I would ever force a woman, I would suggest you don't know me at all."

"Of course I don't," I snapped. "I just met you this morning."

He inclined his head in apparent surrender, then flopped onto his back and laced his fingers behind his head. He slung one ankle over the other, the very picture of a man at leisure.

I blinked, perplexed. Then again, if last night's storm hadn't rattled his composure, why should attempted murder be any different?

"So, now what?" he said. "What do you do in this place?"

I scrambled to follow the latest of his capricious subject changes. "Do? As in...for fun?"

"Yes, for fun. Besides reading, that is. I haven't the patience for that."

"What *do* you have the patience for?" I said, then caught myself. Why was I even engaging in this?

"Not much, I'll admit. I would've liked to find out what kind of noises you make when a man touches you properly, but if that's off the table, I'm open to other suggestions. I mean, this is our life now, isn't it? I'd rather not lie here night after night, talking about our feelings. Not if there's something more interesting to be explored."

"I never talk about feelings," I growled.

"Wonderful. And I don't have any, so that takes care of that."

My thoughts rolled around in my skull like loose marbles. None of this made sense—not the half-naked stranger in my bed, not the quips that kept leaping from his mouth, not the many ways in which Eliana's foreboding letter failed to match the reality.

Harlowe, he will fool even you.

She'd warned me, but still, I couldn't escape the sense that I was one step behind this man, struggling to catch up but never actually making it. Moreover, I felt like I'd missed something. Something crucial.

"I know." He thrust a forefinger into the air. "Why don't we go into town?"

"To...town?"

"Yes. Oceansgate proper is only a stone's throw away. We could go to the theatre. We could go out drinking. We could do whatever we want."

"You want to go to the theatre," I said flatly. There was that feeling again.

"Well, why not?"

"I don't know, maybe because you just married someone who then tried to kill you?"

He waved an airy hand. "Oh, you didn't actually *try*. If you had, I'd be gasping about on the floor right now." He cinched two hands around his neck and pantomimed dying horribly.

I watched his performance to its conclusion. "You are absolutely the strangest man I've ever met."

"You must have led a very boring life, then."

Wow. That was rich—the pampered prince accusing the handmaid of being sheltered.

"Look," I said. "You can go into Oceansgate, if you want. But I'm not. Half the people there hate me, for one, and two, I'm tired."

"Come on, where's the fun in that?"

"We just married each other out of obligation. This isn't supposed to be fun."

He held my eyes for a beat, then pouted. "Well, town sounds much less enticing if you're not going to come along and let me loosen you up a bit."

My whole body went taut. "I never loosen up."

"Clearly."

I slitted my eyes. "I definitely should've stabbed you."

He laughed. "You'll have plenty more chances, I'm sure."

The offhand remark sent me down a rabbit-hole of what ifs. *Would I have more chances?* Was I squandering my best shot at protecting Amryssa? What would happen when Olivian—and Kyven himself, no less—discovered he'd married the wrong woman?

Something burbled in my stomach, then sprang from my lips in the form of a hysterical laugh.

Kyven cocked an eyebrow, but soon joined in. When our laughter died, we stared at one another.

"What was that about?" he said.

"This." I gestured between us. I had the distinct impression that tomorrow, when he found me out, it would be the first and only time I would manage to best him. "This whole thing is absurd. So...I'm just going to go to sleep now. *With* my knife."

"That sounds uncomfortable. But very well. I'll leave you to it. If you need me, I'll be over here, dying of boredom." He chuckled. "See? You won't have to stab me after all. Just ignore me, and the problem will take care of itself."

I shook a disbelieving head and settled into the mattress. I wouldn't make the mistake of turning my back; I didn't trust him for a second.

Kyven closed his eyes. Despite his protestations, he fell asleep almost immediately. Or at least, I *thought* he had. The moment I drifted off, he murmured.

"My Lady Amryssa. I never would've touched you if I'd known you didn't want me to."

I prised my eyes open, wondering when I'd closed them. Had I dreamt that?

Apparently. Kyven looked far, far gone. His chest rose and fell, the stark lines of his body ebbing and swelling in the candlelight.

I battled the sleep weighting my eyelids. Zephyrine help me, who was this man? I'd caught no sign of the emptiness Eliana had described, but this tenacious cheerfulness was just a smokescreen, right? What if he woke while I slept? What if I jolted awake to his hands wrapped around my throat?

The dagger must have sensed my ruminations, because it sighed in my grip. *What do you need?*

After a moment's contemplation, I told it, *Sleep. Make him sleep. Don't let him wake until I do.*

The dagger hummed and sizzled, then went quiet—the sign of a bargain accepted.

I waited another minute, watching Kyven breathe, but fatigue dragged at me, more insistent than a millstone tied to my ankle. I'd barely slept in two days and couldn't hold out much longer.

At last, I let go, praying my enchantment would hold until morning.

8.

Olivian's voice snatched me from sleep. "She did *what?*"

I peeled my eyes open. The wall between my chamber and Amryssa's muffled Olivian's shouts, but there was no mistake—the seneschal was in his daughter's room, and he was *pissed*.

"That conniving little cheat," he bellowed. "I'll kill her!"

I clambered upright. A glance confirmed Kyven was still lost to the depths of slumber and hadn't tried to kill me last night, but I'd sort out the meaning of that later. Right now, Amryssa needed me.

I flung my blanket aside and dashed into the hall. Why hadn't I remembered Olivian had a key to her room? Why hadn't I anticipated this?

I burst in to find the seneschal pacing at the foot of Amryssa's bed. She sat amid the tangled sheets, her eyes like gray glass orbs in a bloodless face.

"Don't yell at her," I blurted. "This was my idea, not hers."

"Oh, was it?" Olivian rounded on me, spittle flying. "Why does that not surprise me, *Your Highness?*"

I backpedaled a step. *Your Highness.* Huh. I...hadn't actually considered that.

"Well?" he roared. "Is that how I should address you now?"

I groped for my dagger, then winced. Shit. I'd left it in my room.

Ah, well. No way out but through. I snapped steel into my spine, since apparently, I now outranked Olivian—all ninety-nine seneschals in Elara answered to the monarchy. "I guess you should."

He snarled. "Because *you* married the prince last night, not Amryssa?"

"Looks like."

"And what do you have to say for yourself?"

"Um. Oops?"

Olivian's glare turned murderous. His fingers flexed, practically glowing with the need to strangle me. "And just what on earth possessed you, girl? What in seven hells were you trying to accomplish?"

I flashed my teeth. "After reading Eliana's letter, you really have to ask?"

He started toward me, violence in his eyes.

I dug my heels in, even while I wondered if I should run. What was I going to do, fight him bare-handed?

Thankfully, Olivian stopped mid-stride, his attention shifting past my shoulder. I turned, expecting empty space, or maybe a particularly provocative torchier, but a bare-chested prince filled the doorway instead, his breeches slung low on carven hips. A sleepy smile clung to Kyven's lips.

He looked...gorgeous, so much that yesterday's hate came crashing back like a punch to the gut. Then I saw what he held.

My dagger.

He offered me the weapon, hilt first. I snatched it, my loathing muddling to something indefinable.

"I figured you'd want that." Kyven winked. "Seeing as how someone in this room sounds *very* cranky, indeed."

For long moments, no one spoke. Olivian used the silence to smooth the rigid cast of his shoulders. "Ahem. Your Highness."

"Seneschal." Kyven's smile played at a smirk. "Good morning. I'm prepared to accept congratulations at any time."

"I'd offer them," Olivian said tightly. "But it seems there's been some...confusion."

"Ah, yes." Kyven eyed me. "For which I apologized last night. Though I can do it again, if your daughter would like."

"Not *that*," I whisper-hissed.

Olivian's eyes narrowed, but he didn't pursue the subject, thank Zephyrine. "Your Highness, it's only...I have to be sure. Which of these women did you marry last night?"

Kyven's brows rose. He glanced from me to Amryssa and back again. "Which of these women? Surely you're joking?"

"No." Olivian's patience was already fraying. "Who was it?"

"Well, if you'd attended your own daughter's wedding, you'd know, wouldn't you?"

At Olivian's glower, Kyven relented, though he was very clearly enjoying himself.

"Why, her, of course." He gestured to me. "The Lady Amryssa."

The seneschal spat a gravelly curse. "Except that's *not* the Lady Amryssa. That is." He pointed at the bed.

The evergreen smile dropped from Kyven's face. "The... What? No. That can't possibly be your daughter. She looks nothing like you."

"I think I'd know my own child."

Kyven studied Amryssa, dubious. "Is she even old enough to marry?"

"At twenty-seven," Olivian growled, "I'd say it's past time."

The prince absorbed that, then turned to me, bewildered.

I inhaled until my lungs threatened to burst. Maybe this would be the spark that finally lit the fire. Kyven's false cheer would burn away, and I'd unmask the monster, right here in front of everyone.

"Is this true?" he said.

I cleared my throat. "It...is."

"But...if that's the Lady Amryssa, then who're you?"

"The keymistress!" Olivian boomed, his control snapping. "You didn't marry my daughter, you married her fucking handmaid!"

Kyven's gaze widened. He looked me up and down as if seeing me for the first time. "You mean *you're* the keymistress?"

I raised my chin. "I...am."

"And you married me under false pretenses?"

"I did."

"But...*why?*"

A glance at Amryssa granted me strength. "Because. I didn't want you touching her."

"Lioness," Kyven breathed, then spent a mile-long minute just staring. "I'm...speechless. I think I'm also rather impressed."

I opened my mouth, readying a defense, then realized I didn't need one and floundered in silence. Well, this wasn't going as expected. At all.

"Enough dithering," Olivian shouted. "Just tell me this can be undone."

I flinched. "Undone?"

"Yes. As in, tell me you didn't consummate this."

I stilled. The consummation. Shit. Like the ceremonial kiss, I hadn't thought that through.

"Well?" Olivian said.

Kyven watched me without blinking. In the silence, the floor tilted, the whole world awaiting my answer. I had the strangest sense that if I lied, my new husband would corroborate me. But that was probably crazy, and besides, lying wouldn't do me any favors. This marriage *had* to bear up under scrutiny. If not, Olivian would only force a repeat ceremony with Amryssa.

No, I needed an honest solution. Or, at the very least, a way to buy time. "We didn't consummate anything," I said. Then, for good measure, "Don't be vile."

Kyven pressed a hand to his chest. "Ouch. You really are a death-blow to my ego."

Olivian released a breath. "Thank Zephyrine. Now come with me." A meaty hand circled my arm as he towed me toward the door.

"Hey." I pitted my weight against his, but I might as well have tried to topple a centuries-old oak. "Let go of me."

He dragged me into the hallway without slowing.

"Where're we going?" I shrieked.

"To my office, so you can write to the king. You'll accept the entirety of the blame for this, then petition him for an annulment."

"An annulment?" I cried. "What? You can't do that."

"*I* can't, you're right. But the king can. An unconsummated union can still be dissolved, as long as he grants an annulment and the two of you sign the certificate."

Ice hardened in the pit of my stomach. "But...what if I refuse?"

Olivian's gaze thinned—a threat. "You won't."

"Okay, well...what if Kyven does?"

His withering look conveyed exactly how likely he considered *that* prospect. "He's a prince. Who just married a glorified housemaid. I doubt he'll have a problem."

I barely refrained from flipping him off. "So that's it? I go to all this trouble to save Amryssa, and you want to throw her to the wolves?"

He bared his teeth. Down the hall, an approaching steward spotted us and abruptly reversed direction. I imagined how we must look— Olivian in a towering rage, me clutching my dagger while being hauled along in my nightgown.

Business as usual, really.

I tried and failed to regain control of my arm. "Let. Go. I'll come with you, just stop manhandling me."

"Fine." The seneschal released me without breaking stride. "But if you run, I swear to Zephyrine I'll haul you downstairs by your hair."

The moment he turned his back, I gave him the finger. Immature? Yes. Satisfying? Also yes.

In Olivian's study on the second floor, he collapsed behind his desk and glared. "You have no idea how thoroughly you've fucked this up."

I crossed my arms and glared right back. Sitting would've put me at eye level with him, so I didn't. "I'd actually say I actually have a pretty good idea, since that was the *entire* point."

"Oh? And was the *point* also to ruin Amryssa's chance at leaving Oceansgate?"

"Her chance at...wait, what?" I squinted, wondering if I'd heard him correctly.

"Leaving!" He slapped an open palm on the desk. "Do you think I actually want her here, suffering nightmare after nightmare? Do you think I wouldn't have sent her to Hightower ages ago, if I could have? Do you think I haven't been trying to arrange a safe place for her for *years*, and now you have the audacity to destroy that for her, you ungrateful, conniving wretch?"

Blood drained from my cheeks. My knees gave out, dumping me hard into an armchair.

"I should wring your meddling neck," he continued, the words hateful and hot.

I sat there, immobilized by the idea that he might actually *care*. "I don't... But...you never said that. You never told me you wanted better for her."

"What do you think this was all about?" he roared, then reined himself in, fisting his eyes and dragging in a breath.

When Olivian looked up again, he'd achieved a sliver of calm, however tenuous. "I had an agreement," he said. "With the king."

"Yes," I said faintly. "For new lawmen. You said."

"But that was only part of it. An insignificant part. The rest involved Amryssa having a place in the capital, once she was wed. She would've been a princess. Eligible to be cared for in Hightower. She would've had the kind of life I can't afford to buy for her in any other way, because our coffers are *empty*, Harlowe. Bled dry. It's cost me everything we had to keep Oceansgate afloat these nine years."

My mouth opened. Closed again.

The seneschal planted his elbows on the desk. "If not for you, Amryssa would've had a home. A *safe* one."

I absorbed that. "But...this is her home. She and Kyven were supposed to live *here* after the wedding."

"For a time. But if she'd outlived Kyven, Hightower would've taken her in. You understand?"

My throat went dry. He'd said *if*, but an unspoken, unmistakable *when* hung in the air.

When Amryssa outlived Kyven.

Olivian stared, his eyes as hard and flat as chips of green glass. His words writhed in my mind until the shape of his plans came into focus.

"Seven hells," I breathed. All this time, I'd glimpsed the tip of the iceberg without once suspecting a behemoth lurked beneath. "The king didn't banish Kyven here at all. He sent him to die. His own son. *That's* what your half of the marriage bargain was. To make the prince disappear."

Olivian said nothing.

"It's true, then?" I continued. "Kyven's a monster? A...killer? So awful his own father wants him gone?"

The seneschal made a gruff, affirmative sound.

I sat back, my mind awhirl. "But who was supposed to kill him? If Kyven had married Amryssa, he eventually would've tried to hurt her, and—"

It clicked.

A bitter laugh fell from my lips. "Oh, goddess. You wanted *me* to do it. I would've murdered him the moment he touched her, and then you could've shipped Amryssa to the capital without getting your hands dirty. I would've been the one to bear the punishment. Is that right?"

He busied himself rearranging a brass paperweight. "That's about the shape of it, yes."

Cold white silence cloaked my mind. Holy shit. Olivian had set me up. He'd taken my measure with frightening precision, then staked Amryssa's life on my homicidal tendencies. If only I hadn't swapped places with her, things would've happened exactly as he'd wanted.

"You can hate me all you like," he said roughly, "but you *will* fix this. I don't care what I have to threaten you with."

I breathed deep. "You don't have to threaten me at all, actually. And I can't believe I'm saying this, but...I don't hate you. Not for this. I think... I think..."

Kyven's words from just minutes ago came tumbling back. *I think I'm rather impressed.*

"I didn't know you had it in you," I said. "I really, really didn't.

More importantly, I didn't realize you wanted better for Amryssa. I always thought you didn't care."

"Of course I care. I'm her father." Olivian's voice was cold, but now I sensed an untapped depth beneath the words. "You and I both know these nightmares are killing her. One of these days, she'll get loose. And when that happens, we'll lose her. Better she be safe somewhere far away than gone forever."

Numbness chewed at my limbs. I flexed my fingers, trying to coax some sensation back into my deadened hands.

"And if you must know," Olivian continued, "Amryssa means more to me than my territory. I care about Oceansgate more than I care about myself, but for her, I'd let it burn."

The sentiment scoured out my insides. All this time, our purposes had aligned, only I'd been too stubborn to realize. Too hard-headed to consider that Olivian's gruffness and inflexibility might conceal deep caring.

I laid my hands on his desk, palms up. It was a gesture of apology, and supplication. "Goddess, if I'd known, I never would've switched places with her. I mean, I get why you didn't tell me. You were trying to toss me off a cliff. But the thing is, I would've let you. I would've jumped on my own, if you'd just come to me and explained. Kyven and Amryssa could've said their vows, and then I would've waited outside her door until she screamed. And once I'd sunk my dagger into his back, I would've held out my wrists for your new lawmen. I would've been *honored* to let them take me away."

He eyed me. "Would you?"

"For her? Yes. Anything."

His posture eased as his fury subsided, some. "Well, you can still do that. Once your marriage is annulled."

"Yes. Give me some paper."

He pushed a fountain pen and parchment into my hands.

I bent over the desk. The pen's nib scratched furrows into the silence, inked pleas flowing from my fingers. I detailed what I'd done and begged for a chance to rectify the mistake.

"I realize you love her," Olivian said gruffly, once I'd finished. "Perhaps I should've trusted that more than I did."

"You definitely should have. You should've told me everything. If you had, I could've been in prison already. Amryssa would be on her way to Hightower right now."

He made a thoughtful sound. Long moments passed, but the abrasiveness of our usual dynamic had faded—for once, we actually understood each other.

"So now what?" I said.

Olivian dripped wax onto my letter and stamped it with Oceansgate's seal. "It'll take a month for this letter to reach the king. Then another for the annulment certificate to arrive back here. Once it does, you and Kyven will sign it, and Amryssa will marry him, as planned."

"And then I'll kill him?"

"Yes."

A small, sad smile etched itself on my face. "Because all the king wants is a convenient death for his son, in some faraway backwater where no one will look too closely?"

"Precisely," Olivian said. "At which point Amryssa will be a widowed princess, in need of care."

I huffed out a dead laugh. Dear goddess, I'd come so perilously close to breaking this. I'd nearly let Kyven make me his wife in full. I'd *wanted* to.

Clearly, something was deeply, deeply wrong with me. Merron was lucky I'd cut him loose.

"You might be given a life sentence," Olivian said. "I'll do what I can to avoid that outcome, but I have very little influence."

"I'd appreciate you trying."

He nodded, businesslike. "While we wait for the annulment, I want you by Kyven's side at all times. Don't let him near Amryssa. Or any other woman in this house, for that matter."

Bitterness flooded my tongue. "You mean...you want me to babysit him?"

"Yes."

"What about at night?"

"Especially then. He can't be permitted to go prowling the halls. You'll have to keep him in your room."

"Oh, great." A laugh scraped up my throat, but I'd dug this hole myself. Now I would have to dig myself out.

"And *try* not to kill him. Not yet. If he makes an attempt on you, you'll have to deflect it without slitting his throat."

I grumbled. "Now you're just taking the fun out of it."

His gaze thinned.

I raised open palms. "Sorry, sorry. Just kidding. Sort of."

"Hilarious," Olivian said stonily. "And do not, under any circumstances, consummate this marriage. If you do, the annulment will be out of reach forever."

The memory of Kyven's tongue stirred a crackling heat inside me, but I shoved the feeling down into the darkest parts of myself. Of which there were plenty, apparently. "Come on. Do you really think I'd stoop so low?"

"You're young. Which is synonymous with idiotic. And Kyven's pretty. Prettier than Merron, at least. Even I can see that much."

Blood crept into my cheeks. I hadn't realized Olivian knew about my dalliances with the steward, but apparently I'd misjudged a whole fuck of a lot. "I'm twenty-seven, not a teenager. I can control my baser urges, thanks. Not that they were ever that depraved to begin with."

"Good." Olivian's attention slid to the corner. He startled, so subtly that I almost missed it, but then that look crept over him again. Haunted. Hunted.

With our typical animosity stripped away, I found the courage to finally ask.

"What're you looking at?" I said. "When you do that. Who is it you're seeing?"

Olivian's jaw flexed. For a moment, I thought he wouldn't answer, but he grunted and said, "My wife."

My eyebrows rose. "Amryssa's mother, you mean?"

He looked away. Not toward the corner again, just...not at me.

"You can see her even though she's gone?" I pressed.

He sighed, irritated. "If she is, that hasn't stopped her from expressing her displeasure at how I've handled things with our daughter."

I frowned. "Is *that* why you want to send Amryssa away, then? Because her mother's ghost tells you to?"

He emitted a cold bark of laughter. "No. Just the opposite. She keeps asking me to turn Amryssa loose. Into the marsh."

My gut lurched. "What? No. Don't listen to her. She's not real."

"I know. It feels that way sometimes, but..." He picked at his leather blotter. "I know. It's just a splinter of the nightmares, lodged in my brain. Mostly, I ignore her."

I nodded, only halfway mollified. I'd never met the Lady Marche—she'd died before I'd been made keymistress, one of the nightmares' earliest casualties. But Amryssa always spoke of her mother in reverent tones, and in Oceansgate, people whispered about how deeply the seneschal had loved his wife. Back then, they said, Olivian had governed fairly. Only after the Lady's death had he descended into callousness and obstinacy.

"That was hers, you know." He gestured to the dagger. "Before that was yours, it belonged to my wife."

I startled. He'd never so much as hinted at the dagger's provenance before. Briefly, I considered asking for more, then decided it wasn't worth the trouble. The weapon wouldn't belong to me for much longer.

Because... Shit. I'd left Amryssa alone with Kyven, hadn't I? The very thing Olivian had asked me not to do. "Well, thanks for the chat." I stood, itching to go.

"Harlowe."

I paused.

"My daughter's lucky to have you." He grimaced, then swallowed, as if the sentiment had sliced his tongue on the way out and now required him to gulp down a mouthful of blood.

Probably not far from the truth. "Thanks," I said, then smiled thinly and closed the door, leaving him to his darkness and ghosts.

On my way back upstairs, the magnitude of my mistake dragged at me like ballast. I'd been so sure that marrying Kyven equated to a masterstroke of strategy, but now I was sickened by what I'd done.

I'd jeopardized Amryssa's welfare. Come *this* close to robbing my best friend of a future.

At least Olivian had gotten my head on straight. And, knowing what I did now, I could fix it. I could bide my time, unmask my new husband's darkness for myself, and dispense with him when the time came.

I would clean up the awful mess I'd made, whatever it took.

9.

That afternoon, in the open-sided cupola on the roof, I sweltered over a basket of mending. Amryssa sat on the far bench, staring out over the marsh. Her lips moved, though her words failed to carry on the muggy air.

Kyven lounged beside me. In a concession to the heat, he'd foregone a waistcoat and rolled his sleeves to the elbow. Rather than expressing anger over my duplicity, he'd spent the day studying me with open interest.

And...shit. I was studying him back. Again. Who knew why, because I hated his face. Everything about it annoyed me, from the squared vee of his chin to the taper of his nose. Even his hair made me angry. It fell across his forehead as if he'd planned it that way, which he probably actually had, the narcissist. The longest, shiniest lock just kissed the arch of his brow, and I couldn't help but notice the chestnut hues matched exactly, unlike most people, whose hair and eyebrows differed by a shade or two.

I forced my attention back to my mending. What entitled him to stare like that? Creep.

"For someone who just vaulted from lady's maid to princess," he said, "you look remarkably unhappy. If I didn't know better, I'd suspect you find your new husband lacking."

My mouth twisted as I jabbed the needle in with unnecessary force. "You're *not* my husband."

"Oh, I beg to differ." Amusement and that stupid, snobbish accent molded his words into a taunt. "I distinctly remember becoming so last night."

"Fine. Maybe you are, for now. But you won't stay my husband for long."

I'd told him about the annulment the moment I'd found him—not in Amryssa's room, as I'd dreaded, but at the breakfast table, working through an assembly line of piled-high plates with his attendants. Just before walking in, I could've sworn I'd caught hissed words in an Oceansgate accent, but Vick had given me a narrow-eyed look upon entry, and I'd paused. All three men were from Hightower, weren't they?

I must have imagined it.

Now Kyven propped his elbows on his knees and gave me a casual once-over. We were effectively alone—his attendants had disappeared to Zephyrine-knew-where, and Amryssa may as well have ascended to another plane.

"How long will this annulment business take, again?" he said.

"Two months, roughly." Stitch, stitch. "Less, if we're lucky."

"Lucky?" He chuckled. "You almost sound as if you mean that."

I gave him a withering look, which he endured without appearing to suffer any ill effects. "This might come as a shock," I said, "but I don't want to be married to you a second longer than I have to. This whole thing was a mistake."

"Hmm." Sparks flew in those skylit eyes. "And yet you didn't seem to think so last night, when you were making that delightful little whimper and inviting me to do my worst."

I spluttered. Something red and angry swarmed beneath my skin.

"Oh, don't look so apoplectic, I'm only joking. And I do have one honest question."

"Which is?" The words hissed from me like steam jetting from a teakettle.

"How much did the seneschal offer you? To annul our marriage?"

I paused my sewing and waited for the punchline, but not a single one of those chestnut lashes flickered. "Nothing. He didn't offer me anything. Why would he have?"

"Well, you're a princess now. You wouldn't just...sign that away."

I tensed. "Is *that* what you think this was about?"

"Well, why else would you have married me?"

I flung the mending into its basket so I wouldn't accidentally shove the needle into my thumb. Or his eye. Zephyrine help me, how would I refrain from stabbing this donkey's ass for two whole months? "I already told you. I married you because I didn't want you touching Amryssa. That was the beginning and end of it for me."

He made a *tsk*ing sound. "Come, now. No one would throw themselves into the teeth of an unwanted marriage just to protect a friend."

"They absolutely would." I spat the words like gravel. "Not that you'd actually understand that. You've probably never sworn loyalty to anything other than your own reflection."

His chin dipped. "You have to admit, it does inspire a certain sense of devotion."

I gaped, wordless. If I'd had any skill at drawing, I would've marched downstairs to the library, pulled the dictionary from its shelf, and sketched in Kyven's portrait beside the entry for 'arrogance.' Maybe the one for 'delusional,' too.

"You wouldn't have gone to all that effort," he continued, "then changed your mind without an incentive."

I slitted my gaze, but...fine, he *did* actually have a point. I just didn't know how to counter it. How much did he understand about his father's motives in sending him here?

I decided to chance something close to the truth. "I just hadn't realized Amryssa...and you...would have a place in Hightower, after the wedding. *That's* what made me reconsider."

Apparently, that didn't set off any alarm bells, because Kyven sighed, a light exhale that failed to stir the heavy air. "Fine, then, don't tell me. I suppose it doesn't matter, anyway. Once we sign the annulment, you can gallop off into the sunset with your newfound riches and try to forget I exist. Not that I expect you'll have much luck."

I flattened my brows, unwilling to dignify that with a response. Who cared if he believed me, anyway? "So you'll marry Amryssa, then? After the annulment?"

His attention arced toward my best friend, his expression softening with the same tenderness he'd faked at breakfast yesterday.

Except...goddess, it didn't *look* fake. Somehow, Kyven had mastered even the smallest tells—his posture loosened and his mouth curved. He looked, for all the world, like a man surveying something fragile. Something he'd rather preserve than break.

I swatted at the errant thoughts. Maybe I couldn't distinguish performance from reality, but that didn't mean Kyven wasn't a monster. Eliana had said so. Olivian, too.

It didn't matter how convincing a show he put on.

"I *did* come here to marry." The prince's gaze swung back to mine, his attention like a boomerang that kept returning to me.

"So...that's a yes?"

"I suppose it'll depend on what's in it for me."

"What's in it for you?" My lip curled. "Wow. How very noble of you."

He smirked. "I'm a prince. I'm noble by definition. I don't have to actually *try*."

I swore under my breath. At least his arrogance made him easy to hate. "Don't you ever tire of hearing yourself talk?"

He laughed. "No, never. Do you ever tire of giving people the sharp side of your tongue?"

"No. I like my tongue the way it is, thanks."

"Mmm-hmm." His attention dropped to my mouth.

Heat climbed the nape of my neck, and I pulled at my collar. Goddess, I hated summers in Oceansgate. There was no escaping this muggy broil. "When you say there's something in it for you," I said, taking back control of the conversation, "what do you mean? Did your father...offer you something? To marry?"

Kyven's focus flicked back up to my eyes, which should have come as a relief but didn't. Who actually had irises that blue? And who looked at people that unwaveringly?

Someone needed to pass legislation against this sort of thing.

"Are we trading secrets, now?" He leaned in.

I fought the urge to retreat. "No. I don't keep any, anyway."

"Oh, I doubt *that*. Everyone has secrets."

My eyes narrowed. "Everyone? Including...you?"

A lazy smile lifted his mouth. "Especially me."

A shudder danced down my spine. Little did he realize I knew all about his private sins. His secrets had arrived before he had, and now I kept them in my armoire drawer, not five paces from where he'd slept last night.

"But I don't feel like sharing unless you do," he said. "So why not tell me what the seneschal's paying you?"

"I already said," I hissed. "Nothing. Now why'd you come? You don't need another title, much less a territory. So what're you hoping to gain here?"

Kyven glanced to Amryssa again. She'd now extended a finger to serve as a perch for a gargantuan purple butterfly—the wretched thing had three wings that shivered and flexed as she murmured to it.

"You wouldn't understand," he said, again with that hint of softness.

Fake softness, clearly. "Try me."

"Try you? I tried with you last night. At which point you made it abundantly clear that you'd rather I hadn't."

My pulse kicked. I groped for my dagger, tried my utmost not to stab him, and only barely succeeded.

"And on the subject of motivations," he continued, "what does it matter whether I marry her? If you can't keep your new title, money's the next best thing, and Olivian must've offered you plenty. So what do you care what happens after the annulment?"

I mashed my lips together, but he didn't warrant the effort of lying. "I *care* because Amryssa can't stay here. She has to go to Hightower."

"Ah." The wrinkle between his eyes smoothed away. "You mean to accompany her, then? Perform a heroic act of self-sacrifice by living in luxury with her in the capital?"

I gritted my teeth so hard my molars creaked. Goddess, this fucker was giving me the mother of all headaches. "You know what? You're wasting my breath. Just marry her when the time comes, okay?" Because in the end, it didn't matter what Kyven hoped to find here. He only needed to live long enough to make Amryssa a princess.

"Oh, I don't know that it's that simple." He rubbed at his jaw. "Now that I've met her, I don't exactly trust her ability to refuse."

I paused, my brows pinching. "What's that supposed to mean?"

"Well, last night, I gave you a choice. But look at her. How's a man supposed to marry a girl like that? Much less bed her? It...wouldn't be right."

I chewed on that. Thinking about them...*entwined* made me want to shove him off the roof, but I didn't plan on letting it go that far. I'd get rid of him right after the vows. "I'm sure you can manage. You married me without any trouble."

"You asked me to."

"Okay. But you had no problem trying to"—I swallowed against a dry throat—"*bed* me."

His eyelids lowered. "And I would've kept you up all night, lioness, if you'd let me. Trust me on that."

Queasiness rolled through me, lifting my stomach and dropping it again. Shit. Why had I eaten that extra biscuit with breakfast? It wasn't sitting right.

"But I've always preferred my women spirited. The Lady Amryssa doesn't appear to have heard the word."

I frowned. "She's stronger than you think."

"She looks like a stiff breeze would carry her off."

"You're underestimating her." My tone heated, as if I could pour enough acid into my voice to scald him. "Not that you care, or even deserve to hear it, but any man would be lucky to call her 'wife.' Amryssa's better than anyone I've ever met. She's generous. Self-sacrificing. She'd take an arrow for anyone without even thinking, whether they deserved it or not. And I don't know about you, but that kind of self-lessness isn't something I come across every day. Maybe not ever again. Which makes her worthy of respect. She's the most unselfish person I know, and I wouldn't have married you for anyone else's sake."

He fell silent. Something in his eyes changed—a subtle clearing of space, almost, like clouds parting, or a crowd thinning to reveal someone I hadn't expected. Someone who now considered me with interest, as if I were a puzzle in need of solving.

"I think you might actually mean that," he mused.

"I mean it with all my heart."

"Hmm."

That was all he said. But the force of his attention coaxed goose-bumps from my arms, despite the heat.

I cleared my throat with enough vigor to throw off the sensation. "Don't tell me you've never met someone deserving of loyalty."

"Never. In my experience, no such thing exists. Most people are unforgivably selfish. Myself included."

I hesitated. Well, we agreed on one thing, at least. "That's my point, though. Most people *are* selfish. So when you find one who isn't, the last thing you should do is pass them by. It's better to give yourself to them. Humble yourself. Because they might be the only person to ever deserve that, and if you miss your chance, you might never get another."

"I...see." Kyven contemplated his palms for a moment, then glanced up through his lashes. "And are you such a person? The kind I ought to give myself to?"

"No." I scooted back an inch. "Gods, no. What?"

The corners of his eyes crinkled. "Well, you would have me believe you acted out of selflessness last night. That your friend's well-being concerned you more than a title. In your own words, you married me to protect her, which would make you one of those exceptionally rare altruists you just spoke of. The kind I should humble myself before. Right?"

My lungs sucked at the brackish air as I tried to parse the dexterity with which he'd turned my argument against me. What he said *sounded* like it made sense, and yet I hadn't meant that at all.

"No. You're...getting it backwards."

"Am I?" The question was mild, but his attention never wavered. That rapier gaze threatened to cut away the bramble of my defenses and leave me with...well, who knew.

Seven hells, I'd wished and wished for him to dispense with those ridiculous half smiles, but now that he had, I wanted them back. Desperately. The way he scrutinized me twisted my insides into configurations I didn't recognize.

"I didn't mean anything like what you just said," I managed. "I'm not anyone special. I'm no one at all, really. Just a girl who found someone to believe in, in a place where everyone's forced to embrace the worst of themselves."

"But not you? You resist your baser instincts?"

I considered. "Only because I have the luxury of being able to. If Amryssa hadn't given me this life, I wouldn't have the option."

He inched closer, infiltrating my personal space with the scent of bracken and brine. His eyes were like wintry lances, aimed at my heart.

My breathing stalled. This was...different. A glimpse beneath the mask, only I didn't see a monster there, but someone quick-witted and inquisitive and...engaged.

"So you're grateful for what you have," he said.

I forced air through a parched throat. "Very."

"And loyal. To a fault, it would seem."

"I try."

"So loyal, in fact, that even though Olivian offered you nothing, you agreed to forfeit your new title simply so Amryssa could have a better life."

My nerves sizzled. Gods among us, why wouldn't he just *blink*? "Not that it matters, but yes."

"And you consider that normal. Just par for the course. You think you're no one of consequence."

"I *know* I'm not."

Long moments spun by. Kyven reached out and, when I froze, tucked my hair behind my ear. I shivered. Something about the gesture felt horrifyingly intimate. The brush of his fingers carried an impossible weight, one that made my heartbeat climb into my throat.

I angled away, trying to calm my reaction.

He dropped his hand and blinked, sobered by my retreat. "Apologies. Your hair was blowing around."

I had no idea what to say. There was no breeze to speak of. Just a ripe, waiting stillness, so thick I could taste it.

He cleared his throat, then rose and strolled away to lean against a pillar. Sweat glued his shirt to his back, accentuating the twin columns of muscle flanking his spine.

I stayed on the bench, trying to piece together my shattered composure. What the fuck had just happened? Just when I'd found my footing with him—a hatred I could safely burrow into—he'd knocked me off-kilter again.

"Harlowe?"

I jolted. It was the first time he'd said my name, and the syllables sounded so foreign in his mouth, the vowels robust, the *r* softened almost to nonexistence. "What?"

"What're they doing down there?"

"Who?"

"Those men."

I smoothed my skirts—and my breathing with them—and went to stand beside him.

A duty, I reminded myself. That was all this was. I would tolerate this awful, beautiful, monstrous prince for a bit, then marry him to Amryssa and widow her. Logical, concrete steps I should have no trouble taking.

Steps I *would* have no trouble taking.

I scanned the lawn with shaded eyes. Below, Merron and the stewards milled at the edge, where the grass gave way to a feral purple tangle. In the swamp, cypress roots jutted from the water like beckoning fingers, inviting the unsuspecting into Zephyrine's corrupted domain.

The men fanned out, armed with shovels and torches. Some dug a trench in the grass while others burnt the outer perimeter. Their combined efforts produced a barren brown line in the earth. "They're containing the spread," I said.

"The what?"

I glanced sidelong, but Kyven's gaze was as open and cloudless as if the moment on the bench had never happened.

"The spread," I said, steadier this time. "Of the rot."

"The rot?"

"Yeah. It's a long story, but...maybe you've heard of our patron goddess? Zephyrine?"

His mouth tilted. "I'm from Hightower, lioness. Not the underside of a rock."

I rolled my eyes. Yep, I'd definitely enjoy stabbing him, when the time came. "Okay, so you might've heard of Zephyrine, but what you probably don't know is that nine years ago, she fell asleep. Or was cursed with some kind of divine slumber. Or...well, nobody knows, really. What happened. But she stopped answering prayers, and started dreaming these awful nightmares, and without her around, the marsh got sick. Just in the middle, first, where Zephyrine sleeps inside her thousand-year-old tree. But the rot's crept outward ever since. The only way to stop it is to burn it, so that's what we do, because any plants or animals affected turn poisonous. Humans aren't susceptible, but if we don't protect our gardens and coops and goats, we'll have nothing to eat."

"Hmm. That doesn't sound so tragic."

"No?" I scoffed. "Big words for someone who ate his own weight in bacon this morning."

"Come, now. I'm not forgoing my rights to a lavish breakfast. I just mean that everyone acted so doom-and-gloom after the nightmare yesterday. So why not just leave? Go elsewhere?"

"And do what?" I crossed my arms. "Beg someone to take us in? No, thanks."

"You wouldn't have to beg. You're rich."

Oh, great. He was no different than the rest of them. "We're not, actually. Everything we had is gone. Everything but what you see here."

Kyven cut me a glance. That had surprised him, clearly, and I belatedly wondered if I'd misstepped. Maybe he'd come here believing Amryssa would make him wealthy. That he would inherit a territory whose coffers he could tap at will.

"So what you're telling me," he said slowly, "is that I should eat less bacon?"

I blinked. Or not. "I'm saying we have nowhere to go. No income. Oceansgate lost its tax collectors when we lost our lawmen. Life has only gotten harder, and at this point, we're hanging on by our fingernails. Olivian's only real hope is for Zephyrine to wake up."

"So you stay," he said, half-question, half-statement. "Nightmare after nightmare. You *endure*."

"I didn't say I liked it." My lips dragged down at the corners. "I hate it, actually. I hate how the nightmares make me feel so..."

He arced a brow and crossed his arms, one boot propped casually over the other. "So...what?"

My jaw hardened. What was I doing? "Nothing. I don't talk about feelings, remember?"

He chuckled. "You brought it up."

"I didn't. And if you're so damn curious, how'd the nightmare make *you* feel? And how'd you show up to breakfast yesterday looking as fresh as a daisy?"

"I'm special." He shrugged one shoulder. "I thought I'd already made that abundantly clear."

I threw my hands up. Ugh. Served me right for trying to have an actual conversation with this jerk.

"Do they need help down there?" he said abruptly.

I eyed him. Here came the subject changes again. He was like a moth, flitting from one shiny candleflame to the next. It was a wonder he ever concentrated long enough to secretly torture people the way he did. "Who, the stewards?"

"I don't see anyone else digging trenches, do you?"

I made a face. "It isn't a suitable pastime for royalty, if that's what you're asking. It's hot and dirty and sweaty and miserable."

"I hope you're not questioning my ability to wield a shovel. And besides, I'm bored. You can't expect me to just...sit around and wilt all day, like your esteemed charge over there." He waved toward Amryssa.

"You're not going downstairs."

"Well, I'm not going to sit still all afternoon. Idleness is one of the few talents I wasn't blessed with."

I glared. "Olivian wants me to keep an eye on you."

"So do it from here."

I opened my mouth to argue, but he was already in motion, blurring past me, descending the stairs to the attic.

"Hey!" I called. "Come back!"

No reply.

I started to follow, then paused to consider Amryssa. Before I could decide, Kyven appeared below. He strode across the lawn, shedding his shirt on the way, then grabbed a shovel and joined the efforts.

Merron and the stewards exchanged glances. A scowl pinched my ex-lover's face, but he grudgingly went to work beside Kyven, who catapulted soil from the trench with startling proficiency. The prince bent and flexed, bent and flexed. Muscle bunched and smoothed, his rhythm unflagging.

My jaw went slack as I watched. Huh. Maybe it wasn't hatefulness that had roughened his palms and honed the cut-crystal lines of his body. Maybe it was...hard work.

Something he was clearly very familiar with.

I drifted toward Amryssa and sat. The butterfly climbed the stagnant air, no longer interested in its communion now that I'd shown up.

She watched it go. "You intrigue him."

I frowned. "Who, the butterfly?"

"No. Your husband."

"What?" I laughed, all hard edges and cold denial. "No, I don't. Don't be ridiculous."

"I think perhaps he intrigues you, too."

"Am, no." I made a sound of revulsion. "He infuriates me. He's head-over-heels in love with himself and probably couldn't act serious at a funeral. And let's not forget the part where he kidnaps seneschal's daughters and hurts them."

"That wasn't him, though. He never did those things."

She delivered the statement with such matter-of-fact conviction that I paused. "What? Who told you that?"

"The butterfly."

The butterfly. I shook my head. Of course.

"It had a message." Amryssa burrowed against me, her bare skin sticking to mine. "It said I'm not who we think. Nor is the prince. None of us, none of this, is as it seems. That's what it told me, just now."

My insides soured. Normally, her ramblings slid right off, but today, the words lodged somewhere south of my heartbeat, in a no-man's-land I didn't dare trespass upon.

"It's all right," she said. "You'll see."

I watched the men work below. I wouldn't see. I would sign the annulment and rid the world of Kyven, then ship Amryssa off to Hightower. I'd spend the rest of my years imprisoned, and that would be that. A small life, now concluded.

I slid an icy shutter down, sealing whatever feelings I had about that future behind a hard, blank wall.

"The butterfly said another thing, too," Amryssa continued. "There's a storm coming. More powerful than any nightmare. And when it arrives, everything will fall apart."

I flinched. *Everything will fall apart.*

That much, at least, was probably exactly right.

10.

Over the next three weeks, I trailed Kyven like a would-be jailer, watchful and suspicious.

Not that my vigilance accomplished much. As if in answer to my scrutiny, the prince doubled down on his carefree image—he laughed easily, did everything with gusto, and seized every opportunity to slip me a wink or a half smile. Moreover, ever since our conversation in the cupola, he often studied me as if sizing up a mountain he planned to climb.

Which unsettled me, to say the least. Mostly because I knew that, however well he disguised it, he was likely thinking about pain. Specifically *mine*, and as the days passed, I almost hoped he would slip. Unleash his sadistic tendencies so I wouldn't have to endure this farce anymore.

But instead of putting me out of my misery, the insufferable man just...never stopping moving. Breakfast usually involved three separate trips to the sideboard, followed by an exhaustive investigation of the manor's rooms in search of something "stimulating." When that inevitably failed, Kyven would pester some poor steward for a job, then spend the afternoon chopping wood, or feeding the hot-water boilers, or wrestling the sheep for shearing. Whatever the task, it usually involved a ridiculous amount of brute strength, and apparently required him to take off his shirt.

Infuriating, egotistical show-off.

Keeping him in my sights exhausted me, and I still had to tend to Amryssa. The only thing making my double duties tolerable was the fact that the prince didn't chafe at my relentless presence. He only ever complained of boredom, and then he did so with his customary half smile in place.

Nothing else seemed to vex him. Not the heat. Not the scalding tea Miss Quist spilled on his spotless jacquard waistcoat one morning. Apparently, not even the fact that he'd married the wrong woman, whose bed he would share for the next eight weeks.

When I told him he would sleep in my room until the annulment went through, he waggled his brows, a wicked gleam in his eye. But he never so much as touched me. He only sauntered around my chamber each evening, his clothing at a minimum. More than once, he caught me running my eyes over his sculpted torso.

"See something you like?" he said one night.

I jerked my attention down to the book in my lap. I'd made it my policy never to fall asleep before he did, so while he puttered around, expending the last of his considerable energy, I took the opportunity to read.

"No," I said.

"Ah, the infamous denial of attraction."

"Attraction?" My fingers clamped around the pages, smudging the ink. "Ha. The only thing I find attractive here is the fact that I'll be rid of you in five weeks."

"Ah, but five weeks isn't an insignificant amount of time." He drummed his fingers against his chin. "If you aren't careful, you'll fall madly in love with me before then."

I grimaced. "You have a zero percent chance of making me fall in love with you. *Especially* in five weeks."

"You know, you're right. My apologies."

My shoulders loosened.

"I'm sure I can do it in three," he added, and winked.

I couldn't help myself. I threw the book. Kyven ducked away, laughing.

Goddess, I hated him. Yet as the weeks passed, some part of me *did* grow accustomed to his presence. I never forgot I was sharing my bedchamber with a monster—one who, by his own admission, was keeping secrets. But that didn't stop me from sometimes, just sometimes, appreciating the way the day's heat dusted him with gold, how he looked as though someone had painted him from light and fire. Not to mention the way my heart beat dull and drunk in response.

A shame, really. All that gorgeousness, wasted on a villain.

The days passed. Each evening, I read until Kyven wore himself down. Then I called on the dagger's enchantment, ensuring he wouldn't wake until I did.

Then I rolled away and ignored him. Or tried. But the heat-drenched silence had a maddening habit of amplifying each sound. There was the cadence of his breath. His sleepy murmurs. The startling frequency with which he dreamed.

All of which prevented me from finding proper rest.

Still, I would've endured a thousand of those unsettled nights in order to see the changes in Amryssa. Without the threat of marriage hanging over her head, she smiled more. Her musical laugh graced my ears with increasing frequency.

Only now did I realize how painfully somber she'd become after Olivian had announced his intentions to marry her off. And if she still spent long hours staring out the window, if she somehow looked frailer than ever, at least the wait for the annulment had given her room to breathe.

All too soon, it would be over.

Soon enough, everything would fall apart, just as Amryssa had said.

~

Vick was up to something.

I couldn't say exactly when I'd realized. Maybe when Kyven tried, for the third time, to distract me when his orange-haired attendant emerged from a room that hadn't been used in almost a decade. Or maybe when I caught Vick sitting in the library, sketching walls and stairwells in the air.

"What're you doing?" I said.

He took my measure, his gaze acute, like he could calculate my innermost secrets if he viewed me from a certain angle. "Making a blueprint."

"Of?"

"The house."

I paused. Vick sat in an overstuffed armchair, his shortsword leaned against the side, but his hands were empty—not a scrap of parchment in sight. "What, inside your head?"

"Where else?"

I blinked. I'd lived here nine years and still struggled to navigate the manor's sprawl, at least when roaming the lesser-used wings. The idea of someone charting this labyrinth in less than a month...

"There's a locked room," he said, unmoved by my astonishment. "On the third floor. If you take two rights from the stairs, then a left, it's the last one on the right. That door's barred. What's in there?"

I frowned. Kyven was off in the corner, entertaining himself by spinning a standing globe, then plunking down a forefinger at random. Absorbed as he was, he didn't look up.

"Does the seneschal keep something in there?" Vick's green eyes bored into mine. "Something important?"

My throat worked. Goddess, Kyven had said Vick didn't do small talk, but this was...intense.

"What business is it of yours?" I managed.

"This is my home, now. Shouldn't I learn the ins and outs?"

I wanted to say no, but...ugh. Maybe he had a point. And my relentless sparring with Kyven had drained me of the will to argue.

So I pondered the question. It took me three tries to mentally conjure the correct hallway, but—

Ah. A locked room. *The* locked room.

Right.

"It's the Lady Marche's bedchamber," I said. "Or it was. Olivian sealed it up when she died. No one's been in there in years. Well, except..."

Vick leaned in, but I had no desire to tell him about the steward who'd taken it upon himself to air out the Lady's chamber five years ago. Olivian had hurled the man against a wall and throttled him to within an inch of his life. I would never forget the way the man's mouth had opened, fishlike, while his face turned a mottled shade of purple.

Nor did I want to talk about how Amryssa, in an unprecedented show of initiative, had thrown herself into the fray. Olivian had shouted in her face, which had allowed the steward to scurry away, at least.

It was the only time I'd seen Amryssa defy her father, and unsurprisingly, she'd only done so for someone else's sake. But afterward, she'd been subdued for days. And while she'd eventually forgotten the incident, I hadn't. I'd come away from that experience knowing the Lady Marche's bedroom was something Olivian would kill over.

Now even I feared to set foot inside. And that was saying something.

Vick cared nothing for my reticence, though. "No one goes in there? Ever? Surely there's a key somewhere?"

"There is," I said grudgingly. "But only one, and it lives in Olivian's pocket. The others were melted down, so you can forget about opening that door. He'll murder you if you even try."

"Will he." Vick licked his lips. I could practically see the desire to chart this forbidden secret unfolding behind his eyes.

"Look," I said. "You really don't want to—"

The library doors creaked. I whirled, fearing Kyven had escaped my supervision, but he hadn't strayed from the corner. Instead, Althea hurried in, brightening at the sight of me.

"Harlowe." She came close, her hands clasped. "I've been meaning to find you. And say thank you, for that nightmare a few weeks ago, when you..."

She trailed off with a glance at Vick and Kyven. "Well. For when you did what you did. I can't lose my position here, not when my family needs me. So...thank you."

Her earnestness warmed me. "It's nothing. Really. Anyone would've done the same."

"Not anyone," she said.

"And what, pray tell, did Harlowe do during the last nightmare?"

I nearly jumped out of my skin. Gods among us, how had Kyven gotten across the room so quickly? Somehow, he stood at my elbow, appraising Althea with keen eyes.

Very keen eyes.

My heart turned over. Oh, no. Nope. Absolutely not. He would *not* be taking an interest in any of the housemaids, not if I had anything to say about it.

"Althea," I said, "why don't you go see if Olivian needs help?"

She hesitated, her attention shifting to Kyven.

He beamed a smile that probably would've disarmed a career mercenary. "Althea. How lovely to meet you. You have a family, you say? One that relies on your help? Tell me more. Do they live in town?"

She opened her mouth, but I cut her off. "Althea. Go. See Olivian. Or Miss Quist. Or literally anyone else. Now."

She gave a surprised squeak at my tone, but hurried away, thank Zephyrine.

Kyven pouted. "Well. That was rather rude."

"You questioning her was rude," I said, hostile. "What business is it of yours where her family lives?"

He shrugged, which made my bones crawl. He'd probably wanted to know whether she would be...missed. Or something. Creep.

"Shouldn't I get to know people?" he said.

"No. You should leave them alone. *Especially* innocent young housemaids."

He raked his gaze over me, amusement kindling in his eyes. "Why, lioness. If I didn't know better, I'd think you were jealous."

Whatever sliver of tolerance he'd earned from me over the past three weeks withered to ash. "Jealousy? Don't be daft. That has nothing to do with it."

"Mmm-hmm. If you say so."

When he smirked, I clutched my dagger so hard my palm ached. If I didn't put distance between us right the hell now, I couldn't be held accountable for what happened next.

So I stalked away. By the time I reached the door, I'd wrestled my wrath into submission. Mostly.

Five more weeks, that was all. Then I could wash my hands of him. Literally.

"Come on," I said. "Amryssa's probably done with her bath by now. I need to go check on her."

No answer. When I looked back, Kyven bent toward Vick, whispering. A look passed between them, heavy with meaning.

My gut clenched. What in Zephyrine's name?

The prince straightened. He came sauntering toward me, that stupid half smile tilting his mouth, as if I hadn't just caught him scheming with his attendant. "If Amryssa needs us, then by all means, lead the way."

I slitted my eyes. What was he up to? Moreover, what was Vick up to, with all this sneaking around?

"You're beautiful when you do that, by the way." Kyven's voice dropped to a velvety croon. "That look of yours...it makes me want to misbehave, if only so you'll scold me, afterward."

"Scold you?" I forced the words through clenched teeth. "I'll do much worse than scold you. So don't test me. You have no idea who you're dealing with."

He set a hand against the doorway, caging me in. "Ah, but that's the thing, lioness. I rather think I do. I think I've had you figured out since that day on the roof."

I tried to retreat, but the jamb prevented it. Kyven leaned so close his breath wafted across my skin, stirring a memory of that same heated exhale—those same lips—blazing a trail down my neck.

I shivered. "Get away from me."

He chuckled. "If you insist." He strolled away.

I stood there, my feet nailed to the floor, my chest heavy with outrage. Well, outrage and...something else. Some nagging awareness of my own heartbeat, one I had no explanation for. I swiped at my hair, smoothing the stray strands his breath had dislodged.

Thankfully, the phantom sensations faded when I glanced at Vick. He still sat in the armchair, watching me.

A smile curved across his mouth, but something about it brought to mind a scythe. It was a smile that said I had no secrets and never would, that this man had weighed me with a glance and found me wanting.

With a shudder, I hurried after Kyven, unable to decide which man unnerved me more.

I I .

Giving Kyven a head start proved to be a mistake. I rushed down the hall, searching for some sign of him.

And found nothing. Just shadows and moth-eaten draperies. How had he gotten away from me so quickly?

My chest tightened. Amryssa was waiting for me upstairs, but I couldn't leave Kyven unattended. I refused to turn my back on him, only to find out later that some unlucky housemaid had disappeared.

I upped my pace, wondering if I should call his name. But I didn't want to draw attention—Olivian might be lurking, and he wouldn't forgive an oversight like this, not on the heels of the shattered bust debacle.

I rounded a bend in the hall and pulled up short. Miss Quist blinked at me, her wispy blonde curls only halfway contained by her cook's cap.

"Harlowe, sweetheart. I almost ran right into you. How clumsy of me."

I waved off her words. "No, no, it's my fault. I was just looking for Kyven. You haven't seen him, have you?"

"Oh, yes." Her eyes brightened. "His Highness went that way, just now. He offered to bring some mushrooms up from the cellar for me.

Isn't that delightful? He might be a prince, but that doesn't stop him from pitching in, does it?"

My mouth tightened. If pissing me off every five minutes counted as 'pitching in,' then sure. He was endlessly fucking helpful. "Right. Yes. Excuse me."

I hurried away, then pushed through the first external door I came to, since the root cellar could only be accessed from outside. Heat and brightness hit me like a slap, but I barely noticed. Across the yard, the cellar doors lay open. Between them, a dark tunnel sloped into the earth.

I hurried over and plunged inside. The temperature plummeted as I went, the air thickening with the scent of barley and dried apples. My eyes struggled to adjust, the rapid shift from bright to dark rendering the tunnel little more than a shadowy smear.

"Kyven," I called into the darkness. "Are you down here?"

No answer.

Loose earth squished beneath my shoes. Soon, the passageway widened, delivering me into the cellar proper. Shadows moved within shadows, and I stopped. For the second time in as many minutes, I'd almost collided with someone.

Before me, a figure crouched, rooting through a crate that probably held the dregs of last year's scraggly potatoes, or maybe the stunted mushrooms Miss Quist had requested. I couldn't tell, what with the sunbursts still lingering on my retinas.

"Just so you know," I said, "I don't appreciate having to chase—"

The figure straightened and whirled. A fist caught me by the windpipe, then forced me backward until my shoulder blades hit the wall. Dirt rained down, grit clogging my eyes.

I flailed, trying to fend off my attacker, but the hiss of a blade leaving its sheath made me freeze.

Because that wasn't just any blade. It was *my* blade. My dagger. The belt at my waist suddenly felt much too light.

My pulse sped as panic pumped along every nerve. Without my weapon, I was defenseless. "Give that back."

But the grip at my throat only tightened. Cold steel pricked my jaw.

Gods among us. If I could've drawn a proper breath, I might have actually laughed. Kyven had shown his true colors. *Finally.*

"I knew it," I wheezed. I sounded borderline hysterical, but I was about to be murdered in a root cellar by my own husband, so I couldn't judge myself too harshly. "I always knew you—"

"Shut up." The knife-tip dented my skin.

My mouth snapped shut, my mind spiraling into nothingness. Because that voice didn't belong to Kyven. It was...a *woman's.* I blinked, trying to clear the debris from my eyes.

Slowly, features emerged from the darkness. A long, elegant nose. Full lips. Dark hair, braided into a coronet around a heart-shaped face.

I stared. I'd never seen this woman in my life. She didn't even look to be from Oceansgate—instead of a shabby, thrice-mended dress, she wore a man's tunic over deerskin leggings.

I stared. "Who the hell're are you?"

When she didn't answer, suspicion hatched in my mind. "Wait. Are you one of those outlaws, from the woods? What're you doing here? Are you *stealing* from us?"

"Stealing?" Her nose wrinkled. "Since when is taking from the rich considered stealing?"

"I don't know," I hissed. "Probably since laws were invented?"

Her gaze narrowed.

I glared right back. I probably shouldn't have goaded her, but I was sick to death of the misconceptions. The *judgment.* "Look, lady. Just so you know, no one in Oceansgate is rich. Least of all Olivian. So how about you piss off, back to the woods? Go tell your little bandit friends to stay away. There's nothing here for you."

My outburst earned me a jab of the knife. I winced, though she hadn't *quite* broken skin.

"We're hungry." She leaned in. "And you've got food. Seems simple enough to me."

I sneered. "You realize there're twenty-eight people living in this house, right? Look around. There's hardly anything here. If you take our food, we'll—"

"Unhand her."

I froze, my mouth clicking shut. Because *that* voice, I recognized.

Shadows rippled as Kyven emerged from the tunnel behind my assailant. "Now."

The woman stiffened. "My...lord?"

My brow wrinkled. *My lord?* She couldn't even see him. How did she know to call him that?

Then again, that ridiculous accent gave him away. That, and the imperial command he somehow laced through every word.

"I'm ordering you," Kyven said coldly, "to put down the knife. Don't make me say it again."

The woman sucked in a breath, but a moment later, both fist and blade vanished from my throat. She backed away, her hands raised. "I'm sorry, my lord. I didn't think—"

"What, that I'd take issue with you threatening my wife?" Censure bled from Kyven's tone. Apparently, he *could* have a serious conversation. "Because I do. And it's as she said. There's nothing here for you. Even if there were, that doesn't give you the right to go around putting daggers to people's throats."

The woman wilted.

I gaped. Good goddess, what would it be like to just...*prince* your way into making people feel bad about themselves?

Clearly, I hadn't been utilizing this princess thing to its fullest potential.

"Go." Kyven's command held no room for argument. "And don't come back here."

The woman made to move past him, but he extended a hand, palm up.

"Leave the knife."

She gulped and set my dagger in his grip, then rushed off. He stood unmoving. With the tunnel backlighting him, I couldn't make out his expression.

Seconds ticked past, each one snarling my nerves tighter. Because now we were alone down here, and Kyven had my knife *and* the perfect alibi. People would have asked questions if I'd turned up dead in our bedroom, but here in the root cellar? He could simply blame my murder on the outlaw who'd tried to rob us. Easy.

A crazed laugh burbled from my throat.

"What," he said, "is so funny?"

"This." The intensity of the last few minutes jarred something loose, some violent rush of emotion. It would be a relief, finally, to know. To see that the man I slept beside—the one who waltzed through these halls looking the way he did, who charmed people left and right, who was in the maddening habit of calling me his wife, no less—was no more than a monster.

I only hoped he'd make this next part quick.

"Go on." I gestured to the dagger. "You have my knife. And all the privacy you could want. You can finally do everything you've been dreaming of doing to me."

No answer. For long moments, he didn't move. Then he came toward me. Light gleamed on the point of my dagger—a bright star of pain, just waiting to be delivered.

A red wall of rage rose within me. Goddess, what a graceless, stupid way to die. How had I even gotten myself into this situation? How could I leave Amryssa alone like this?

But when Kyven's face came into focus, his mouth snicked up. "I assure you, lioness, the things I dream of doing to you *don't* involve a knife."

His hand moved. I braced for the bite of metal between my ribs, but he simply slid my blade into my belt-sheath. Then he just...

...stood there. Committing exactly zero crimes against my person. If anything, he looked like he was trying not to laugh. "Surely you didn't think I'd hurt you?"

I stared up into his face. What? *What?* I wanted to scream. I wanted to slap him. I wanted to fall to the floor and thank him for saving me from that thief, only the fact that he had didn't make sense, none of this did, and mostly, I just wanted him to stop *looking* at me like that.

Like he knew me. Like we had some kind of rapport.

"Now." Warmth colored his voice. "I have some mushrooms to deliver, and you have a seneschal's daughter to attend to. Shall we go? Or would you prefer to stand here making baseless accusations all day? I really could go either way, myself."

I opened my mouth. Closed it. Nonsensical tears pricked at my eyes. "I...don't understand you."

His mouth quirked. "Really? I wonder why that is."

I just stood there, helpless. Lost.

"Have you considered," he said, "it might be because you haven't actually tried?"

He flashed me a wink, then walked off, snatching a burlap bag on the way. Mushrooms, presumably.

I stared after him. Seven hells, I...what? My mind melted to a wide white roar, a slate that had just been wiped clean. I'd been so sure he was evil. I'd been utterly convinced. But now...

Kyven's footsteps faded. A full minute passed before I finally shook myself and hurried into the passageway. I might not understand what had just happened, but I did know one thing.

I wouldn't be letting the prince out of my sight again.

12.

The incident in the root cellar stayed lodged in my thoughts for days, like a splinter I couldn't dig free.

I took to watching Kyven closely, almost obsessively. I scrutinized him over breakfast when he rushed to take a laden tray from Miss Quist. Then when he helped the stewards split kindling in the yard. And again on the afternoon he plucked a still-yellow dandelion from the marsh's edge, then gave it to Amryssa for no reason at all.

In private, I reread Eliana's letter, wondering if I'd missed something. But her warning remained clear: Kyven had a dark side.

I just...couldn't seem to actually find it. Not even a glimmer.

As the midpoint of my marriage approached, I wondered. Had Eliana been mistaken, somehow? She'd believed what she'd written, clearly, and Kyven *was* keeping secrets, but nothing added up. I felt like I'd been handed a jigsaw puzzle, only now the pieces refused to produce the image on the box.

All I knew for sure was that Kyven was hiding something. He'd said so himself, but I'd also caught him whispering with Vick a dozen more times, their exchanges growing heated. The fox-faced attendant wandered the house at all hours, and whenever our eyes met, he smiled that razorblade smile.

Yes, I'm up to something, it said. *And no, I won't tell you what.*

At this point, I didn't know what to believe.

"I think Vick hates me," I told Kyven one night, by way of bringing up the subject. I knew if I asked outright, he'd only turn the question around on me, so I'd resolved to come at it from another angle.

"So?" Kyven said. "Just hate him back."

He lay on the far side of the bed, his eyes closed, his hands propped beneath his head. His bare torso caught the candlelight and threw it in my face.

Sweet Zephyrine, he was always doing that. Just...*glistening*. The absolute nerve.

"That should come to you naturally enough," he added.

I frowned and rearranged my nightgown. It was hot tonight, and I would've given anything to dispense with my nightwear completely. "Did you just call me hateful?"

"Oh, don't sound so scandalized. It's nothing you wouldn't lay claim to yourself."

"Oh, really? Says who?"

His mouth curled, though his eyes didn't open. "Are you saying you *aren't* hateful?"

"Well...no. Of course not. I hate you, don't I? You and your attendants, both."

He chuckled. "Oh, come, now. No one hates Lunk. It's physically impossible."

I huffed, but he had a point. Lunk's tears at my wedding, plus the man's endless, jagged-toothed smiles—not to mention the raging crush he'd developed on Miss Quist—had the inconvenient effect of deflecting any ill will.

"Fine," I said. "Lunk's all right. But Vick? He's creepy. I mean, why's he always poking around, acting like he's looking for something?"

Kyven cracked a lazy eye. "What would he be looking for?"

"I don't know. You tell me."

He managed a shrug, even though he was lying down. "Nothing. Not to my knowledge, anyway."

I held his gaze, scanning for some hidden meaning, but he only crooked a mischievous smile. Goddess, he was good. Or innocent, maybe. Or...ugh. Who the hell knew, anymore?

"You're feisty tonight," he said. "Seeing as how you have all this energy, you know what we ought to do?"

I groaned. I *did* know, because he suggested the same thing every night. "Go into town," I recited, in unison with him—snooty accent and all.

He laughed. "Excellent. You're catching on. Should I go get dressed, then?"

"No. I'm not going anywhere with you. Exactly the opposite."

"Hmm. So I should go get *undressed*?"

"No. Stop." I slapped at his shoulder, then instantly regretted finding out how solid it was. If Merron ever spoke to me again, I'd have to tell him not to let Kyven chop so much wood. "I hate that you always do that."

"Do what?"

"Needle me. On purpose."

"I do no such thing." Mock scandal suffused his voice. "I only meant I'd have to get undressed, first, in order to dress for taking you into town."

I threw him an exasperated look, but his words swirled in my mind like water around a sluggish drain.

Would it be so terrible to go with him, just this once? Amryssa was already asleep for the night, and the house's cheerless halls had grown downright oppressive, lately. These days, I just...itched. Spending every waking moment with this pompous prince had made me feel bound and chafing, as if my skin had grown too small to contain the errant reactions he provoked.

"Come on." Kyven rolled toward me, all those muscles shifting in concert, which I tried my best not to notice. "I'll take you to the theatre. Then for drinks. We'll have fun."

I crossed my arms, but...goddess, when had I last indulged in a drink, much less a show? My trips to town always involved errands done as quickly as possible, in an effort to minimize the whispers.

Witch, witch, witch.

But I'd never gone into Oceansgate with Kyven. And, for all that I detested him, I couldn't deny he had a certain...magnetism. He carried a whirlwind force about him, a potency that couldn't be contained or denied. Only endured.

Maybe accompanying *him* to town would make for a different reception. And maybe, if I got a few drinks in him, I could loosen his tongue regarding Vick.

Vick. That decided me. My bristliness hadn't gotten me any closer to unmasking Kyven's secrets, but maybe plying him with alcohol would.

"You know what?" I said. "Fine. As long as we're back before Amryssa wakes up."

Those obnoxiously blue eyes brightened. "Really?"

"Yep. Let's go."

He rocketed off the bed as if he hadn't had a foot planted in the world of dreams just minutes ago. "A marital victory, at last. What a rush." He disappeared into the bathroom and emerged minutes later, clad in such princely finery that my insides constricted.

Goddess. I would never marry—not truly, not considering what I'd soon sacrifice for Amryssa. But if I had, I would've wanted my future husband to look something like this.

Just...minus the part about being a liar. And possibly a sadist.

I sighed and went to my armoire. In the bathroom, I exchanged my nightgown for an amethyst dress with lace spills at the sleeves, then eyed my reflection, thankful my dagger had managed my corset laces for me. I would've rather flung myself out the window than asked for Kyven's help.

When I emerged from the bathroom, he gave me an appreciative once-over. "Ready?" He offered an arm.

I ignored it. "As I'll ever be."

We stole into the hall and down the stairs. With each step, a fizzy lightness crept over me, a thrill that buzzed in the back of my skull. I hadn't done anything like this in...well, ever, and I almost felt as though I'd slipped into someone else's life. Like I was sixteen years old, escaping the watchful eyes of my parents. Shedding the burden of duty, if only for a night.

Not that I actually was. Tonight's purpose involved coaxing some kind of truth out of Kyven. But as we slunk through the candlelit halls, I swore the shadows made way, then curtained together again behind us, the darkness itself accommodating our passage. As if we'd locked the world out of some shared secret.

Outside, the marsh's salt-heavy tang blanketed the evening. The worst of the heat had broken, and the stars hardened to fiery diamonds. The swamp's glow rose from the trees like spectral purple fumes.

I paused to contemplate the house's unlit windows, then the sky. A month had passed since our last nightmare, and before that, we'd only had an eight-day reprieve. But the nightmares usually passed through every six weeks or so, which meant we *should* have another fortnight of peace.

Kyven drew close, as if he could sense my mental abacus clacking. "If we see so much as a cloud, we'll hurry back. We won't leave her alone."

My breath caught. Was he that perceptive, or was I that transparent? "You swear it?"

He pressed a fist to his heart. "On my life," he said, and swept an exaggerated bow, like some knight of old.

I huffed at his over-the-top theatrics. He was clearly lying, but...so what? Town wasn't far. Only a mile and a half. I'd be minutes from Amryssa, at most.

Kyven straightened and sauntered off, into the sultry darkness. I followed, knowing that if the weather turned, I'd rush back, with him or without him.

On the road, gravel crunched beneath our feet. Kyven attempted to draw me into a conversation and, with no other way to pass the time, I let him. It was a real discussion, even, about Lunk's newly minted love for Miss Quist.

I'd been there three weeks ago to witness its conception. One morning, our rosy-cheeked, frizzy-haired, gloriously plump cook had brought a tray of eggs into the breakfast room, and Lunk had lost his heart.

I hadn't known a man could fall in love in a single moment, but the giant's cheeks had slackened and his blunt features softened to a glow. He hadn't spoken, but he'd quit breathing and hadn't started again until the kitchen door had swung shut behind Miss Quist.

Now I conversed with Kyven in low tones, my attention still on the sky. "Has Lunk talked to her yet?"

"No," he said, "and I don't believe he plans to. He has a habit of taking himself out of the running before he even gets started. I've seen him do it before."

"Why? Because of his...?" I gestured to my face.

"Mmm-hmm. I've told him that any woman worth her salt will realize how much he has to recommend him, and that we can't *all* win the genetic roll of the dice. But he never listens. Most likely, he'll moon about, admiring her from afar, and eventually write a despairing poem or two. If nothing else, I take comfort in the fact that you'll have to suffer through the recitation with me."

I digested that. Despite having two attendants, Kyven mostly looked after himself, so I'd only spoken to Lunk a handful of times. The giant always covered his mouth when he talked, as if a raised hand might conceal the lisped *s*'s and bee-buzz *th*'s his underbite produced. Yet he'd struck me as intelligent and open-hearted, a man worthy of someone as sweet as Miss Quist.

Warmth fuzzed beneath my ribs, and I caught myself. Goddess. Charitable thoughts about *two* people in one fell stroke? I was losing my edge.

At least Kyven still made me want to stab something whenever he walked by.

"You should tell Lunk she's not the type to judge on looks," I said, in an attempt to regain my balance. "And that she reads even more romances than I do. They're more scandalous, too. Maybe they could bond over that."

Kyven arced an eyebrow, but he passed up the opportunity for a jibe, much to my surprise. "He won't listen. Though I *did* ask him about his newfound passion while he and I were outside the kitchen yesterday."

I narrowed my eyes. "Oh. So...you're planning to trick him into confessing?"

He smirked. "I wouldn't say I'm *planning* it."

"Oh, no, of course not." I sniffed. "Let me guess, you had some convoluted justification, didn't you? What did you tell yourself, that you were *creating an opportunity where none currently exists?*" I mimicked his stuck-up accent, my nose thrust into the air.

He laughed. "Gods, lioness. You're adorable when you mock me. Truly."

The compliment stole half the air from my lungs, and I scolded myself. Stupid. Stupid, pretentious, condescending prince. Stupid me for indulging in his bullshit. Stupid Olivian for burdening me with this man long enough that he was starting to feel familiar.

I faced forward, effectively closing the door on our repartee. We'd almost reached town, and in the dim embrace of night, Oceansgate stood as a remnant of its former self. Derelict houses sagged against one another. Moonbeams striped the ragged cobblestones. In the distance, the sea reflected starlight, and abandoned anchors rusted on the beach—vestiges of ships that no longer sailed these waters.

Once, this had been a bustling port town, the terminus of the trade route from the distant southern islands. But with the advent of the nightmares, our harbor had fallen into disuse. Now, instead of shipping goods along our overland route to Hightower, vessels sailed past us to Stormbow. The harbor there was shallower and less protected, the waters plagued by the weather that had given the territory its name, but at least their squalls weren't the suicide-inducing kind.

Kyven surveyed the ramshackle buildings. A breeze lifted, carrying the scent of saltwater and seaweed. "It's charming."

"It *was.* Now it's just...faded. And I'm sure it has nothing on Hightower."

"Oh, no place does. But this one looks lively enough, all things considered. Where's the theatre?"

I pointed to a distant building, where torchlight caught on ivy-laden walls. Cracks split the stucco, stained black by the sea air.

We descended the last hill into town, and Kyven was right—a surprising number of people were out, rendering the streets lively. Women in bright skirts beckoned from crumbling doorways while men in faded tailcoats spouted ragged, drunken choruses.

A strange energy came over Kyven, almost as if he belonged in a place like this. He reached for my hand, his grip vibrating with excitement.

I started to pull away, then reconsidered. He was like a fox in a henhouse here—liable to duck down an alley and eat somebody. At least with our fingers linked, I could keep him on a leash. So I left my hand where it was.

Ugh. I'd have to send Olivian a bill, once this was over. One that included a hefty fee for my pain and suffering.

Within minutes, we joined the influx of theatregoers. Threadbare waistcoats and handheld paper fans gleamed in the torchlight. Kyven dropped a few coins into the ticket-seller's hand before leading us to our red velvet seats.

I settled in to absorb the scene. The auditorium's proscenium arch, once gilded, now bore a patina of neglect, but the chandelier made up for it, sparkling with a thousand dangling crystals. Anticipation fizzed in the air. As we waited, someone tossed a pair of underwear onto the curtained stage, prompting ripples of laughter.

A few moments later, the curtain lifted. Kyven's grip on my hand tightened.

Pirates swaggered onto the stage, accompanied by a creaking ship powered by ropes and pulleys. In the background, drums and cymbals clashed out a thunderstorm.

I leaned in. For the next half-hour, two rival pirate captains—a dark-skinned woman and a brown-haired man—tried to kill one another. When that failed, they grudgingly fell in love instead, culminating in a fiery love scene complete with a satin-draped bed and bare, heaving breasts.

They were beautiful together. Incendiary. So much that something fluttered in the base of my stomach, and I couldn't stop myself from glancing over at Kyven.

He gazed back at me, his eyes like blazing blue stars. His expression crackled with lust, but also with something else—a glittering delight, a joy I'd previously glimpsed only in passing. Now it had found a new home in the sweep of his brows, in the imperial tilt of his nose.

"I love this," he whispered. "The theatre. I love it more than anything in the world. I could come here every night and never tire of it."

I searched his face. "Really? But...what happened to you not having feelings?"

"Oh, lioness." His eyes softened. "Haven't you figured it out? You shouldn't take anything I say seriously. Only half of it has any basis in reality."

I stared, caught up in him, somehow. The sheer delight pouring from him felt so...real. So authentic the plaster ceiling could have fallen in and I wouldn't have looked away. "Does that mean...you *wouldn't* have kept me up on our wedding night, then?"

The moment the words emerged, I clamped my lips together. What the hell? I could've said anything, and I'd said...*that*.

Kyven grinned. Not halfway this time, but full and white, as wide as a promise. "Ah, but that's the fun part. Figuring out which half to believe."

He held my eyes a moment longer, then returned to the play. And he really did look like a boy on Solsticetide Evening, breathless and radiant, eager to hang his lantern outside the door so Zephyrine could leave her gifts on the longest night of the year.

The play's action rose, but failed to recapture my focus. Kyven was like a blue-and-red flame beside me, a bright, burning thing that tangled with thoughts of Eliana and Amryssa.

That wasn't him. He didn't do those things.

Seeing him like this, I could almost believe it. After all, Kyven had let me go, in the cellar. He'd *protected* me. And how could a man with a raw love for theatre, with a ready laugh and a zest for...well, *everything*, it seemed...delight in hurting people?

Possibilities threaded through my mind. I was missing something here. I could feel it.

The play ended. Cheers erupted, Kyven hollering louder than anyone else. When the curtain fell, we rode the crowd out into the sticky evening, where he reclaimed my hand and whisked me down a side street.

A block later, he paused before a rain-stained bulletin board. Ancient flyers advertised shows that had come and gone, while others detailed job postings that no longer existed.

Kyven tapped a Wanted poster. "What's this?"

I scanned the yellowed parchment. The headline offered a reward for the leader of the swamp brigands, then listed the man's crimes: robbery, highway banditry, tax evasion. The accompanying portrait was generic and washed-out, and could have been anyone.

The poster must have been years old, considering no lawmen remained to collect a reward from. "It's about the outlaws living in the woods. The same group that woman in the cellar was from."

Kyven ran a finger along the bottom of the poster, where someone had scrawled a handwritten addition. *The true seneschal of Oceansgate.* "And this?"

My mouth tightened. "I don't know. They're common thieves, but...their founder has become kind of a mythic figure, at this point. People act like he's the champion of the downtrodden. The noble thief who helps the poor, that sort of thing. Maybe because he gives away money. Or used to, when the nightmares first started. And he's made sure everyone in Oceansgate has a set of chains. But calling him 'the rightful seneschal' is ridiculous. I guess Olivian just hasn't cultivated the people's love, like this guy has."

Kyven tore the poster off the wall and folded it into the pocket of his tailcoat.

"What're you doing?"

"Research." He flashed a sunlit smile. "I want to know everything about my new home."

I gave him a skeptical look, but he was already pulling me by the hand again. A brisk walk later, we veered through a doorway, and I found myself sitting at a wooden table in a crowded pub.

The place was wide open—high-ceilinged but dark, all warm black walls and gray stone floors. It was old, too, in a way that settled into my bones and gave weight to the air.

Amid all those shadows, Kyven gleamed, as fresh and bright as a copper penny.

He ordered two ales and a plate of fruit. The waitress set everything on his half of the table, leaning in so far her bosom nearly spilled into his face.

Not that he noticed. He pinned me with a look, then set to peeling an apple in one continuous spiral. I tracked the progress of his paring knife, wondering if I should have done something to keep him from having a blade.

But I didn't actually feel threatened. Not with Kyven studying me like he was paying attention with his whole self. Like he could scorch away my layers with the frosty burn of his eyes.

"Did you enjoy the show?" he said.

I shifted on my stool, trying to get comfortable. All around, laughter mingled with the clink of glassware and the pungent tang of sweat. "I can't believe I'm saying this, but yes. Your company was actually tolerable, for once."

"Careful." His mouth hitched. "Compliments like that are guaranteed to go to my head."

I scoffed and guzzled my ale. "*Everything* goes to your head. Compliments, insults, doesn't even matter."

"Hmm. You may have a point."

Great. There he went with the *hmms* again. I'd learned to be wary of them, because Kyven usually chased them into meatier territory, drawing me into a conversation that sounded light on the surface, but wasn't.

Sure enough, he leaned in, his elbows planted on the table.

"There's nothing quite like it, is there? The theatre. It's possibility in its rawest form."

I grimaced. A philosophical discussion was the last thing I needed right now. "I have no idea what that means."

His knife circumnavigated the apple. "It *means* that inside that auditorium, there're no rules. I'm not a prince. You're not a keymistress. The curtain goes up and we're free to become pirates, if we like. Or rivals, or lovers, or friends. In there, we can be whatever we want. Write any story we wish."

My skin tingled. Shit. I hated that this angle interested me. "And you...enjoy that? That freedom?"

"Freedom, yes." His face lit up. "That's the word. Theatre isn't just possibility, it's freedom, in its purest form. Because every time I go, I'm reminded that I can reinvent myself, just like those players do on stage."

I pondered that. Huh. "And what would you like to become, exactly?"

"Well." His smile took on a mysterious edge. "That depends on the day. On my mood. Which changes rather frequently, if you hadn't noticed."

I drained my ale to give myself time to think. I wouldn't argue his capriciousness—he habitually flitted from one thing to the next. But his flightiness had a...steady quality, almost. He was predictably unpredictable, and always cheerful, always upbeat.

Which, all this time, I'd assumed was manufactured. But his expression, inside that theatre...

"And you, lioness? Who would you be, if you could reinvent yourself?"

My musings evaporated as his question made my tongue stick to the roof of my mouth. Funny—in some ways, I *could* reinvent myself, but the dagger's gifts ended at the surface. That was the irony, I supposed. I could alter my face all I liked, but no amount of magic changed what lay beneath. None of my adjustments made me less...*me*.

Now words flooded my throat. Honest ones. Goddess, I shouldn't have drained that mug so quickly.

Maybe another drink would reinstate my sanity. I waved the waitress down.

But when the second mug arrived, sipping from it only lubricated my thoughts. "If I could've been anyone," I said slowly, "...I think I would've liked to be good, like Amryssa. Worthy."

A crease formed between Kyven's brows. "Worthy? Why in Hyperion's name would you think you aren't?"

"Well, it's like you said. Most people are selfish. Me included."

His knife paused mid-swipe. The now-lengthy peel trailed onto the table, its ruby richness lurid in his hands. "Would you like to know what I see, when I look at you?"

I leaned in. "No."

"Well, lucky for you, I'm going to tell you anyway, you stubborn woman. Because someone needs to inform you you're absolutely worthy. Of course you are. You're ferocious, in fact. Most people shy away from that side of themselves, but you? You're tyrannical and not the least bit sorry about it. Not when it comes to the seneschal's daughter, and not when it comes to your loyalty. Which means you take a hangnail more seriously than I take a knife to the throat, but that single-mindedness is your greatest strength. It means you can be trusted. Relied upon. You don't change your mind along with your clothes. You're ironclad, and if that's not the single rarest and most precious quality a person can have, I don't know what is."

My blood thundered in my ears, loud enough to drown out the surrounding din.

What.

The.

Fuck.

I'd been unfailingly short with him. Cruel, even. And he came back with this? This...*gift* of an interpretation?

I buried my face in my mug, desperate to soothe the erratic leap of my pulse.

Kyven resumed his peeling, apparently unbothered by my silence. "Now, what I'd like to know is what the Lady Amryssa did to inspire your devotion in the first place."

His words were airier than dandelion seeds catching on an updraft, but they brought me to a standstill, anyway.

"What do you mean?"

"I mean you're not a woman who trusts easily. Yet you stuck your neck into the marital noose in order to spare hers. She must have done *something* to earn that from you."

I stared. Kyven's knife scritch-scritched, depriving the apple of its armor, exposing the soft core beneath.

How had he guessed that? Especially when Merron had assumed the opposite?

Then again, the two men had nothing in common. While Merron took everything personally, Kyven seemed immune to my opinions. Trying to insult him was like trying to injure a well by throwing a dart into the water—all I earned was a ripple of amusement, and once it faded, the surface adopted the same configuration as before, utterly unperturbed by what had just happened.

He wasn't the kind of man I could hurt. Not by accident, probably not even on purpose. Which was...oddly freeing, now that I thought about it.

"Amryssa saved my life once," I heard myself say. "When I was eighteen."

"Nine years ago." He dropped his eyes, slicing the apple into sections, now. "The same age as the nightmares. Interesting. What happened?"

I hesitated, but either the heat or the ale or the way he studied his apple—as if intentionally granting me a reprieve—pried my tongue loose.

"It was after... Well, I didn't have any family, then. I didn't even have a home, just a shanty I'd pieced together in the swamp. I used to dig for mussels out there. Bring a bag to town each week, barter it for bread and soap and matches." My words grew halting as I stumbled over the memories. "But everyone in Oceansgate avoided me, even back then. They called me names. Swamp-girl. Bog-wraith. Seemed like they came up with something new every week."

And later, once Olivian had given me the dagger, the whispers had inevitably included the word *witch*. People had taken to crossing their fingers when I passed, attempting to ward off whatever evil spirits I must have appealed to in order to alter my face and hair.

But I left that part out.

"They never welcomed me. It didn't matter that my parents had taken me into the swamp and just...left me. The townspeople saw a raggedy, penniless girl, and they shunned me. Everyone except Amryssa."

Kyven's gaze didn't lift. As if he knew. As if he understood I hadn't spoken of this in years, that the words were too raw and fledgling to survive direct observation.

"I don't want your pity," I rushed out.

"I don't recall offering it." He sounded like he was commenting on the weather.

I breathed. Guzzled more ale. Kyven betrayed no hint of impatience, and that, more than anything else, prompted me to continue. I'd started this, for Zephyrine knew what reason. I might as well finish it.

"Anyway," I said, "one week on my way to town, I ran into an alligator. A nasty one. He wanted my mussels, and I didn't want him to have them, and by the time we'd finished arguing about it, he'd laid my leg open from hip to heel. I was bleeding so badly I couldn't find a clean patch of clothing to staunch the flow with."

Alarm flickered across Kyven's features.

Hesitation sank steel-tipped claws into my windpipe, but I swallowed it down. No sense stopping now. I would get this story out. Drop my past into his lap, if only to see whether maybe, just maybe, he had a heart that beat, after all.

"I staggered into town, trying to get to the surgery, and Amryssa was passing in the street. I remember she was wearing a white dress that day. I'll never forget, actually, because I'd never seen anyone so beautiful. So angelic. And I couldn't believe it when she helped drag me inside. She let me bleed all over her perfect dress, and when the physician said I'd lost too much blood to survive, she volunteered to give me some of hers."

Kyven's knife pierced the apple's heart and stayed there.

Another gulp of ale. Another breath. "I don't remember much else, because I kept losing consciousness. It's just...flashes. Cut-up bits of memory. But I remember the surgeon opening my vein and hooking some kind of tube from Amryssa's arm to mine. Supposedly there wasn't much chance of it working. Something about one person's blood not usually agreeing with another's. But in our case, it did. The physician sewed up my leg, and Amryssa gave me so much blood that she passed out, and afterward, she needed weeks to recover. Olivian was so pissed. But here I am. Still alive, because of her. Because she refused to turn her back on me, even though she could have. Even though she probably should have."

Kyven's throat bobbed, as if he were fishing for his next words somewhere deep within. "But she asked something of you in return, did she not? For you to become her keymistress?"

"No, no." Denial pitched my words low. "That was a gift, too. The storms had just started, and her mother had just died. Back then, the nightmares weren't as bad as what we get now, but they could still kill, and Amryssa needed someone to look after her. So she gave me a choice. A chance to get out of the swamp. The truth is, I haven't done a thing to deserve it. If it weren't for her charity, I'd still be out in the marsh. Alone."

Kyven let go of the apple, letting the slices unfurl like petals. He raised his eyes.

My head seemed to come unstuck from my body. For all the many looks he'd given me, none had laid me bare the way this one did. It was like he was looking through me. *Into* me.

"You're very much...not what I expected, when we met," he said. "I've known that for weeks now, but I don't think I realized the full extent until this moment."

My throat tightened. I had no answer for that.

"Perhaps the Lady Amryssa isn't, either. Perhaps...I've underestimated her."

"You wouldn't be the first." I fiddled with my mug, if only to give myself something to do. "Everyone treats her like she's made of eggshells. Even me, to be honest. But her kindness is...fierce. She might seem soft on the outside, but inside, she's strong. Strong enough to weather any bullshit life throws at her."

"Bullshit?" Kyven's trademark smile tickled to life. "My poor, virgin ears."

"Sorry," I said, not really thinking. Mostly, I was just profoundly, grotesquely relieved to have moved on to another subject.

"Are you?"

I considered. "No. I'm absolutely fucking not."

His smile stretched. "Ah, well. In truth, my ears aren't any more virginal than the rest of me."

At that, a memory arose—a deft tongue, tracing shivering lines against my throat. No, he wasn't virginal in the slightest. That I knew.

A fiery arrow glided down my spine. Gods, would my mind never cease to revisit that place? Whenever Kyven got too close, too *attentive*, my thoughts went careening downhill.

I relived our wedding night way more often than I wanted to.

To distract myself, I plucked an orange from the fruit plate and dug my nails into the peel. When I looked up again, Kyven's eyes glittered—whether because he'd divined the direction of my musings or drawn that story out of me, I couldn't say. But he looked like a man who'd labored over a jigsaw puzzle for weeks, then found the last piece lodged beneath the carpet.

"I want you to call me Ky," he said, apropos of nothing.

Itchiness tightened my skin, a warning prickle, like I'd looked around and realized I'd strayed too close to an open flame. Next thing I knew, it would burn me, and I'd have no one to blame but myself. "I'm not doing that."

"Why not? Afraid you'll like it?"

"No." The word was hardly more than a scoff. "Nicknames are just way too...familiar."

"Well, they do say familiarity breeds contempt. So, seeing as how you're so intent on hating me, perhaps you ought to let your guard down a little. It might help your cause."

My head swam with the circularity of his argument. I had no idea how he came up with things like that on the fly. "What? That doesn't even make sense."

"It makes perfect sense."

"It doesn't. And you're infuriating for even saying it."

"You like that I infuriate you."

"I don't."

"Keep telling yourself that. Perhaps you'll even believe it, someday. Because I certainly don't." He grinned and popped an apple slice into his mouth. I hadn't known a person could chew *smugly*, but he managed.

Ugh.

"Hungry?" He offered a piece of fruit.

I set aside my mangled orange and snatched at the apple, if only to get Kyven to stop looking at me like that. Like he'd unearthed some private shard of me and tucked it into his pocket.

The fruit exploded between my teeth. As I chewed, a new sound joined the hubbub—the wheeze and whine of tuning instruments.

Thank goddess. A distraction. In the corner, a fiddler, a percussionist, and a banjo player were setting up.

"It's about to get loud in here," I said. "We should probably go."

"Go?" Kyven downed his ale in one throat-bobbing swallow, then plunked down the empty mug. "Absolutely not. We're just getting started, and I'm very much looking forward to this next part."

My stomach did a slow capsize. I'd heard him say that before, hadn't I? "Next part? What next part?"

Those blue eyes glinted with their own internal light. "The part where I convince you to dance with me."

I3.

D ancing.

Was that what we were doing? It felt more like having different parts of myself flung in different directions, moment by moment.

Kyven dipped and spun me, seemingly without effort. And I'd downed so much ale that I let him—a willing partner, pliant in his arms.

At least he made it easy, his instinct for the music impeccable. If I hadn't known better, I would've sworn he actually knew this song, because he seemed to anticipate every twang of the banjo and rattle of the tambourine. But that was impossible. This song was pure Oceansgate—bayou music, fiddle-heavy and chaotic, not remotely suitable for the rarefied rooms of Hightower.

Which could only mean he was a natural. I briefly wondered if his innate sense of rhythm carried over into other...activities, then promptly stopped wondering, because what?

Fuck, I was drunk. I had no other excuse for the rogue thoughts tainting my mind. Or for the staticky thrill that shot through me every time Kyven steered me with a hand on my back or a nudge of his hips. Still, I didn't stumble once, not until a stout patron with an inflamed nose bumped into us and sent me reeling.

Kyven caught me neatly and wheeled me back in, nestling me in the crook of his arm. "Excuse us."

The man only glared, unplacated. "Hmph. If it isn't the bog-witch and the prince. Descended from your towers to rub elbows with the likes of us, eh?"

My scalp tightened. The man lurched away, clearly deep in his cups.

I watched him fade into the crowd, surprised to realize our presence hadn't gone unnoticed. At all. Half the women stole glances at Kyven, while the men put up a wall of flinty glares. In the corner, someone flashed crossed forefingers in my direction.

"They haven't been doing this all night," I said. "Have they?"

Kyven smirked. "I was wondering how long it would take you to notice."

"A...while, apparently." Shock cut my words into stilted pieces. Usually, the townspeople's hostility drilled into me, impossible to ignore, but tonight... "I must not have been paying attention."

"Yes, well. I tend to have that effect on people."

I peered up at him. How strange. Even now that I'd realized, I didn't care what anyone thought. Not right now. "Are you saying you're distracting?"

His grip tightened, bringing me closer. "I prefer the term 'all-consuming', myself."

All-consuming. It was a ridiculous claim. Outlandish. But my pulse surged, drawn by the gravity of those lunar eyes. I groped for a retort and failed to locate so much as a breath.

His other arm came up, pulling me into him, chest to chest. The music rollicked onward, stranding us amid a flurry of sound and activity.

"All-consuming?" I finally found a pocket of air in some unexplored region deep in my lungs. "You think way too highly of yourself."

Kyven searched my face. This close, his scent drowned me—wild marsh and woodsmoke and lonely, star-strewn nights. Except those long-ago evenings had never felt like this one, so hot and close and intimate. Out there, no one had ever stared at me like they could map the exact shape of my soul if they spent long enough trying.

"I think every bit as highly of you," he said. "If it's any consolation."

"It's not," I said, but my fingers seemed to disagree, because they closed around his shirtfront as if trying to draw him closer.

His lids dropped. "Careful." He made the word into a mouthful of warm honey.

Careful. It was probably the most honest thing he'd ever said to me, a word to heed, but my body had apparently undergone a spectacular divorce from logic. I quivered inside, my breath a ragged starburst, and didn't let go of his shirt.

"If you keep looking at me like that," he said, "I might have to do something about it."

I missed a beat, then another. "Do something? Like what?"

"Well, I had no plans to kiss you tonight. But I could absolutely be prevailed upon to change my mind."

Hot needles swarmed in my gut. My eyes dropped to his mouth. He would taste like apples, I was sure. Sweet and crisp and delicious. Except...no. He was awful. The very idea was awful, and I hated everything about it. "I wouldn't kiss you if you were the last man on earth."

"No? Then why did you come?" His mouth snuck up at the edge, that tug pulling a corresponding hitch from my chest. Gah. No matter what else he was, he truly was beautiful. Annoyingly, disgustingly so. "Were you in it for the sparkling conversation? The free ale? Or did you intend to stare at my mouth all night and pretend not to find it interesting?"

I swallowed a shaky breath and heaved my eyes up to his. With more effort than it should've taken, I unhanded his shirt and shoved.

Except he didn't move. His arms circled me like hot iron bands.

My heartbeat expanded to claim my whole body. Sweet Zephyrine, how had we ended up here? I'd meant this to be an investigation, yet I hadn't asked a single question. I'd gotten distracted. Drunk on gorgeous eyes and a soft, inviting mouth.

And booze. Yes, definitely the booze.

"Don't read anything into this," I said. "I only came because I wanted to know about Vick."

"Vick?" Kyven's gaze thinned. "What do you care about him for? Don't tell me you'd rather *he* kiss you?"

I made a face. "No, of course not. I hate him."

"The same way you hate me?"

"More." I shook my head. "Or...no, less. Obviously less, because I hate you most of all. Goddess, would you stop *doing* that?"

"Doing what?"

"Asking loaded questions." I pushed again, and this time he released me. "Ones that damn me no matter which way I answer."

"If a mere question can damn you," he said, "maybe it's time for some self-reflection."

I stemmed a gasp. "You're horrible."

"Come, now. I don't think you actually mean that."

I gaped, mostly to cover up the fact that some twisted part of me was busy sighing in agreement. Seven hells, what was happening? I needed to get away from him before I said something I'd regret.

So I whirled and stomped off, not bothering to circumvent the other dancers. I just stampeded through, shearing couples in half, ignoring the hisses and hard looks my flight earned me.

Kyven caught up to me at the edge of the dancefloor, grabbing my hand and whirling me around. The look on his face—triumphant, almost predatory, had me backing away until my shoulders hit the wall.

Which proved to be a mistake. He surged close, trapping me with a palm splayed beside my head.

My breathing spiraled from my control. Goddess, he smelled so maddeningly familiar. He looked it, too, and I wished I didn't know every sound he made in his sleep, the exact texture of the drowsy chuckle he sometimes did in his dreams. Or that if I unbuttoned his collar and pushed it aside, I'd find a birthmark under his left collar-bone, a pale splotch in the shape of a half-moon.

What had Olivian been thinking, sticking me with him? Then

again, the seneschal had warned me against temptation, and I'd been haughty enough to declare myself above it.

Which had obviously been incredibly fucking stupid.

Kyven leaned down. "Do you want to know what I think?"

"No," I snapped, even as my pulse staged a rebellion in my veins. "I couldn't care less."

"I think you like me," he crooned. "And it frightens the ever-loving shit out of you, because you know I like you, too. What's more, I think you only refuse to give me an inch because you know you'd end up offering me a mile. And you also know I'd take it, and so much more besides."

I barely resisted the urge to slap him. "You're delusional."

"*You're* in denial."

"I'm not. The only reason I came is because I needed to know about Vick. It had nothing to do with you."

His eyes slitted, but that didn't dampen the victory igniting there. As though he could see through my protests to some secret even I couldn't decipher. "Fine. If you're so desperate to know about my attendant, then ask whatever you like. I'd be more than happy to get that out of the way."

I raised my chin, which I realized, too late, had the unfortunate effect of bringing my mouth closer to his. Now all I would have to do was go up on tiptoes. Which, obviously, I'd rather stab myself than do. "Fine."

"Fine."

"Tell me what Vick's looking for. At the house."

Kyven's jaw flexed. "Money. Valuables."

Shock blinkered my vision black for a moment. I couldn't believe he'd actually answered that. Honestly, it would seem. "You mean he's trying to rob us? What in Zephyrine's name makes him think he has the right?"

"If you must know, he thinks Olivian's hoarding riches. That all of you are coddled. Which, in your case, couldn't be further from the truth, but Vick doesn't know you like I do. Next."

A swallow scraped down my throat. Vick could search the house top to bottom and not find a single stashed-away penny, so he could waste his own time all he liked. I elected to ignore the rest of what Kyven had said completely. "Okay, so your attendant's a thief. Fantastic. But is it more than that? Does he...hurt people, sometimes?"

That caught him off-guard. His eyes flared before he modulated his reaction. "Only when necessary."

My thoughts wheeled. What the hell did that mean? Did Vick and Kyven make some kind of demented two-man team? "Do *you* hurt people?"

Kyven held my eyes. "No."

"Really? You've never harmed a woman in your life?"

He frowned. "I thought this was about Vick."

An icy fist wrapped around my stomach and squeezed. "Just answer the question."

A muscle ticked in his jaw. Across the room, a dropped glass shattered, but it might as well have been miles away for all that it affected me. "Lioness, I'm no hero. Quite the opposite. But I have *never*, nor will I ever, take pleasure in causing anyone pain. Least of all a woman. So no. Never in my life. Though I can't conceive of why you're asking."

That answer plunged into me like a rock into a well, causing an explosion of ripples. Seven hells, he looked—and sounded—so utterly sincere. But *someone* had to be responsible for the dead animals, for terrorizing the seneschal's daughter.

I gathered my thoughts. "Right. Then...Vick, he's always been with you, right? Always been your attendant? Traveled with you wherever you've gone?"

"No." Not a moment's hesitation. "I've known him just shy of a year."

A year. The reply punched a clean hole through the nascent theory taking shape in my head. Yet Kyven's blunt delivery rang with significance, enough that I sensed something here, some puzzle I could click together if only I could arrange the fragments properly.

"Is that all?" Kyven's breath fanned across my lips, warm, sweetened with apples.

I shuddered. Or shivered. Who could tell. "No. One more."

"Yes?"

"Who are you?" I jabbed a finger into his chest. It felt like poking iron. "In here. Who are you, really?"

A parade of emotions crossed his face—alarm, resolve, triumph. "It's as I said. Whoever I want to be. Whatever I feel like becoming in the moment. I'm a prince, and a pauper, and oftentimes a pirate. And right now, I'm also a man who wants to kiss you very, very badly."

My breathing stuttered and died.

He zeroed in on my mouth. "That's the thing, lioness. What I want above all else is to experience everything life has to offer. I want to go everywhere. Do everything. *Be* everything. Reinvent myself like those theatre-players do, find out which shape suits me best. And right now, with you, I get to be something I've never been before. Something entirely new."

"Which is?"

He leaned closer. "A husband."

"A...husband."

"Yes. If only for four more weeks. And husbands are generally known for kissing their wives."

I searched for a defense and latched onto the first one I could find. "But I'm not even nice to you."

He chuckled, low and sultry. "I don't need you to be nice. I need you to be interesting. And gods above, are you interesting. You have *layers*. Buried under thorns, maybe, but that only makes me want to see what's there all the more. What treasures you're guarding so jealously."

Tingles swept up my spine. "There're no treasures. I'm just...hard work." Which normally worked to my advantage. Being difficult had always kept people at arm's length.

But with him...

"Tell me." His lids lowered, his lashes splaying across his cheeks. "After seeing me in the yard, do I strike you as a man who shies away from hard work?"

My lungs quivered. An eternity swept past, marooning us inside a swollen, aching silence. Far away, the crowd buzzed. The music rolled on. But my awareness narrowed to our mingled exhales and the way his heartbeat battered against the fingertip I hadn't yet reclaimed from his chest.

"Well?" Kyven whispered.

"I hate you," I whispered back.

A laugh rolled from his throat. "That doesn't bother me in the slightest. And nothing prevents you from kissing a man you hate."

I tried to list the myriad reasons why I shouldn't touch him. Why this damnable attraction was inconvenient at best and catastrophic at worst. Because there were a thousand reasons to resist him. A million.

I just couldn't think of a single one, right now.

My fingers curled around his shirtfront. And—

Clang. The peal of a warning bell smashed the night apart. Then another. *Clang.*

Kyven's eyes shot wide. He snapped upright as the crowd devolved into a scribble of panic. People fled for the exits, men shouting over one another while one woman wailed louder than a newborn.

"The Lady Amryssa," Kyven said, low and urgent, but I was a step ahead of him, already moving.

Oh, goddess. I'd left my best friend. Sleeping and unchained, with her bedroom door locked but her window unbarred.

I'd left her *alone.* Then completely forgotten to watch the sky.

And now Amryssa had no one to protect her from the incoming nightmare.

14.

I ran.

My stomach roiled as I shoved bodies aside in my quest for the door. Who cared about these people? Not me—they were only steps from their chains. Meanwhile, a mile and a half separated me from the girl I owed my life to.

The girl I'd now abandoned.

I exploded into the street. I'd lost Kyven in the melee, but it didn't matter. He was a distraction. A stupid, intoxicating puzzle I had no business wasting time on, much less almost kissing.

I sprinted through the emptying avenues. To the north, a purple monstrosity crackled over the trees. *That* was the real danger. The wolf in the henhouse I'd turned my back on while preoccupying myself with the fox. Stupid, stupid, stupid.

But I would fix it. I would get to Amryssa.

I had to.

Gravel fountained from my churning feet. I bolted along the road to home, my muscles screaming. But wasted seconds might make the difference between life and death, so I shoved past the pain.

Go. One foot in front of the other. Agony, but it didn't matter. Faster.

What was Amryssa doing? Only just waking? Jiggling the lock on her door? Turning to the window, realizing her chance had come?

The nightmare growled. Shit. *Shit.* The thing was already so close. The bells had been rung too late, and everyone at the house would be chaining themselves, not realizing a full ten minutes separated Amryssa from her keymistress.

My lungs sucked at the steaming air. The char of burnt paper rained ashes down my throat, warping my determination to despair.

You are nothing. A throwaway. You had one purpose, and you couldn't even do that.

The poisonous thoughts battered me, each word rammed home by the sound of hoofbeats. Which was...a new hallucination.

But wait. Were those *real?*

I glanced behind me. A shadow barreled from the night, a demon-dark horse and rider. Even in my fevered state, I recognized that glint. Blue heat.

Surprise nearly sent me stumbling.

Kyven didn't slow as he drew alongside me. By some miracle of agility and brute strength, he fisted the back of my dress and hauled me up, planting me in the saddle in front of him. His arm locked around my waist. The horse bent and stretched, its muscles like oiled coils in the darkness.

I clutched at the saddle's pommel. "Where'd you come from? And where'd you even get this thing? Is it yours?"

"I hope you're not suggesting I'm immoral enough to steal some-one's horse." Kyven's voice was low beside my ear. "Because if so, you'd be absolutely right."

I squeaked. "You *stole* a horse?"

"I did."

"For Amryssa?"

"No. For you. I gave you my word, didn't I?"

"Yes, but..." I hadn't actually believed him. Not for a second. "What happened to you not taking vows seriously?"

Kyven's hold tightened. He didn't answer. Maybe he'd surprised even himself.

Whatever. I'd sort through it later. For now, I pulled myself low, trying to minimize my wind resistance. Kyven leaned in, too, a steely wall at my back.

My mind raced. I could help. I *had* to. I gripped my dagger and called its magic.

Overhead, the nightmare roared. My head spun, but I slapped a palm against the horse and poured out magic in the form of energy and speed. The diseased purple trees smeared as the beast surged faster.

Kyven grunted in surprise.

Within moments, the manor appeared over a rise, an imposing mass of columns and gables. My gaze scaled the heights to Amryssa's tower. Shit.

Her lamp was lit. Worse, her silhouette darkened the window.

Every nerve stretched to a length of razored wire. My veins emptied of blood, then filled back up with night and rage and darkness, as if I could recruit the storm to help me. As if I could forge it into a blade wicked enough to cut apart the intervening distance.

I poured more power into the horse.

Close.

Closer.

Nearly there.

Up in the tower, Amryssa unlatched her window. The sky screamed as she swung the panes outward.

"You'll have to catch her," I hollered.

"What?" The rising cacophony almost stole Kyven's answer.

"When she jumps. You'll have to catch her."

He stiffened. I could practically feel him measuring the distance, the impossible drop. Even if he tried, the fall might kill her. It might kill them both.

But I would chance it. And if *he* wouldn't, I'd make him. I'd save her through sheer fucking will, if I had to.

I fisted my dagger tighter.

Our horse rocketed into the drive. Amryssa clambered onto her windowsill as I launched myself from the saddle.

I hit the ground in a tumble. Crumpled limbs. Gravel everywhere. Pain. Wet blossoms of blood, and then I was up again, sprinting. Just yards to go.

I skidded to a stop under Amryssa's window. She balanced on the sill, her hair a flying white pennant, her nightgown a wind-torn tumult. Gray eyes reflected the storm. Her mouth moved, but the gale snatched the words.

Somewhere nearby, the horse screamed. Kyven appeared, pawing at my skirts.

"What're you doing?" I swatted at him.

"Making a landing pad," he shouted. "It'll make for a softer touch-down than I will."

He fisted my hems and whipped my skirts wide, opening a cradle of fabric. Which...okay, actually made sense.

Amryssa lifted her foot into nothing.

Time splintered. The world hung suspended, a teardrop *thump-thumping* in time with my heartbeat. There was sound. Wind. *Fear.* Unassailable, unstoppable fear.

Amryssa jumped.

A scream ruptured my throat. I flung up a hand, and all my love, all my willpower, exploded in a jet I could *see*, a purple funnel that spiraled from my palm. I jerked back, but quickly managed to steady myself. The magic poured from the dagger, but also from the storm—I could *feel* it. Energy coursed through me, lighting my veins, bending to my will.

Amryssa plunged earthward. But my spiraling magic netted her, coiling around her limbs.

She slowed, then floated, then came to rest in my skirts as gently as a babe laid in its cradle. The violet magic blipped from existence.

Kyven looked at me as if I'd grown an extra head, but his shock barely registered. I dove for Amryssa, checking her for injuries. To my relief, she was unharmed, the only blood on her the stuff I'd smeared there myself.

Kyven shook himself, then bundled her into his arms.

"Can you get inside?" he shouted. "Or should I carry you, too?"

A thundercrack rent the air. I bent double, my vision heaving, my blood a blackened oilslick in my veins. Just moments ago, the storm had aided me, but it had already switched sides again. Set its gnashing fangs against my throat.

Kyven moved to help me, but I forced myself upright.

"Don't worry about me," I gasped. "Just get her upstairs."

He nodded and dashed toward the house. I pelted alongside him, hauling open the doors, not bothering to close them again. We streaked through the grand foyer and up the stairs.

Amryssa moaned. "Let me go. Let me out."

Kyven's jaw hardened. The nightmare ran hungry claws across my mind, but I stitched my focus to that badge of resolve. To his unwavering steps, to his utter lack of give.

Atop the stairs. Down the hall. Up the spiral staircase to the tower. Toward our rooms, and then we burst into Amryssa's, where Kyven pinned her to the bed. I ripped the manacles from the drawer and snapped them in place. Plucked my keyring from my pocket. Locked everything tight.

A few cranks of the chains later, it was done.

I swayed on my feet, my bones like hot jelly. I tried to take a step but couldn't, too lost over the horizon of my own relief. "I'm sorry, Am," I warbled. "I'm so, so sorry."

Her gray-green eyes held mine, two shining pleas in a pallid face.

"Now you," Kyven said behind me.

I almost laughed. Me? Who cared about me?

Everything melted. The wallpaper broke into heaving towers of insects. Thoughts pricked at me—angry hornets, stinging, stinging, stinging. *Nothing. Worthless. Empty.*

"Harlowe," Kyven hollered. "Come on."

I turned to him, and...oh. No claws, this time. No, this time, he shone.

"*Now.*" He pulled me toward the door.

In my room, he heaved me onto the bed and snatched the keyring from my slackening fingers. The house rattled and wobbled and tried to crunch me in its jaws. Shadows unfurled from the ceiling, venomous worms that sought my skin and wriggled through.

My eyes rolled as slimy darkness coursed beneath my skin. Something clicked around my wrists, then my ankles.

Manacles. But...how? I couldn't have made it on my own.

Kyven cranked my chains and climbed atop me, caging my face with calloused fingers.

I blinked up at him, forcing myself steady. Something ruptured inside my chest, a gush of molten fear.

Oh, goddess. I'd have to watch him die. He'd just saved me—*again*—and now he would end himself right in front of me. "Go," I said, knowing it was already too late. Shit, why had I told him I hated him? He'd die believing that. "There aren't enough chains here for us both."

He ran a thumb over the arch of my cheek. "Then it's a very good thing I don't need any."

His words landed in my ears and sat there, nonsensical. I searched his face for proof of the lie, but...there was nothing. No wince, no gritting of the teeth, no throaty convulsion as he swallowed back horror.

He just gazed at me, clear-eyed, the blue no longer that of ice or frost, but of a wide warm sea on a windless day.

"Impossible," I croaked. A scream tried to splatter out, but I gulped it back.

"It's not. Lioness, listen to me." His touch anchored me, even while the world battered itself to pieces around us. "The nightmare can only take you if you let it. So just...listen to my voice. Feel me against you. Nothing else matters. Only me, and I'm not leaving you."

My eyes darted. Behind him, the wallpaper bulged and broke open. Dozens of insectile arms thrust through the gap, a many-limbed monster hissing my name, promising to nibble me down to limp, wet strings.

"*Harlowe.*"

My attention jerked back to Kyven.

"What is it?" he said. "That you see? What does the nightmare tell you?"

The answer boiled up from somewhere deep. "That I'm worthless. Nothing. Insignificant."

"That's not true," he said. "You *know* that, don't you? Because if so, the storm can't have you. But you can't just believe you're worthy, you have to know it. Like I know it. Like Amryssa knows it. Maybe your imbecile parents didn't, but what they did would've crushed a lesser woman. Only you didn't break, because queens never do. Queens are ironclad, remember?"

"But..." I battled for air. The nightmare fought to pry my fingers loose from the anchor-line of his gaze. "I'm no queen. Just a lowly princess."

He blinked, then laughed, the sound so unexpected that it infused me with a dose of control.

"That's my girl," he said, stroking my cheeks, my hair. "My eight-week wife. What's your name?"

"My...name?"

"Yes. You're Harlowe, but Harlowe what?"

"It's..." I blocked out the storm's wildfire roar, the way blood was oozing down the wallpaper. Queen. He'd called me a queen. Think about that. "I don't have a last name. Not anymore. My parents took me into the swamp and walked away and...I buried their name out there. In the marsh. Now I'm just Harlowe."

The nightmare screamed. My hands curled into claws, my arm yanking against its socket in a quest to dig my own heart from my ribcage.

Kyven took hold of my wayward wrist and pinned it to the mattress, so much more gently than the manacle did. "All right, then, just Harlowe. Listen to me. Right now, I'm just Ky. All right?"

I nodded. "Ky." I hefted his name like a shield.

"Yes, good. Now here's what's going to happen. You're going to stay with me. Because this storm, it's nothing but fear, trying to swallow you up. Everything it says, everything it shows you, is a lie. And while it's strong, you're stronger. You might be just Harlowe, but you're also a survivor."

"I'm...not."

"You are." He imbued the words with steel conviction. "You survived the swamp. Years of solitude. A homicidal alligator, for Hyperion's sake. And you've survived these nightmares. Countless times before."

Amryssa was screaming. So was Olivian and everyone else, their cries saturating the walls, vibrating up through the floors.

I was losing.

I knew before it happened, anticipated the break of the dam just before the flood carried me away.

The nightmare ripped me from the haven of Ky's arms. He called my name—once, twice, again, but I couldn't hear him anymore.

I was drowning, dragged into the depths by the monsters that would gnaw me into nothingness. I tried to claw my way back, but he was gone, my bright oasis swathed by darkness.

I sank into the murky fathoms. Down, down, down, to where nothing remained but the screaming.

I 5 .

Consciousness seeped in, layer by layer.

Soft, gray light.

A steady heartbeat. Pattering rain.

Then pain. Lots of it. Deep and old, laced along the framework of my skeleton.

I groaned and forced my lashes apart, expecting an eyeful of ceiling. Instead, I got a rain-studded windowpane, an expanse of red sheets, and a bare, solid chest beneath my cheek.

I was...lying on my side. Unchained. Wearing only a chemise. With a half-clothed prince serving as my body pillow.

I raised my head, my cheek unpeeling from its resting place, then abandoned the effort when the room began a sick whirl.

"Ugh." My face thwacked back down. An arm tightened around me, and I craned my neck to find crystalline eyes trained on me.

"Good morning," Kyven said.

My belly rippled. I probably would've thrown up all over him if I'd had anything in my stomach to eject. "Is it?"

"I can't say I have any objections to waking up this way, so yes. It is. At least from where I'm standing."

"But you're lying down." My voice sounded like a rusty tap being forced. "And you could at least *pretend* not to be so fucking cheerful."

His chest hitched with suppressed laughter, which had the inconvenient side-effect of ramming an icepick through my skull.

I squeezed my eyes shut.

Thankfully, Kyven took the hint and stilled. His fingers curled around my upper arm, firm and hot. Our thighs wove together, and his heart thudded against my ear—serene, steady, slower than mine had ever been. Probably a function of all that wood-chopping and sheep-shearing. In the background, the rain dripped a soft chorus.

Once my head stopped stabbing itself, the overall effect was...nice. And since moving had proved agonizing, I didn't try again.

Instead, I probed my mind for an accounting of last night. I remembered screams flaying my throat. The dwindling throes of the storm. Kyven—Ky?—unlocking my chains and unfastening my dress, then shedding his clothes and pulling me against him. Murmured reassurances. *It's over, lioness. It's finished. You're safe.*

And before all that, Oceansgate. Theatre and ale and dancing. A hazy whirl of panic that had ended with the man I'd married saving two lives. Not just mine, but—

I jerked upright, my head shearing itself in half. "Amryssa!"

Kyven pulled me back down. "Is downstairs at the moment, eating her breakfast."

"What?" My throat cracked around the word.

"Mmm-hmm. I gave your keychain to Miss Quist. Told her you could use a morning's reprieve. She was surprisingly amenable to getting the Lady dressed and fed. Said Miss Amryssa needs to eat more, anyway, and she'd get an entire breakfast in her if it was the last thing she did. If you ask me, that woman is in dire need of someone to force-feed."

I processed that. "You mean you got up already? Then came back to bed?"

His hand found my hair and smoothed the strands through his fingers. "I didn't want you waking up alone. You spend all your time looking after the Lady Amryssa, but as far as I can tell, no one ever looks after you."

A hollow ache opened within me. He might as well have sunk a knife between my ribs and twisted. I heaved myself half upright, propping my forearms on his chest.

Kyven gazed down his cheeks at me, a hint of smile contouring his lips.

And something very strange happened.

It started beneath my ribs—the flutter of a thousand delicate wings taking flight. Warmth lightened my limbs, then sighed outward, sparkling its way down to my fingers and toes.

He looked...different. Maybe it was the aftereffects of the storm, but his beauty moved me on some seismic level I couldn't explain. The lines of his face came together like a symphony, harmonic and familiar, yet somehow startlingly new.

My gaze flickered away, but then I found myself staring at the half-moon birthmark beneath his collarbone. My fingers quivered with the need to find out whether it felt as smooth as it looked.

Which I resisted. Barely.

"You..." I murmured to his chest, "...saved me."

Spare words, but backed by a whole wide wall of wonder. Kyven could have done anything last night—hurt me, abandoned me, consigned me to the storm. I'd been as vulnerable as a tortoise stranded belly-up, but he'd *protected* me. Again. Me and Amryssa, both.

Goddess. If our positions had been reversed, I would've left him.

"Before you make me out to be some kind of savior," he said, "it cost me nothing to do what I did. I'm only sorry I didn't manage to guide you through it better."

My fingers edged toward his birthmark. *Had* it cost him nothing? He'd stolen a horse for my sake. Helped break Amryssa's fall, then brought her to safety. And through it all, I'd tasted his urgency as sharply as my own.

No, that couldn't have come for free.

At the realization, conviction hardened within me.

Eliana's letter was wrong. It had to be.

I didn't know how, or why, only that this man wasn't the monster she'd described. I would've staked my life on it. I had, really, last night. And he'd acquitted himself.

Which didn't answer even one of my questions. If anything, it only created more. Who *was* this man? What secrets was he keeping, if not those?

"Who are..." I started. "How did you... When the nightmare..."

Goddess. I couldn't think properly with him stroking my hair like that.

He made a humming sound. "We both have rather a lot to explain, don't we?"

I lifted my eyes. "Me? Why me?"

"Oh, I don't know. Perhaps you'd like to tell me how a woman falling from a third-story window can come fluttering to earth as softly as a feather?"

I swallowed. Okay. Fair point.

But I couldn't explain that to myself, much less him. I'd never managed anything like it before. In the past, the dagger had only ever worked subtly, and at close range.

Then again, I'd never channeled magic with last night's desperation, or come so close to losing Amryssa. Still, something more had been at work. The nightmare had *joined* me for a second. As if our agendas had aligned.

"I've seen magic before," Kyven said. "In Hyperion's temple, in Hightower City. People offer prayer candles, and the wicks ignite on their own to show he's listening. But what you did last night... I've never seen magic wrought by human hands. I don't believe it *can* be wrought by human hands. Which makes you...what? Some type of goddess? I don't suppose you're Zephyrine herself, hiding in plain sight?"

I blinked at the absurdity of that.

"Because if so," he mused, "I suppose *I'm* the one who married up, here."

A chuckle warmed my throat. Now he was only teasing. "No, I'm just a person. And I can't explain last night. All I can tell you is that the magic comes from the dagger."

One eyebrow skewed upward. "The dagger?"

"Yes. The one Olivian gave me. There's something inside it, an...enchantment, I think. But last night—well, I don't know what happened. The magic's never been that strong. I've definitely never *seen* it, and I've never drawn power from the storm. I didn't even know I could."

Gears turned visibly in his head. "Maybe Zephyrine's inside that knife of yours, somehow?"

I gathered a protest, then stopped. Huh. Why had I never considered Zephyrine?

Maybe because she'd vanished years ago. Or maybe because, in Oceansgate, the bayou seemed to harbor a magic of its own. While Hightower boasted a central, official temple, Oceansgate revered its thousand-year-old oak, and, by extension, the marsh itself. Here, people believed in nature's witchery, in a whole second world that lurked beneath the mirrored waters. They feared witches and wights, boogeymen and ghosts. Not to mention hexes and evil eyes and apparently abandoned little girls who couldn't brush their own hair. Belief in the supernatural permeated Oceansgate's collective consciousness, and I'd bought into that myself, ascribing the dagger's power to some kind of witchcraft.

But someone from Hightower would analyze this the *sensible* way —by setting aside superstition. And if magic indeed came from the gods, then Zephyrine might not be sleeping, but...stuck. Inside the blade Olivian had given me.

The idea rocked me. Seven hells. Had Amryssa's mother snared the goddess inside her knife, somehow? If so, did Olivian know? And why did the dagger's inhabitant feel so...incomplete?

"I can't think of any other explanation," Kyven said.

"No, me neither," I said slowly. "Aside from witchcraft, which, you're right, probably doesn't exist."

"Probably not."

Facts wheeled through my head. The Lady Marche had died in the third nightmare, after getting caught out in the marsh. Back then, the storms had been weaker, enough that I'd survived the first two unchained, but by the third, everyone had known what to do. Which meant the Lady should never have ventured into the swamp without a way to protect herself.

What had she been doing out there?

I thought. And thought. Until my headache swelled to an impossible size and my mind ran so many circles it started chewing on its own tail.

Kyven seemed to sense my struggle. "It's nothing we have to solve this morning."

"No, I guess not." With reluctance, I shelved my deliberations for later, when I had a clear head.

Kyven studied me. His hand drifted from my hair to my face, cupping my cheek in a rough palm. The touch wasn't any different from last night's, but this time, a prickle shot across my skin.

I cleared my throat. *Focus.* I wasn't the only one who'd done something inexplicable.

"The nightmare," I said, trying to piece together a sensible question. "You'd...done that before, hadn't you? Resisted like that? You must have. You must've done it your first night here."

A half smile. "Yes."

"But...you're from Hightower. How could you possibly have known how?"

He paused. "To answer that, I'd have to tell you my whole life story."

"Okay. Go ahead. It's not like I have anywhere to be, apparently."

Heat crept into his eyes. "Oh, but I can think of better ways to spend our time alone. *Much* better ways."

I moved to swat his shoulder, but he caught my wrist and held it fast.

A zing eddied into me from the place where his fingers circled my forearm, prompting the very potent realization that I was practically lying on top of him. Which was...probably sending the wrong message.

I tugged my hand away. I might have decided he wasn't a criminal, but really, what did that matter? This man was destined to marry Amryssa. All that had actually changed was that pesky little detail about me killing him in cold blood.

Which was...fine, really. It would've been a shame to let a face like that go to waste, anyway.

"I'd much rather continue last night's conversation than tell you my deepest, darkest secrets." His voice took on the consistency of hot, wet silk. "Because I believe we were at the part where you were about to fall hopelessly in love with me."

"No, we were at the part where I was about to slap you." I eased off him, though it cost me every ounce of energy and a not-insignificant amount of throbbing pain.

Goddess, why did everything hurt? So much more than usual?

Then I remembered. I'd launched myself from that horse last night. And hit the ground *hard*.

I looked down. Crusted scrapes littered my arms. Everything ached, though not so much as to suggest I'd broken any bones.

Kyven's gaze followed mine. "I suppose I *could* share, if you'd care to join me in the shower. I always do my best confessing while naked. I do most things better while naked, actually. I'd be happy to demonstrate."

I rolled my eyes, ignoring the mysterious response that prompted at the juncture of my thighs. "I already told you my story. For free. No joint showering required."

He heaved a theatrical sigh. "That's true."

"The least you can do is return the favor."

"Well. My life isn't actually all that interesting."

"Somehow, I doubt that." I held his eyes for a beat, and wow, did he make dishevelment look good. Dried sweat stuck his copper-dark hair to his forehead. Two-day stubble dusted his jaw, just begging to be touched, while scarlet smears adorned his chest.

My blood, not his. Evidence of how close he'd held me last night.

Seeing my own marks on him did something strange to me, so I kicked my legs over the bedside and went in search of my dagger. Best give him space, like he'd done for me over ale last night.

Best give us both space. Much-needed, much-desired, absolutely critical *space*.

Once I had my dagger in hand, I claimed a seat at my vanity. Kyven scooted to the mattress's edge, his eyes meeting mine in the mirror.

"Would you like to see?" I said. "What it can do?"

He nodded and made to stand, but I waved him back. I'd never shown this to anyone before. Then again, no one had ever saved me from a nightmare, either. Now this would have to serve as my tit for tat, since Kyven wasn't getting his hands on any other kind.

I went to work, smoothing away a cut.

He sucked in a soft gasp. "That's...astonishing."

"Just tell me your story. While I work."

Eventually, he must've come to grips with seeing my wounds knit into fresh, unblemished skin, because he said, "Last night, do you remember me saying I wanted to go everywhere? Do everything? *Be* everything?"

I quelled a shiver. Given the circumstances in which he'd delivered those words, I couldn't have forgotten if I'd tried. "Yep." I concentrated on a particularly nasty scrape, one that required me to pick out a chunk of gravel, first.

"Well, that wasn't always true. At its root, my story isn't all that different from yours."

I frowned. Whatever growing up as royalty involved, I doubted being dumped in a swamp ranked among the perks.

But I'd listen. I owed him that much.

"I wasn't...wanted, you see," he said.

I paused. I didn't detect any hint of resentment, just a bare laying of facts.

His gaze turned distant in the mirror. "My parents...well, they had me by accident, and they never missed an opportunity to let me know. I was the last of my siblings, and my mother and father were tired by then. Enough to consider me a burden. The lesser of all my brothers and sisters. And you'd hardly know it now, but I felt that judgment so keenly. I was a quiet child. Sullen. After all, my parents thought of me as a mistake, so why shouldn't that be true?"

A lump formed in my throat. "That's hard for me to imagine. You being..." *Unwanted*, I almost said, then veered. "Sullen."

He laughed. "Oh, but I was. Enough that I resolved to leave home as soon as I could. Which I did, when I was still young. Probably too young to be finding my way in the world, but I can't say I have any regrets about it now."

I made a sound even I didn't know the meaning of. I had difficulty imagining a prince being permitted to just...go forth, but he *was* the youngest. So far down the line of succession as to be practically ineligible for the throne. And an early launch would explain some of his more surprising tendencies—chiefly, his willingness to spend his days lathered in a dirt-soaked sweat.

I guessed he *hadn't* grown up in opulence, after all.

"Anyhow," he said, "after I left, I traveled all over. I think I was trying to find a better family than the one that hadn't wanted me. But it turns out no matter where you go, people are much the same. Mainly interested in themselves. *Loyal* only to themselves. In short, not like you."

My shoulders curved as if to deflect his words. I wasn't special. I didn't know why he insisted on seeing me as such.

"But one night, I made peace with all that, in a dingy little theatre in Gray's Reach."

My hand slipped from the cut I was mending. Gray's Reach? That was as far north as one could go in Elara—the frosty terrain of the patron goddess Gelidra, a territory renowned for its icy mountains and cruel winters. I could barely conceive of traveling that far. The journey would take weeks. Months. "You've been to Gray's Reach?"

"I've been to ninety-eight territories, if you can believe it. Only one remains. But Gray's Reach was ten years ago, now. At the time, I was nineteen, and had never seen a play before. I'd also never drunk that much ale, but the show grabbed hold of me, anyway."

"And that...changed your life? A *play*?"

He fought a smile. "Mmm-hmm. It was like a whole new world opened up, one I'd never known existed. Those people on stage, they were whatever they wanted to be. Whatever they said they were. And

I thought...why shouldn't the same be true for me? Maybe my parents hadn't wanted me, but so what? What prevented me from wanting myself? What if the only person who could define me was...me? And in doing so, I could become whatever I wished?"

My breathing did something funny. It couldn't be that easy, could it?

"When I sobered up, the first thing I did was join that theatre troupe. Which turned out to be everything I'd hoped for. We traveled all over Elara together, and each night, I tried on a new face. Figured out which ones felt like mine, be they the hero's or the villain's. I've been a pirate in my time, and a horseman. A warrior and a poet. I've even been a woman. I've also died a shocking number of times."

Something tickled at the back of my mind. "And...you often fell in love in the evening, and out of it again by sunrise?"

He laughed. "You clever thing."

Color stung my cheeks. Goddess, I'd thought he'd meant something very different by that.

"Anyhow, that was my life," he said, "for a very long time. I tried on every identity I could. Kept the pieces I liked best, let go of the others. And along the way, I sampled every food. Soaked up every vista. Learned every accent I could wrap my tongue around. Which happens to be all of them."

"*All* of them?"

"Well, all but one. I can do Oceansgate, if you like," he said, his inflection so identical to mine that I forgot what I was doing.

He caught my shock in the mirror and grinned. "Or would you prefer Stormbow?" His voice had changed again, filling with stilted consonants. "Though I have to say Crystal Hollow is my favorite, without a doubt."

My jaw slackened. I'd never even heard that last one. Ever. But I could see why he liked it. It was melodic. Like a song compressed into words.

When I managed to sift through my surprise, I said, "That's incredible. *You're* incredible."

"Ah. You've finally noticed."

I flushed. "But...after all that traveling, you ended up in Oceansgate?"

"I did."

"Where you stayed a while?"

"Mmm-hmm," he said.

"This was recent?"

A pause. "Yes."

"How long have you been here?"

"Ten months."

I chewed on that. Nearly a year. "But if you've been to ninety-eight territories, you can't have stayed anywhere else for that long."

"No. By the time my wanderings brought me here, I'd made myself into this and I liked it. It felt natural. Right. And, if I'm honest, I was curious about the nightmares. I'd heard the stories and..." He shrugged. "What can I say? I wanted every experience. Not just the pleasant ones."

I refrained from gaping, but only just. "You came because you *wanted* to live through a nightmare?"

"Well, why not? At least, that's what I thought. And then I had my first one and the confidence I'd spent a decade building fell apart so quickly. But I saw something there. Inside the eye of the storm." Wonder snuck in, silvering his words. "I could *taste* the possibility. I thought...surely if I knew myself down to the molecule, if my self-belief was unflinching, if I could belong to myself in every sense, I might battle a nightmare and win. And I'd already worn so many faces. Played so many roles. But this was the most challenging yet. The most exhilarating. So I stayed, and made it my mission to conquer the storm."

I scanned his reflection, dumbstruck. He perched at the edge of the bed, one elbow draped over a knee, the opposite palm propped against the mattress. The spare, hungry lines of his body radiated their usual power, yet I'd completely misinterpreted its source. Twice, now.

"It took me more than half a year," he said, "but I managed."

"But...that should've been impossible."

He lapsed into a secretive half smile. Because clearly, it wasn't.

The silence thickened to bursting. When I could stand it no longer, I pushed back from the vanity. This time *I* was the moth answering the beckoning shine of the flame. I went and stood before him, so awed I couldn't think past my own amazement.

All his self-assurance was apparently...completely genuine.

No wonder my insults never affected him.

"I didn't realize people like you existed," I said.

"I could say the same." He looked up at me, steady. So steady. "It's funny. In plays, people are always risking themselves for others, but I've never actually met anyone with that kind of conviction. That kind of *loyalty*. Not until you."

Heat blossomed along my neck.

"It's always men, too, in stories." His smile turned wry. "I suppose it should come as no surprise that in reality, it's women who have that kind of courage."

I searched for words. "I think I've...catastrophically misjudged you."

Silence. Consideration. Then, "I was no less guilty. I thought... Well, I thought what everyone else did, when I came here. That you were pampered. That everyone in this house was."

We stared at one another. I held my breath, waiting, waiting, for...what? The hand that dangled between his knees twitched, his fingers flexing, but he made no move for me, nor I for him.

In the quiet, questions whined in my ears like diving mosquitoes. One landed to sting. "But if you'd spent time in Oceansgate, how come people didn't know you in town last night?"

Slyness slid into his eyes. "Because. I didn't spend those ten months in town. I spent them in the woods."

"In the *woods*? What, with the brigands?"

"They call themselves 'liberators,' thank you very much. But yes."

Shock harpooned me to the floor. "Wait. So...you knew that woman, then, down in the cellar? Is *that* why she called you 'my lord?'"

His eyes flashed. "Mmm. Yes. Kyra's always been...impetuous. I'm not surprised that she threatened you, but you should know that isn't what the liberators are about. Redistributing resources, yes. Holding knives to people's throats? No."

I blinked at him. Blinked some more. "I don't... Wow. Okay. You really were one of them."

He surveyed me, a long, lazy look that ended with a smile. "I've surprised you."

"You've shocked me. I mean...what was that even *like*? Living in the forest?"

"Uncomfortable," he said. "And wet, and surprisingly demanding. We couldn't drink the water, so we had to harvest the rainfall. Not to mention hack apart the forest for firewood. But food was the biggest challenge. Things were easier when there was still traffic along the road to waylay, but now the situation's getting dire. If the liberators don't find a new food source soon, they'll have to go elsewhere."

"Oh. But...why not just move to town, then?"

He gave me a knowing look. "Because. Their leader prefers anonymity."

I thought back to Kyven's pocketing of the Wanted poster last night. At the time, I'd written that off, mainly because he'd *acted* like it didn't matter. But I should've realized. "You know him, then? This...bandit chief?"

"He and I have met," he said, and I had the distinct impression that he was enjoying this.

"What's he like?"

"Oh, very mysterious. Very...bandity. And very committed to playing the hero. I can't tell you much more, because I wouldn't be any sort of friend to him, if so."

I pondered that. "Can *he* resist the nightmares, too?"

Kyven held my eyes for a heartbeat, then another. "As far as I know, only I can do that."

Bits of the puzzle he posed locked together with a click, backed by the soft thrum of rain. "So *that's* where the rumor comes from, then, about the brigands not needing chains. From you. Of all people. But...Vick. You said you've known him less than a year, which means you must've met him in the forest, right? Is *that* why he and Lunk don't wear the royal livery? Because they're not actually from Hightower? Because they're nothing more than common thieves?"

His answering smile nearly blinded me. I'd pleased him, I could tell.

"Wow." I trotted the revelations around in my mind. No wonder Vick's accent didn't match Kyven's. It sounded stiff because it was fake, because Vick hailed from my own back yard. At least Lunk's lisp papered over any clues to his origins. At least *he* hadn't lied.

"Don't tell them I told you," Kyven said. "Lunk in particular would be sorely disappointed to know you no longer think of him as over-trained and equally overpaid."

A strangled laugh worked free. "Okay. But...you'd been back. To Hightower. Right?" He must have. Eliana had met him in the capital just months ago. In Burdock Street, whatever that was.

"I spent time there, yes. Off and on." Kyven studied me from beneath his lashes. I couldn't tell if he was playing coy or dissembling. Or both. "When it suited me."

Gods among us. This story almost disproved Eliana's letter in and of itself—she'd made it sound like the crimes in the capital had been continuous. I almost blurted as much outright, then yanked it back.

There was something in the way Kyven was looking at me. A challenge, almost. An expectation. One puzzle piece I was still failing to grasp.

I strained toward it, but it felt like trying to do long division in my head. The solution promised to fall into place, only I couldn't juggle the moving pieces long enough to get there.

But while I was many, many things, I wasn't stupid. That I knew. If I demanded answers, Kyven would only evade, like when I'd asked about Vick, or the Wanted poster. But if I waited, combing through every unguarded word he said, I would piece it together, whether he wanted me to or not.

"This explains so much," I said, leaving him to his secrets. I'd have the rest out of him, and soon. "But...what does this mean, exactly? For us? How does it affect the next month?"

One bronze brow arched. "Are you asking what I want from the rest of our marriage?"

"I... Yes. I think so."

He chuckled and made a fruitless attempt to straighten his hair. "Something very different than you do, I'm sure."

"Which is?"

He heaved a breath, as if squaring for battle. "I want...everything. To experience all life has to offer. Which means that for as long as I'm your husband, I'd like to actually *be* your husband. In every sense. I want to live it. Breathe it. Map it from the inside until I can draw it in the dark. I want to sink into it. I want to bury myself inside you."

At my startled look, he laughed. "Not like *that*, lioness. Well, no, that's absolutely a lie. I do want to bury myself inside you. *Like that.* But that's not precisely what I mean, in this case. It's more like..."

"Authenticity?" I offered, in a feeble attempt to recover. "Is that what you're saying?"

His mouth snicked up. "Just so."

My bare toes wriggled against the carpet, searching for purchase amidst this dizzying conversation. "*That's* what you meant when you said there was something in this marriage for you?"

"Does that surprise you so much?"

It did. It really did. Although I now understood why he'd refused to explain, up on the roof that day. If he had, I wouldn't have believed a word.

But now that I'd seen him throw himself into one experience after another with unfailing enthusiasm, it almost made sense that he would approach marriage the same way.

"Surprise aside," I said slowly, "what does authenticity mean to you, exactly? You want to...what? Share my bed? Stare into my eyes? Cuddle me? Fuck me?"

"I'm not talking about *fucking*." His tongue trailed over the word, tasting it. Caressing it. His accent reshaped it from something crude into something luscious. "At least, not *just* that. If it were up to me, I'd take that, of course. And the staring, and the cuddling, and the bed-sharing. And some of this, too. Where I look after you, like I did last night. That's part of this whole matrimony business, if I'm not mistaken."

I ignored the sudden fluttering inside my ribcage. "But if we did all that, we'd be married. Completely. With no way to annul it."

"Oh, but if there's one thing I've learned, it's that things are what you make them." His voice smoothed, like honey across satin. "As far as I'm concerned, no king, no law, can tell me who or what I am. The same is true in this. What you and I are to one another is ours alone. It's decided here, in this room, and nowhere else. Certainly not in Hightower, or by some crusty old monarch. Which is what I meant when I said I don't take vows seriously. I didn't mean I don't take *myself* seriously. Only words forced upon me by other people."

My throat worked. It took me three tries to produce a response. "So no matter what we do, you'll sign the annulment? Marry Amryssa?"

He didn't blink. "Is that what you want?"

My pulse stumbled, then righted itself. It absolutely was. Kyven was her only route out of Oceansgate. Her only chance at safety. "More than anything."

"Then why not? But you should know I have no intention of repeating this with her. Once it's done, I think it's best if I move on. That's what I'd always planned, truth be told."

"What, to...leave?"

His smile flattened, turning rueful. "Yes. Your Lady can have her place in Hightower, without me. And I'll walk out into a nightmare, never to be heard from again."

I digested that. "But everyone would think you were dead. Wherever you went, you wouldn't be a prince anymore."

"I've spent most of my life not being a prince. It wouldn't be anything new."

My thoughts whirred, but this was...perfect, actually. He could live as he liked, no arranged marriages or royal fathers to answer to. The king would consider his problem solved, and Amryssa would have a wonderful life. I could even accompany her to Hightower, something I hadn't dared hope for. "But where would you go?"

He shrugged. "Fairmont, probably. The only territory I haven't seen. The last accent I have left to collect."

Fairmont. Smack-dab in the middle of Elara. He'd be far enough from both Oceansgate and Hightower that we wouldn't chance seeing him again.

A thrum started up in my veins. "I like this idea."

"Oh?" His voice dipped into husky territory. "Which part? All of it?"

"Well, not the part with the fucking."

He chuffed a soft, hollow laugh.

"Or the cuddling. But the bed-sharing, I can do. More importantly, I can help you get your freedom. I just have one request. Something you have to do for me."

He gave me a look. A sultry, up-and-down, *I-sincerely-hope-this-involves-us-getting-naked-somehow* perusal that set my stomach quivering. "Anything for my wife," he said, so throaty he sounded like someone else.

What. In the actual hell. Where had he learned to do that? On the stage?

Annoyance flared, and I clung to it. If this prince thought he could do that scorchy-scorchy shit with his eyes and not suffer some kind of retribution, I would disabuse him of that notion, and quickly.

"Anything?" I said, matching his seductive tone.

"Anything."

I stepped in and leaned down, as if to kiss him.

He tipped his face up, eager, his lips parting as his lashes sought his cheeks. He slid a hand into my hair, but I stopped, my mouth a hairsbreadth from his.

He deserved a little torment. Probably more than a little.

Still, I hovered there for much longer than necessary. Just a fraction of an inch, and I would know what he tasted like.

And goddess, I wanted to find out. Something swelled in my ribcage, so insistent it felt like a tempest trapped inside a thimble. Because while, on some level, I'd found him beautiful since I'd first laid eyes on him, *this*—the temptation of his scent, his nearness, waking up to him the way I had—it was...

Well, something I couldn't indulge in, at any rate. Because despite Kyven's claims, our annulment *had* to stand. I would secure Amryssa a place in Hightower, one nobody could dispute.

Moreover, until Amryssa walked down that aisle, everything could still fall apart. Which meant I needed a backup plan. A way to make Oceansgate livable for Amryssa, if possible.

"I want you to help me find out if Zephyrine's in my dagger," I said, not so much speaking as breathing the words directly into his mouth. "And if so, how to get her out. How to stop these nightmares."

Kyven's eyes snapped open. He was so close I could count the diamond flecks in his irises. Feel every needy pull of his breath.

Goddess, if I kissed him, I wouldn't offer him an inch. Not even a mile, like he'd said. I'd give him a fucking light-year.

So I pulled back, leaving him straining toward empty air. He groaned, but I swore I clocked a note of appreciation in it.

"You're ruinous, do you know that?" His voice had gone tauter than a bowstring. "I swear you'll be the death of me."

I forced a chuckle. I wouldn't, although I very nearly had been, that first night. If only he knew how that tongue of his had saved him.

"But...I'll help you," he continued. "Of course I will."

"Thank you." A knock came at my door, and I moved away, grateful for the distraction.

It was probably Miss Quist, come to deliver Amryssa. Except when I swung the door inward, a steward waited in the hallway, his face pinched. "Harlowe. Your Highness. The seneschal wants everyone downstairs, in the library. He's putting together a search party."

"A search party?" My blood chilled. "What? Why? Is someone missing?"

The man wrung his hands. "It's Althea. Her chains weren't used last night. Or if they were, they were stowed away first thing this morning. And she didn't show up for her duties. We've searched her room, but...nothing. It's like she's vanished."

Vanished. I turned to Kyven, seeking reassurance, but when our eyes met, ice frosted my bones.

Because, for just a moment, he didn't look at all surprised.

16.

On the way downstairs, I glanced back to where Kyven trailed after me.

His expression radiated quiet concern, but I couldn't forget the flash I'd seen in my room. Or the fact that he'd been so interested in Althea last week. *Or* the knowledge that he'd been unchained during last night's storm, because while he'd comforted me, yes, I couldn't be sure he'd stayed. At the nightmare's peak, he could have gone anywhere, done anything, and I wouldn't have known the difference.

My stomach soured. Just minutes ago, I'd been so certain of him, but that had been before he'd admitted to spending the past decade as an actor. As a *liar*. One adept enough to wield any accent at will.

Now confusion cycloned within me. Who was he? What was he hiding? By the time we reached the library, my head throbbed.

Vick had already arrived—he stood in a corner with folded arms, his expression guarded but his eyes as incisive as ever. I wished I could turn that acuity back on him, because while the proceedings didn't appear to surprise him, they didn't appear to *not* surprise him, either.

Gods, what if *he'd* taken Althea? What if neither of them had? Ugh.

Olivian cleared his throat, signaling for quiet. Most everyone was in attendance, except Miss Quist and Amryssa. Lunk occupied an armchair, his expression somber.

"As many of you know," the seneschal began, "one of our housemaids was discovered missing this morning."

I grimaced. I barely knew Althea, but I hoped to Zephyrine she was all right.

Olivian mostly repeated what the steward had said, though he looked markedly less put-together while doing it. Blood vessels laced his eyes. His hair appeared to have been combed with a fork—if it had been combed at all—and I marveled that he'd managed to mobilize the staff for Althea's sake. Then I realized that, for him, her disappearance represented a tool gone missing from its toolbox. One less housemaid meant fewer hands to churn the butter, to gather the eggs and hang the washing on the line.

Olivian didn't actually *care*. He just didn't want the household's manpower diminished.

"It goes without saying," he said, "that if Althea failed to secure herself last night, her body might be somewhere on the grounds. Be prepared for that possibility."

I winced. Olivian concluded by dividing the staff into pairs and instructing us on where to search.

"We'll reconvene in two hours. If she's not found—" Olivian faltered, and I followed his glare to an empty nook. I could practically see his wife's ghost hovering. Taunting him.

But he seemed to have finished. Housemaids and stewards sorted into twos and drifted off.

"Well," Kyven said. "You and I are to search the third floor, it seems."

My jaw tightened. More alone time with him. Hurray. "Yup. Might as well get going."

"Let's. Because the sooner this is over, the sooner I can partake in some recovery bacon."

I paused, my gaze narrowing. "Recovery bacon? And what exactly do you have to recover from, if the nightmares don't affect you?"

"Oh, it's nothing to do with last night." He gave me a saucy smile. "More that *someone* in this house is adept at working up my appetite, then leaving me wanting."

I opened my mouth, then snapped it shut. It didn't take a genius to figure out he was referring to the way I'd taunted him with that almost-kiss upstairs. "You deserved that."

"Oh, I don't dispute it. And I didn't say I didn't like it. Just that it left me...hungry."

I turned my burning face away and headed out of the library. This man. With him, the upper hand always seemed to elude me.

On the third floor, Kyven and I searched the eastern corridor, room by room. I avoided his gaze the whole time, unwilling to brave another volley of flirting.

For his part, he gave the search an honest effort. Or seemed to, at least. He flipped the heavy drapes aside, coughing at the resulting billows of dust, then got on his knees and hunted beneath the beds.

No Althea. I couldn't decide whether that heartened or discouraged me.

When we reached the end of the hall, we came to a locked door. Kyven jiggled the handle and frowned. "What's in here?"

"You really don't know?"

"No." He blinked down at me. "Should I?"

I crossed my arms. This was the room his attendant had expressed such an interest in, right before I'd caught them whispering together. Except it turned out Vick wasn't Kyven's attendant, but...what? His subject? Underling? Certainly not his friend...their interactions had never been warm enough for that. And lately, Vick's glares had grown even colder. "Well, Vick was dying to know all about it. Right before you two got all chatty together."

Kyven's brow furrowed.

"Do you know where Althea is?" I blurted, unable to help myself.

His expression didn't flicker. "I imagine I do, given that anyone in their right mind would tire of these nightmares. Anyone would *leave*.

I'm sure she's far away, breathing a sigh of relief at never having to suffer another storm like last night's."

I cataloged his every word, every blink. "So you didn't steal her?"

He snorted. "Hardly."

"And you didn't have Vick steal her? Use this room to hide her, maybe? Because he seemed dead-set on getting through this door."

His look turned dubious. "If Vick has any interest in this room, it's because he suspects it holds something of value. Just what are you accusing me of, exactly?"

I studied him for long moments, then pressed my palms to my eyes. Seven hells, I didn't actually know. I only knew that this morning, my feelings had undergone some tectonic shift, transitioning toward trust, toward this bone-deep need to *believe* him.

Even now, a quiet certainty pulsed within me, a stillness that said I was safe with this man. Could I trust it?

My breathing grew shallow. Maybe Althea *had* left on her own. Maybe she'd taken her family and fled. Maybe Kyven whispering to Vick was just a coincidence, and—

"What in Zephyrine's name are you doing?"

I whirled.

Olivian stood in the hall, his head lowered, his stance wide, like a bull on the precipice of charging. "Why aren't you two back downstairs with the others?"

I backed away. Anywhere else, I would've held my ground, but here? An image flashed—of that poor steward, mottled and air-starved, Olivian's hands around his neck.

Goddess, I never should've come near the Lady Marche's room.

Kyven stepped in front of me. "This door's locked. It's the last place we have left to search, but we can't get in."

"Because it's private." Every line of Olivian's body was strained to breaking.

"Well, you did say every room." Kyven sniffed. "If there were exceptions, you should've specified."

"There're exceptions," Olivian hissed. I'd never heard that tone from him—as cold and sibilant as a blade being drawn. "No one comes near this door. Not the keymistress, not even a prince."

Kyven drew himself up. His height didn't equal the seneschal's, but he *held* himself like a much taller man. And he was still plenty big enough for me to hide behind, thank Zephyrine.

"Very well." He sounded almost...bored. "The thrill of playing hide and seek was wearing thin, anyway."

With that, he took my arm and guided me away. I went, too shaken to protest. I doubted he had any idea how close that had come to violence.

Back downstairs, everyone had reassembled. I calmed my trembling breaths and said a prayer for Althea. No one had found her, apparently, and I hoped she was halfway down the Oceansgate road, well on her way to a better life.

But then Miss Quist and Amryssa entered, and my musings evaporated. I rushed toward my best friend, forgetting Kyven. Vick. Everything.

Amryssa looked awful, as if the nightmare had carved out a chunk of her vitality and cast it into the fire. Her bones prodded at skin as diaphanous as wet silk, and deep hollows lurked beneath her eyes. And...had she somehow lost weight since yesterday?

"Am, what happened?" My hands fluttered over her, as if by rearranging her dress, I could rearrange *her*.

"Nothing." She tried for brightness and fell miserably short. "I only...well, I'm tired. That nightmare...it was a cruel one."

Miss Quist's wide-set blue eyes reflected the same helplessness filling my heart. "She ate, but it hasn't helped much. I don't know what else to do, except send her upstairs for a nap."

I gulped down the thorny ball forming in my throat. Amryssa looked like she was dying. Actually dying. Slowly but surely, these nightmares were killing her, and I couldn't do a goddess-damned thing about it, except—

No. Wait.

I straightened. Purpose leached into me, chasing away the ache in my marrow. Like I'd told Kyven upstairs, I could free Zephyrine from my dagger. Stop the nightmares.

Because, looking at Amryssa now, I wasn't convinced a royal marriage would save her.

At this rate, I wasn't sure she'd survive to see the wedding at all.

17.

I spent the day fussing over Amryssa. A nap and a bath revived her a little, enough that by evening, I'd decided she would live. *This* time. But the nightmares were escalating, and if the next storm arrived before the annulment certificate did...

I shuddered. I had a month to free Zephyrine, maybe less.

The following morning, I threw myself into investigating my dagger. I installed Amryssa in the library, which would stay cool all day, given the continued rain, and set out to find Olivian. When I spotted his broad shoulders down a hallway, I sped after him and caught at the sleeve of his morning coat.

He turned. Annoyance leapt into his features, like he'd been holding it in reserve for precisely this moment. "What?" he barked.

Before I could get a word out, he fired more questions. "Why aren't you with the prince? Didn't I tell you to stay with him? Do we really need *another* housemaid going missing?"

"Althea left on her own," I snapped, and goddess, how I hoped that was true. "You know that's the most likely explanation."

He grunted—in concession or impatience, who knew.

"And Kyven's in my room, showering. I locked him in, so there's no need to get snippy."

"Fine." Olivian waved a contemptuous, *out-with-it* hand. "Then what do you want?"

I lifted my chin and just...dove in. Amryssa couldn't afford for me to hesitate. "What I *want* is for you to tell me how a piece of Zephyrine ended up in my dagger. And where the rest of her is. And why the nightmares seem to have a vested interest in keeping your daughter safe."

The seneschal went ashen. His mouth opened, but nothing came out. A falling feather would've made more sound.

I chronicled every telltale twitch. Half of what I'd just said had been a stab in the dark, but the raw panic filling his eyes told me I'd hit the mark.

Seven hells, he'd *known*. All along, Olivian had understood where Zephyrine was and hadn't done a thing about it.

No wonder I hated this prick. The goodwill I'd granted him that day in his study dissolved like a sandcastle in the first high wave.

"I don't know what you're talking about," he said, but his denial arrived much too late. "If the dagger told you that, it's lying."

A breath jetted from my nose. So he knew the knife spoke, too. Unbelievable. "The dagger didn't tell me anything. I figured this out on my own." Or...Kyven had, really, but I didn't need to go awarding the prince any gold stars at the moment.

"You're mistaken." Olivian's words sounded like they'd been wrenched from his throat by force.

"I'm not. Clearly. Which means you know how to undo these nightmares, don't you? How to free Zephyrine."

I hadn't thought the seneschal could look any more apoplectic, but he managed. He made a choking sound as his pupils shrank to fevered pinpricks. "You have no idea what you're asking."

I sucked at my teeth. "Maybe not, but remember how you said we only got into this bride-swapping mess because you didn't trust me when you should have? Don't you think this might be another one of those times?"

He leaned in, making full use of his height. "I absolutely do not."

I widened my stance, unwilling to back down.

"And if you love my daughter as much as you say, you won't breathe a word of this. Not to her or anyone else. Do you hear me? Do your job. Protect her. I don't want to hear of this again." He bulled past me, his rage so palpable I swore the flocked wallpaper cowered as he passed. Each stomp rattled the glass sconces in their sockets.

Well, then. If *that* reaction was anything to go by, Amryssa was indeed a part of this. A very large part.

But Olivian clearly wouldn't give me a damn thing. I'd have to dig up the truth myself. Wrest his secrets from the crumbling woodwork and assemble them on my own.

Where to start? The library, probably. Our only real repository of information. I'd have to hunt through every book, see if I could find mention of the dagger, or the Lady Marche, or any kind of clue.

I was still standing in the hallway, staring out the window, not really seeing the silver wetness sheeting down the pane, when footsteps approached.

I turned to find Merron. Fatigue and wariness dulled his features.

"Hey." I reached for his elbow, but he stepped back.

"Your Highness," he said stiffly.

I winced. Well, his avoidance this past month had definitely been intentional. "Yeah, about that. I—"

"I just need to know one thing," he said. "That day, when we were together. Did you know? Had you already decided you were going to marry him that same night?"

My mouth went dry. "Merron..."

"Just tell me." His eyes shimmered, accusation held at bay. "I need to know what that was. If that was why you told me to forget you, afterward."

A prickle invaded my throat, and I bought a moment's delay by squeezing my dagger. *Zephyrine, help me.*

I'd never meant those words so literally, but now I knew I had a goddess on my hip—one I hadn't treated with much courtesy, or any deference to speak of. In fact, I'd done an embarrassing amount of swearing in front of her.

The dagger hummed. *Yes?*

I tried to make up for my heathen ways by adopting a tone of supplication. *Tell me what to say to him. Please. I can't stand making him suffer.*

A laugh murmured against my palm and faded.

I frowned. Unhelpful vixen.

The truth it was, then. "Yes, I...knew."

Pain bled through Merron's stoicism. "And you didn't tell me?"

"Because you would've tried to stop me." A pleading note snuck into my voice. "You know you would have."

He swallowed in silence, and if nothing else, I appreciated him not coming out with a denial we both would've known to be a lie.

"I deserved better," he finally said. "From you."

Oh, goddess. I wanted to pull up the carpet and crawl underneath, then tack it back down to the floorboards. "You did. You absolutely did. And I'm sorry. I hate that I hurt you. I have no excuse. This whole marriage thing was a mistake, and I'm stupid for having done it."

"Then you...regret it?"

"Deeply."

He recoiled like I'd delivered an aimed blow. "Goddess, Harlowe, that's even worse."

"Worse? What? How?"

"Because." His brows drew together. He looked so...woebegone, with the silvered light robbing his skin and hair of their rich brown hues. "If you regret marrying him, that makes this whole thing a waste. It means I lost you for nothing. It means I feel this way for no reason."

My chest caved in. A thousand excuses bubbled in my throat—aspersions on Kyven's honor, promises of an annulment, denials that I could feel anything for some russet-haired prince of Hightower. But none of it would've helped. I'd ground Merron's heart to a fine powder, and I couldn't seem to stop doubling down on that process.

So I said the truest thing possible. "I did it for Amryssa."

"Amryssa." A hard wall went up behind his eyes. "Right. Of course."

Shit. Why had I gone with that? If I stuck my foot into my mouth any further, I'd start digesting it. I tried to explain, but he fended me off with a raised hand.

"Don't. Just don't, okay? I don't want to hear another word about how you'd go to the ends of the earth for her when you refuse to do a single thing for me."

With a shake of his head, he swept past. I watched him go, my every breath laced with remorse.

Gods among us. I was a terrible, horrible person. No heart to speak of. Which usually came in handy, but with Merron, I always walked away painted in a fresh layer of shame.

And right now, I had never felt so small.

18.

On my return to the library, I found Amryssa and Lunk sitting cross-legged on the carpet together, laughing.

I paused, letting their lightheartedness soothe the sting of my disgrace. It helped that they weren't just laughing, but outright *giggling*—her with a silvery twitter, him with a rumble akin to furniture being moved.

I watched them until my heart quieted.

Because...this was it, wasn't it? *This* was why I loved her, why I'd give anything. Why I'd marry Kyven all over again if necessary. Because even after the nightmare had brought such suffering, Amryssa shone like a diamond in a coal mine, like a lamp on a foggy night. She was the best and brightest humanity had to offer, and she deserved a little peace.

She glanced up at my approach. Her white curls spilled down her back and trailed onto the carpet. Amusement brightened her face.

And...wow. I'd have to leave her with Lunk more often. He'd done more to revive her than anything else I'd tried. Affection for the man surged through me, so potent my eyes stung.

"Harlowe." Amryssa patted the floor. "Come sit. Lunk was just telling me about the time he tried to slaughter a chicken, but it made off with his underwear, instead."

The giant ducked his head. "Oh, the keymistress doesn't need to hear about that." *Keymistress* came out as *keymithreth*, while *doesn't* became *doethn't*. "No doubt she's got better things to do."

He was right, of course—there were four massive walls of books here for me to hunt through. A million leatherbound possibilities that might describe the rise of the nightmares, or the Lady Marche's dagger, or...well, I didn't know what I was looking for, exactly.

But I *did* know Lunk was simply being shy. Amryssa had an undeniable softness, a tranquility that encouraged confessions about underwear-pilfering chickens, but I was decidedly less inviting, and the giant often slanted away when I came near.

I smiled, trying to soften the harshness of my features, but Lunk's dark eyes sought the floor and stayed there.

Well, no chicken stories for me today.

"Don't mind me." I moved away. "Pretend I'm not even here."

"Oh, but you are." Amryssa pulled a pale curl through her fingers. "And without your husband, at that. Where is he?"

My *husband*. I wished she wouldn't call him that. Somehow, on her lips, the word sounded much too real.

"I'm right here," came a voice behind me.

I turned to find Kyven striding through the doors.

My heart momentarily forgot its cadence. He looked fresh and clean and perfect, his wet hair glinting like polished mahogany, that sky-blue waistcoat accentuating his eyes. As I stood there, trying to quiet the fireworks in my bloodstream, he rolled one snowy shirtsleeve to the elbow, then the other. Those sinewy forearms hooked my gaze and held it.

I tried to shake off my reaction. All he'd done was resist a nightmare—okay, he'd also done a mild amount of saving my life—but that shouldn't have granted him the power to affect me like this. Especially because logic implied he might also be kidnapping the housemaids.

I just...gods among us, I didn't believe it. I couldn't *make* myself, not when he was standing there like he was ready to work. To help me save the person I loved most.

"How'd you get out of my room?" I said, hating my own breathiness.

He shrugged. "I picked the lock."

"Picked the..." I pressed my lips together. I didn't want to know where he'd learned *that* particular skill. Or why. I didn't want to know anything except how to free Zephyrine, because every word I exchanged with this man only drew me further into his thrall.

"I assume," he said, "that when I agreed to help, I agreed to do research. So where do we start?"

"Didn't you say you don't read?"

He made a face. "Gods forbid. But this isn't *reading*, really. More like solving a puzzle. Conquering a challenge, you could say."

"Which is...something you enjoy," I said, more statement than question.

He started toward me. I swore I caught Amryssa smiling from the corner of my eye.

"It absolutely is." Kyven came close. His voice dropped, his vowels filling out even further. "And the pricklier the challenge, the more liable I am to throw myself at it. I'm especially fond of the ones that seem impossible at first blush."

A heatwave rolled up my spine. Were we still talking about books? Something told me not.

A sound like a suppressed snicker broke into my awareness. I glanced around to find gray eyes and black ones taking our measure. For all that the colors differed, both pairs shone with repressed mirth.

My gaze narrowed. Great. Lunk and Amryssa were clearly in cahoots, now.

"Right." I turned back to Kyven, my tone brusque. "Why don't you start at the other end, then, and I'll stay here. We're looking for...ledgers, maybe. Diaries. Anything that might chronicle the years around the start of the nightmares. Or that might mention the dagger."

He nodded and moved off. I watched him go, earning myself another round of giggles from the peanut gallery.

I briefly wrestled with the compulsion to flip Lunk and Amryssa the bird, then stalked to the nearest bookcase without lowering myself to their incredibly childish level. Moral high road, and all that. Because wasn't I just a paragon of fucking virtue.

Hours dragged by. I flipped through books and books and more books, but progress was slow. At one point, Vick wandered in to survey the library. His attention moved from me to Kyven, a sneer twisting his lips.

I frowned. What was *that* about? Every time I saw him, he seemed increasingly resentful, and now I wished he would just get on with his plans to rob us elsewhere.

Or whatever the hell he was doing.

By mid-afternoon, my back ached. The books had no apparent order—fiction was jumbled with treatises on inter-territory commerce and textbooks on astronomy. I even found a volume about something called paleography, which turned out to be the study of ancient handwriting.

I tossed that one aside, frustrated. How did Olivian get anything done in here?

Then again, he mostly didn't. He spent his time holed up in his study, arguing with the Lady Marche's ghost.

With an aggrieved sigh, I thought better of my desecration of literature and bent to retrieve the paleography book. It had tumbled beneath an armchair, and when I reached for it, I spotted a bundle of withered weeds beside the splayed pages.

Wait. Not weeds.

My breathing picked up. No, those were the peonies Kyven had given me on our wedding night. I'd ditched them beneath the chair, then forgotten them completely.

I snuck a furtive glance, but he stood atop the sliding ladder by the window, thumbing through a massive tome. Meanwhile, Lunk and Amryssa huddled around a boardgame they'd unearthed.

Nobody was paying me any attention, so I snatched the flowers.

The stems had shriveled, but the blossoms retained some volume, their champagne petals preserved in a perpetual state of bloom.

My mouth edged downward at the corners. How fitting that Kyven had chosen a flower that barely lasted. What was it he'd called me the other night?

My eight-week wife.

Eight weeks. Just a blip. Ephemeral and meaningless. Like these peonies.

"I think I've found something."

I whirled, one hand flying to my chest when I found the subject of my ruminations standing right behind me. I shoved the flowers under my skirts, then winced at the snap of breaking petals. "What is it?"

He gave me a puzzled look. Shit. I'd spoken much too loudly for the rain-drenched gloom of the library. I composed my face, trying not to look too deranged.

"It's only a sentence." Kyven hefted the weighty tome. "And I'm lucky to have seen it at all. I only happened upon the right page. Otherwise, this book holds nothing but the lethally boring ramblings of some old steward who apparently considered the daily state of the larder to be worthy of immortalizing in ink."

I blinked, digesting that. The peonies crackled again, and I forced a concealing cough. "Okay. Tell me what it says."

"It's dated from thirty years ago." He read aloud in an immaculate Oceansgate accent. *"Aside from waging war on the larder's rats, I worry for the Lady Marche. She copes with her childlessness by writing feverishly in that little brown diary of hers, as if enough scribbled pleas to Zephyrine might buy her a babe."*

Childlessness. My mind swiveled and swooped around the word. I hadn't realized Amryssa's mother had had difficulties with her conception. Then I raked over the rest, and a spark simmered in my chest. "A 'little brown diary?'"

"Exactly. Something like that would have to be around here somewhere, wouldn't it?"

It would, and that was exactly the sort of thing that might provide clues to the dagger's origins. But when I scanned the room, the internal spark flickered and died. These shelves housed thousands of books, half of which were brown, and while Kyven's find might have narrowed our search, we'd still need weeks to sort through them all.

I glanced up to find him contemplating me, his head tilted.

"What?" I said.

"I'm just wondering if there's any particular reason you're crouched there on the floor."

A flush warmed my neck. If I stood, he would see the peonies, and that was the last thing I needed. If he thought he'd caught me mooning over some meaningless trinket he'd given me, this cocksure prince would grow even cockier. Or...cocksurer? Cock—

Never mind. Probably best to move on from that word entirely.

"Nope," I said. "No reason. I'm just...admiring this chair. It's very nice, don't you think?"

He snapped the tome shut. "I didn't know you were such a connoisseur of furniture."

"Oh, but I am." Panic set in, heating my insides to a glow. "Furniture is so...functional. You can do all sorts of things with it. Sit on it. Or...not sit on it? So many options."

Kyven slitted his eyes, a silent proclamation that I'd lost my mind.

Which wasn't off the mark. Someone had clearly stolen my body and was now using my mouth to spout gibberish. Briefly, I considered hurling myself through the nearest window, if only to escape this disaster of a conversation.

"Well," he said, after approximately a decade of silence. "Carry on, I suppose. Though I'm a bit disappointed to hear you don't have more stimulating uses for the furniture. I can think of at *least* a half dozen, myself."

When he strolled away, a slow breath leaked out of me. I tucked the peonies behind my back and stood, only to find Amryssa and Lunk watching me with undisguised glee.

This time, I *did* give them the finger. And afterward, I wasn't even sorry about it.

〜

We didn't find the diary the next day. Or the next.

The rain continued for a week, dampening the world, cloaking the manor in gray. Amryssa and Lunk played games while Kyven and I combed the library. Vick continued his relentless search. The whole time, water trickled down the panes, and I swore the rain filtered through the gaps in my ribs, drip-drip-dripping into some hollow chamber nestled beneath my heart. Into the same secret place that housed the fluttering wings I'd first felt while looking at Kyven after the last nightmare.

In light of Althea's disappearance, I knew I should have suspected him. Hated him. But that same sparkly feeling kept rearing its head, determined to outstay its welcome. It assailed me in the unlikeliest of moments—like at the dinner table, when Kyven buttered Amryssa's bread and set it on her plate with a big-brother smile. Or in bed, when he propped a hand behind his head and tugged idly at his breech-laces, a suggestive smile playing over his lips. And the time Olivian barreled into the library, intent on upbraiding me for some infraction or another, only for Kyven to divert him into a discussion about the merits of alligator leather while simultaneously throwing me a wink.

Then, those wings would stir, and I would look away. Do my best to escape him.

But at night, I didn't have that luxury. Each evening, Kyven would croon his flirtations and do everything in his considerable power to fluster me. Which worked. Ninety-eight percent of the time, it worked, though I did my utmost to hide the betrayal of my staccato breathing. Eventually, he would roll over and sleep, which always left me feeling like he'd laid out a banquet for my benefit, then smiled knowingly when I'd refused a single bite.

Out of desperation, I stopped using the dagger's enchantment. Maybe if Kyven didn't look so damn *contented* at night, I could exorcise this increasingly urgent...awareness. But he slept nearly as soundly without the dagger's influence. Meanwhile, I tossed and turned. And sometimes, in nighttime's youngest hours, I just...breathed. Held him in my nose.

I couldn't seem to help it.

Tonight, I lay on my back, watching the swamp-glow shimmer on the ceiling. The rain-streaked pane made it look like purple firelight, dancing to a tune no one could hear.

"Lioness," Kyven murmured.

My heart nearly burst out through my mouth. I rolled toward him, breathless, but whatever I'd anticipated went unfulfilled, because he wasn't even awake.

His eyes fluttered beneath closed lids. Was he...dreaming? About *me*? The way he'd said my name was unfamiliar—hungry and windswept—and I ached to hear it again.

But he only sighed and rolled over, stealing himself from sight, though the view from behind wasn't anything to complain about, what with all those ripples and lines laid out like a feast for my eyes.

Still, I barely slept that night. A hollow throb chased me into slumber—an uneasy sense of incompletion, as if I'd gone into town half-remembering I'd left a pot on the hob to burn. That something critical had gone undone.

And, to my dismay, the same thing happened the next night.

And the next.

19.

The night the rain stopped, I dreamed of my parents.

I was eight years old, surrounded by the swamp, the rustling tupelo trees. This was my first time seeing the part of Oceansgate that ran wild, and I didn't care for it one bit.

My mother stood before me, her hands on her hips. "I want you to wait, Harlowe. Right here."

"Wait?" I whined. My lank brown hair drifted against my elbows, stirred by a breeze that didn't touch the heat. "But why? Where're you going?"

"Not far." My mother used *that* tone. The one that meant she couldn't wait to be done with this. With me. "Your father and I will be right back."

I stamped a foot. "But I hate this place."

Her mouth tightened.

Some distant, grown-up part of me—the one that understood what was happening—cringed at my mother's impatience. But child me met with petulant confusion. Last night, from the ratty cocoon of my blanket, I'd heard Ma arguing with Da, and while I couldn't have said what about, I'd caught a few choice phrases. *Too much. A handful. Can't do it anymore.*

Now the words buzzed in my ears along with the mosquitoes. "Why can't I come with you?"

"Because. I said so."

"But—"

"For once in your life, Harlowe, can you just listen?" she snapped. "Do as you're told?"

I pouted, but I obeyed. Zephyrine knew why, but I obeyed.

My mother walked away. Didn't look back. But my father did, and even within the hazy confines of the dream, that simple act took on a life of its own. His brown eyes considered me, vast and deep and wondering.

Goddess, how I wished he hadn't done it. I wished there hadn't been a point at which he'd considered returning for me and decided not to.

My mother slapped at the back of his head, and he faced forward again. Blue shadows swallowed them, Da's white shirt winking out.

I was alone.

I waited there, swatting at bugs and anticipating my parents' return, until long after the sun set. Even though I knew, deep down, that I'd been abandoned.

The cold hoot of an owl jerked me awake. I heaved upright in bed, my chest surging like a bellows, my skin slicked with sweat. Gods, I hadn't had that dream in ages. Now I ran my hands down my face, trying to scrub the memories from my skin.

Calm. *Breathe.*

Somehow, Kyven had slept through my violent awakening. He sprawled beside me like some wayward god, thoughtlessly taking up enough space for his own temple.

Seven hells, but he was beautiful, each bold brushstroke of him like someone's answered prayer. And I couldn't handle it right now, not with my nerve endings pruned to rawness by that dream. Not with the stain of *unworthiness* left behind.

No, I needed to get away from him. Go...anywhere else.

I slid from bed, pausing only long enough to grab the throw blanket from the armchair.

Downstairs, in the kitchen, I gulped cold water from the faucet. But the dream still moldered in my throat, rancid and clinging.

Air, then. I needed air.

I hurried back into the hall, pausing when Merron's door slid from the gloom. Was he still awake? Because if so, I knew of one surefire way to calm the nausea laying siege to my innards.

I got as far as reaching for his doorknob, then froze. No. What was I doing? Last time had ended in disaster, and I refused to sink to that level of selfishness again. Besides, it wasn't *his* touch I longed for. It was...

It was...

Well, who knew, but appealing to Merron wasn't right. I could not, *would* not, hurt that man any more than I already had.

I snatched my hand away and hurried onward.

Upstairs, on the rooftop, cool night air brushed at my cheeks. The rain had cleared, revealing stippled stars, and I stood at the roof's edge, my blanket wrapped tight.

Tomorrow, the heat would return with a vengeance, but for now, the swamp glowed beneath a cloudless, moon-chilled sky. Out on the lawn, fireflies danced like amethyst stars.

It was beautiful. And deadly. And a reminder that I needed to hold myself together if I wanted to help Amryssa, not fall apart at the first sign of a nightmare. A perfectly mundane one, at that.

A foot scraped against stone. "Harlowe?"

I whirled. Merron stood beneath the cupola, his arms spread, his nightshirt rippling on the breeze. He looked...terrified.

"Merron? What's wrong?"

"Don't," he choked out. "Please. Just...think about this."

I furrowed my brow, mystified. But then he shot a shiny-eyed glance at the drop behind me, and I understood.

He thought I meant to jump.

I couldn't help it. I snorted. "Really? I only came out here because I had a bad dream. So you can go ahead and close your mouth."

He didn't close his mouth. Whatever he tried to say next stalled in his throat.

I sighed. "Come on. After all these nightmares, you think I'd just give up? If nothing else, you should know I wouldn't leave Amryssa like that."

That seemed to reach him. His mouth snicked shut. "Okay. You're...okay? You're sure?"

I wasn't, not really, but I wasn't *not okay* in the way he feared. "I'm fine."

"All right. But...will you come here? You're scaring me."

I frowned. "No. I like it here."

He eyed the scant inches separating me from a dizzying earthward plunge. "Okay. But...did I hear you downstairs? Just now? Outside my room?"

I paused. Shit. I had no feasible way to explain that.

Thankfully, the shadows rustled, saving me from an answer. Kyven wandered out of the darkness, looking tousled and decadent and utterly unsurprised at finding us here.

"Lioness." He scrubbed at his mussed hair. "Bad dream?"

I gave Merron a *See?* look. "Yep. I just came to get some air."

"Mmm." Kyven stretched, catlike. When he raised his arms, his entire torso rippled, muscles standing out in places that seemed physiologically impossible.

It was absurd. So ridiculous that even *Merron* watched. But then the steward's face closed up. "What're you doing out here, Your Highness?"

"Trying to lure my wife back to bed." Kyven scanned Merron with abject disinterest. "What's your excuse?"

"I'm..." Merron glanced to me for help.

I shook my head. If he expected me to admit to lingering by his door in front of my temporary-but-still-very-legal husband, then...nope.

Not going there.

"I'm trying to get her away from the edge," Merron said uncertainly. "I don't like her standing so close."

Kyven snickered and strolled to a bench. "How unfortunate for you. Because last I checked, she could stand wherever she damn well pleases."

At that, my stupid heart swelled and swelled. Kyven draped himself atop the bench, perfectly at ease. Meanwhile, Merron tensed like a matchstick curved against two thumbs.

They were both looking straight at me. But seeing two completely different people.

"Go back to bed, Merron," I said, softening my dismissal with a step away from the brink. "I'm sorry I scared you."

He studied me, plainly affronted, then threw his hands up and padded back down to the attic.

Once he'd gone, Kyven winked.

I expelled a sigh. "Don't do that."

"What?" A smirk curved his mouth. "I didn't say a thing."

"You didn't have to. Your face did all the talking."

He laughed, then extended his arms. "Come. Sit. Tell me about this dream."

I drifted close. I'd come out here to escape him, yet here I was, unable to resist the allure of that insouciant half smile. Or the fact that he apparently considered my will to live a foregone conclusion.

But once I neared the bench, I hesitated. I had nowhere to sit except in a straddle atop him, which he seemed to expect, because he flicked beckoning fingers at me.

I scoffed. "I'm not going to use you as a seat, if that's what you're thinking."

He pouted. "Why not?"

"Is that a serious question?"

"Oh, come on. I had to endure all of five minutes in bed alone. The least you can do is cuddle me."

I wrinkled my nose. "Not a chance."

"You'd deny a poor, lonely husband the minimum of attention?"

"You're a big boy." I settled into our familiar sniping, the dream's aftertaste finally receding. "You'll live."

"Oh, come on," he said. "We're both wearing clothes."

"Not enough for *that*."

A shimmer moved in his eyes, one that said he *knew* I wouldn't surrender, but he enjoyed putting the effort in, regardless.

"Besides," I added. "Last I checked, I could sit anywhere I damn well please."

He laughed and dropped his hands. "Well, I can't argue with that. It was obviously said by someone incredibly wise." He heaved himself upright—complete with an obscene amount of abdominal rippling—and patted the now-empty half of the bench. "There. Happy?"

I eyed the space he'd cleared. Goddess. He both eased and sharpened the ache inside me. Like an addiction. The more I got of him, the more I wanted. And the more I wanted, the harder it was to keep him at arm's length.

This was dangerous. *He* was dangerous.

So dangerous, in fact, that I couldn't stop myself from settling on the bench and drawing up my legs. I tucked my nightgown close, at least, so as not to provide any encouragement.

Not that Kyven needed such things. He stacked his forearms on the apex of my knees and rested his chin on top.

I sucked in a breath. Starlight and bayou-glow danced across his face, rendering him breathtaking. Even more so than when he slept.

"You're staring," he said.

I cleared my throat. "You happen to be in the direct path of my eyeballs. It has nothing to do with you."

He laughed softly. "You're *staring*."

I huffed. "Okay, fine, well, so are you."

"Mmm. Because I like your face. I like your hair. I like *you*."

Heat throbbed in my cheeks. Looking at him did things to me, but being looked *at* piled a whole set of other things right atop the first. "You *do* know I still hate you, right?"

His smile deepened. "Oh, I'm well aware of how you feel about me."

The air thickened. Gods, how did he do that? Say one thing and mean another entirely?

Time to change the subject, since I couldn't win at this little game.

"As delightful as your arrogance is, I actually... Can I ask you something?"

He hiked a brow in invitation. Or challenge, maybe. "Go ahead."

"I want to know..." I picked at a loose thread on my nightgown. "...What did the nightmares show you? When you first came here?"

His face blanked.

I almost smiled. Finally, I'd managed to surprise him. Ha.

But it didn't last long. A divot formed between his brows as he considered. "The storms told me...I wasn't enough. Not charming enough, not witty enough. Not enough for anyone to want."

Shock bloomed, but I tamped it down. That was so close to my own fear, yet he and I couldn't have been more different. "And so you conquered that by...what? Changing yourself? Making yourself so charming, so witty, that your shortcomings didn't matter?"

"Shortcomings?" His smile edged toward slyness. "Lioness. Are you suggesting I'm compensating for something? Because I assure you, there's nothing *short* about me. Not where it counts."

I shook my head. Sweet Zephyrine, he could probably sexualize a conversation about a potato.

When I didn't rise to the bait, he sighed, apparently deciding to grant me mercy. "The thing is, it wasn't about that. When the storms came, it didn't matter what I was. Only what I *believed*. Which meant I didn't have to become more charming. I had to realize I already was. Define myself so the nightmares couldn't. Because they don't tell any kind of truth. When they say you're worthless, that's simply your own fear, aimed back at you. The storms' only weapons are the ones you hand them yourself."

His words settled into me, heavy and warm. The nightmares had always felt so inescapable, like truths shouted from the exact center-point of the universe. But maybe that was just another one of their illusions. "You just...figured that out? On your own?"

"It took time," he admitted. "Months. But once I understood, half the battle had been won."

"And now you resist by just...believing you can?"

"No. By knowing it."

Something squeezed inside my chest. "What's that even like? Having that kind of faith in yourself?"

"It's..." His eyes glossed over as he searched for an answer within. "Freeing."

I stared. My whole being boiled down to a complex simmer of reverence and envy.

"But you'll have an easier time than I did," he said. "You'll conquer the nightmares with hardly any trouble."

My brow crinkled. I hadn't once imagined myself accomplishing what he had. Not when I was so susceptible, and he was so...I didn't even know. *More.* More than me. Larger than life. "Why do you say that? Because I have you to help me?"

"No. Because you're immoveable."

I side-eyed him. "Is that a fancy way of calling me stubborn?"

He chuckled. "I value my life much too highly to admit to *that*. I only mean...you're strong. Strong enough to handle me, at any rate, and I can't tell you how rare that is. I tend to run roughshod over people, if I'm not careful."

Well. That much, I believed.

"But with you...I don't have to worry. You're ironclad. And no nightmare in the world can rob you of that."

I dropped my gaze. I didn't feel ironclad, not around him. I felt...soft. Breakable. As bare and unprotected as the apple he'd skinned that night in Oceansgate.

Time for another subject change.

"I *am* stubborn, though," I said. "Which has never helped me with the nightmares."

"I wouldn't call you stubborn. You're more like...strong-willed."

"Come on." I leveled him with a look. "I'm difficult."

He cocked his head. "I believe 'spirited' is the word you're looking for."

I rolled my eyes. "I'm prickly."

"You're assertive."

I puffed out a breath. "I'm a handful. Too much."

"Well," he said. "As one handful to another, I think you're just enough."

My pulse misfired, robbing me of words, even though his claims were ridiculous. I knew I wasn't in danger of winning any personality contests anytime soon.

Still...a dark thrill flickered against the backdrop of my quickened breathing.

"You're welcome to keep going." His eyes flashed a challenge. "I could do this all night."

"You're impossible," I said.

He laughed. "Well. That much might actually be true. Now, if you're fresh out of self-deprecations, why don't you tell me what you dreamed?"

The thread unraveling from my nightgown became newly fascinating. But I had no reason to hold back. He already knew my secrets. "It was...one I've had before. Lots of times. About my parents leaving me."

"Ah." He slid his arms down over my knees, hooking my thighs, pulling me closer. His torso was like a slab of hot stone pressed against my shins.

The contact woke something inside me, heat uncurling from some haven deep within my bones. Each nerve sparked like a shooting star.

Briefly, I closed my eyes, overcome by the rivers of sensation coasting through me. Goddess, I was fucked. Royally so.

Pun definitely intended.

"Your parents were idiots," Kyven said.

"That's the thing, though," I said breathlessly. Better to lose myself in protests than in him. "They weren't. They were just normal people whose kid made them miserable. It's no surprise they got rid of me."

"No. If they were miserable, it was because they'd decided to be. It had nothing to do with you."

I paused. "Is that really what you think? That life is just...what you make it?"

"It's what I know."

"That sounds too simple."

"The truth often does." His head tilted, his cheek heating my kneecap. "And once you realize that, your parents won't be able to touch you. Neither will the nightmares. Neither will I, for that matter. You'll have everything you've ever wanted. Anything you desire."

Anything. For some reason, my focus dropped to his mouth.

A mouth that now lifted under my gaze. "You're a force of nature, lioness. Once you embrace that, nothing will stand in your way."

My lungs contracted. Gods, how I longed to curve toward his certainty, like I would a fire on a frigid night. What could I become, with his assurances? Who could I be, with him to bolster me?

Except...there was no us. No future. Just a thousand reasons to keep my distance. A hundred uncertainties hovering between us.

Yet when I met his gaze, all those fell away, because right now, his eyes looked infinite. Like a summer sky above an open plain. Or an endless candle, burning against the dark.

Something must have shown on my face, because his breathing changed. His heart thudded against my shins, its steadiness giving way to something urgent.

His hold on me tightened. "Harlowe..." His voice had gone thick. Soaked in smoke.

A sizzle unfurled within me, so vast and wild and terrible I wondered if I would combust. Leave Kyven hugging nothing but ashes.

Because seven hells, what was I supposed to do when he said my name that way? Except tell him to stop looking at me like that, maybe. Make it clear that people like me didn't *get* blue skies and infinities.

Ever so slowly, he slid a hand down my thigh, his coarse palm catching at the silk of my nightgown.

My pulse sped, each heartbeat slamming against the next. When Kyven reached my hip, he seated his grip and squeezed. That pressure became the epicenter of a full-body shiver, one that somehow ended between my thighs.

He must have sensed my reaction, but he didn't push. His eyes held mine, a molten question.

And yet I sat unmoving. Not because I needed to annul this

marriage so he could marry Amryssa, or because I hadn't deciphered the last of his secrets, or because he'd leave me like everyone else had, but...

Well, it was all of those things. And none of them.

Hell, I didn't even know.

I just knew I had to scoot back, so I did, breaking his grip and smoothing down my nightgown. "I'm tired," I said, averting my gaze. "Take me to bed?"

A beat passed, then another. The sparks in the air cooled and frosted over.

"Of course," he finally said. "Whatever you need."

For once, his answer held no innuendo. No heat at all.

Even though I'd given him the perfect opening.

2 0 .

Another week passed, during which I cranked tighter. I swore the manor was shrinking around me, a vise closing me inexorably in its grip.

I was determined to free Zephyrine. And annul my marriage. Yet the search for the Lady Marche's diary proved fruitless, and my obsession with Kyven only grew.

I prayed. I asked for Zephyrine to help me find the journal, or for Kyven to decide he'd had enough of this and go already. For a fucking housefire to burn the house to ash so I wouldn't have to face the thing brewing in my depths.

I whispered to the goddess in every moment of weakness, like when I ducked into the defunct music room to escape the blue searchlight of Kyven's gaze, and again two days later, when I caught him staring at me from across the library and the air between us lit like a flashfire.

Gods among us, that *look*. Being struck by lightning would have affected me less. And by the way he held my eyes for half an eternity before a smile snuck across his mouth, he knew it, too.

I grabbed for my dagger and rushed from the room. *Zephyrine, help me. Under no circumstances can I sleep with this pompous ass. Or...sorry,*

199

incredibly arrogant man, that's what I meant to say. Because if I do, Amryssa can't marry him, and that would be a disaster. For so many, many reasons.

The dagger zinged against my palm, giving me the distinct impression that Zephyrine was laughing at me before she faded away.

Well, then. On my own again.

Wasn't that just great.

Somehow, I survived another week. By now, I'd wasted three quarters of a month looking for a stupid diary, and now the final days of my marriage stared me in the face. Which should have come as a comfort —the annulment certificate would arrive within the week. But I dreaded a nightmare arriving first.

Amryssa had faded nearly to nothingness. Today, I found her sitting cross-legged in the library, staring out the window.

"Hey." I was barely able to get the word past the hundred-pound weight in my throat.

She glanced up, sadness etched in her smile. Her hair hung in drab curtains, and even her eyes had lost their hint of green. "Hi."

"Are you all right?"

Her fragile shoulders rose and fell. "It's calling to me. Again."

"What is?"

"The marsh."

I sucked in a breath. In the past, I'd always brushed off her yearnings, but now they filled me with foreboding. What if there a reason she longed for the swamp? What if freeing Zephyrine took her away from me, somehow? What if...

Seven hells, I probably didn't even understand all the what-ifs.

I cleared my throat, telling myself not to panic until I had something to panic *about*. If only I could find that damn diary. Then I'd have some idea of what all this meant. "Can I ask you something?"

Amryssa nodded. "Of course."

"What do you remember about your mother?"

She blinked. "My mother? Hmm. Warmth, I suppose. Laughter.

Brown skin. Shiny black hair. Fingers stained with charcoal—she was always drawing. And a smell like...bergamot tea, maybe? Oh, and hugs. Lots of them."

My heart squeezed. "She loved you a lot?"

"Oh, fiercely. Me and Father both. Sometimes I think..."

Her throat worked. I waited.

"I think she'd be sorry to know what's happened to us. Where we've ended up."

That rammed an arrow through my chest, but I forced myself to continue. "But what about the dagger? It was hers, right? Do you remember much about that?"

Amryssa's attention fell to my belt. "Oh, yes. She used to wear it, just like you. I always thought it was because...well, I don't know. I suppose I never asked. It's an heirloom, perhaps."

Her gaze strayed to the window again. The sheer longing in her eyes made me wilt inside. Goddess, I *had* to help her. I had to fix this.

So I devoted the rest of the afternoon to sifting through the last brown books in the library. Hours later, I was sweating, cursing myself into a foul mood, when I slid the final volume from its shelf. I cracked the cover to find a primer on...ornithology.

Birds. Freaking birds.

Something snapped inside me. I hurled the book and sank to my knees, my face buried in my hands. I'd failed. I'd pinned my hopes for Amryssa to this, and had nothing at all to show for it.

A pent-up sob cooked the inside of my chest. A moment later, a warm hand landed on my shoulder. I looked up to find Kyven smiling down at me. The collar of his shirt hung open, exposing the smooth column of his neck.

I shouldn't have stared, but I did. I liked that he so often left that button undone, that I could see the ripple of muscle when he ate, the bob of his throat when he laughed. Moreover, the sight of him—that *thing* that blazed inside me whenever he came close—chased away the shadows clogging my veins.

Right now, it was probably the only thing that could.

"The diary might not be in the library," he said, "but that doesn't mean it isn't in this house."

I scrubbed at my cheeks. "We don't know that it actually exists, though. What if that steward was wrong? What if the Lady was writing letters? Or...I don't know. Shopping lists?"

"She wasn't. He called it a diary. He sounded sure."

"Maybe. But if she kept a journal, it should be here."

A mischievous spark flared in his eyes. "Well. There is one more place we could look. A rather obvious one, actually."

I rocked back on my heels, suddenly wary. Oh, gods. "Why do I have the feeling I know exactly what you mean?"

"Because you do. Of course you do. Great minds, and all that."

I swallowed. Or tried to, but my throat had gone drier than sand. "We can't," I whispered, even though no one was here to overhear. Lunk had taken Amryssa to dinner, bless his soul. "If Olivian finds us in his wife's room, he'll kill us. Actually kill us."

"Then he won't find us. We'll make sure of it."

I fisted my skirts. There were few things I feared, at least physically, but the rage the seneschal had unleashed on that steward was one of them. "We have no way to get inside, though. Olivian keeps the only key in his pocket."

Kyven's lips twitched. "You're forgetting my many talents."

I frowned, but... Right. He could pick locks.

Like any normal person.

"I'd be happy to do a little breaking and entering," he said. "It beats reading, at any rate."

I rubbed at my temples, but really, what was there to consider? Asking Amryssa about the dagger had gotten me nowhere, and my questions to the blade itself had gone unanswered. I almost suspected that whatever bit of Zephyrine lived inside had forgotten its divinity. Or else never understood it in the first place. And now I was running out of both time and options.

I sighed. "Okay, fine. But if we end up dead, I'm going to be incredibly annoyed with you."

"You're already incredibly annoyed with me."

I huffed. "Yes, but only because—" When I snapped my teeth together, he arched a brow. His smile turned knowing, as if I'd spoken out loud.

I dropped my eyes. "I hate you," I finished, with no vitriol whatsoever.

"Noted," he purred.

I cleared my throat. "So when are we embarking on this suicide mission?" This, at least, made for a safer conversational topic than whatever the hell that last thing had been.

"How about tonight? After everyone's asleep?"

"Tonight," I said. "Great. Who needs to see another sunrise, anyway?"

I had no idea how long lock-picking was supposed to take, but I was fairly sure it wasn't ten seconds flat. Which was why I stared at Kyven in horrified wonder when he pushed on the Lady Marche's door and it actually *opened*.

He'd made it look so easy.

He offered the hairpin I'd handed over, now broken into halves. "Impressed?"

"Yes." I pocketed the makeshift lockpicks. "Entirely against my will, but yes."

He grinned, and I glanced around. The sconces in this wing stayed unlit at night, and moonlight threw odd geometries onto the carpet, courtesy of the hallway's grimy windows.

"We ought to shut ourselves in," Kyven said. "In case someone passes by."

I nodded. The chances of a visitor here were slim, but we would take every precaution. I grabbed his hand and tugged him into the Lady's room.

And abruptly flung his fingers away when they curled around mine.

Kyven's disembodied chuckle floated from the darkness, followed by the creak of the door and the scrape of a match. Brightness flared as he lit a candle he'd brought in his pocket.

I spun a slow circle. The wavering light revealed a room that had once been the height of luxury—a four-poster bed stood against one wall, the mattress so high I would've needed a stepstool to climb atop. In the corner, a paneled screen served as a rack for a once-lavish dress. A mirrored vanity occupied another wall, cosmetics pots and brushes laid out on top.

I squinted. Dust caked the vanity, but streaks marred its surface, as if someone had fondled the Lady's things. Recently.

"Someone's been in here," I said, my breath hitching.

Suddenly, a sick possibility occurred to me, and I did another sweep of the room. But...no Althea. Not even anything of discernible value, like Vick had speculated. Just half-rotted, moth-eaten luxuries, the remnants of a life cut short.

Kyven went to the vanity and ran a finger through the dust. "The seneschal must visit sometimes."

My gut squeezed. *That* little tidbit only fueled my impatience to get in and get out. If Olivian found us in here...

Seven hells. I'd rather be caught outside in a nightmare.

"Then let's make this quick." I hurried to the standing screen and peeked behind, then patted down the hanging dress for hidden pockets. Kyven went to work, too, rifling through the vanity's drawers.

The minutes stretched like hours. My stomach cramped with urgency, yet as I flipped up an area rug and hunted through the dusty nether regions of a chaise longue, a dark hole opened inside my chest.

Useless. This was all useless. The next nightmare would come and I'd be no closer to freeing Zephyrine, and—

"Lioness."

I glanced up to find Kyven standing by the door, one ear cocked.

"Did you hear that?" he said.

I curled my lip, prepared to tell him just how unfunny I found his little joke, then choked on my reproach. Footsteps sounded in the hall, so heavy and lumbering they could only belong to one person.

My heart flung itself up my throat. "Oh no. No, no, no. You've *got* to be kidding me."

Kyven burst into motion, crossing the room in two strides and taking me by the arm. Panicked as I was, I didn't resist, just let him propel me toward the bed, where he motioned for me to get underneath.

"Hurry," he hissed. More footsteps, closer now.

I threw myself onto the carpet and wriggled beneath the bed-skirt. Darkness swallowed me up, so complete that only the dust stinging my nose assured me I still existed.

Kyven must have snuffed his candle, because no light accompanied him when he squeezed in beside me. He settled so close that his body heat warmed my arm.

The footsteps stopped in the hall. A key grated in the lock.

My pulse roared. Would Olivian realize the door was already open? Smell the tang of the extinguished candle? Notice the dust smears we'd left behind?

A whimper snuck from my lips. Kyven inched closer, pressing his chest against my side. A warm hand landed across my mouth.

"No sound," he breathed, so quietly I couldn't even call it a whisper. "If I have to, I'll go out and face him, but no matter what you see or hear, you stay here. All right?"

I nodded, knowing he could feel my agreement, even if he couldn't see it.

We lay like that, unmoving, hardly even breathing, while the seneschal trudged inside. For long moments, Olivian just...stood there, not three feet from where the bed-skirt hid our shoes.

A tremor took up residence in my limbs. Did he know? Did he suspect?

Kyven must have felt me trembling, because he curved closer, his breath stirring my hair.

Out in the room, a match scraped. Faint light rimmed the bed-skirt. Kyven's hovering face came into focus, the dimness leaching his irises of color.

He glanced pointedly at the hand covering my mouth, then raised questioning brows. When I nodded, his fingers left my lips. He planted his hand beside my head.

There was hardly any space under here. Just enough that he could brace himself over me, assurances in his eyes. I clung to the promise I found there, to the steadiness he radiated.

Then a growl broke the silence. "Show yourself."

My heart rammed against my breastbone. Shit. Shitshitshit.

"I know you're here." Naked fury rode Olivian's every syllable.

I bit back a cry. Kyven's brow knitted, his eyes filling with something like regret. Or maybe resolve. He laid a finger across his lips, then pointed to himself and out toward the room.

Terror crashed over me like a breaking wave. No. No, fuck that. I might've agreed to let him go, but who cared what I'd said? I wouldn't hide here while Kyven had the life choked from him. While blood vessels burst in his eyes and all his teasing—his arrogance and half smiles—winked out of existence forever.

He levered himself over me, but I clamped my arms around him, then my legs, trapping him as he tried to wriggle free.

We struggled in silence, but I refused to let go. I didn't care what I had to do, who I had to stab. How much of Zephyrine's magic I had to borrow to ensure he walked out of here alive. I would do anything, I would—

"Coraline," Olivian growled. "You've been dogging me all day, so you might as well show your face. I'm not leaving until you do."

I froze. So did Kyven. We stared at each other as realization dawned.

Sweet Zephyrine, the seneschal wasn't talking to *us*. He was addressing his dead wife.

The bed frame shuddered as a heavy weight settled atop the mattress.

The spasm in my chest eased, if only by half. I pictured Olivian hunched above us, his brows lowered as he waited for a ghost.

"Ah," he said, at length. "There you are."

I frowned. His voice had changed. I hardly even recognized it, full of tenderness as it was.

"You're so beautiful. I always forget how much." He laughed—a strange, crooked sound, and... Goddess, he'd gone mad. Well and truly mad.

What followed was the most bizarre conversation I'd ever been privy to. Olivian seemed to fracture into two people, first praising his wife, then scolding her. He professed his love in one moment, and in the next, railed at the Lady for asking him to release Amryssa into the marsh.

"You can't have her," he shouted. "I won't hear of it, so you might as well stop asking. Our daughter's place is here, now. You made that choice. We both did."

Now. The word caught in my mind and held. What did that mean? Had Amryssa's place been somewhere else, once?

Olivian went on, spewing love and fury, the line between the two growing increasingly blurred. The whole time, Kyven and I stayed still as stones.

At last, the invective wound down. When Olivian finally stood, he did it in stages, as if he'd aged a decade in the last twenty minutes.

"I love you," he told the empty room. "And hate you. And gods among us, how I wish you hadn't left me."

His footsteps receded. Hinges creaked. The key clinked in the door.

I blew out a mile-long breath. The seneschal had locked us in, but Kyven could always use the picks from this side. Olivian had also left a lamp burning, but considering what I'd just heard, I doubted he was in a frame of mind to realize, much less return to rectify his mistake.

"You can get off me now," I said.

Kyven didn't budge. He just lay atop me, much as he had on our wedding night.

"I could." His half smile resurfaced. "But 'can' and 'want to' are two vastly different things."

I studied him. Gods, I was already getting annoyed again. Mostly because if I didn't, I'd get unreasonably turned on by the press of his hips against mine. "Okay. I *want* you to get off. How's that?"

"How badly?" he crooned.

I narrowed my eyes.

"As badly as you wanted to stop me from going out there?" he continued. "As badly as you wanted to keep the seneschal from killing me? Because, for someone who professes to hate me, you seemed awfully invested in my survival."

I considered that, then reached up to cradle his stubbled cheeks. "The only reason I wanted to keep Olivian from killing you," I said sweetly, "was so I could do it myself."

He blinked, then broke into a smile. "Gods, lioness. You're a terrible liar. The absolute worst."

I was. I really was. And we both knew it, but that didn't stop me from bucking hard enough to dislodge him. He rolled aside with a sound that was half chuckle, half groan.

"Whatever," I said, "I don't—"

I froze. And stared at the underside of the mattress, at the spot I hadn't yet glimpsed, what with Kyven looming over me that whole time.

"What?" he said. "Don't tell me you miss me already?"

"No, you insufferable prince. I just... Just..." I jabbed a finger upward, indicating the leatherbound book wedged between the slats. The *brown* leatherbound book. "*Look.*"

Kyven rolled onto his back and followed my finger. A long silence spun by.

"Well," he said. "Would you look at that?"

Somehow, I was certain of what we'd found before we even opened it. The diary had a sheen, a well-worn patina that buzzed against my fingertips.

The moment Kyven locked us into my bedroom, I cracked the book's cover. Sure enough, the first page bore a portrait. Of Olivian. Younger and beardless, without any of the anger now cemented into his features. The artist had rendered him mid-laugh, eyes glinting.

Underneath, it said, *My sweet Ollie, overflowing with smugness after this morning's Great Donut Incident.*

Ollie. I couldn't imagine anyone referring to the seneschal that way, and I had no idea what a donut incident was, much less a great one, but clearly, we'd struck gold. This book had belonged to the Lady Marche. No one else could have transmuted love into each sweep of the charcoal like this.

"Ky." Urgency slanted my voice upward. "This is it."

I turned pages, revealing flowery handwriting, plus more drawings: the ancient oak at the heart of the swamp, then Zephyrine, dark-eyed and brown-skinned, wearing her usual attire of palmetto leaves. Something about the goddess looked familiar, but I couldn't place it. And—

My pulse jumped. There was the dagger, in crisp and perfect detail. And a few pages later, a sketch of a baby who could only be Amryssa.

"We found it," Kyven said.

I grinned up at him.

"And," he said softly, "you finally called me Ky."

My brow wrinkled. I had, hadn't I? "It just...came out. I don't know why."

His mouth tilted. "Probably because of that whole familiarity business we discussed. Accompanied by a commensurate amount of contempt, I'm sure."

"I'm sure," I echoed, faint.

Something in his eyes shifted. "Would you like to read this alone? Or together?"

I considered. "Alone" was the obvious answer, and I opened my mouth to tell him so.

But something else came out.

"Together. If you want."

Apparently, he did want, because he stripped to his usual nighttime breeches and stretched out on the bed with the diary while I ducked into the bathroom to change. When I reemerged in my nightgown, Kyven—Ky?—opened his arms, gesturing for me to join him.

I drifted toward the bed, contemplating how best to refuse him. And then I just...

Stopped.

Seven hells, I didn't have it in me right now. Not when all I *really* wanted was to nestle against his side. To let the thud of his heartbeat assure me that while he'd almost died—trying to save me for a *third* time, no less—we'd both come out of that room alive and no matter what this diary said about Zephyrine, or Amryssa, everything would be okay because we'd make it okay, and tonight I just wanted to forget that I still didn't know Ky's secrets, and that he'd soon marry Amryssa and desert me, because couldn't I worry about all that in the morning?

So I gave in. I crawled across the mattress and settled in the circle of his arms, my head pillowed on his shoulder.

He didn't move. When I glanced up, pure shock was splashed across his features.

"What?" I said.

"I just...didn't think that would work. Not for one single second did I think that would work."

"Are you complaining?"

"No." He cinched an arm around me and propped the book on his chest, where we could both see it. "Complaining is the last thing I'd dream of doing right now."

"Okay. Good."

"Are you ready, then?"

"Probably not," I admitted. "But it's now or never."

The Lady's Marche's story started out innocently enough. The diary's early entries detailed her marriage and subsequent move to the house —"happy events," in her words—followed by paragraphs about her hopes for a baby. But when pregnancy eluded her for a year, then two, her optimism lapsed into despair.

Ky turned pages. In them, the Lady chronicled how, in her third year of marriage, she turned to Zephyrine. She made routine treks into the marsh, armed with cakes and wine she left beneath the holy oak.

There, the Lady swore she could feel Zephyrine's presence. Hear a divine whispering. But her prayers went unanswered, despite the offerings she laid at the goddess's feet.

In the fourth year, the Lady turned to the hex-casters and healing-women, the ones the townspeople snubbed in daylight but visited by night anyway, pleading for love tonics and beauty salves. There, the

Lady paid exorbitant sums for pills and potions, for poultices she let dry on her belly.

Nothing worked.

But I believe I've found the answer, she wrote. *The woman I saw last night told me hope doesn't lie here in town, but in the swamp. I just haven't gone about getting Zephyrine's attention the right way.*

It takes blood, the healing-woman said, and doesn't that make sense? The patron goddess of things that go slithering in the shadows has no need for wine, but blood.

At that part, I pressed closer to Ky.

"This isn't going well at all," he said. "If only the Lady had attended the theatre, she would've known not to make a blood pact with a goddess. It never turns out the way it's supposed to."

I smiled grimly. "Somehow, I don't think that would've changed anything. She was obviously desperate."

"Hmm. You're probably right."

We read on, about how one day, the Lady slipped into the swamp when "sweet Ollie" went to town. At the foot of the giant oak, she opened her vein. A chalice full of blood later, Zephyrine finally heeded her call.

How can I describe her, other than to call her dazzling? I was dizzy by then, so dizzy I could barely see straight, but that didn't stop me from recognizing divinity. Zephyrine shone, her skin the color of a cypress's heart, her hair like dark oil. She wore nothing but leaves and vines, yet I'd never seen anything so breathtaking.

I begged. I threw myself at her feet, told her I would do anything for a child.

Zephyrine knelt. Laid a hand on my belly. She peered into my eyes and told me my wish can't be granted. That something is wrong, inside of me. Not made right for nurturing a child.

The news almost broke me.

But then she offered a boon. My years of pleading hadn't gone unnoticed, Zephyrine said, and my blood had bought her favor. She said she could birth a child for me—one that would be part of her, of divine origin. I could have the sweet daughter I've always craved.

But there's a catch. Because isn't there always?

I can only keep the child for a time.

At that, a pang twisted my stomach. Ky's fingers tightened around the book.

"Is that possible?" I whispered against his chest.

"I don't see why not. The gods are mysterious. And powerful."

"So *that's* why Amryssa doesn't look like Olivian? Because she's not actually his? *Or* the Lady Marche's? She's...Zephyrine's?"

He made a sound I couldn't interpret.

Mind churning, I flipped back a few pages, to the sketch of the goddess rising from the swamp. *That* was why Zephyrine had looked familiar. Because she had Amryssa's face, or a version of it. Their coloring was so different I hadn't immediately made the connection, but now that I had, there was no mistake.

The concept of the goddess bearing a daughter rocked me, yet the more I mulled it over, the more sense it made. My best friend was so much better than other humans, so of course she wasn't one. No, she was something more. Something godly.

"Maybe you'll get to marry up, after all," I told Ky.

He said nothing. When I glanced up, his expression was tight.

The unfamiliarity of it gave me pause. "This doesn't change anything for you, does it?"

"I never imagined I'd marry a goddess," he said slowly. "Aside from the one I already have, of course."

"Oh, stop it. I'm no goddess."

He made a tutting noise. "I thought we'd established that you're exceptional. And that I'm a fount of wisdom and truth."

I rolled my eyes. "And bullshit, clearly. Lots of it."

"Only half the time."

"Uh-huh. And which half are we dealing with right now?"

He aimed a fond smile at me. "The truthful one, of course."

My chest fluttered, which I ignored. "Fine. Then if I'm a goddess, you should listen to what I tell you, and I'm saying you *need* to marry Amryssa. Now more than ever. Because if the Lady Marche made some kind of promise to give her back, then broke it, I need to get Amryssa as far from here as possible."

For long moments, he didn't answer. His chest rose and fell beneath my cheek. "Does that mean you'll tell her? What she is?"

"I..." Silence welled. I didn't like that question. "Can we just keep going?"

He didn't argue. He propped up the book again, and we read on, about how the Lady Marche had faked a pregnancy while Zephyrine carried a true one. Olivian knew, but no one else, and on the day the child was born, the Lady went into the swamp. She emerged not only with her long-awaited baby, but an antler-hilted dagger, gifted from the goddess.

The knife holds a piece of Zephyrine, she wrote. *One she cut from her own breast and forged into a weapon. It will help keep my daughter safe until her eighteenth birthday, at which point I'll return her to the swamp.*

Because if I don't, Zephyrine will fall into a peaceless sleep that will bring ruin to all Oceansgate. And the goddess will never stop looking. Never stop trying to dream her child home.

A cold shimmer rolled down my spine. I flashed back to the night Amryssa had leapt from her window, when the nightmare had helped me. *And* the dagger, both. They'd conspired to save her.

Which made sense, now. A terrible, horrible, sickening kind of sense.

Few entries remained after that. The Lady Marche had apparently taken to motherhood like a muskrat to the reeds, because the intervals between updates grew. Two sketches accompanied the dwindling entries—one of the dagger, another of Amryssa as a toddler.

I try to remember this time is temporary, the Lady wrote after a three-year lull. *But Amryssa feels like mine. I don't know what I would feel for a child born of my own body, but I can't imagine a greater love than this one. I care for her so much that I fear what I'll someday do. Or not do, as the case may be.*

The next page was blank. And the next.

Ky set the diary aside. Quiet blanketed the room.

"I doubt any of that's what you wanted to hear," he said.

"No. It's really, really not." My voice cracked. It was obvious which choice the Lady had made, just as it was obvious that ending the nightmares would mean giving Amryssa back.

I couldn't have one without the other.

Shit.

Ky rolled toward me, leaving his arm in place as my headrest. He toyed with the ribbon adorning my keyhole neckline—not in an attempt to take off my nightgown, I knew. Just playing with the tie, without any motive.

"You have a choice to make," he said. "A very difficult one."

I swallowed against a raw throat. "Doom Oceansgate by taking Amryssa to Hightower, or end the nightmares and lose her forever."

"Yes."

An icy dark nothingness hardened within me. I waited for Ky to laud my strength, to assure me I could survive the loss of the one person I'd ever truly loved. The only one who hadn't left me, like everyone else had. Like he soon would.

He didn't, though, thank goodness. A line formed between his brows. "Did you ever see her, out there? In the swamp?"

"Who, Zephyrine?" I tried to scrub the arid despair from my voice, with little success.

"Mmm-hmm."

I weighed that, grateful for the subject change. "I caught...glimpses, sometimes. I'd hear laughter on the breeze, or see a woman from the corner of my eye. Or feel something behind me and turn to find flower petals fluttering through the air. And once, in the beginning, when I hadn't eaten in days and hadn't figured out how to dig for mussels yet, I found a fish laid out on a stone. Like an offering. It was cold, still. And I assumed it came from Zephyrine. In some weird way, I knew it had."

"She looked after you," he said.

"Yes."

"And now you have the option to return her child to her. Or not."

I quieted. He hadn't loaded any accusation into the statement. The words rang with fact and nothing more, a decision he would leave to me.

And yet there was no decision to make, not really.

The mere idea of losing Amryssa crouched on my chest, driving all the oxygen from my lungs. In the emptiness left behind, Olivian's words came back to haunt me. *I care about Oceansgate more than about myself. But for her, I'd let it burn.*

Gods. Only now did I understand what he'd truly meant, how very alike he and I were. Because I already knew what I would do. I didn't have to measure anything on the scales of justice or the greater good.

Amryssa wasn't going into the swamp. She was going to Hightower, because the world needed her sweetness and light. So did I. Without my friend, I'd be nothing but an orphan again, without purpose. Without worth.

I burrowed against Ky. He seemed to sense what I needed, because he tucked my head beneath his chin, his breathing deep and even. I was so profoundly grateful that he hadn't pushed or judged me that I couldn't hold back any longer.

I touched his birthmark. It was *right there*, a pale beacon just inches from my face.

A muffled gasp escaped him. The hand he'd cupped around the nape of my neck tightened.

I froze. "Sorry. Did I hurt you?"

A pause. "No," he said thickly. "It's only...that's a sensitive spot. One I very much like having touched."

I should've pulled away. But the skin below his collarbone was smooth and enticing, and the groan that rumbled from his chest when I resumed stroking fired bolts of warmth through me. His breathing accelerated, though he didn't take my attentions as permission to touch me back.

And goddess, I adored him for that, for granting me that control. For gifting me a shard of power in this horrendous situation.

When I glanced up again, his lips had parted. His eyes were low blue flames.

Seven hells. Talk about a distraction. I let my fingers still and stop.

He growled a soft protest. "You wouldn't be so cruel as to leave me hanging, would you?"

I gave him an impertinent smile and curled my hand against my chest. "Of course I would. It wouldn't be any fun if I didn't."

"Oh, I beg to differ. I can't think of anything more *fun* than me pinning you to this bed and fucking you hard enough that you forget what we just read."

Want ignited in my breast, pure and unadulterated. There was something perversely erotic about hearing such filthy words in that silken accent. "That sounds like a terrible idea."

His tongue swept over his bottom lip, leaving it gleaming. "It sounds like a fantastic idea. The best idea anyone's ever had, anywhere, in all the world, throughout the entire history of time."

"You're being ridiculous," I said, but I sounded breathier than a maiden being laced into her first corset.

"Maybe." Scorching promise lit his eyes. "That doesn't mean you wouldn't enjoy yourself."

My thighs ground together. Zephyrine, I *would* enjoy myself, of that I had no doubt. But...

The truth, deep down, in a place too clandestine to see the light of day, was that I craved more than just pleasure. I didn't want the inch, but the mile. I wanted...shit, the same thing he did. To map him from the inside until I could draw him in the dark. To bury myself inside him.

What I *didn't* want was to give it all back in a handful of days. To have it wrested from me.

To be left. Again.

But I would, because he would make Amryssa a princess and disappear. Just as I'd asked him to. So I disentangled myself and turned my back.

Ky groaned. "My cruel, wicked wife. You have no idea what you do to me."

"Of course I do. Why else do you think I do it?"

"Mmm." He nuzzled against me, one arm still beneath my head. "Probably because you hate me."

"I really, really do." A feverish sound escaped when he nestled my hips into the crook of his. "I hate you more than I've ever hated anyone, anywhere, in all the world, throughout the entire history of time."

He laughed, his breath tickling my nape. "Lucky for you, that doesn't bother me in the slightest."

"It should."

"It doesn't. I'll still worship you all night, when you finally let me."

A full-body, molten shiver claimed me. "*If* I let you."

"No," he purred in my ear. "When."

I lay there, humming inside, quietly exploding, torn between turning over so I could beg him to do exactly that, and thanking him for distracting me from the horrors of the diary.

"And lioness?" he murmured.

"Yes?" I sounded squeaky. Like a shrunken mouse.

"I can't wait. I really, truly cannot *wait*."

I wasn't sure I could, either. Volcanic need laced my veins, a thousand fiery rivers all leading to him. But before I could gather the resolve to turn over, his breathing lengthened.

I laughed, a silent hitch I kept buried in my chest. Was this damnable prince serious? He'd just threatened to fuck me stupid, then promptly fallen asleep, draped around me like a scorching, muscled blanket.

Ass. Infuriating, tantalizing, exasperating man.

I lay there, unable to imagine spending a night glued together like this, not in this heat. But I didn't want to wake him, so I closed my eyes and tried to drift off.

To my surprise, sleep came on like a lullaby. And it lasted, a rest more restorative than any I'd had in weeks.

2 2 .

Of course, tranquility didn't last beyond the point at which I opened my eyes.

I rolled from bed while Ky still slept, then spent the day mired in dread. The idea of telling Amryssa the truth tied me in knots, because what if she left me?

But I couldn't bear to lie to her.

I dropped the brush while combing her hair. Twice. Then misaligned her corset and had to re-lace the entire thing. At breakfast, I overfilled her cup *and* the saucer that caught the runoff, then took her back upstairs to exchange her dress for one that didn't have tea dribbled all over the skirts.

All the while, knowledge pulsed inside me like a poisoned heartbeat.

Amryssa was Zephyrine's. And the goddess wanted her back.

By afternoon, my head throbbed, to say nothing of my heart. Up in the cupola, Amryssa read a book while I sweated over the mending. Ky had busied himself in the yard below, lashing together a frame for some leggy tomato plants.

All the energy he'd accumulated during our weeks-long search of the library seemed to be pouring from him at once. Once he finished with the tomatoes, he weeded the entire vegetable garden, then jogged over to the wood-chopping stump. The thing saw frequent use, given how much fuel the hot water boilers consumed, and we also had an unending supply of diseased purple wood to dispose of. Not to mention an axe-wielding prince who apparently had more drive than he knew what to do with.

An exquisitely tempting prince, at that.

I wrenched my gaze away from all those sweat-slicked muscles. Four more days. Then the annulment certificate would arrive, and Ky would cease to be my problem. He wouldn't be anyone's problem but his own.

At dinner, Amryssa listlessly pushed bits of trout around her plate. Olivian chewed in silence. Ky sat opposite me, his so-called attendants stationed behind him. Vick glared at the back of Ky's head as if he could drill a hole into it.

A bite of fish scraped down my throat, but dinner didn't interest me any more than it did Amryssa. I forked a green bean and dropped it again. What the hell was I going to tell her? What if she refused to go to Hightower, once she knew?

The kitchen door opened.

Miss Quist bustled in, carrying a tray of chipped ramekins filled with thin gray pudding. My eyes shot to Lunk, who straightened.

Goddess, he must be pushing seven feet when he did that. He puffed out his barrel-like chest, making the day's first smile itch to life on my lips. No way could he hold his breath like that for long, but it'd be fun to watch him try.

Miss Quist distributed the puddings. Rosy color dusted her cheeks. Blonde ringlets framed her face like frizzy wisps of sunshine.

"Dorothea," Ky said, and I jolted. Since when was he on a first-name basis with our cook? "How lovely to see you."

Miss Quist's perennial color flamed higher. "Your Highness."

"Just Ky," he said good-naturedly. "How many times do I have to I tell you?"

"At least once more." She placed a double serving of pudding in front of Amryssa. Lunk tracked her every movement, stars in his eyes.

"You know, Dorothea, I've been thinking..." Ky rested his chin on his hand. "It's been ages since I've had a good Snogberry Fizz."

My brows snapped together. A...what?

"Do you make those here in Oceansgate?"

Miss Quist paused while setting down Olivian's pudding. "I've never heard of such a thing, Your Highness. I'm sorry."

I slitted my eyes at him and mouthed, *What're you doing?* Because I was about a hundred and eighty percent certain Snogberry Fizzes didn't exist.

Ky winked and blew me an airy kiss. I glanced around, but no one had noticed except Vick, who weighed our exchange with narrow-eyed calculation.

I narrowed my eyes right back, wondering what he'd look like with green beans all over his jerkin. Maybe mashed into that orange hair, too. What was his problem?

"We make them all the time, where I'm from," Ky was saying. "I'd love to take up the habit again. Maybe you could bring Lunk here back to the kitchen? Have him show you how they're made?"

Lunk's besotted expression shifted to one of such transparent alarm that I fought the urge to throw my fork. What was Ky doing? And did he have to be so *obvious* about it?

But Miss Quist seemed delighted by the idea of the giant remedying her culinary deficiencies. She pressed a hand to her bosom. "Oh, I'm always up for learning something new. Come on, Henry, why don't you carry this tray for me? Zephyrine knows you're strong enough to take all the dishes at once." She bustled around the table, clearing our plates.

I gaped. Henry? Was that Lunk's real name? How did she even know that?

Goddess, I needed to pay more attention.

Lunk—Henry?—came dutifully forward, his face flaming, whether because of the impending need to invent a Snogberry Fizz or because Miss Quist had complimented his brawn, I couldn't say. But he stoically bore the loaded tray to the kitchen. The door swung shut behind them, leaving us to our sallow puddings.

Well, then. With the excitement over, I stuck my spoon into my ramekin and swirled. Ky reclined in his chair, those forget-me-not eyes brimming with satisfaction.

What the hell was that? I mouthed.

Pure artistry, he said back, in silence.

I blinked. I couldn't believe I'd understood that. *It was ridiculous.*

You loved it.

I hated it, I countered. *Almost as much as I hate you.*

He shook his head, smug. *You love me. What you actually hate is admitting it.*

My eyes dived to my pudding, which I'd apparently slopped over the sides of the ramekin with the consummate skill of a two-year-old.

How absurd. Of course I didn't love him. He didn't mean it, anyway, not like *that.*

A fact I repeated over and over in order to keep the wings beneath my heart from erupting into a flurry.

Olivian's gruff baritone cut through the clink of dinnerware. "What in Zephyrine's name?" He rose from his chair to glare at the windows.

The heat in my cheeks faded. Outside, the light had dimmed to a dusky caramel, but something purple glowed on the lawn. I laid an instinctive hand on Amryssa's shoulder. I didn't know whether I meant to shield her or reassure her, but it was just a raggedy little dog out there. A forked tongue hung from its mouth while two tails twitched behind. The puppy tottered across the lawn, glowing amethyst.

Ky went to the window. "It's sick." Wherever the poor stray had come from, it had picked up the rot on the way.

Olivian grunted. "Kill it."

My heartbeat turned to mush when I realized who he'd directed the command at. "Who? *Me?*"

"Yes, you," he snapped. "Unless you'd rather Amryssa do the honors?"

I found the hilt of my dagger and squeezed. This prick. If it was so easy, why didn't he go? Not to mention I'd never killed anything before. Okay, maybe a few billion mosquitoes over the years, but never a diseased puppy. I probably would've had an easier time murdering a grown man.

Actually, I'd tried that once, hadn't I? And look how *that* little endeavor had turned out.

Ky glared at Olivian. "I'll do it." The words were clipped, not at all like his usual.

But the seneschal didn't seem to notice. "Fine. I don't care who snaps its neck, so long as the cur doesn't infect the hens and leave us with poisoned eggs for breakfast."

Ky opened his mouth, then reconsidered and whisked past me in a rush of cypress-scent and firesmoke.

My head whirled. Partly because of the onslaught of his scent, but also because he'd just volunteered to kill something. To murder a helpless animal. Maybe not because he wanted to spare me, but because he just...wanted to?

Oh, gods.

I pushed back my chair and hurried after him.

The dining room doors swung shut behind me. Down the hall, Ky pushed out through a side exit. Anger tightened his posture, and that, along with the heat and the horribleness of the day, squeezed my throat in a vise grip.

Seven hells, could Eliana have been right, all this time? Had I just refused to see it? Had I let myself develop all these capital-F feelings for a murderer?

I mean, not that I *had* capital-F feelings. I just...

Oh, for fuck's sake. I was wasting time.

I reached the door Ky had used and burst out into the muggy evening. He was already halfway across the lawn. When he reached the puppy, he scooped it up without slowing.

A whimper scalded my throat.

Ky hopped over the trench rimming the yard and ducked into the forest. Which made sense—he wouldn't want to do this in view of the windows. But I needed to see. I had to know, once and for all.

I scrambled after him. At the lawn's edge, I plunged into the forest, into an alien realm of violet trees and snarled underbrush. The smell of decay weighted the air. I squelched between the ferns and palmettos, one hand atop my dagger.

Ahead, in a clearing, Ky set the puppy down. I ducked behind a corrupted cypress and peeked around its trunk. The dog gazed up, its dual tails flicking, as if undecided on whether to wag or curl between its legs.

Ky knelt. He clamped a hand around the dog's neck.

My heart plummeted, snagging my stomach on the way down. Shit. Shitshitshit. I didn't know how best to save the puppy—use the dagger's magic on Ky? The dog?

But it was already too late. His hand moved, and I winced against the inevitable crunch. When it didn't come, I opened my eyes to find him...

...petting it?

I loosed the longest breath of my life. Ky ruffled the pup's fur and, when it capsized in wriggling delight, scratched at its belly. The dog's twin tails thumped against the ground.

"There now," Ky crooned. "How about a bit of cheese?"

He dug in his waistcoat and came up with a chunk of white stuff. The dog snarfed the offering without a moment's pause.

My head lightened, threatening to float off my shoulders. I stepped out from behind the tree, my hand falling from my knife.

Ky glanced up. "Oh, lioness, I didn't see you there. Would you care to pet him? He smells repugnant, but he makes up for it with sheer enthusiasm, at least."

"You're not...going to kill him?"

"Kill him?" He looked affronted. "Of course not. Who would kill an innocent dog?"

A creeping heat suffused me. Shame or relief—I couldn't untangle the two.

"Except that bloodthirsty old fossil you call a seneschal," he continued. "Who, by the way, you should tell to go fuck himself next time he speaks to you that way. I can't remember the last time someone's made me so angry."

A spiky laugh fled my lips. Gods among us, how could I have suspected him of being a killer? Even for a moment? He wasn't. Clearly. He was just...*him*. A cocky prince. A man who knew himself so thoroughly that the nightmares couldn't touch him, who disliked the seneschal's attempts to control me just as much as I did.

"You know, I *have* told Olivian that," I said. "Many times. But he's strangely immune to insults. Kind of like someone else I know."

"Well." Ky dusted his hands and stood. The puppy dashed into the underbrush, apparently having gotten its fill of cheese and attention. "In that case, I'll tell him myself. A royal command to go fuck oneself isn't to be taken lightly."

My heart melted like warm butter. This silver-tongued devil. "Ky. I have...something I should tell you. Something I got wrong."

He came toward me, his eyes gleaming lilac in the swamp-glow. "What is it?"

"I—"

A branch cracked. Our heads whipped around.

The bracken rustled, and Vick emerged, his shortsword in his hand. I frowned. What was *he* doing here?

Ky's expression closed up. "Oh. It's you."

Vick studied the span between our bodies as if mapping its exact dimensions, its *meaning*. He didn't say anything.

Ky expelled a sigh. "Feel free to open that delightful mouth of yours at any moment. And Harlowe knows you're not from High-tower, so you can lose the terrible accent."

Vick surveyed me for so long that my pulse ticked up. What did he plan on doing with that sword? Moreover, why did Ky sound so chilly?

"What'd you do with the dog?" Vick finally said. "Is it dead?"

I recoiled at hearing an Oceansgate accent come from his mouth. I'd known, but still. He suddenly seemed like a different person. One that set my teeth on edge, even more so than before.

"I let it go." Ky sniffed. "Though I'll thank you not to share that with the seneschal. Now, why don't you run along? I was about to have a word with my wife."

Vick laughed, as if the princely request carried no weight at all. "I'm sure you *were* about to have a word. Among other things."

My skin tightened. There was something wrong about the way he was talking. As if to an overbearing parent, not royalty. And while *I* felt entitled to direct my impudence at the prince—I'd married him, after all—outrage scorched my throat when Vick did it.

Which probably didn't make much sense, but whatever. I'd never claimed to be rational.

Ky's look turned flinty. "What I do with my wife is none of your concern."

"Oh, but it is. We had a deal, or don't you remember?"

I stiffened. A deal? What deal?

Ky glowered. "It would be difficult to forget."

"Good. See that you don't." Vick sheathed his blade with effortless competence. Clearly, he could do some damage with that thing, if he wanted to. "Oh, and Ky?"

"What?" The word came out as a hiss.

"Next time, kill the damn dog. Because if you don't, someone else will." Vick flashed a cold smile and melted back into the underbrush.

Ky stared after him.

"What the hell was that?" I said.

"I..." His voice shook with barely contained emotion.

My heart writhed against my ribs. I'd never imagined anything could hold the power to throw him so off-balance, but he looked like he'd just swallowed spoiled milk.

"I'm starting to dislike that man," he said. "Intensely."

"You're not the only one. But what was he talking about? What deal?"

Ky stabbed his fingers against his eyelids and exhaled.

"Don't think for a second you're getting out of explaining this," I warned.

"No, I know, I just..." He made a sound of frustration. "If you absolutely must know, Vick and I made an agreement, before coming here."

I frowned. "What agreement?"

"We agreed that once I died, or...more accurately, once everyone *thought* I'd died...everything of mine would go to him."

I blinked. "What? Why?"

"Well. I needed *some* kind of successor. And choosing him made sense when my intent was to marry, get my fill, and walk out into a nightmare. But all this waiting has made him antsy. I think he's starting to suspect I might not leave at all. That you and I might..."

I waited, but he didn't continue. "What? We might what?"

"Have something." He met my eyes. "Something that might entice me to stay."

A pained squeak came out of me. I didn't know how to respond to that, so I focused on the last part. "But...what exactly is he so impatient for? Money?"

"No." His eyes shone with something I couldn't name. "He wants to succeed me."

I blinked. I didn't know much about royal titles and inheritances, but I grasped the basics, at least. "But...it doesn't work that way. He can't become a prince just because you say so."

"No, not that. It's..." He trailed off, chewing at his lip. "He wants to lead the liberators."

My heartbeat ground to a halt. "What?"

Ky smiled without humor.

"Wait." I spluttered, trying to gather hold of myself. "You mean... You're not saying...*you're* the bandit chief?"

He raised his hands in a "surprise" gesture.

My thoughts spun. "But...no. The brigands've been out there for nine years. You only came to Oceansgate ten months ago."

"True," he said, drawing out the word. "But for the last four of those months, the liberators have answered to me. Because I inherited the title from the last man, who inherited it from the one before him, and so on and so forth. It's never been just one person, lioness. There've been five of us, over the years. Before I showed up, Vick was slated to be next. But along came this charming upstart, and of course old Charley decided to put me in charge when he left. Vick's wanted me gone ever since. And I was finally ready to leave. To let him have his turn."

I stared, my mind a confetti whirl. But gods, this would explain that woman's reaction to Ky, down in the root cellar. And Vick's increasingly sour looks. It would even explain why Vick had been combing the manor all this time—he probably wanted to return to the forest flush with riches, plucked from Olivian's supposed trove.

"So...Vick's a power-hungry thief? Who's angry that you took his place in line?"

A smile flickered around Ky's mouth, then died. "Yes. But the thing is, lioness, he isn't harmless. I'm not entirely sure he didn't threaten you just now."

My brows pinched. "Threaten me? He didn't threaten me."

"Oh, but he did. The sword? The dog comment? Trust me, those meant something different than they seemed."

"But..." I groped for words. "If he's so dangerous, why don't you just send him away? Issue one of those royal commands you were just talking about?"

He let out a long exhale. "Because. He isn't beholden to me. Not in the way you think."

I stepped toward him without thinking, folding his roughened fingers into mine. "Okay. Then if he won't listen to you, we'll have Merron and the stewards throw him out."

He swore under his breath. "That's just it. You wouldn't like what would happen if we tried. Vick would...retaliate. He'd ruin everything you've asked me for."

"What do you mean?"

His throat bobbed. "I *mean* he could destroy this second wedding you want so badly. With little more than a word."

A thousand thoughts tumbled through my head. "Are you saying he has something over you, then? Something that could affect Amryssa?"

He stared for long moments, then glanced to the sky and dragged his free hand down his face. "Yes. And Hyperion help me, but I never intended to make such a mess of this. I never intended..."

He trailed off, looking more pained than I'd thought possible.

"What? What didn't you intend?"

"Any of this." His voice turned low and rasping, an intensity of feeling bleeding through and doing something strange to his accent. "Gods, lioness, but I didn't intend to *care* for you like this. I thought I'd be marrying a pampered girl, not some woman of fire and steel. And yes, I wanted to try out marriage, but I never thought it'd feel so...consuming. Or that I'd end up wanting you like this. Or that I'd have to spend every day chopping wood because exhausting myself is the only way I can keep my hands off you. I never intended any of that, but you know how I feel about challenges, and here you are, the most spectacular one of all, because no one's ever made me work this hard, or demanded so much of me, or commanded me to become the best version of myself merely so I could earn the right to stand in their presence, and now that you have, I fear I might be addicted, because I can't imagine doing anything less with anyone else."

He cut himself off, breathing hard, and I gaped, so stunned I could barely locate a breath. "You...what?"

"I'm fairly certain you heard me."

The swamp had ceased to exist. I felt like I was hanging in mid-air —falling into those eyes of his, into warm, wide pools of violet. My insides dissolved until my skin contained nothing but glittering heat.

Ky squeezed my fingers. "I never intended any of that, but now it's happened, and I've dragged you into the middle of it, and I can't see any way out that doesn't involve me disappointing you. And believe me, that's the very last thing I want to do. But...I need to tell you the truth. All of it."

I dropped his hand, reeling from the enormity of everything he'd just said. "There's *more*, then? More than just you leading the brigands?"

His lips pressed together. "Yes. A very big something. About who I am."

My stomach slid sideways. "But...you're not the one who hurt all those animals. Right? You can't be."

"I—" Ky's brow knitted. "Wait, animals? What animals?"

I gulped against a raw throat. "The dead ones. From when you were younger. And the seneschal's daughter. The one you left the ball with, who disappeared for a week. That couldn't possibly have been you. I *know* it wasn't."

He peered at me as if I'd spoken in some foreign tongue. There was no spark of recognition in his eyes. Just pure, unadulterated confusion.

"I'm...lost," he said. "What are you talking about?"

"All those crimes." My voice veered upward, as if taking flight. Why did he look so *baffled*? "In Hightower. The horrible things everyone blames on Prince Kyven Windermere, but which can't be things you've actually done."

He blinked, and finally, *finally*, an ember of understanding flared. "Gods above. Is *that* why you've hated me all this time?"

I swallowed a dead laugh. I didn't hate him. I hadn't hated him in weeks.

He took a tentative step, as if afraid I would back away. Which I didn't. I was done with that.

"None of that was me, lioness. I've never hurt anyone or anything, I swear it. It's not in my nature."

My eyes swept the length of him. He shouldn't have looked so achingly beautiful like this, draped in the eerie glow of the marsh. Especially because, for the first time since I'd met him, he actually seemed unsure of himself.

But we'd finally dug to the heart of what lay between us. We'd skinned the apple and sliced it open, exposing the constellation at the core. This was the real Ky, heartfelt and vulnerable, no mask in sight, and he was so damn glorious that my heart contracted painfully inside my chest.

"I believe you." My voice came out steady. "But if you've been keeping some other secret, I need to know what it is."

He nodded. Took a deep, preparatory breath. "I know. And it's... I'm—"

The clang of a bell cut him off.

I froze. Dread dropped through me, reducing my brain to an overheated puddle. The alarm bells, but...no. Zephyrine, not now. Not when Amryssa couldn't make it through another nightmare.

The bells clashed again, echoes blaring through the swamp.

I closed my eyes, trying to wish the sound away. It didn't work. When I looked again, Ky's mouth twisted with regret. "She needs you."

"Yes." I nearly choked on the word. "I'm sorry. I have to go."

"Do you want me to—"

"Yes," I said. Because I knew what he was asking. "Please."

He nodded. "All right. Then I'll see you upstairs."

I backed away, then turned and bolted. Palmetto leaves slapped my skirts as the nightmare wakened behind me. The sting of charred paper rode the breeze.

I swatted aside curtains of moss. At my hip, the dagger awoke, then began its ritualistic murmur. *Protect, protect, protect. Guard her where she belongs.*

I clenched my jaw and ran faster. *I will, but you're going to help me. You have to make sure Amryssa survives this.*

The dagger didn't answer, at least not in words. Only with a spark that wobbled and wavered, as if in confusion.

But I refused to let the nightmare take Amryssa. I didn't care if I had to go toe-to-toe with Zephyrine herself.

I jumped the trench and shot across the lawn, then hauled open the same door I'd escaped from.

And pelted down the hallway, fully prepared to do battle with a goddess.

23.

The nightmare came on quick. So quickly that Amryssa started screaming before I'd finished chaining her.

Thunder crashed outside, rattling her bedroom. The walls rippled. Already, this nightmare outstripped the others—shadows boiled around us while worms writhed between the floorboards. The sight made my stomach churn, but I lashed myself together with resolve. I could not, would not, fall apart. Not when my best friend needed me.

More thunder boomed, drawing a shriek from Amryssa. I cranked her chains and clambered onto her bed.

"I love you," I said, aiming my words into the gap between screams. What would Ky have said? Something profound, probably. "And I want you to know your friendship saved me. I didn't deserve it, but you gave it anyway, and that means the world to me. So just...try to remember that. Even when this thing is beating down the doors inside your head."

That must have meant something, because her next scream guttered in her throat. "I love you, too," she gasped. "Always. But go, Harlowe. You have to *go*."

The world wobbled and surged. Chittering insects spewed from beneath the bedskirt, transforming the floor of Amryssa's bedroom into a heaving black sea. Outside, the nightmare roared, making the entire tower sway.

My insides swayed along with it, but I took Amryssa's face in my hands. "Listen. You're going to get through this. We both are."

Pain rippled across her brow. "I don't know if I can. Not this time. I want... Out. I *need* to go outside."

My lungs pinched. I growled a denial and unsheathed my dagger, calling the magic I'd used a thousand times before. *Help her. Carry her through this.*

The knife flared and sizzled, snarling at me in a way it never had. *Guard her where she belongs. GUARD HER WHERE SHE BELONGS.*

My lip curled. All this time, that hadn't meant what I'd thought it did. "I will, but she doesn't belong in the swamp. She belongs right here."

The dagger pushed at me, and I pushed back, in what amounted to an invisible clash of wills. Amryssa bucked against her restraints. The nightmare screamed. The shutters rattled in their frames, the slats groping toward us like fingers.

I gritted my teeth so hard my mouth flooded with the taste of metal. Ironclad. Ky had called me that once, and I believed it now, *made* myself believe it. Zephyrine could fight all she wanted, but I'd bend her.

I'd break her, if I had to.

The dagger shrieked. *GUARD HER WHERE SHE BELONGS.*

A cry tore from my throat as I plunged the knife into Amryssa's headboard. "You guard her, for fuck's sake! You're her mother!"

Whatever shred of Zephyrine lived inside capitulated. I *felt* it recoil like a kicked puppy. Then it circled back, more softly this time. *Yes*, it sighed. *Help her. Guard her.*

The dagger glowed violet. Skeins of magic unfurled and slid down the headboard, seeking Amryssa's skin. The tendrils seeped into her, and within moments, her brow smoothed. The straining line of her throat softened. "Harlowe? It... What did you just do?"

"Kept you...safe..." I said, then threw out a steadying hand, because her coverlet had melted. Caustic goo adhered to my skirts, burning my skin wherever it touched. The room kaleidoscoped around me.

Panic flickered, but I pressed its spiky edges flat. I could last another minute. I *would*. After all, I'd just cowed a goddess, or a piece of one.

If I could do that, what else was I capable of?

"You have to go," Amryssa whispered.

"I know." I kissed her forehead, then scrambled off the bed. Black beetles swarmed my shoes, their tiny mandibles snapping, snapping, snapping.

"I'll be back in the morning," I gasped, and ran.

Dark thoughts chased me from the room. *You'll die here, and no one will care. Nothing will mark your passage from this world but a heap of picked-clean whiteness.*

"Shut up," I hissed as I locked Amryssa's door and stumbled toward mine. The hallway rocked like a raging sea as blood welled from beneath the baseboards.

I ducked into my room and slammed the door. Ky awaited on my bed, wearing nothing but breeches. My chains and manacles were already assembled, needing only my wrists and ankles for completion.

His lips tilted. "Another few seconds, and I would've come for you."

For a moment, I just stood there, buttressed by the sight of him. He'd ironed himself out since our confrontation in the swamp, and now confidence glowed off him, brighter than the myriad candles, more solid than the inhuman shapes scaling the walls.

Because those weren't real. *He* was.

I was, too.

The moment I realized it, the nightmare's illusions dulled. I took a tentative step, then another. True steadiness escaped me—my legs wobbled and my muscles squirmed atop my bones—but I made it to the bed and planted my hands atop Ky's shoulders. And...goddess, he was so intensely solid. Like sun-warmed stone beneath my palms.

He peered up, wonder in his eyes. "You feel it."

My stomach flip-flopped, but the longer I gazed down, the more the storm's efforts receded. It was like I was inside the nightmare, yet apart from it, somehow. "I feel *something*."

He took hold of my waist and stood. I stared up. My fingers glided from his shoulders to his neck, then up into that glossy hair.

He shivered. For long moments, we just stood like that, an island of stillness amid the maelstrom.

"You should probably chain me now," I said, husky.

He nodded and let his hands drift to my dress, unfastening the hooks that ran down the front. "We won't continue our earlier conversation. Not yet."

I shook my head. No, now wasn't the time. Whatever the truth, whatever he had to tell me, I set it aside. I only cared that he was here with me. *For* me.

That right now, in this moment, I was seeing him with utter clarity. And that, in all the time I'd known him, he'd never once hurt me. He'd only proven himself, over and over, in a thousand different ways. He'd *cared* for me.

Whatever Vick had over him, then, whatever Ky had to confess, it wouldn't change that. "No, I'd rather talk about something else."

"Such as?"

"I don't know. Something...happy?"

He finished with my dress and tugged it off. That done, he reached around for my corset laces. The surety of his fingers told a story, of how he'd done this many other times, on other evenings, in other bedrooms, with other girls.

But I set that thought aside, too, storing it on a high shelf, to be taken down and examined later. Or not. The past didn't matter. Not right now.

"Something happy, hmm?" he said. "If you like, you could start by admitting how breathtaking you find me. I can't think of anything happier than that."

He yanked my corset loose and let it fall to the floor.

I stood there in my chemise, caught by his gaze. I'd never realized such pale eyes could command such depth, but that sky-deep expanse seemed to stretch forever. "You *are* breathtaking. So much that it hurts to look at you, sometimes."

Shock leapt in his eyes, then smoothed into delight. His hands skated down my sides. He lifted me onto the bed and moved over me, his touch leaving flames in its wake.

I lay there, limbs splayed, a flashfire shiver starting somewhere deep. I'd never imagined being chained to a bed could feel so...sensual, but Ky infused the process with both tenderness and promise. His thumbs lingered along my pulse points as the cuffs clicked shut. First my wrist, then my ankle. My other ankle, another wrist.

When he finished, I tested my restraints and, for once, didn't chafe at the vulnerability they conferred. Goddess, the things he could do when I was helpless like this.

He cranked my chains and climbed atop me, his weight like a spear pinning me to the now. Somewhere distant, the hurricane raged. Bits and pieces filtered into my consciousness— something monstrous hunched in the corner, its knobby spine rippling while a different something crunched wetly between its jaws.

But I drew a curtain down between myself and it. There was me, here. Ky.

That was all.

"I don't believe you've ever complimented me before," he said. "I think I like it."

"Don't get your hopes up," I said. "It'll probably never happen again. I *do* still hate you, after all."

He chuckled, a smoky sound that slid fire along my nerves. "Of course you do."

Incredible. Here we were, mid-nightmare, and I couldn't keep from melting at the sound of his laugh.

He leaned close, locking us into some private orbit. "Now, how would you like me to distract you? We could try what we did last time, or...something new."

My breathing sped. Pressure built behind my eyes, an ache I recognized as the storm edging into my mind, but I'd already lasted longer than I should have. A heady sense of triumph joined the zing of his nearness, propelling me to some new height.

Fuck, this was a rush.

"Touch me," I breathed.

His eyes heated. "Well. If you insist." He caged my jaw with a hand, turning my head to expose the delicate skin of my earlobe.

I whimpered. The ceiling oozed fingers of shadow, but I steered my attention away, back to Ky.

"Where's the line?" he murmured.

"Don't kiss me," I said. An inch, a mile, and all that. Because even here, even in the midst of all this, I knew he had to marry Amryssa. "Just...touch me. Please. Lick my neck, like you did on our wedding night. And talk to me. I know you don't have feelings, but...maybe pretend like you do. Just for tonight."

"Oh, I have feelings." He made a thrumming sound deep in his throat. "When it comes to you, I have plenty, as it turns out. Tender ones. Awestruck ones. Filthy ones. Ones that tell me I need to taste this place beneath your ear again."

His mouth descended, gifting my neck with liquid heat, and I loosed a moan that sounded like a thousand voices all begging at once.

Around us, the nightmare shrieked, but Ky was doing that thing with his tongue again, the one I'd dreamed about, and I couldn't be bothered to care.

"Gods," he murmured between strokes of his tongue. "Sometimes I want you so badly I can hardly see straight."

Longing swelled, lacing my veins with fire. "Only sometimes?"

He chuckled and kissed a path down to my collarbone. "No, always. It's like I told you when we met. There's something captivating about you. And that feeling's only gotten worse."

He tongued my collarbone, plucking another involuntary cry from my throat. He glanced up, his look devilish. "Hmm. I do believe you like that."

"I hate that," I said, wanton now. Pleading. "I hate everything about it."

"Mmm. What about this?"

He sucked hard enough to make my spine arc. "Even worse," I croaked.

The suction only increased, driving a lightning-tipped spear into the base of my stomach. I writhed beneath him. How bizarre and wonderful that I could feel his attentions in a place he hadn't even touched.

He lifted his mouth and circled my neck with his hand again. He didn't squeeze, just rested his fingers there, the suggestion of force held in check. "Tell me." He hovered, staring into my eyes. "How badly do you want to put a dagger to my throat *this* time? Scale of one to ten?"

"Eleven," I managed. "Definitely an eleven."

His mouth twitched. "Well, at least I get a reaction."

Goddess, did he ever. It was all I could do not to tilt my chin up and nip at his bottom lip—it waited like a juicy berry, just begging to be bitten into. But that would have opened a whole new door onto a whole new set of problems, ones that didn't need visiting tonight any more than whatever confession he'd tried to offer in the swamp.

Ones that hopefully didn't need visiting *ever*, though I was starting to worry I wouldn't last four more days. Sometimes, I didn't think I'd last four more minutes.

My arms flexed, my wrists yanking against their chains as my body slipped from my control. The nightmare battered at me, demanding to be let in.

Kyven angled his forehead against mine. "Not yet. Stay with me."

I nodded. "I'm trying. Talk to me?"

"About?"

"Anything," I said. "Tell me something I don't know. About you."

"Something you don't know. Hmm. How about...I think about you all the time. Did you know that?"

"I meant something *true*."

"That is true." His lashes fanned across his cheeks as his attention dropped to my mouth. "There I'll be, chopping wood, or milking the cows, or sifting through some terminally boring book at your behest, and some part of my mind never lets you fade into the background.

You're always there, on some level. Like a candle that never burns down."

"Really?"

"Truly."

My throat thickened. "And what do you think about? When you think about me?"

His gaze lifted, colliding with mine again. "Your years in the swamp. How alone you must have been, how afraid. Then I think about how, in the end, that experience made you what you are. And that makes me lose my breath, sometimes. Knowing you didn't fall apart under pressure. That instead, you crystallized. I think that's half of why you're so beautiful to me—because you looked desertion in the face and answered it with loyalty. And sometimes, I wonder what it would take to earn that devotion for myself. What it would feel like to belong to someone who's capable of believing in me that much."

I searched for my voice and finally found it wedged somewhere between my lungs and my stomach. "But you don't need me to believe in you. Not when you already believe in yourself."

"Oh, but I want both." He grinned. "That's something you *do* know. I'm unforgivably selfish, and I want everything. All of it. Every last thing I can get my hands on."

I chuckled, but when his smile faded, so did my laugh.

"The truth is," he said, "I've spent so much time rebuilding myself that I've never taken the time to build something with someone else. I've never even stayed in one place long enough to try. But being married to you, it's... I don't know. Made me wonder if being a husband might be something I have a talent for."

The sentiment strummed an aching chord within me. "Among your many other talents, of course."

That earned me a smirk. "Yes, well. I'm glad you've finally come to terms with how impressive I am."

"I didn't say *that*."

"You implied it. Which is nearly the same thing."

The walls heaved, threatening to collapse on us, but I immersed myself in his reassuring scent. "I think about you, too, you know. Way more often than makes sense."

His thumb skimmed along the underside of my jaw. "I should hope so," he murmured. "I'd hate to be all alone in this preoccupation of mine."

I tried to smile, but the gesture never made it to my face, because he stared at me with such liquid intensity that the world spun away. He could have called me by any name he'd wanted just then, and I would've answered, because I had never felt so...wedded to anyone. Not in the legal sense, but like he'd stitched some offered-up part of me to an equivalent one of him. Like this moment had finally carved away the bullshit and misunderstandings and let us stand before one another, bare-faced and without pretense.

The ghost of a warning solidified in my mind. Fuck, *was* I going to fall in love with him?

It certainly felt like it, just then. Something was coming, heavy and inevitable, and any attempt to fight it would amount to nothing more than me shouting protestations at an approaching dawn.

At the thought, my equanimity frayed. My arms jerked, my fingers clawing as I buckled beneath the nightmare's influence. A wheezing breath leaked from my throat.

Ky didn't blink. "Not yet." He slid his hands up and laced our fingers together. He flattened himself atop me, locking us into an age-old position that was nothing short of carnal.

Gods, he was all muscle. A slab of carven stone.

Lust flared, hot and insistent, edging out the storm's foothold. I tilted my splayed hips upward, pressing into him, unable to help myself.

He shut his eyes and laughed softly. "Gods above. You're more difficult to resist than this nightmare, do you know that?"

"I should hope so," I teased, with my best attempt at a Hightower lilt.

He laughed again and ran his nose down the side of my throat, inhaling deep.

The storm shouted into the echo chamber of my mind. *You are nothing. Trash. Worthless.*

Liar, I railed back. And, to my amazement, some part of me believed it. Because wasn't this moment, this prince, this husband of mine, who trembled with yearning as he pressed his face to my neck, tangible proof?

I mattered. I'd made a mark on the world just by existing. People *cared* for me. Maybe I hadn't done the greatest job of caring about myself, but that didn't mean I wasn't capable. Maybe I just had to decide. Like this man had.

The possibility hung in my mind, a teardrop poised to fall.

"Ky," I whispered.

"Harlowe." He spoke raggedly against my neck. His fingers clamped mine tighter, as if he could transmute his strength into me, palm to palm, straight through my skin.

"I have something to tell you," I said.

"What?" His breath was like a heated forge against my skin.

"I think...I'm glad I married you. I think I don't regret it."

He whipped his head up. The sheer elation in his eyes bought me one last lucid moment. He opened his mouth to reply, but I never got to hear it, because the nightmare cracked my mind like an eggshell.

The darkness poured in, carrying me downward into the sooty, seething black.

2 4 .

T his time, awareness came on like a hammer strike. My head pounded. *Boom.* My fingers ached. *Boom.*

Except...that dizzying thump came from outside my skull, not within. Because someone was at my door. Banging.

Loudly.

I opened my eyes. "Ugh."

Strong limbs tangled around me, but their laxity told me my bed companion was still asleep. I raised my head just as the door opened. A brown-haired man peeked in.

A frisson of alarm shot through me. "Merron? What're you doing here?"

He surveyed my bedroom, whatever opinions he had about finding me entwined with Ky locked behind an opaque wall. He stepped in, probably figuring that since we were halfway decent, there was nothing keeping him in the hall. "Sorry to wake you. But I need to borrow His Highness."

I blinked. My eyeballs felt gritty, like I'd spent the night fighting my way through a sand-laden gale. "Okay."

Ky made a sleepy sound. I glanced up to find those luminous blue eyes fluttering open. When he caught me staring, he brought a hand to my cheek. "Mmm. A little early to be contemplating my perfection already, don't you think?"

"We have company," I stage-whispered, and cut a sidelong glance. "Company that's here to borrow you, apparently."

Ky's attention slid to Merron, who stood straight-backed, his gaze locked on the middle distance.

Ky barely reacted. He didn't even take his hand from my face, just lifted lazy brows and said, "Yes?" in the most regal tone possible.

Merron cleared his throat. "It's the rot, Your Highness. It jumped the trenches and infected the lawn overnight. The stewards are down there digging and burning, but we need help, and..." He flicked a glance at me, then resumed his study of the wall. "Well. You happen to be an excellent trench-digger."

Ky's attention swerved to me again. "I am, aren't I? It's probably my most impressive talent of all."

I mustered a smile and peeled myself away. Or tried. Ky tightened, his grip, and in the pause, I read a reluctance in his face, a tick of uncertainty that belied the easy words.

No one else would have caught it, but I did. "What? What's wrong?"

"It's..." He held my gaze, even as he addressed Merron. "Can I join you in a moment? I need a word with my wife."

The head steward hesitated, his silence as good as any answer.

I searched Ky's eyes. We *did* need to talk, yes, but the rot superseded any of our petty secrets. If the coops or gardens or pigpens were lost, we'd be ruined. "Just go. This is way more important."

He studied me for a moment, then pulled me close. "I will," he said, low enough that only I could hear. "But I want you to stay away from Vick today. *Far* away. I don't think he'd actually lay a finger on you, but...I'd rather not find out."

Surprise gnawed at my stomach. Here I'd thought he wanted to finish yesterday's confession, when in fact, he was worried about my safety. "Okay. I promise."

"Good. I'll be back as soon as I'm able. Then we'll talk."

Suddenly, I wanted to cling to him. Beg him to stay. But I forced myself to swing my legs to the floor. This man would only be mine for three more days. Now was *not* the time to start needing him.

"Your Highness," Merron said tightly. "You're needed downstairs. Now."

Ky nodded, and that infernal half smile flickered, assurance settling over him like a mantle. He pushed aside my castoff chains—he'd unlocked me some time just before dawn—then rolled out of bed and hunted for his shirt, which he buttoned on.

"I hope you realize I'll need some bacon, first," he told Merron as he sailed into the hallway. "Not even I can perform acts of heroism on an empty stomach."

Even after he'd gone, Merron lingered, his hands flexing at his sides.

My heart tilted on its axis. Gods, how must he have felt, walking in on us like that? "I'm sorry," I said. "You shouldn't've had to—"

An exhale shot from his nose. "It's not that. Honestly. It's just…"

I shut my mouth and waited.

Merron took a fortifying breath. "Look. I know you think I'm mad at you for marrying him, but it's not that. It's not jealousy. I mean, I *am* jealous. Obviously. But mostly, I'm just mad at myself. For not being able to reach you. For not saying or doing whatever he has that's actually gotten through to you."

I blinked. "I—"

"Like him," Merron cut in. "Obviously you like him. You've never once slept with me like that."

I didn't know how to respond. "Even if that were true," I said carefully, "it doesn't mean anything. I'm not staying married to him."

Merron's look turned pitying. "Maybe you should, though. Have you thought about that? Maybe you should do something just because you want to, not because you think it's best for Amryssa."

With that, he marched out, leaving me slack-jawed and staring.

Gods among us. I'd been right about one thing. I didn't deserve him. I never had.

The knowledge cast a shadow across my mind, but I pushed past it and went to pull on my discarded dress.

Amryssa. She was waiting, and a heart-to-heart with Ky wasn't the only one I had on my schedule today.

Right now, I needed to scrounge up the courage to tell my best friend where she'd come from.

And pray like hell that it didn't end with her leaving me.

Despite my trepidation, once I started talking, I couldn't stop. Mostly because Amryssa didn't seem to believe me. Somewhere in the middle of my third attempt to explain her godly origins, I gave up and went to my room for the diary. Let the Lady lay it all out.

When I returned, Amryssa sat cross-legged on her bed. She reached for the book, a few moonlit strands catching on the knob of her elbow. My eyes snagged there, too. She was so skinny, barely there at all. How had that happened? *Why* had that happened, after I'd persuaded the dagger to help her last night?

Goddess, I needed to get her out of Oceansgate. The moment she married Ky, I would take her away.

Amryssa read in silence, turning pages, occasionally backing up again. When she reached the portrait of Zephyrine, she studied it for so long my chest tightened. I feared whatever she would say next.

So I went to the window and studied the lawn, which had been hacked to bits. Tainted sod had been piled up, and bonfires raged in the heat, sending rippled plumes into the sky. Ky had joined the efforts in the trenches. Sweat poured down his spine as he jabbed his shovel into the earth. Bits of grass stuck to his glistening shoulder blades.

As I watched, Merron's words swelled in my ears. *Maybe you should do something just because you want to.*

For a moment—one selfish, stolen second—I pretended I could. That I wasn't Amryssa's protector. Just Ky's wife, and not in this half-cocked, purgatorial capacity, but for real.

Images filled my head—of me standing by the door in the after-noon, welcoming him in from chopping wood. I would kiss his sweaty skin. Tell him about my day. I'd mock his fancy accent, and then, when he tried to win me over with a laugh and an arm clamped around my waist, I'd take him upstairs for a bath. Once there, I'd watch with eager eyes as—

"What's this?" Amryssa said behind me.

I whirled. She stared down at the diary, which lay open to the last page.

I shut my useless daydreams into a locked steel box. Mere days from now, Ky would marry Amryssa. Then he'd leave.

The end.

"What's what?" I said, a shade too brightly.

Thankfully, Amryssa didn't notice. She frowned down at the pages. "It looks like a letter. Addressed to me."

I frowned and approached the bed. Sure enough, the Lady had inked an entry into the back, where Ky and I hadn't thought to check. We'd stopped when the pages had gone blank.

I leaned in. *My dearest Amryssa,* it began.

"I didn't see this," I said, my heart thumping. "Can I read it with you?"

"Of course."

I crawled onto the mattress, then propped my chin on her bony shoulder.

My dearest Amryssa,

Blood of my blood, flesh of my flesh—I love you so very much. Enough that the word 'love' is only a pale descriptor for how I feel.

If you've read the preceding entries, you'll know we're not kin, at least not in the strictest sense. But in my heart, in some place in me that runs deeper than a soul, I am your mother, and you are my daughter. This will never not be true. Time could fill an ocean, then another and another, and still not diminish my belief.

Which may explain why I stopped writing in this journal years ago—you became mine. We became family. I only came across this diary again this morning, and I was surprised to see I hadn't written in over a decade.

You're eighteen, now. We celebrated your birthday just last week. I'll never forget the way you blew out the candles, because I loved you for granting me that indulgence, for not proclaiming yourself too old to partake in such silly traditions. In our all-too-brief time together, I've cherished our silly moments most of all. This was no different, even if the occasion was one I've dreaded all your life.

As you've no doubt guessed, when the sun set on our celebration, I didn't return you to the swamp. Zephyrine help me, but I couldn't.

I hope you can forgive me, my sweet daughter. Especially because I know you dream of leaving us, even if you don't understand why. I see it in your eyes sometimes.

But I can't let you go. I can't let you vanish. So tomorrow, or next week, or maybe the week or month after that, I'll go to the goddess myself. You see, there was one part of our bargain I didn't write about here, in case your father ever went snooping. I didn't want him to know, because I didn't want him to stop me if I decided to exercise the option.

Zephyrine gave me a choice, all those years ago. When you came of age, I could return you to her, or offer myself instead, thus buying you an entire lifetime out here in the world. It comes at the cost of my blood—all of it, this time—but I can't think of anything I'd rather spend it on.

Still, it's hard to say goodbye. I keep falling prey to the lure of one more day, one more laugh, one more hug. The nourishment of hearing you call me Mother one more time.

It will never be enough, but I doom Oceansgate by staying. I know that.

Soon. I'll go, I promise.

I have to.

And I'll hide this in a place your father will never think to look. I only hope it finds its way into your hands someday. I want you to read this and understand why I'm gone, that it's not because I didn't love you enough, but because I loved you too much, enough that I couldn't bear for you to miss out on all the moments that have brought me such joy.

I want you to fall in love someday.

I want you to forge friendships that remake your idea of the world.

I want you to laugh, and cry sometimes so the moments of laughter shine even brighter, and I want you to travel, and have children of your own, and see a thousand sunrises and maybe, when you're old and wrinkled and exhausted, return to the swamp smiling. When you're ready. When you've seen and done it all.

Or maybe you won't want any of that. You're a goddess, or borne of one—I still don't understand exactly how that works—so maybe your desires will be different than mine. That's all right, too.

Most of all, I just want you to have a choice.

So this is my gift to you, my beloved girl, blood of my blood.

A choice. It's yours. Do with it what you will, and know that I gave it freely.

I love you, forever and ever, through life and death and everything in between.

Your adoring mother,
Coraline Marche

When I finished reading, quiet tears drenched my cheeks. Amryssa wept, too. She pressed one hand to her mouth, her fingers trembling against white lips.

"That's... Wow," I whispered. "Are you okay?"

"She died for me?" she warbled. "*This* was why she went into the swamp that day?"

A sob escaped her, one that sounded like it had cracked her chest open, and I caught her in my arms. She cried against my shoulder. All the while, the letter ran on a loop in my mind.

Goddess, but that was love. Real and true. Amryssa was lucky...and cursed, for having lost her mother that way, but so unbelievably lucky to have experienced love like that in the first place.

I smoothed her hair. She eventually pulled back, leaving a gluey mess of tears and mucus along my neckline.

"This explains so much." Her voice fractured into quiet pieces.

"It does? Like what?"

"Like why I've always felt so...apart. Why I've never truly fit, why

I'm not shaped like other people inside. Why I sometimes feel like a shadow of something greater, or like there's this hole in me where something more should be. Why the swamp calls and calls and calls to me and never stops."

I stiffened. "*That's* how you've felt? Always?"

She trained tear-bright eyes on me.

I felt like I was choking. "Why haven't you ever said so?"

"Because." She sniffled. "I didn't want you to worry. I know it hurts you when I'm unhappy. So I've tried. I truly have. I've tried to be content."

I inhaled sharply. "You're not, though?"

"I am," she said, averting her eyes. "Sometimes. With you, when we're laughing. Or when Lunk tells me chicken stories. But it's hard, Harlowe. The swamp. It shouts louder every day."

I took the diary and set it aside, needing a moment to concentrate on something other than her crumpled face.

How I wished things had gone the way the Lady Marche had intended. But they hadn't—not only did Amryssa not want the same things, but her mother's sacrifice had gone awry. When the Lady had finally ventured into the swamp, she'd been waylaid by a nightmare. She'd died before offering herself to Zephyrine, thus leaving Olivian with an impossible choice: consign his daughter to the marsh, or curse Oceansgate with the nightmares.

But at least this explained why the seneschal had stayed. He was responsible for this.

My next question stuck in my chest, blocking my airway and squatting on my heart. I had to ask, yet the prospect terrified me.

So I closed my eyes and took a cleansing breath. After all, I'd battled a nightmare and *almost* won. I could do this.

"What do you want?" My words were about as firm as last night's pudding, so I repeated myself, louder this time. "Now that you know, what do you want to do about this?"

Amryssa's chin trembled. She stared and stared and stared, and in the quiet, the two halves of my heart declared war on one another. *I need you to be happy, but gods above, please don't leave me.*

"Let me ask you something," she said. "Would you be all right, if I went?"

Oh, goddess. I caged my answer against the roof of my mouth, feeling like a monster for having it ready.

"That's not fair, I know," she rushed to add. "But I want you to tell me the truth."

I tried a few versions out in my head, then shaped my denial into something suitably gentle. "I'd be...lost."

She nodded, as if she'd expected that. "And my father? Do you think he'd be all right?"

"No," I blurted, because that had no shades of gray. Olivian had gutted his territory for her. Knowing what I did now, I suspected losing his daughter might actually kill him.

He'd have nothing left. Just ghosts and guilt and nightmares. Ones he'd brought on himself, but...still. He hadn't made any choices I wouldn't have. "No. He wouldn't."

"Then I think...I have to stay." Amryssa scrubbed at her cheeks, her eyes solemn. "Because I could never hurt him like that. Or you."

The iron band around my ribcage loosened. "Really?"

"Really."

"But is this actually what you want?"

"Yes." She squared her shoulders. "I want...this. My life. My family."

I missed a beat, then threw myself at her, my lungs expanding in a rush. "You'll marry Ky, then? Go to Hightower with me?"

She patted my arm, then attempted a giggle. It was a sallow, trembling thing, but a giggle, nonetheless. "I will."

"Oh, goddess, I want that so badly," I said into her shoulder. She smelled like flowers. Like night-blooming jasmine and plumeria, which must have been some kind of goddess thing, considering no one in this house had been able to afford perfume for years. "But only if it'll actually make you happy."

"It will." She patted my arm. "Also, you're choking me."

I eased back, my limbs syrupy with relief. I felt heavy, like someone had poured me full of molasses. "Thank Zephyrine. I mean, not Zephyrine—that's actually kind of rude to say, now that I think about it—but thank *you*. Zephyrine can wait. She can have you back when you're eighty."

Amryssa mustered a smile and fondled the diary. "Until then, what do we do with this?"

I considered the journal. If Olivian found his wife's letter—if he learned about the blood-price—he would offer Zephyrine his life. Of that, I had no doubt. But that would kill Amryssa as surely as fading into the swamp would. "I'll keep it hidden, in my room. Olivian can't know. No one can."

"All right. And Harlowe? Do you think I could have some water? I'm thirsty. And tired. And I think I need to lie down for a minute. This is...a lot."

I jumped to my feet, ready to go join the stewards' lawn war, if necessary, so immense was my relief. "Of course. I'll go grab some from downstairs. Be right back."

She lay down, her shoulder blades jutting beneath her dress like wings. I strode into the hallway, then dug for my keyring and locked her door, just in case Vick was prowling around nearby.

But in the end, I shouldn't have worried, because Vick didn't come for Amryssa.

He came for me.

2 5 .

I was nearing the stairs, my steps whispering against the tatty carpets, when a shadow darkened the corridor behind me. I glanced back, and...shit. Vick was headed my way, clearly on a mission.

My stomach sank. Goddess, Ky had asked me to do one thing today. *One thing*.

I veered into a side hallway and chose a random corner to turn, then another. After ducking through a door, I found myself in what had once been a nursery, complete with pastel curtains and a cradle with a bug net draped over the top.

I leaned against the wall, my chest heaving. Had I lost him? A minute ticked by, then another, and I allowed myself to hope.

But then the knob turned. When the door opened, Vick slipped inside.

Dread flash-boiled in my stomach. As usual, he wore his short-sword. A disembodied section of my mind calculated whether anyone would hear me if I screamed.

Probably not.

Vick smiled, a slow bleed that sharpened to a wolf's grin. A few carroty curls had escaped the tie at his nape and frizzed in the heat.

I sidled away. "Don't mind me. I was just on my way downstairs."

He was on me in a flash, barring me from retreat with a hand planted against the wall. He leaned close, one hand rested casually atop his sword pommel.

I froze, eyeing his weapon. If he drew, I could go for my dagger, but I had no illusions about how *that* would go. I wasn't a fighter. The best I could do was lure unarmed princes into sucking on my neck before catching them off-guard with a blade to the throat.

Vick, unfortunately, was not an unarmed prince. Nor was I about to offer him my neck.

"Just the person I wanted to see," he said. "You're a tough one to get alone."

"Yep. Great to see you, but I'll be going now." I made an attempt for the door, but he pinned my shoulder to the wall.

"Ah, ah," he tutted. "It's past time for us to have a chat, *Princess*."

My skin writhed in his sweat-dampened grip. "Is it? Because I'm pretty sure I'd prefer we never speak again."

His fingers dug into my arm. "You think you're so clever, don't you? Talking like that. Marrying Ky like you did. Trying to get yourself a title."

A laugh knifed its way up my throat. "You think I married him for a *title*?"

"Of course I do."

I almost guffawed in his face. This conversation was even less amusing the second time than it had been the first.

But then the sparkling accusation in Vick's eyes sobered me. Sweat beaded his upper lip where a few blond hairs had escaped the razor, and...goddess, he looked so young. Younger than Ky, but also harder and grimmer, enough that arguing while trapped in a room with him seemed like an incredibly stupid thing to do.

So I didn't. "You know what? You're right. I'm a double-crossing gold-digger who just wanted to be royalty. Sucks that it didn't work out the way I planned."

Vick's nose twitched, making him look more foxlike than ever. "Oh, I know. I know all about people like you. You don't care if others go hungry while you hole up in your little castle, eating sausage every day. You're the kind that thinks you deserve everything even though you contribute nothing."

Well, then. Don't hold back, or anything. Though I supposed this was the liberator in him talking. "Yep. You've got me pegged. Well done."

His eyes flashed. "Are you mocking me?"

"I would *never.*"

He grunted, a warning. "Here's what's going to happen, Princess. However your little tricks with Ky started, I'm not an idiot, and I see the way he looks at you now. Which is fine. You can give him all the moon-eyed looks you want, wrap him around your little finger, I don't care. But when the annulment comes, you *will* sign it. And then you'll send him away."

I tried to tug my arm away, but it was no use. Despite Vick's compact size, hard living had bought him a sinewy strength I couldn't match. "Fine. I'd be glad to."

His eyes slitted, as if he were trying to work that out. "Do you understand? If you so much as *think* of asking him to stay—"

"What, are you going to run me through?"

"What? No. What kind of question is that?" A snarl wrinkled the bridge of his nose. "I don't *run women through.* What do you take me for?"

I clamped my lips together. I was about ninety-eight percent sure he didn't actually want me to answer that.

"I'm the good guy," he said. "Not the villain. Which means that if I have to hurt you, it's only in the name of the greater good. That'll be on you. Not me."

I scowled. And here I'd thought *Ky* was the master of circular reasoning.

"But," Vick said, his grip tightening, "while we wait for all that, you're going to tell me where to find the damn valuables in this house. Because I've reached the end of my patience. If Olivian won't share with the territory he's supposed to govern, I'll make him."

"There's nothing here, though. No money. We ran out of all that years ago."

"You say that." His smile approached a sneer. "But there's *something* in this house, I can feel it. Something that'll help the people the seneschal's supposed to serve."

Alarm bells clanged in my brain. I considered my dagger, then the diary—the only things of value under this roof. Well, and Amryssa.

But Vick couldn't have any of that. He'd have to gut me, first. "I don't know what you're talking about. We have nothing. Barely enough to eat."

"Fine." His smile gleamed with cold light. "If you won't tell me, then you've forced me to do this. Just know that this was your decision, not mine."

He reached for his sword.

Cold terror spiraled through my gut. *Zephyrine, help me.*

At my summons, the blade awoke. I inhaled the goddess's energy, funneling it into my palm, willing it into a weapon. Planting my free hand against Vick's chest, I cannoned Zephyrine's magic straight into him.

He reeled backward, clutching his heart, his sword halfway drawn. His mouth opened and closed soundlessly.

I darted away. I probably hadn't done any permanent damage, but I had no desire to stick around and find out.

Adrenaline shrieked in my veins. I pelted down the hallway, my feet barely touching the steps as I descended the stairs.

Only once I'd reached the kitchens, where Miss Quist and Lunk bent over a bubbling pot together, did I glance behind me.

Vick hadn't followed.

Which was cold comfort, because I had a feeling that I'd just made an enemy.

26.

Ky didn't make it to dinner that evening, occupied as he was with the battle out on the lawn. Neither did Vick, though obviously for different reasons.

After the meal, I tracked down Lunk in the library, mostly in an effort to gauge whether or not Vick had survived.

When I asked about his absence, Lunk only shrugged. "He wasn't feeling well. I think he went to bed early."

"Oh. Is that all?"

"Yes. Why?" He held a hand over his mouth, like he always did when speaking to me. He didn't do that with Amryssa, but no surprise there—she was divine, while I was just...me. "Did you need something? Should I wake him?"

I shook my head, my nerve endings buzzing. It would probably be too murdery to pray that Vick never wake again, but I went ahead and did it anyway.

"No." I tried to sound casual. "Just wondering."

Lunk made to move off, but I caught at his wrist. His arm was too substantial for me to circle entirely, but he got the idea and stopped. "Is there something else, keymistress?"

"Yes." I chewed at my lip. "It's just...seems like you and Miss Quist have gotten close, and I want you to know how happy that makes me. She deserves a man like you. Someone good."

Crimson flared in his cheeks. "Well, she's amazing," he said. "Not just beautiful, but industrious. And kind. So incredibly kind."

I risked a smile. "Then I hope you'll stay with us. With her."

He ducked his head. "I'd like that. It's just..." His gaze slid away.

When I he didn't continue, I frowned. "What?"

He rummaged in his pocket and produced a compact book. It was Miss Quist's favorite—I recognized the sapphire cover, the scuffed and twice-cracked spine.

"I don't know that I'm what she wants." Lunk smiled bleakly, then opened the book and handed it over. I inspected the page, which showed a curvy woman embracing her fierce-eyed pirate lover. The hero had flowing black hair, brown skin, and glistening muscles.

"She lent this to me, but..." Lunk gestured at the drawing. "See? It's her."

I blinked. Huh. The heroine did indeed resemble Miss Quist, complete with blonde corkscrew curls and rosy cheeks. I couldn't believe I'd never noticed before. "Wow. It is."

He pointed at the pirate. "But Captain Dash..." He trailed off, and I could practically hear him proclaiming he could never compete with the pirate lord.

"I think this might be her way of letting me down easy," he said.

I snapped the thing shut and handed it back. "No. She's not like that, and besides. It's just a book."

"It's not *just* a book. Believe me, when you look like this"—he waved to indicate his face—"you grow up believing in the fictional world more than the one around you. In some ways, it's more real. More just."

I fell silent, not knowing what to do with that. I hadn't grown up around books. I'd cut my teeth on pure survival, on endless worries about which berry bush would ripen first and how many mussels I could dig up to trade for candles. I hadn't encountered the luxury of literature until I'd joined Olivian's household and Eliana had taught me to read.

And while I thoroughly enjoyed books, I'd never considered them a haven, the way Lunk apparently did.

"But they're just stories," I said slowly. "Idealized versions of life, not the real thing. Because in the real world, good men wear all kinds of faces. Miss Quist knows that as well as I do."

A sad smile stole over his features. "That's easy for you to say when...well, when you look like that." He made a vague, complimentary gesture in my direction.

I trailed my fingertips across the features I'd chosen. "Well. To be honest, I didn't always look like this. I was born plain. Less than plain, actually."

His brow furrowed. "You...what?"

"I know. It sounds strange, but Zephyrine gave me a...gift. One that lets me remake myself however I like. I might look like this now, but I didn't used to. I spent years being invisible."

He blinked at me.

I stepped closer, an idea sparking. I'd never reshaped anyone else's face, only my own, but why wouldn't it work the same way? "Actually, I could do the same for you, if you want. If you'd rather look like"—I gestured at the book—"someone else. Or some slightly different version of yourself."

He stared, nonplussed. Clearly, that was a lot to take in.

"I'm not trying to talk you into anything. Just making an offer. Here, watch."

I palmed the hilt of my dagger. Zephyrine awoke, her warmth bristling against my skin. Guilt needled at me, some rational part of me cringing at using the goddess's power while also plotting to keep her daughter from her, but I pushed the feeling aside. This was for Lunk, not me.

I passed a hand over my eye, letting the magic seep in, changing one dark iris to shimmering green.

At least, I hoped I had. I'd never done this without a mirror before. But apparently it worked, because the giant's bronze cheeks went stark white.

He opened his mouth, closed it again. "That's...witchcraft?" He sounded strangled.

I changed my eye back to its preferred brown and released the dagger. "No. It's Zephyrine's magic. I just get to borrow it."

"I..."

I waited. Maybe I shouldn't have shown him that, but something about this man felt so irrefutably safe. Moreover, Ky trusted him. So did Amryssa. Which meant I did, too.

"I've never seen anyone wield magic before," he finally said. "You're saying you'd share that with me?"

"I would."

He contemplated the book, then tucked it back into his pocket. Conflict warred in his expression. "That's kind of you. I just...don't know if I could trust it."

"It's not painful. And if you didn't like how it looked, I could always change it back."

"No." His jutting brow crinkled. "I mean, I don't know if I could trust how people would treat me. It's funny. If you'd asked me a year ago, or maybe even a month, I would've jumped at the chance. But meeting Dorothea... It's made me wonder if someone might actually see me, someday. Really see me. If I looked like Captain Dash, I'm not convinced I'd ever know for sure."

I let that sink in. That was...wow. Admirable. "I get it. But let me know if you change your mind, okay?"

He smiled, his whole face softening. "I will. And thank you."

"Of course."

I moved off. I didn't know what had possessed me to bring all that up, only that the prospect of tomorrow didn't seem nearly as certain as it had this morning.

Upstairs, I readied Amryssa for bed, but the events of the day formed a dark, sucking hole beneath my feet.

What would Vick do once the effects of my assault wore off? Would he come after me? Ruin Amryssa's wedding?

Bile slicked the back of my throat. I was such an idiot. I should never have pissed him off like that, except he'd threatened me and I'd just...lost myself. Seen red.

Now I drew up Amryssa's coverlet and extinguished her lamp. After locking her door, I made for my room, hoping to find Ky waiting.

But the bed was empty.

My heart slid into the bottom of my stomach. A glance outside confirmed he was still hard at work with the stewards, digging up the glowing bits of rot they'd missed during daylight. From the looks of it, they'd be out there for another few hours.

I grumbled and changed into my gauziest nightgown, then tried to read. But the words swam before my eyes, and I eventually lowered the book, my head swirling.

Vick. The liberators. Ky. Whatever he'd tried to tell me in the swamp yesterday taunted me—I had all the pieces now, I could feel it. But they were jumbled and out of order, and no amount of mental rearranging produced a sensible answer.

With a scoff, I tossed my book aside. Ky would tell me his big secret as soon as he came upstairs, and it would probably be something stupid. Something that wouldn't change anything, because *nothing* would change anything. We'd annul our marriage, then he'd marry Amryssa and leave. I'd take her to Hightower, and that would be that.

I just had to make sure Vick didn't screw it up.

A knock broke the silence, and I frowned. That wasn't Merron's signature pattern. And Ky would've come right in.

Sure enough, when I opened the door, Olivian loomed in the hallway. He held out a letter—one with an ornate seal stamped across the front.

My heart splattered against my ribs, then went quiet.

The annulment certificate. Three days earlier than expected.

I made no move to take it. Instead, I just stood there, wondering how something so innocuous could wield such power.

"Well?" Olivian said. "I don't have all night."

I shook off my stupor and grabbed the thing, resisting the urge to pinch it by a corner, like I would a rat dangling by its tail.

"Sign it and give it back to me tomorrow," he said.

I forced myself to respond. "Okay. Sure."

"Amryssa will be married first thing in the morning. And this time, I *will* attend." He gave me a significant look, which he shouldn't have bothered with, considering I was the last person in this house who would interfere. "And Harlowe, this *is* still valid, isn't it?"

I missed a beat, but his meaning quickly became clear. "If you're asking whether I've lost control of myself and had some kind of sex marathon with the prince, then no. Of course I haven't. Don't be ridiculous."

He gave me a narrow look. "It would require far less than a marathon."

I grumbled. "Exactly zero sex has taken place."

He grunted, but seemed satisfied. "Good. Fine. Then sign this, and have Kyven do the same. Your marriage will be dissolved the moment that certificate has two signatures on it. And whatever you do, don't lose the damn thing."

I heaved an exhale. "Where would I lose it, Olivian? Down the front of my nightgown?"

He shot me a look that would have sent a younger Harlowe scurrying for the corner. "Just don't screw this up again."

"Trust me, I have no desire to. I'll be there tomorrow with bells on."

He grunted again and traipsed off, scrubbing a hand through the mess atop his head. I watched him go, wondering if he cut his hair himself or if someone did that to him on purpose. The black locks stuck out at all angles and all different lengths, like each one had been hacked off at a random interval.

The seneschal reached the spiral stairway, then disappeared downward. With all distractions removed, I had no choice but to confront the letter in my hands. The seal had already been slit, and I thumbed it open to find a document nullifying the unconsummated marriage of one Harlowe X and His Royal Highness Prince Kyven Windermere, on the grounds of "deceitful claims on the part of the bride."

Well. I couldn't argue with that. Not that the king needed to be so snooty about it.

At the bottom of the paper, dual signature lines awaited—two long, bare marks that stretched like these endless hallways.

I coughed out a cold laugh, slammed my door, and scrounged for a pen at my vanity. This document was the key to Amryssa's future, absent only a few dashes of ink.

I spread the parchment on the vanity and stared at it. A minute passed. Then another.

But I managed, in the end. I signed the damn thing and went to bed, leaving the annulment certificate folded on Ky's pillow.

He finally came in sometime around midnight.

At least, that was my best guess, because I was drifting in the velvet reaches of sleep when sounds infiltrated my awareness—first the click of a latch, then the rustle of paper.

I surfaced, mostly, and lay unmoving. Ky was somewhere nearby, obviously aiming for stealth, but when footsteps shuffled and hinges creaked, I gave in and cracked an eye.

He stood in the bathroom doorway, his outline blurred by the candleglow from within. He was filthy, coated in bits of grass, his hair a sticky, sweaty mess.

Gods help me, he'd never looked more enticing.

At the thought, a silent scream hollowed me out. This man would cease to belong to me in a matter of hours.

Or...minutes, actually. Maybe even seconds. He held the annulment certificate and pen, staring down as if he'd never encountered anything like them before. Which, I guessed, he hadn't.

He glanced up at me.

I rammed my eyes shut. The silence did its utmost to crush me, but

Ky must not have caught me looking, because long seconds ticked past in which he didn't say anything. Neither did I.

Because sweet Zephyrine, I wasn't ready. I hadn't expected the annulment certificate so soon, and I couldn't face the prospect of talking it over with him. Not tonight. If I did, I'd have to find some way to smile. To shrug, nonchalant, and keep from yanking the pen from his hand. Keep myself from throwing it out the fucking window.

Because goddess, I just wanted one more night. One more chance to wake up in his arms before I had to give him away for good.

Except...then a new thought elbowed its way to the forefront of my mind.

Once Ky signed the annulment, anything could happen. I could spend all night beneath him, and it would amount to nothing more than mindless pleasure for us both. It would no longer be the irrevocable binding I'd done my damnedest to avoid.

My heartbeat crested in my throat, forceful enough to bruise, and I opened my eyes, intending to tell him to sign the thing and come to bed already, sweat and grime be damned.

But he'd closed the bathroom door. Seams of candlelight glowed around the frame. Metal squeaked within, followed by the muted thunder of water falling into the tub.

I lay there, contemplating, for much, much longer than I should have.

But I was being stupid. Surrendering to him wouldn't come for free. Of course it wouldn't.

In the end, I closed my eyes and tried to sleep again—the only course of action that wouldn't bring consequences with it.

27.

Someone murmured my name.

I cracked my eyes, expecting daylight, but shadows still swathed the bedroom. I rolled over and checked the bedside clock, which I could just make out in the sallow marshglow from the window.

Two in the morning.

I rubbed at sleep-heavy eyes, wondering what had woken me. Then a husky laugh warmed the quiet. I frowned, wondering what Ky could possibly find amusing at this hour, especially because he was clearly fast asleep, his head thrown to the side.

"Lioness," he said. "Gods, yes."

At that, my heart stilled, deliberating its next beat. Wait, was he...?

He made a sound—half chuckle, half moan, entirely sexual.

I sat up and shoved the coverlet aside. Oh, no. No, no, no. Him sleep-talking my name had been torture enough, but *this*? Outright warfare. No way could I lay here while he dreamed his own pleasure, not if it was *my* face he saw in his mind.

"Ky," I hissed.

He didn't respond, too busy smiling at whatever sordid thing dream-me was doing to him. "Mmm."

In desperation, I heaved astride him and clamped my hands around his shoulders. "Ky. Wake *up*."

"For the love of Aerelis," he said. "Yes, like that."

That stopped me. *Aerelis*. What the hell? Wasn't Aerelis the patron goddess of...

My mind spun, combing through the lessons I'd absorbed from Amryssa's books. Aerelis. The patron goddess of...Windfell?

Yes, that was right, but Windfell was nothing. A territory even more insignificant than Oceansgate, a microscopic eastern peninsula populated by howling gales, barren cliffs, and a few unfortunate sheep.

Why would Ky invoke the patron goddess of Windfell?

"Fucking hell, lioness," he crooned.

My thoughts slowed, his words digging into me like barbs. There was something different about the way he was talking. Something wrong.

Then it hit me. His accent. This wasn't the rarefied lilt of Hightower, but something unfamiliar. No doubt one of the myriad dialects he had in his lexicon, but why would he dream in a different accent than the one he'd been born to?

Unless... Unless...

My blood slowed to an ice-water trickle. Oh. Oh, no. Oh, goddess. Oh, seven fucking hells.

The puzzle pieces finally came together like a hand had reached down from the sky and arranged them for me. I thought of Vick and Lunk—not royal attendants, but criminals. Brigands who, according to that Wanted poster, staged highway robberies along the Oceansgate road.

And the way Vick treated Ky as a resented superior, rather than a prince. Because who was Ky, really?

An actor. An impersonator. He'd said as much himself. He'd taunted me with the truth, only I hadn't reached out and taken hold of the very thing he'd dangled in my face.

Not until this moment.

"Ky," I shouted, shaking him.

He jerked, his lashes whipping apart. "What? What is it? What's the matter?"

"Everything," I hissed, hating the accent still coming out of his mouth. The Windfell one. The *real* one.

Because each one of those harsh-sided words told me Kyven Windermere had never made it to our doorstep at all. No, the *true* prince had been waylaid by brigands, like everyone else who chanced that perilous road. He'd been ambushed by Vick, Lunk, and the bandit chieftain lying beneath me. Who'd then dared to take his place.

That was why Kyven's crimes had been so unfamiliar to him.

"Was I dreaming?" He blinked, clearing the haze of sleep. "I think I was. About you."

Those barren syllables caved my chest in. Something must have shown on my face, because alarm brightened his eyes.

"Oh, no," he said, transitioning smoothly back to Hightower. "This isn't... Listen to me, lioness—"

I made a sound of disgust and scrambled off him, retreating as far as the bathroom doorway. "Don't you dare call me that. Don't pretend to know me when I have no idea who the fuck you actually are. Other than someone who isn't actually Kyven Windermere."

He grimaced and struggled to his feet, one hand raised in entreaty. "That's—"

"True. Don't even try to deny it."

He swallowed. "All right. But I wasn't keeping it from you. I *tried* to tell you yesterday."

I glanced around for something to throw, but nothing lay within reach. This asshole. Every vowel, every swallowed *r*, was a lie.

His brows crooked. "And you know I would've told you this morning, if Merron hadn't needed me. I even would've done it now, if you hadn't been asleep when I came in."

I flashed my teeth, hoping naked aggression would soothe the fury scouring my insides. What should I do? Scream? Run? Go tell the stewards we had an impostor in our midst?

Except... Shit. I fisted my hands in my hair. If anyone found out this man wasn't Kyven, Amryssa's wedding would be canceled. Then she'd be stuck here. Forever.

That was what Vick had in his arsenal, then—the power to destroy Amryssa's future simply by telling the truth.

"Who are you, really?" I spat. "And don't you dare lie. Because I swear to Zephyrine, if you spout one more line of bullshit, I'll stab you like I wanted to that first night. Obviously it was a mistake not to."

Ky—oh goddess, that wasn't even his name, but what was?— padded toward me. "Bullshit? None of this has been bullshit."

"It has. All of it. From the beginning. You *liar.*"

His expression darkened, going from contrite to indignant. "Liar? Hardly. I told you *one* lie over a breakfast table, months ago, before I even knew your name. Apart from that, I've been entirely truthful. I've been nothing short of authentic with you from the moment we met."

"Authentic?" Stark fury colonized my insides. "Go to hell. You used me."

That seemed to anger him, because a snarl scrunched the bridge of his nose. But his approach didn't slow, even when I flung out a finger to stop it.

He simply walked into my hand, letting my finger stab into the thick muscle over his heart. He stared down at me, his eyes a glittering accusation.

"I have not," he said, the words chiseled from ice, "nor will I ever, *use* you."

"You pretended to be someone you're not." I shaped the accusation into a fiery whip. "Then *married* me, for Zephyrine's sake."

"Oh, is that a punishable offense, now? Because I seem to remember you doing exactly the same to me. I also seem to remember forgiving you for it. Without a moment's hesitation."

I opened my mouth, stumbled over a protest, then tried again. "That was different. I had a reason."

"And you think I didn't?"

"I don't know! What could you possibly have to gain from impersonating a prince? When you're nothing but a thief? A brigand?"

"I'm not a *brigand*." His eyes flashed. "Why are you always using that word?"

"Because that's what you call people who steal things!"

"I stole nothing," he said, low and lethal.

"Except Kyven's entire identity," I sniped back.

His nostrils flared. "I may have played a role. But I'm no thief. I'm an actor, like I told you. And before that, a shepherd's son. One nobody wanted. *Also* like I told you."

"But you're from Windfell," I hissed.

"Yes."

"Not Hightower."

"No."

I stabbed his chest again, doing my best to make it hurt. "Then every moment we've spent together has been a lie."

His jaw hardened. "No. You know me, lioness. Inside and out. I've shown you every scar. I've told you all about my past, my parents, how I left home when I was young. About the play I saw in Gray's Reach when I was nineteen. Which not even Lunk has heard about. He's known me for nearly a year, ever since I left my theatre troupe and came to conquer the nightmares, but I've never once shared with him what I have with you. You might not have known me for long, but you *do* know me better than anyone on this earth."

I bit my lip, my eyes stinging. "Don't do that."

"Do what?"

"Make us sound close. Make us sound intimate."

A sharp light blazed in his eyes. "We *are* intimate. You're my wife, for Hyperion's sake. What's more, you understand me."

"I don't understand shit." I pushed at him again, but it was like shoving against a steel wall. "I don't even know why you're here. Why you bothered to pretend."

He hauled in a breath—once, twice, like he was shoring himself up. "Officially? Because we wanted into this house, and I knew I could pass as Kyven with ease."

"Oh, right. Of course. Because you wanted to rob us, too. You and Vick, the oh-so-noble heroes."

His eyes narrowed. "We *help* people, lioness, like it or not. We got Althea out, didn't we? And her family. Lunk and I would've gotten Miss Quist out, too, if she'd actually wanted to go."

I gaped. "You told Miss Quist about this?"

"I didn't tell her I'm not Kyven. But that I'd smuggle her out of Oceansgate? Yes."

I breathed and breathed and breathed, but no amount of indrawn air could lessen my rage. "So you knew where Althea was, that day we went searching? You knew this *whole time*? Even though you told me you didn't?"

His jaw worked. "I believe my exact words were, 'I'm sure she's far away, breathing a sigh of relief.' Which I was, because she was."

I bared my teeth. "That's a technicality."

"No, it was the truth. So were the reasons I gave you for coming here, that night in town."

"Screw your reasons," I spat. "It sounds like you wanted to just come in and steal everything."

"*I* didn't." His voice hardened to steel. "Vick might have imagined he'd raid this place and then return to the forest. Take up the reins I'd abandoned. But *I* came here to be a husband."

"Oh, please. You expect me to believe you went to all this trouble just for some new role to play?"

His lips peeled back. "Not *just* that. If you must know, I also intended to do the Lady Amryssa a favor. I meant to satisfy my curiosity, then disappear. She could've had Kyven's title without bothering with all the rest, because no woman deserves to be saddled with a husband she didn't choose. My sister suffered that fate, and I wouldn't wish it on anyone."

Emotion rose up in me, thick and cloying. "You wanted to help Amryssa?"

Air jetted from his nose. "Yes. It's like I told you—the liberators help people. And I'd heard the gossip, in Hightower. Suggestions that Kyven wasn't the kindest of men. Though I didn't know a thing about dead animals or seneschal's daughters until you told me in the marsh yesterday."

The power of his regard proved too much. I dropped my gaze, only to find myself eye-to-eye with that birthmark I loved so much.

Had loved so much. Had, past tense.

"Where is he, then?" I managed. "The real Kyven?"

"Dead."

I jerked my gaze up again.

The intensity of his focus sliced into me. "And before you go giving me that look, know that I had nothing to do with it. His carriage overturned on its own, for no other reason than he was driving too fast on a road that's been filling with potholes for years. He died in the accident, and his attendants fled, and it fell into our laps, Harlowe. The carriage, the prince's clothes...the whole thing, like an opportunity offered in an open palm. And it made sense to me to take it. Everyone would've gotten what they wanted. Including you, if only..." He pressed his lips together.

"What?" My voice rang with challenge. "If only I hadn't taken Amryssa's place?"

"Yes, but..." He grabbed my hand and pressed it to his heart, splaying my fingers against hot skin. "I'm *glad* you did. I'm so unbelievably grateful it was you, because I never would've known what this was like, with her. I wouldn't have known what this was like with anyone but you."

I hissed between my teeth. "There is no *this*."

"There absolutely is. Don't you dare deny it. Every word, every look, every nightmare you've ridden out with me, every confession, it's all been real. This insignificant question of my name doesn't change that."

The urge to cry crowded my breathing. I couldn't name this darkness inside me—fury, or broken-heartedness, or some perverse melding of the two that had somehow mutated into an undercurrent of desire. I wanted to hit him. I wanted to dive into his arms and stay there. I wanted to scream until I shattered, then shout that this was all his fault, that now it was his job to catch all the pieces.

"Fuck," I muttered. Tears scrabbled up my throat and stabbed at my eyes. I blinked, unwilling to let them fall. "What even *is* your name?"

He sidled closer, his familiar scent raveling me into a chaotic knot.

"The same one you've been calling me." Something raw boiled beneath his words. "The one I've *asked* you to call me. It's spelled differently—K-A-I—but I've been truthful, even about that. About everything. Gods know I tried not to be at first, but acting didn't feel like acting, with you. It felt like lying. So I just...didn't."

"Kai." I tested the name on my tongue. "What, you're telling me you have half the prince's name, just by random chance?"

"If any of this is random." He stared me down. "I've never put much stock in the gods, but I have to wonder if Zephyrine can do more in her sleep than just dream people into a frenzy. Because all of this seems...strangely convenient. As though someone designed it this way."

I blinked, unwilling to let him distract me with philosophy. "Ky. Kai. Fine, your name's the same, but that accent? The way you talk? Lies."

"No," he said, with the same dark edge that had flavored his words in sleep, or in moments of high emotion, though I hadn't understood the significance until right now. "This is me, lioness. At my truest. I've spoken this way for years. To friends, to lovers, to everyone who knows me. Windfell belonged to the sullen boy who hated himself. Hightower is for the man who claimed sovereignty over his own life. So you can't tell me I need permission to speak this way, or some nonsensical birthright. Not when this is what feels like mine, what *tastes* right in my mouth."

"It's not what you were born with," I snapped. "Which makes it a lie."

"It's not," he growled, his anger rising. "No more than that face you wear, which, if I'm not mistaken, you weren't born with, either. At least if Lunk is to be believed."

I gaped up at him, wildfire sparking in my breast. "How dare you?"

"How dare *you*? You of all people should understand what it means to define yourself. Because you and I are the same, lioness. How can you not see that? We're people life tried to sweep under the carpet, only we stood up and refused. We reinvented ourselves and didn't waste a moment on apology. I didn't then, and I won't now."

"No, apology is obviously completely beyond you."

"I'm *sorry*," he said. Despite the fury tightening his words, he sounded like he actually meant it. "But only for telling you I was Kyven. I'm not sorry for coming here. Or for marrying you. Or for falling half in love with you. Or for convincing you to fall half in love with me."

"What the fuck are you talking about?" I shrieked. "I'm not half in love with you."

"Now *that*," he said, leaning closer, "is a bald-faced lie. As far as I'm concerned, that makes us even."

"I should slap you."

"Go ahead." Kai stared down, his mouth tight. His eyes were licks of blue fire, scorching away the air in the room until nothing remained but the stillness before a lightning strike. "But slapping me won't stop me from wanting you, and it certainly won't stop you from wanting me."

I stared, too stunned and angry to answer.

"So do it." His gaze dropped to my mouth. "Slap me as hard as you can. I *beg* you. So long as you kiss me, afterward."

My breathing grew harsh and frantic. Oh, goddess. Something was happening inside me, some unquenchable thirst rising up, transforming every heartbeat into a fresh ache that cried his name. Ky. Kai. It was the same, wasn't it? And so was he. Because when I looked at him now, I saw the same man who'd held me in the darkness and winked at me over the dining table. Who'd guided me through the nightmares and painted fire across my throat with his tongue.

Not only that, but he was the only one who could do this to me. Who could steal my breath and feed it back to me in the form of knowing looks and heated words. Who could take my heart and reshape it in his hands. Who could soak up the candlelight like some fiery, avenging angel—one who'd marked me for capture and now held my eyes with the focus of an archer sighting down the shaft of an arrow.

His fingers tightened around my hand. Gravity bent me closer, threatening to suck me into his orbit. I wanted...

Seven hells, I wanted *him*. So very, very badly.

My nostrils flared. If I didn't escape him right this second, I was going to do something incredibly fucking stupid.

So I shoved him away and stalked off in the only direction available—the bathroom. I stomped into the candlelit circle of mirrors, my reflection breaking into a hundred shimmering shards. Kai followed and stopped behind me. In the mirrors, shadows honed his face to a collection of blades—sharp eyes, sharp cheekbones, sharp fury that demanded some kind of response.

"You were supposed to be a prince," I accused his reflection. "Who was supposed to marry a seneschal's daughter. And instead, you're just...nobody, married to some other nobody. It's actually kind of hilarious, if you think about it."

A warning flashed in his eyes. "I am *far* from nobody. And you couldn't be less of a nobody if you tried."

His response carved out a hollow space within me. And...shit. I couldn't stop myself.

I whirled around and slapped him. *Hard.* Fire lashed my palm as his head snapped to the side. The crack of flesh reverberated from tile and marble and glass.

He straightened slowly, his breathing turbulent. When he swept his hair back from his face, embers smoldered in those chilled-fire eyes.

As if he'd *liked* that.

I flexed my stinging palm. "That's for not being Kyven Windermere."

He ran his tongue along his teeth and smiled, predatory, and I could no more squelch the need surging up in me than I could stem the gush of a burst dam with bare hands. Because my anger had multiplied, sharpening into a double-edged blade that sliced at me with such savagery that I couldn't distinguish anger from desire.

Fuck, I didn't care where he'd come from. I just wanted to inhale him. Punish him. Tear him into pieces and consume each one. If only this once.

I stepped in and yanked his face to mine. Our mouths collided in what amounted to the fiercest kiss of my life.

It was like breathing lightning. Like drinking an inferno. His mouth was hot and demanding, his tongue a delirious force that obliterated all reason. His hands captured my ribs and crushed me close.

My body went molten, and I broke away, dazed. He tilted his forehead against mine, my ribcage still folded in his vise grip.

"And that?" he breathed. "What was that for?"

"Also for not being Kyven Windermere."

He gave a gravelly chuckle. "Well, would you look at that. All I had to do was get angry for you to finally admit you want me."

"Fuck you," I spat.

He pulled back just enough to let me glimpse the heat crowding his eyes. "That *is* what happens next, yes."

I studied him. He licked his lips, his eyes fanatical and gleaming, and I was lost. Utterly and completely. I had never wanted anything the way I wanted him, with every molecule. Because prince or not, he was still *him*, and I craved him like I craved my next breath.

This prick.

"Fine," I said. "Do it. But you're not allowed to enjoy it."

Before my lips finished shaping the words, he was devouring me again. This time, it wasn't a kiss, but something beyond that. A starburst, exploding me into blazing need.

"I promise to hate every second," he said against my lips, then grabbed my ass and hoisted me, his muscles bunching as he carried me to the counter and set me down. Our mouths went to war. I clutched at him, barely able to make sense of our fevered whimpers. I didn't know whose they were, only that I was drowning. Falling. Flying apart into a wondrous expanse of crackling heat and want, want, want.

His hands roamed the contours of my breasts and belly, and I pawed at him with equally frantic fingers. He yanked my legs apart and pressed close, grinding his desire against me. He kissed me so deeply I wondered if he could taste the hunger I'd been bottling up for weeks.

Oh, goddess. He was going to annihilate me. I could already tell. An inch, a mile, and so much more besides.

His scalding fingers skated down the outsides of my thighs. He gripped the hem of my nightgown and lifted.

"Don't stop kissing me," I gasped into his mouth. "Don't you dare fucking stop."

He answered with a hungry sound and moved his hands to my neckline, instead. Then he gripped the keyhole closure and just...

...ripped. Down the middle. Like it was easy. Like it was nothing.

His mouth never left mine as he flung the halves of my nightgown apart. Air hit my bare skin, and I forced my legs wide, opening to him, granting him every scrap of control. His tongue plunged into my mouth, and I bit down hard enough to earn a groan. My hands scrabbled at his back, fingernails etching lines into his skin.

I'd broken some invisible barrier. Strayed far beyond the point of surrender. But I might as well wreak some havoc now that I'd resolved to climb onto the pyre and set myself ablaze.

Kai's rough hands collared my waist. He finally broke the kiss and pressed me back until my elbows hit the counter. We stared at each other, panting. The marble wicked the warmth from my skin.

He perused the length of me, his dilated eyes lingering on the swell of my breasts, then the valley between my legs.

"You're exquisite," he said. "Exceptional in every way."

Before I could respond, he dropped to his knees. I barely had time to coil in anticipation before his tongue slid against my wetness. No pause. No break. Just dazzling destruction unleashed.

I cried out as my head fell back. Sweet Zephyrine, if I'd thought that thing he did with his tongue felt good on my neck, letting him do it *there* made me want to levitate off the counter. He licked and lapped and sucked. My eyes crossed behind closed lids, my entire body quaking as the void threatened to engulf me.

Then he slipped two fingers into me and I nearly rocketed free of my skin. The boundaries of myself collapsed to a shimmer.

He kept going. And going. Until I started to fold inward, a star verging on implosion.

"Oh, *fuck*," I gibbered at the ceiling. "Fuckfuckfuck, you have to stop. Please. Or..."

His tongue slowed as his fingers disappeared. When I opened my eyes, he stood between my splayed legs, his face hard as he yanked his breech-laces from their eyelets. "Or what?"

"I'll come." I sounded as parched as a person could get.

"The problem being?"

"I want to do it with you. Around you."

"Well." He flashed a half-smile, this one rigid with promise. "That doesn't sound *entirely* unenjoyable."

He jerked his pants down, then gripped my thighs and yanked me to the counter's edge. My nightgown rumpled beneath me, still caught around my elbows, the torn halves trailing into the darkness. A glance into the mirrors offered me a thousand versions of sculpted magnificence—the rippled texture of Kai's ribcage and the high globes of his ass. The creamy, cabled length of his thighs. The rounded crowns of his shoulders, bronzed from the sun.

My breath thinned to a standstill. I slid my attention back to him, then downward, to where he'd already lined himself up.

My tongue went dry. Goddess, it would hurt for a second. Maybe for a few. And right then, I could have wept, because I absolutely needed it to. I needed to feel him, all of him, needed to transmute this bottomless craving into something I could name, something I could lose myself in.

He paused, one hand drifting to my waist. It was the first tender touch all night, but I knew it wouldn't last. It was a prelude, the last lull before he unleashed all the ferocity caged into the straining lines of his body.

"Gentle?" he said. "Or rough?"

"Rough." I widened my legs. "If you're gentle, I'll kill you."

"Gods. My vicious wife. I was hoping you'd say that."

Wife. The word bounced around in my head, nonsensical, because hadn't he signed the annulment already? I gathered a breath to ask, but his grip clamped around my waist, and he buried himself in me in one clean thrust. Everything in my head vaporized to white-hot silence.

Fucking.

Hell.

He eased out, then drove in again. My spine arched, bending me back onto the marble, baring my throat to him. He filled me up painfully, perfectly, oh-so-right, and I made a sound that might have been a word or an appeal or maybe the death cry of every moment in which I'd resisted him, probably knowing the whole time that I would end up right here, entirely at his mercy.

He surged into me. A groan tore from his throat, delicious enough to feast on for weeks. He wasn't fast, but he wasn't slow, either. Just forceful and unforgiving, and it was everything I'd wanted and more.

More, more, so much more, because this wasn't the quiet fulfillment of Merron or the others, but something knife-edged, a totality of pleasure that pushed me toward some desolate brink. Kai claimed me again and again, and I began to unravel, the layers of myself falling away with every buck of my body against the counter.

"Squeeze my throat." My whisper was barely audible over the sound of my own fade to extinction. "Just a little."

He obeyed, circling my neck with a calloused palm.

Pressure thinned my airway—not much, but enough to ignite bright stars in my vision. Every sensation daisy-chained itself to the next. Weight became desperation became pleasure became ecstasy.

Oh, goddess. I was going to die, in bliss. And yet I'd never felt more alive.

My awareness shrank to the scrape of breath against silence, the dearth of air in my lungs, the gift of Kai's body in mine. He gave himself to me, swift and certain. Somewhere within me, greed sprouted wings and grew a heartbeat of its own. I cared about nothing but him, the friction of him, and more and faster and yes, yes, yes, just like that.

Then he stopped, abruptly. The pressure at my throat vanished as he withdrew. I was empty, suddenly. So empty it hurt.

"No," I wailed, propping myself up on my elbows. At first, I thought he meant to punish me, but he gathered me up like a ragdoll, pulling the shredded nightgown from my arms and throwing it aside. He carried me to the bedroom, then tossed me onto the bed.

Before the mattress had even finished bouncing, he was on me again, inside me, the angle even deeper this time, though I would've said such a thing was impossible.

My eyes rolled back. He curled over me, fastening one hand around the nape of my neck as he drove into me, faster now, brutal and beautiful and consuming.

I let go. Between one heartbeat and the next, I dissolved into a cataclysm of pleasure. He was a paradise of heat and firmness, a living artwork I couldn't stop touching.

That angle. Oh, shit, that angle. He was exactly where he needed to be. Nothing else mattered. Just him, on top of me. Around me. In me.

That abyss surfaced from the deep, coming to claim me, and I bucked my hips, wanting nothing more than to fling myself into its blissful black reaches.

"Come for me, sweet wife," he whispered, and bit down on my earlobe.

That silver flash of pain joined the roar inside me, giving me the last push I needed to crest the rise and go careening down the other side. I spun apart, a billion star-studded pieces cascading through the dark. Wave after wave consumed me as I called his name.

And then he was doing the same, mincing my name with silken curses as he buried himself deep and stayed there, his whole body contracting. The pinnacle lasted and lasted and finally released him. He melted atop me, an inescapable weight.

I lay there, boneless, my legs twitching. Aftershocks rippled through me.

Moments passed. Or minutes. Maybe a lifetime.

"Fuck," he said, imbuing the word with at least ten times as many vowels as it actually had. "That was..."

"Awful," I hurried out, unwilling to hear anything else.

His chest heaved with formless laughter. "Right. Precisely the word I was looking for. I don't know that I've ever suffered anything that torturous."

I slid my hands along the planes of his back, finding him slicked with even more sweat than his lawn battle had earned him. Something about that delighted me, knowing he'd had to work harder for this than for anything else. "It was...unique, though," I said. "As experiences go."

"Yes, well. I would've called it singular, myself."

Singular. Even that was an understatement. Zephyrine knew I loved sex, but I hadn't known it could feel like *that.* Nor did I know how I was supposed to content myself with the stock variety again, now that I did.

He lifted his head. Sweat dimmed his hair to dark bronze while a rosy afterglow lit his face. "I suppose we'll have to do it again. See if it can get even worse."

My stomach tightened. Which verged on comical, considering I'd just had the best orgasm of my life, five minutes ago. "You're right. You'll probably have to try everything you can think of."

One eyebrow kicked up. "Oh, really? *Everything?* Because I can be surprisingly creative, when I put my mind to it."

A flutter rolled through me. "Is that a threat?"

"Do you want it to be?"

I lifted my chin. "Maybe."

"Fine." He chuffed a soft exhale. "Then yes. But you'll have to tell me where the line is."

Something twinged beneath my ribs. "There isn't one. Not tonight. You can do whatever you want to me."

"*Anything?*"

"Well, within reason. I'll tell you if it's too much."

His expression darkened into something diabolical, and my pulse gathered speed like a stone bouncing downhill. I might regret this in the morning. Goddess, I hoped I would regret this in the morning.

"What about you?" I whispered. "Any hard lines I should know about?"

His blue stare skewered me to the bed. "Yes. There is one thing. Something I absolutely, unequivocally refuse to do with you tonight."

"What's that?"

"Sleep," he said.

I squeaked, then caught myself and glowered. "Fine. I guess I can live with that. If I absolutely have to."

28.

I lost track of the many times and ways in which Kai dismantled me, only to piece me back together and do it all over again.

Some things, I committed to permanent memory, like the way his every muscle contracted when I sucked on his birthmark, or how his neck arched when I wrapped my hands around it and rode him like it was my only purpose in life.

Eventually, a dull yellow glow brightened the windowpane, and Kai brought me over the edge one final time. I knew this was the end because he didn't join me, just slowed to a stop while the blissful ripples ebbed from my limbs. He hovered, smiling like a cat who'd just nabbed a whole coal-mine's worth of canaries.

Once my vision stopped wobbling, I oriented myself to the north star of those blue, blue eyes. Goddess, but he was magnificent. So much that a flood of tenderness broke loose inside me. I tucked a lock of damp hair back from his forehead, my heart fracturing.

"Well?" he murmured.

"Well what?"

"Are you willing to admit you're half in love with me *now*?"

Sharpness bristled beneath my ribs. "No. Just because you fucked me stupid doesn't mean I don't still hate you."

"Hmm. But you *are* willing to admit I fucked you stupid?"

I paused. "I'll admit that inexhaustible energy is a lot more useful than I ever realized. And that trench-digging *isn't* actually your greatest talent."

He laughed and kissed me, so much differently this time, with a softness that made my eyes prickle, and a familiarity that made me feel as if we'd condensed years of mapping each other's bodies into a single night. I swore we somehow had, especially with him still sheathed in me like this, our tongues tangled as he bound our bodies together in two places at once.

I gave myself over to it, etching the moment into memory, tattooing the perfection of it onto my heart. Because this was the beginning and the end, both.

When he pulled back, a tear slipped from between my lashes, which I hurried to wipe away.

"Lioness." A crinkled formed between his eyes. "Are you crying?"

"No." I sniffled. "Why would I be crying?"

"I don't know. You tell me."

"Okay, one, I'm not crying, and two, I don't talk about feelings, remember?"

I expected him to smile, but the light in his face dimmed. "Don't do that. Don't hide from me."

"Why not?" I scoffed. "It's over. I'm not your wife anymore. An hour from now, you'll be married to Amryssa."

He studied me for long moments. "You think you're not my wife?"

"I *know* I'm not. We signed the annulment, didn't we? Before all this."

His face went carefully blank. He eased out of me, then crawled off the mattress and gazed down. He was a heavenly mess, rumpled and sticky and crisscrossed by scratches, only half of which I could claim responsibility for, the other half having resulted from his efforts with the lawn.

The bite marks, though...those were all mine.

"Don't be angry." Kai ducked into the bathroom and returned with the annulment certificate. He held it out.

My pulse stopped, then restarted, double-time. I stared at the offering, then up into his face.

"It wouldn't have mattered, anyway," he said, neutral. "It isn't my name on here."

I nodded, not daring to form an opinion on what that meant, and took the paper. When I didn't unfold it right away, he said, "I'll go clean up."

Good. Yes. That was easier. I didn't want him to see my reaction. "Okay."

He retreated. When the bathroom door clicked, I swallowed my jangling nerves and opened the annulment certificate. And found...nothing. Just a blank, waiting line where his signature should have been. Or Kyven's, rather.

I couldn't help myself. A choking sob rushed up my throat. The ache between my legs intensified, proof that no matter where he went or who he pretended to marry, I would be his wife. Even if no one realized it.

I yielded to a bewildering crush of emotion and wept.

But only for a minute. By the time Kai emerged from the bathroom, I'd dried my cheeks, though the wariness in his face told me redness still rimmed my eyes.

"You're angry at me," he said.

"No." I waved the paper. "But you do need to sign this now."

He hesitated. "I will, but it means nothing. It annuls a marriage that never took place. It has no effect on ours."

"I realize that. But nobody else does, so you have to pretend to be Kyven, still. You have to marry Amryssa and walk off into a night-mare. Then I'll declare you dead and take her to Hightower and... Everyone'll get what they want. Even Vick. He can go play bandit chief to his heart's content."

Kai stared at me as if searching for the lie in my words.

I lifted my chin and let him. He could look as deeply as he liked—there was nothing to find.

"That's still what you want?" he finally said. "Even after all that?"

"It'll always be what I want. Amryssa needs to go somewhere

Zephyrine can't reach her. And you need to go to Fairmont. Visit your last territory. Collect your last accent. You know, experience everything."

"And then...what?" He shifted his weight. "Just never see my wife again?"

And there it was. The question that made my insides ice over. I was a frozen tundra, a blank white space awaiting the inscription of an answer.

Except I *knew* the answer, because it didn't matter whether I wanted him, or if he wanted me. My duty was to Amryssa, first and foremost. Not to Kai, or even myself.

"Who knows?" I said, trying for levity. "Maybe we'll run into each other again someday. Maybe when we're eighty."

His eyes darkened. "What if I don't want to?"

I recoiled, more stung than I had any right to be. "Well, that's rude. I mean, it's one thing to think it, but you don't have to say so."

He waved a hand. "Don't be absurd. I don't mean I never want to see you again. I mean I want to leave here with you, not without."

I weighed that. "As in...what? Disappear *together*?"

"Mmm-hmm. And since I know you won't go anywhere without Amryssa, we could bring her with us. Go to Fairmont together. Because really, I'd like nothing more than to keep keeping you up all night. Even if the first time was the most wretched experience of my life."

Thickness clogged my throat. I opened my mouth but couldn't force anything out.

"Romantic, I know," he said. "Try not to swoon."

I couldn't stop myself. I *was* swooning, succumbing to a rush that started in my toes and fountained upward. Except...no.

This was no different than Merron's offer. A temptation that might promise bliss, but wouldn't last, because nothing ever did. In the end, everyone always left me. Everyone but Amryssa.

"No." I hated how broken I sounded. "I have to take Amryssa to Hightower, where she'll be cared for. Not off on some lark to Fairmont, where anything might happen."

He eyed me, speculative. "So you're refusing me because I'm not a prince?"

"No. I love that you're not a prince. I love—" I cut myself off, changing tack. "I like you better this way, actually. Now that the shock has worn off. I like knowing you're like me and not like them. But I'm going to give Amryssa the best life I can, no matter the cost."

"All right. Then I'll go to Hightower with you."

"What?" I squeaked. "No. You can't."

His brow furrowed. "Why not?"

"Because...well, look at you." I waved a hand.

He glanced down, taking in his own awe-inspiring nudity. His expression betrayed not a sliver of comprehension.

"You look like Kyven but aren't." I rolled my hand in the air, trying to lead him to the obvious. "Don't you think people would find that odd? Besides, Amryssa can't lie. When people ask questions, she'll answer, and everyone will realize she never married Kyven at all. This whole thing would unravel."

He crossed his arms and slitted his gaze. "You've thought this through."

I picked at a stray thread fraying from the coverlet. "I have." Maybe without actually meaning to. But if I agreed to be his, then what? I'd cease to be one of the challenges he loved so dearly, and his attention would wander.

Which would kill me. This time, being abandoned would actually kill me.

For long moments, Kai said nothing. When I looked up, speculation had dawned in his eyes.

"What?" I said, wary. "What're you thinking?"

"Only that you can make this as difficult as humanly possible, if you like. But I'm up to the challenge. I'm up to *any* challenge. Because you know that when I set my sights on something, I'm relentless. I keep on trying, until it's mine."

I attempted to shrug off his words. How was he so freaking *sure* of himself all the time? Especially when I'd just flat-out rejected him?

"I'm not some kind of carnival game. You can't just keep tossing the ring until you land it around the bottle."

"Oh, but I can," he said. "Watch me."

"No." My voice rose. "I'm not a thing to be conquered."

He snorted. "If you had no desire to be conquered, you should never have conquered me, first."

I swallowed a fresh flood of emotion, but nothing about my silence felt quiet. It was more like internally screaming into a pillow.

I shoved the annulment certificate at him. "Look, just sign this and marry Amryssa, okay?"

"I will, if that's what you want. But this conversation isn't over."

"It is," I snapped.

"On the contrary. It's just getting started."

"It's not. This whole *thing* is over. This marriage."

"No," he said, with force. "Not unless you look me in the eye and tell me you're not in love with me. Half in love, even. Say that with utter sincerity, and I'll leave it be."

I flashed my teeth. "I already told you I'm not going to admit that."

"I'm not asking you to admit it," he countered. "I'm asking you to deny it. Tell me no part of you feels for me what I feel for you."

I scrambled off the bed, trying to escape the desperation percolating in my ribcage. What was I doing arguing over nothing, anyway? "This is stupid. I have to go. It's past sunrise, and Amryssa's probably already awake."

"You're hiding again."

Anger sparked beneath my breastbone. Anger and something deeper, something I didn't want to look at in the eyes. I marched up to him, my soles dragging across the carpets.

He smiled, so smugly it made me want to slap him again.

Or kiss him. Oh, goddess, I really did want to kiss him again. I wanted *everything* again, even though he was already all over me—his sweat, his scent, his essence. And still, I craved more. I wanted to rub it all in, soak him up until he became a permanent fixture in my pores.

What a useless, pointless wish. "Get out of my way."

"No."

I crossed my arms, mirroring his pose, though my chest didn't flex and bulge the way his did. "You're being ridiculous."

"Well, we both know that's nothing new." His eyes gleamed a challenge. "And all you have to do is say five words. 'Kai, I don't love you.' That should be easy, considering how adamant you've been about hating me."

I tried to do exactly that, then gave him a silent snarl when the words wouldn't come. They lodged in my chest, nowhere near making it to my throat.

Because I *did* love him. Of course I did—halfway, or all the way, or who fucking cared, really? It didn't matter. This wasn't *about* me.

"I'm going now," I snapped.

A flash of victory illuminated his face, and... Gods among us, I knew that look. Great. Now I would never get rid of him.

Thankfully, when I angled past, he let me go. I stomped away, whisking my clothes from the floor and slamming the bathroom door. Curses sprang from my lips as I dressed.

By the time I reemerged, the bedroom was blessedly empty. The annulment certificate lay on the bed, complete with a second signature. I snatched it up on my way to Amryssa's room.

When I threw open her door, she beamed.

"What?" I snarled. I'd never been so short with her. "Just what the fuck is so fucking amusing to everybody this morning?"

She tried to smother her laughter with a hand. With no success whatsoever. "I'm glad to see you in such high spirits."

I glowered. "I'm not in high spirits. I'm in pissed spirits."

"But why? You're married now. Completely. And were incredibly loud about it, might I add."

"Oh. Gods." Warmth drained from my cheeks. "You heard that?"

"It was impossible not to. At least the first time. Well, and the second. And the third. And the—"

"All right." I flung a palm in the air. "You've made your point. Just..." I cast a frantic glance around, then remembered the annulment and thrust the paper at her. "Here. This came, and it's signed. Which makes Kai not my husband anymore. In a few minutes, he'll be *your* husband."

That sobered her. The amusement dropped from her face. "You and I both know that's not valid."

That gave me pause. I couldn't fathom how she knew that.

"I told you weeks ago he wasn't who we thought," she continued.

I stiffened, but she was right. She *had* told me, and I'd deemed it nonsense. For years, I'd deemed her musings nonsense, when all this time, she'd seen things more clearly than I had. Maybe because she was divine, or maybe just because I was an idiot.

Either way, I shrank inward, collapsing on myself. "Okay, yes, you did. And I should've listened. All this time, I should've listened to you. I'm sorry I haven't been better about that."

"It's all right." She gifted me with a smile I definitely didn't deserve. "You've done your best."

"I've...tried." I went to the bed, suddenly meek, and sat. "I hope you know that everything I've done, I've done for you."

"I do know. Though I wish you'd put yourself first, sometimes."

"I have, though. I do." I heaved a sigh, my anger spent. "I mean, that's all last night was, Am. Me being selfish. Because I definitely shouldn't have had sex with your husband all those times. I just...I don't know. I couldn't help myself. I'm sorry."

"I'm not," she said.

A fleeting smile passed over my lips. "Well, whatever. It's finished. Now we'll get you to Hightower and start over. I'll do a better job of listening to you, and you'll eat all the food we can find, and things'll get better. There won't be any nightmares to deal with. No swamp goddesses whispering your name."

Her gray eyes turned solemn, her regard steady. "And you'll be happy there."

"Yes. You, too. I just need you to marry Kai, okay? Without telling anyone who he is. Or isn't. Please."

She pressed her lips together. "All right. Then I'll wear the dress, if you want. Stand in the library. Say the words. I'll even let him kiss me, if it pleases you."

I swallowed hard. It would do the exact opposite of please me, but whatever.

I'd survive.

Within minutes, I was standing at Amryssa's vanity, pinning up her hair while she fiddled with her gown. It was the same dress I'd worn months ago, and I tried to shut out the memories it evoked.

But I could practically feel the scratch of the cypress vine around my wrist. The weight of the marriage crown circling my scalp.

My thoughts wandered. What would've happened if I'd stopped Kai from untying our vine that night? If we'd left it on until morning, as intended, would Zephyrine have blessed our union?

Goddess. I shook myself. *Get a grip.*

I forced my focus back to my task, pinning a crown of braids atop Amryssa's head.

Her gaze caught mine in the mirror. She gave me a hopeful smile. "Ready?"

I smiled back. "I think I'm supposed to be the one asking you that."

"Oh, but I've been ready since the beginning. Or willing, at least. I'm just glad that this time, I don't have to be afraid."

My smile wavered, but she was right. This wedding was a definitive upgrade from the last one, seeing as how it didn't involve me having to murder anybody.

She dropped her eyes and smoothed the white lace over her lap. "I do wish my mother were here, though."

"Your mother? As in...Zephyrine?"

"No. My *mother*. I wish... Well, I know this wedding doesn't actually mean anything. But I wish she could've seen it, anyway. It would've brought her joy."

My chest ached, and I gave her bony shoulders a squeeze. "I wish that, too. But...do you want the diary, maybe? You could read her letter again. Before we go downstairs."

Her smile returned. "I'd like that."

"Then I'll go get it. It's in my room."

I moved to the door. When I opened it, there stood Olivian, his fist raised to knock. He turned his nose up and sniffed, as if my very existence offended his sensibilities. "Did you sign the annulment?"

I ironed out the sneer already taking shape on my face. "Of course. It's there on the bed."

"Good. Then find somewhere else to be for a minute. I need a moment with my daughter."

I flashed him a cold smile and slipped past.

In my room, the bathroom door was closed. Most likely, Kai had already inhaled his morning allotment of bacon and returned to put on his wedding attire. I approached the closed door, regretting my caustic words from earlier.

I'd simply have to explain that we had no future. That my future had been decided the moment I'd met Amryssa.

I lifted my hand to knock, but a sound stayed my hand. Paper rustled behind me, like a page being flipped.

I turned. "I thought you were in—"

My words died on my tongue. Because there was Vick, sitting on my bed, casual as can be. And he was reading the Lady Marche's diary.

29

Cold hit the back of my neck like an icy hand.

Vick smiled, as foxlike as ever. "Well, well. Isn't this interesting? It turns out I was right about this house having secrets."

When his eyes dropped to my belt, my heartbeat skipped. My hand found my dagger, as if I could shield it from the cut of those green eyes.

"You know," he said, "magic like that would be useful in the swamp. Indispensable, even. What could I achieve, with Zephyrine at my disposal? How many people could I help?"

I shuddered. He sounded...hungry.

"This knife's mine," I said.

"Not for much longer." Vick swung his legs off the bed and stood.

But his bearing wobbled. Clearly, the magic I'd zapped into him yesterday hadn't left him *entirely* unaffected.

Behind me, the bathroom door opened, and Kai appeared in my peripheral, clad in white. He inhaled sharply. "Vick."

"Kai." Vick's tone was cold.

"Why're you here? What do you want?"

Vick laughed. "Want? To leave this horrible house, mostly. But to do it with your girlfriend's dagger. *And* this book. Imagine what everyone will think when I come back with these."

My composure frayed. He could *not* take the dagger. It was my failsafe for Amryssa—the power to protect her, given physical form. "No. Over my dead body."

Vick's eyebrows rose, his hand straying to his sword.

Okay. That had probably been a poor choice of words.

Kai stepped in front of me. "If you so much as *look* at my wife," he said, "I'll gut you."

Vick laughed. "Oh? And with what sword skills? The ones you've played at on stage?" He made a few mock slashes and parries in the air.

Kai's pearlescent tailcoat glinted in the sunlight. "I don't need skill. I'm taller than you, and stronger. And you're looking somewhat worse for wear, my friend. Legs a bit wobbly, this morning?"

Vick's lips peeled back in a snarl. "I never liked you. You always thought you were so special. Swooping in and talking Charley into putting you in charge when we all know it should've been me."

"I know no such thing," Kai said. "And if you ask me, you want it for all the wrong reasons."

Vick sneered, but the insult had clearly landed, because a moment later, he charged.

A shriek tore from my chest as Kai surged forward. They collided in a whirl of flexing limbs and labored breaths. Vick swung; Kai swung back. Fists connected, followed by grunts of pain.

Fear slicked my insides. I could hardly tell what was happening, only that Kai seemed to have a minor advantage. Or he would have, if he hadn't been so focused on keeping Vick's sword in its sheath. Every time the man went for his blade, Kai wrenched his hand away. Which told me that if the blade came out, this would be over.

I edged sideways and grabbed a candelabra off my vanity. I resolved to whack Vick over the head with it, cause some damage. But they were grappling in earnest now, the fight carrying them out of the room and down the hall.

I dashed after them. Amryssa's door creaked open as I passed. Olivian emerged, shouting for someone to explain themselves.

At the top of the spiral stair, I slowed, because Kai had Vick's chest pinned to the wall. "I want you gone," he growled. "Not just from this house, but out of Oceansgate. I'll name someone else as my successor. Anyone but you."

Vick's expression darkened. Kai took him by the scruff and marched him down the stairs. I dropped the candelabra and followed, my breath a fiery torrent. We would throw Vick out. Tell Merron and the stewards to make sure he didn't come back.

And it would've worked, maybe, if Vick hadn't halted at the top of the grand staircase, forcing Kai to stop with him. When Vick turned his head, chilly calculation flashed in his eyes.

"Watch out," I warned. "He's going to—"

Too late. Vick flung himself down the steps, taking Kai with him.

They tumbled, limbs tangling. Kai's coattails pinwheeled as bodies thudded against the carpeted stairs. I winced and bolted after them, coming to a halt when they settled at the bottom.

Because somehow, Vick had unsheathed his sword.

And now he stood behind Kai, his blade pressed to my husband's throat.

30.

Behind me, Olivian bellowed. "What's the meaning of this?"

I didn't move, too caught in the grip of my terror. Kai held my eyes, but the way he craned his head told me some part of him believed Vick would actually cut his throat.

My stomach hollowed out. No. No, no, no. If Vick killed Kai, I'd hunt him to the ends of the earth. I'd murder him in the most inhumane way possible, then feed the leftovers to the alligators.

I stumbled down another step.

"Just stop right there, Princess." Vick flashed a smile. "I don't want that dagger of yours getting too close."

I halted, my blood congealing in my veins. Kai gazed at me without blinking. *Steady*, he seemed to say. *I'll be all right.*

But *I* wouldn't. I wanted to throw up. Or pass out. Or hurl my dagger and bury the blade between Vick's eyes, which I probably would have tried for, if he hadn't been standing so close to a man I'd rather have lopped off my own hand than hurt.

"What's the meaning of this?" Olivian yelled to Vick, the question even frostier than the fear chewing through my insides. "Do you have any idea what the penalty is for cutting a royal throat? For even *threatening* to cut a royal throat?"

Vick snorted. "Considering your lawmen are a distant memory, nothing. We all know no one's coming. Besides, this is between me and the keymistress."

"The *keymistress*? What does she have to do with this?"

"Very little, actually." Vick's smile turned feral. "Except that I want that dagger of hers."

My grip snuck to my waist. The knife hummed, Zephyrine's magic flowing into me.

Stand down, I ordered Vick. *Lower your blade and step away from him.*

His forehead creased. His sword dipped, but stabilized a moment later.

I screamed a silent curse. Just like with Kai at breakfast that morning, it wasn't enough.

"Try that again, Princess, and you'll be mopping his blood off the floor. Now, hands off the knife. I know what it can do."

My molars ground together, but I raised spread hands.

"What in goddess's name are you talking about?" Olivian said. "That dagger is just an heirloom. It's worthless."

"Oh, really?" Vick snapped. He gestured to the diary, which had somehow survived the scuffle tucked within his waistband. "Because your wife's journal would suggest otherwise. So would this." He flipped up his tunic to reveal a livid bruise where I'd unleashed the blade's magic on him yesterday.

Olivian made an enraged sound. "You read my wife's diary?"

"I did. And now you can either command your keymistress to hand over her dagger, or bid your precious prince and your fancy little wedding goodbye."

My heartbeat swelled to fill my entire throat. I couldn't breathe, couldn't think, couldn't see anything but the lethal silver line indenting Kai's neck.

"Go fuck yourself." Olivian's bellow sounded like stones rattling in a can. "No man reads my wife's private diary, and no one tells me what to do in my own house."

Vick's eyes narrowed. His sword-hand flicked.

A scream tore from my throat. "No!"

Kai's eyes widened. The blade bit through his skin, and a crimson dribble slid down his neck. Blood flowered on his white collar, but he was still standing. Still breathing, thank Zephyrine. Thank every god that had ever walked this earth.

"I'll give you anything," I heard myself blubber. "Just don't hurt him. For the love of all that's holy, please don't hurt him."

"Harlowe," Olivian warned.

Vick made an impatient, get-on-with-it gesture. "The dagger, then. Hurry up."

My stomach pitched and rocked. I grappled with my belt, scrabbling at the buckle until it came undone.

"Harlowe," Olivian roared. "Don't."

"Shut. Up," I hissed, then ripped off the belt and tossed the entire bundle down the stairs. I didn't even look at where it landed, because I couldn't wrench my gaze from Kai's. I needed him to be okay. I needed him not to die.

"Why, thank you." With an exaggerated smile, Vick toed the belt and dagger across the parquet, then snatched them up without lowering his blade from Kai's throat.

Something moved in the background. Lunk and Miss Quist, along with Merron and the stewards, wandered from the library. No doubt they'd gathered for the wedding, then heard the commotion.

"Nobody move," I said. "Just let Vick go. Let him leave."

Olivian started down the stairs. "He isn't going anywhere."

Vick flicked his sword again. "Stay back."

Kai grunted. More blood leaked from his throat. I muffled my cry in a fist and came within a hairsbreadth of vomiting.

Olivian stopped, two steps down from me now, vibrating with fury. "Unhand him, you conniving little shit. You have your knife."

"Oh, me, conniving?" Vick arced his brows. "That's rich. If you think *I'm* conniving, you should hear the story the prince here has to tell you."

Oh, no. All my blood dived into my feet and stayed there. I knew exactly where Vick was going with this. How he planned to divert everyone's attention long enough to escape.

But...I wouldn't stop him. If I had to choose between Kai's life and getting Amryssa to Hightower—well, I'd choose both. I'd just have to take my best friend to the capital on my own.

"Tell them, *Kyven*," Vick said. "I'm sure the seneschal would love to know who you really are."

Olivian's focus shifted. "What in Zephyrine's name does that mean?"

Kai's unfailing half-smile kicked into place. "I'm afraid you won't like it."

Vick's attention darted—first to Olivian, then to Merron and the stewards—before settling on the front door. "Tell them. Don't make me cut it out of you."

He applied pressure, more blood leaking from Kai's neck. A grunt tore from my husband's chest as he raised splayed hands. "I'm no prince," he rushed out. "All right? The real Kyven Windermere died on the Oceansgate road when his carriage overturned. I'm just...well. An actor. Here at the urging of the gentleman who's about to saw my vocal cords in half."

The stewards gasped. Olivian's hands curled into fists at his sides. "An...*actor*?"

I wanted to scream. *That* was the important part in all this? Really?

Kai gave a *sorry-not-sorry* shrug.

"And you thought you could marry my daughter?" the seneschal said, low and trembling. "You thought my Amryssa would marry an *actor*?"

Kai's gaze slid to mine. "What can I say? I'm nothing if not optimistic. And I do have a habit of shooting for the stars."

"Get. Out," Olivian said. Then, louder, "Out! Get out of my house!"

Vick shoved Kai toward us and ran, taking the dagger and diary with him. He hauled open the doors and disappeared before Olivian had even made it down the stairs. The stewards hovered, frozen.

Meanwhile, relief screamed through me, so complete that my knees buckled. I half-slid, half-scrambled toward Kai, who just stood there, bleeding, like he had exactly zero plans to retreat from Olivian's advance.

I made it between them just in time. I skidded to a stop and faced the seneschal with my arms flung out. "Don't touch him."

"Lioness," Kai said from behind me. "There's really no need."

Olivian lowered his head, the tendons of his neck sharp enough to slice. "Get out of my way."

"No."

"Go ahead," Kai said. "Let him hit me, if he likes."

"No," I gritted out. "Only I get to do that. If *he* does, he'll break your face, and you won't be nearly as pretty, afterward."

Kai laughed softly, and gods, I wanted to drink the sound. Build a shrine to it, because it meant he was alive, that he would be fine, that he could walk out of here and not look back and live a whole life in Fairmont or wherever the hell he ended up and never think about this place again.

"Just go," I said.

"Go?" He sounded offended. "Surely you don't think I'm *leaving*?"

Olivian flashed his teeth. "Step aside, girl. Or I *will* go through you. He tried to marry my daughter, and he'll answer for it."

Oh, that was it. I'd had enough of the threats. Of Olivian's bullying and glowering and stomping around. I stepped in and shoved my finger in his face, exactly the way I'd dreamed of doing for years. "Just stop it, will you? Stop throwing your weight around. Stop intimidating people all the time. Stop refusing to look past the end of your own stubborn nose, and give me thirty seconds to talk to Kai without you threatening us, you brutish, tyrannical, hate-mongering *failure* of a seneschal and a father."

Olivian jerked back, his eyes wide.

I shook my finger again, scarcely daring to believe I'd actually cowed him. "Look. You can throw him out, if you want. It's your house. But let me talk to my husband first, for pity's sake."

He blinked, his green eyes traveling between us. "Your...husband?"

"Yes." Acid dripped from my tone.

His mouth twisted. "But the annulment."

"Didn't matter by the time it got signed. And it wasn't Kai's name on that paper, anyway."

Olivian took that in. "You're married to this charlatan? Of your own choosing?"

"I am."

"You *care* about him?"

"Yes," I hissed.

He made as if to come at us, then stopped. His attention flickered to the corner, and something surfaced in his expression. A glimmer I recognized.

The Lady Marche. She must have been hovering again, because Olivian's eyes glinted. Some whisper—some ghost of an emotion— reached him, because he grunted and turned away. "Fine. But he's not staying. You can leave with him if you like, but I won't tolerate him under this roof."

My chest inflated as I let my hands fall. "Thank you."

"Thirty. Seconds. That's all."

I whirled and grabbed Kai's arm, then towed him past the bewildered stewards. At the doors, I grabbed the lapels of his wedding jacket.

He peered down, his infuriating smile as crooked as ever. Ruby slickness coated one side of his throat, but he paid the wounds no attention. "Well, that was rather dramatic. I think I preferred my first wedding, to be honest."

A buzz filled my ears. This man had almost died, right in front of me. How *dare* he? "For once in your life, can you stop making jokes? It's a terrible way to say goodbye."

"Goodbye?" He stiffened. "What, you're just going to let him toss me out?"

"Of course I am. It's not my decision."

"Well, no. But whether you come with me is."

Now I stiffened. "What? No. Olivian won't let Amryssa go, so...you can't possibly think I'd leave her. And I've already told you how this ends. I said so upstairs."

He stared into my eyes. Something built inside me, a growing shadow that tinted my vision dark. He'd almost died. He'd nearly left me, permanently, in a way that would've replayed itself on the insides of my eyelids until I was old and wrinkled. Even then, I still would've seen him leaving me. Making a graceless exit from my life, never to be patched over or apologized for, just borne forever. He would've carved an unhealing wound into me that would've chased me into old age and beyond.

The nerve. The unbelievable audacity of this man.

"What, no last-minute change of heart?" he said. "No third-act realization about how you can't live without me?"

"No." I nearly choked on the word. "This isn't one of your plays."

"But what if I want it to end like one?"

"It doesn't. You were always going to leave, and I was always going to let you. I was *always* going to put Amryssa first. And now I have to get her to Hightower, some other way. So go. To Fairmont, like you wanted. See your last territory. Get your last accent."

A scowl marred his perfect features. "That doesn't matter to me nearly as much as you seem to think it does."

I held that wide-sky gaze. Oh, goddess. Part of me was crumbling, collapsing, each word from my mouth a wave battering at my resolve. Except...he'd almost *left* me. The knowledge was like a fist around my heart. I had to hide, had to get away. "Just think of me sometimes, okay?"

His expression darkened. "This is absurd."

"It's not."

"Come with me."

I swallowed the stone in my throat. "No. I already told you. I've been telling you this whole time. That isn't how this works."

His face hardened. His eyes chilled, but he straightened, tugging at his ruined coat. "So that's it, then? You're absolutely certain?"

"Yes."

"Well." He sniffed. "Even I can tell when I'm not wanted."

A steely weight descended on my shoulders. Goddess, I couldn't manage another word. If I tried, I would break.

He leaned in and kissed my temple. Tears invaded my throat, but I walled them off.

"Goodbye, then, just Harlowe," he murmured.

"Goodbye, just Kai."

He scanned the great hall, then nodded at those assembled. "It's been a pleasure."

Nobody said anything. After a moment, Ky turned and walked into the glowing morning. For the second time in my life, I watched a white-clad back fade into the distance.

I stood there until the beacon of his jacket winked out.

I didn't cry. I closed the front doors, then trudged past Merron, who shook his head at me, then the stewards. Past an oddly silent Olivian. Then up past Amryssa, who stood on the stairs, a vision in white lace, a glinting, priceless jewel in this tarnished crown. She reached for my arm, but I shrugged her off.

Only once I reached the safety of my room did I allow myself to cry.

And then, it was so much more than crying. It was me completely falling apart.

31.

A week passed. And another.

With Kai and Vick gone, an uneasy peace descended on the house, and I threw myself into caring for Amryssa. She continued to shed weight at an alarming pace, each day solidifying my conviction that she couldn't stay here. Especially because I'd lost the dagger, and now had no way to protect her from the nightmares.

I had a month, probably less, to get her out.

I begged Olivian to let me take her to Hightower, royal marriage be damned. But ever since I'd publicly rebuked him in the great hall, he mostly communicated in grunts and sneers.

"She's not going anywhere," he growled, when I finally pestered him into answering. "I won't just send her out into the world with no guarantee. It'll chew her up and spit her out. She's too soft. Too fragile."

Tears pricked at my eyes. "But that's my point. She *is* fragile. So fragile she's wasting away. She can't stay here."

Olivian's reddened eyes did their best to scorch a hole in me. "This is the safest place for her, now." His insistence carried a hint of the same madness I'd heard that night in the Lady's room, and I knew, then—he would never let her go. Maybe he never would have.

So I decided to steal her.

Over the next week, I squirreled away every bite of food I could lay hands on. I stashed rye bread and hard cheese, dried jerky and berries. I also "borrowed" two waterskins from Miss Quist, though I didn't tell her what they were for. I figured she probably knew, and since she gave them to me anyway, that equated to approval, in my mind.

As the days passed, the heat of summer broke, the heavy humidity giving way to afternoon rainshowers that peppered the windows. Each time the clouds cleared, the honeyed sunset arrived a few minutes earlier.

In another week, I'd have enough supplies to last us. Then we would disappear.

Multiple times, I wondered where Kai was. At first, I'd mentally tracked his progress along the Oceansgate road, but by now, he would've made it back to civilization, maybe even to Fairmont. Or maybe he'd changed his mind and gone somewhere else entirely.

I hoped not, though. Some part of me liked believing he'd accomplished his goal, that I'd gifted him with that last experience he'd wanted so badly.

Still, that didn't keep me from missing him. Horribly. Every reminder of him—the clothes he'd left hanging in my armoire, the dried peonies I'd now enshrined in a vase on my nightstand—added footprint upon footprint to the trail of pain stretching behind me, which seemed to lengthen with each passing day.

Not that I doubted whether I'd done the right thing. Kai had nearly died, and I'd protected both of us by sending him away. There wasn't any way I could have joined him. Even if I'd done the impossible and left Amryssa, things would've eventually fallen apart.

Three more days limped past, during which Miss Quist announced that she and Lunk were engaged. She'd begged the seneschal for amnesty on the giant's behalf, and, to my surprise, had it granted. In answer, Lunk had found the courage to put a ring on her finger, complete with a tiny seed pearl I'd helped him choose in town.

At that, the household revived a bit. People laughed again. There was talk of how, come equinox, we'd have a second wedding, after all.

Meanwhile, I waited, and prepared. But each day felt emptier than the last, and I swore the hours stretched like putty.

Which was stupid, but I couldn't seem to stop missing my husband. At night, I wondered where Kai was sleeping, whether he'd had enough to eat today. Whether he was warm enough tonight.

Whether he'd ravished anyone else on a bathroom counter yet.

If he had, I couldn't seem to manage the same. Once, Merron came to my room, but I could tell he understood there was no real hope, because when I rebuffed him, he actually chuckled.

"What?" I said. "What's so funny?"

"Nothing. I'm actually kind of relieved, to be honest."

"Relieved? Why?"

"Because. This proves you have a heart." Merron's smile grew rueful. "I don't like knowing it's broken, but I *do* like knowing it exists."

I rolled my eyes and shooed him out, then lingered by the door, pretending his fading steps belonged to someone else—that Kai had just laughed and given me one of his obnoxious half-smiles and gone off to chop wood or rebuild a pig trough or weed the gardens or whatever the hell else he felt compelled to exhaust himself with today.

I stood there for far too long, pretending he would be back. That any minute, I'd see him again.

Even though I knew I never would.

Amryssa only tolerated my moping for so long. Three and a half weeks after Kai's departure, she turned to me in the hallway, took me by the shoulders, and shook me.

I stood there and let her, too shocked to resist. "What're you doing?"

"Snapping you out of it," she said. "That's what people are always doing in books, aren't they? Did it work?"

I brushed my hands down my front, then glanced at my upturned palms. "I don't think so. I don't feel any different."

She blew out a breath. "Well, we need to do *something*. Because watching you scowl all day is making me itchy."

I considered. "Have you considered that you might be allergic to something?"

She crossed her arms. "Harlowe. I hate seeing you sad, but I can't bring Kai back to you. So you're going to have to let me... I don't know. Take you into town, maybe. Why don't we go drinking? Or do some dancing? What was it that made you happy before Kai came?"

A beat of silence spun by. What *had* I spent all my time on, before? "I don't know. I was always so focused on taking care of you."

Her smile looked almost apologetic. "Then you ought to let me take care of you, for once. Starting with a night in town."

A scorching weight settled in my chest. "You don't have to do that."

"I do, though. You're my friend. My sister, for all intents and purposes."

She said it just like that, as if it were the plainest truth in the world, and my throat thickened. I didn't have the heart to tell her a night in town would only remind me of Kai *more*.

I really had to get my mind off him, in any way I could, and I couldn't possibly refuse Amryssa when she called us kin. "Okay."

"Really?" she said, her eyes bright. "Tonight?"

I hesitated. "Will Olivian even let us?"

"Let's go ask."

We did. The seneschal paused perusing some documents and leveled a look at us over his desk. "You want to go to town? Tonight?"

"Yes." Amryssa squared her shoulders. "Harlowe needs cheering up. I'd like to spend some...what do you call it? Girl time?"

He blinked at her. "Girl time."

"Yes."

He sat motionless, his face like a granite slab.

Amryssa's courage dried up. She aimed a pleading glance at me, as if I had a say in any of this.

"I'll have her home by ten?" I offered.

Olivian deployed another glare, but this one contained a glimmer of the same thing I'd caught in the great hall a few weeks ago.

Compassion. Bruised-up, maybe—buried deep, shackled by bitterness, but that was compassion, nonetheless. Somewhere in the depths of his stony heart, the seneschal felt sorry for me. Probably because he'd lost someone he loved, too.

He sighed. "Fine. But you're taking Merron with you."

"Merron?" I arced a brow. "Why him?"

He shot me a glare. "Because you saw fit to give away Zephyrine's dagger, and now you're of little use to me, beyond the keeping of the keys." He opened a desk drawer and rummaged around, then slid a sheathed dagger across the desk. "You can take this, but it isn't anything like the last one, so you'll have to take the head steward with you. Just in case."

I took the weapon and fastened it to my belt. "In case *what*?"

"You see Vick again." He gave me a hard stare. "We don't know what he plans on doing with Zephyrine's dagger."

"Feed people, I imagine." That was really all that man had wanted. To play savior to a broken people. "Or maybe change his hair to a less offensive color."

Olivian lowered his brows, unamused. "The point is, you'll need someone capable."

I slitted my gaze. "A man, you mean?"

"Yes, a man. And Merron happens to be one. Take it or leave it."

"We'll take it," Amryssa said quickly.

Olivian resumed shuffling his papers. "And be back by nine, not ten. We haven't had a nightmare in weeks, and I don't trust the weather not to turn. I want all of you back here before it can become a problem."

Amryssa nodded and swept out before her father could change his mind. I swallowed the burn in my chest and followed, but Olivian grumbled my name.

I turned back. "What?"

"I..." He cleared his throat and looked down, as if the papers in his hands had offered up brand-new information in the last two seconds.

"...just wanted to say...I was perhaps...a bit hasty, when I banished your husband."

My feet turned leaden. I couldn't have moved if I'd tried. "Kai. His name's Kai."

"Right. Kai. I..."

I waited, my breath held.

"Look. You can write to this Kai of yours. Let him know he can come back, if he likes."

My stomach somersaulted. This was...unprecedented. By a long shot.

My silence seemed to fluster him. He grabbed a pen and tapped it against his papers. "He *was* remarkably useful when it came to chopping wood."

I gave a slow nod. "That's...probably the kindest thing you've ever said to me."

"Kindness has nothing to do with it. He was useful."

"Sure. Still. Thank you. And I might've been a little hasty myself, when I said all those things to you that night."

"No. Every word you said was true."

Shock cascaded through me. Olivian tugged at his collar, clearly uncomfortable with that admission, and I hurried to change the subject. "The thing is...I have no idea where Kai went. And even if I did, it wouldn't matter. We never would've worked. But thanks for the offer."

"You're welcome." He still didn't look up. "Now do me a favor and get the hell out."

I laughed. For the first time in days, I laughed, then did exactly as he'd asked.

That evening, Amryssa and Merron and I went dancing.

I couldn't bear to visit the theatre, much less the pub where Kai had conquered my defenses over ale and an apple. Thankfully,

Amryssa found some other place—a back-alley hovel where yellow lamplight and fiddle music spilled from the door.

Inside, we joined a throng of bodies, the crowd so dense that I exhaled in a way I hadn't in weeks. I lost myself in the jaunty music, the shout of conversations, the scent of spilled gin.

Still, people stared at me, and a few raised crossed fingers in my direction. But when Amryssa began whirling in time to the fiddle, a glittering hush spread through the crowd. Gazes followed her, people orienting to her without realizing, everyone subconsciously answering the draw of Zephyrine's child.

I smiled and closed my eyes, letting the music carry me. When I looked again, Merron caught me in his arms and twirled me across the floor.

I anchored my hands to his shoulders. His brown eyes beamed, his smile like a balm to my heart.

"I've been meaning to tell you," he said, barely audible over the music. "I'm leaving Oceansgate. And I won't be back."

My stomach clenched, but I nodded. I'd been expecting this. I was only surprised it had taken him so long. "Where will you go?"

"Crystal Hollow. I have a cousin there, a farmer. He and his wife just had triplets, and they could use some extra hands. Which means I'll have a home there. At least until I decide where to build my own."

I forced a smile. "I'm glad. I mean, not that you're leaving. But that you're moving on. Moving up in the world. Doing what you've always wanted."

He flung me out in a spin, then reeled me back in again. He didn't have Kai's skill, but our dance was looser, in a way. Easier. Less fraught, since it didn't require me to lie to myself or violently skewer any errant feelings through the heart.

"Thanks," he said. "And you know I wish the same for you. I hope you and Amryssa make it to Hightower."

"We will." I raised my voice to compete with the shrieking fiddle. "Come hell or high water, we will. I'll make sure of it."

Another fond smile. "Knowing you, I believe that. And Harlowe? You'll be okay. It might take a while, but you'll be okay."

~

As we made our way home along the graveled road, the evening hummed around us, a rhythmic pulse of cricket-calls and frogsong. In the glow of the swamp, Amryssa's hair gleamed amethyst. I followed it through the dark, replaying Merron's words in my head.

You'll be okay.

I would, eventually. It would take me a long time to accept Kai's absence, but then again, maybe that wasn't the root of the problem. Maybe *I* was. Because maybe, just maybe, I'd sent my husband away out of fear, not foresight.

Tiny stones scuffed beneath my shoes. Up ahead, Merron and Amryssa walked with their arms linked, chuckling about something I hadn't paid attention to. I heaved a sigh and thought back to our last nightmare.

I'd tasted equanimity then, sensed it hovering within reach. In that moment, it had felt so possible to decide, to believe in my own merit. But I hadn't taken hold of it. Instead, I'd booted Kai out of my life and told myself that what I wanted didn't matter.

I rubbed at my temples. All this time, I'd been so loyal to Amryssa, but maybe that was because being loyal to her had been easier than being loyal to myself. Maybe—

A shriek sliced my line of thinking in half. My gaze jumped to Merron, who stood with his arms outstretched, every line of his stance a warning.

I followed his wide-eyed gaze toward the forest.

And froze, my nerves strangling one another. Vick. That prick. He stood at the edge of the trees, and he had Amryssa. Her frail frame trembled as Vick held her by the hair, the white rope of her strands wrapped around his fist. The woman from the root cellar—that same damn woman—stood beside him, smiling at me.

"Let her go!" I shrieked.

Vick barely cut me a glance. He just grinned and backed into the diseased swamp, dragging Amryssa with him. The woman disappeared, too.

Cold dropped through me. I pelted after them, crashing through the glowing bracken, screaming Amryssa's name. But it was no use. Nothing answered me but crickets and squelching mud.

They were gone.

I swatted away a curtain of moss and tried to rein in my pulse. What the hell had just happened? Why would Vick possibly want Amryssa?

My thoughts wheeled, then settled abruptly. It didn't take a genius to figure it out. Vick had the Lady Marche's diary, after all.

Goddess. The fucking *diary*. I should've considered what that meant, because of course Vick-the-would-be-hero would want Amryssa. He'd want to stop the nightmares. Help Oceansgate. Even if it meant wiping my friend from existence.

My stomach shrank to a cold, hard pebble. Shit. Why hadn't I thought of this earlier?

Burning breaths heaved through my lungs, but I pushed aside my self-recrimination. Time enough to hate myself later. Right now, I needed to think. What would Vick do? Take Amryssa to Zephyrine, no doubt. To the holy tree. But it would take him an hour to bush-whack through the swamp.

Meanwhile, I knew this marsh better than he did. Or I had, ten years ago. Its topography still lay in my mind, like a flower preserved between pages. If I ran the road to the manor, I could beat him. I could cut through the marsh, head straight for the oak, and...

Yes. It would work.

I whirled and rejoined the road again, stopping just long enough to toss an order at Merron. "Go find Olivian. Tell him what happened."

He just nodded, his expression crumpled.

I took off sprinting. If Vick thought he could take Amryssa from me, if he thought for one second I'd let him give her back to Zephyrine, he'd messed with the wrong damn keymistress.

3 2 .

By the time I hurtled into the drive, my lungs had caught fire. Sweat soaked my dress.

I stumbled to a stop. The swamp beckoned, but I couldn't just dive in unprepared. Judging by the clouds scudding across the sky, a nightmare was brewing, and I'd need some way to secure myself.

My thoughts spun. I could take the shackles from my armoire, anchor myself to a tree if need be. Because I wouldn't make the same mistake the Lady Marche had.

I would *not* die before reaching Zephyrine and offering up my life for Amryssa's.

I sprang into motion, tearing open the manor's doors and racing up the grand staircase. Candlelight shimmered in the hallways, but I encountered no one.

I burst into my room. The doorknob cracked against the wall, but I didn't spare it a glance. I vaulted toward my armoire, yanking open the bottom drawer, flinging aside scraps of silk in search of my chains.

Behind me, fabric rustled. "Lioness."

My heart went splat, as if an invisible hand had pitched it against the wall. That smoked-velvet voice. That ludicrous accent. That...

What? No. My thoughts fuzzed over, my mind filling with warm white blankness.

I turned, slowly.

All the air left the room. Because there he was, sitting on my bed, as casual as anything, his copper hair falling across his forehead, his starlit eyes searching my face. A plain linen shirt clung to the strong lines of his body. He rested his elbows on his knees, his fingers interlaced.

My pulse restarted, a one-two punch against my sternum. *"Kai?"*

One side of his mouth slid upward. "Who else?"

"But..." Oh, goddess. Was I dreaming? I had to be. My longing had ballooned to such proportions that it had assumed a solid shape. "Are you really here?"

He glanced down at himself. "It would certainly seem that way."

"But...what're you doing?"

He aimed raised eyebrows at the open drawer behind me. "Trying to figure out what you're searching for so desperately."

A skeletal laugh rattled out of me. "You... No, I mean... What're you doing *here*? In Oceansgate? You left. To go to Fairmont. Or you were supposed to."

His head tilted. "Is that so? Because I could've sworn I was supposed to be right here."

"I..." Hot mist slicked my eyes. "But you walked out. You said you could tell when you weren't wanted."

"Well, I can."

"Then why're you here?"

He lifted a shoulder and dropped it. "Because. This was not one of those times."

My throat worked. Emotion crashed through me, splintering me into pieces. Then I was running, hurling myself into his arms, toppling him onto the bed. A grunt flew from his mouth as his back hit the mattress.

His arms circled me, and I clung to him, his heartbeat a full-throated chorus against my ear. I raised my head, then mashed my lips against his with enough fervor to slow time.

He matched the intensity of my kiss, burying a hand in my hair. When I pulled back, he gazed up at me, wonderstruck. "I'll admit, I was hoping for a warm welcome, but this exceeds even my expectations."

"Seven hells, I missed you." My words were garbled, salted with tears. "I thought I was never going to see you again."

"Well." He pushed a handful of hair behind my ear. "You haven't been listening to a word I've said, then."

"I can't believe you came back."

"I didn't *come back*, lioness. I never left."

I laughed, or sobbed, or some combination of the two, and burrowed my head against his chest again.

I allowed myself a second. A flawless, diamond moment in which nothing else existed. I didn't care where he'd been, or who with, or about anything except that he was *here*, solid and reassuring and even more breathtaking than I'd remembered.

He hadn't abandoned me. He hadn't *left*. Even though I'd tried to make him.

That simple truth of that saturated me with such feeling that I came unstuck from gravity. Then reality crashed back, and I scrambled up, scrubbing at my cheeks.

"Vick has Amryssa."

His expression didn't change. "I know. That's why I'm here. I mean, I'm here for you, but also because I've been in the forest these past weeks, watching the liberators. Vick has them convinced he's going to stop the nightmares. I'd hoped he wouldn't go so far as to steal Amryssa, but once I realized he would, I knew you'd need help."

Renewed emotion surged through me. "So you came to save her?"

"Of course." He propped himself up on his forearms. "And I wasn't about to let you rush off into the forest and get yourself hurt. Or killed."

I nodded, unable to speak.

"And frankly, I'm hoping there's something in it for me." His look grew heavy with meaning. "You know. The ring toss that finally lands around the bottle."

Another dizzying wave of feeling crashed up from my depths. Goddess, I could hardly withstand all this intensity, but I was glad he was here. Flabbergasted, really, and so filled with gratitude that I felt like one of Olivian's overstuffed armchairs, thread creaking along every seam.

I wouldn't have to do this alone.

But... My throat soured. Kai had no idea what I planned to do. He hadn't read the Lady's letter to Amryssa, had never learned about the blood-price. He assumed I meant to get my friend back, not reach Zephyrine first and offer myself in her place.

I forced a smile. I couldn't tell him. I also couldn't do anything *but* sacrifice myself, because we had no chance of getting Amryssa back, otherwise. Maybe if we'd had time to rally Lunk and Olivian and the stewards, but considering the weather—

A bell clanged, across the house. Then another. The sound cut through the silence.

"Well, that's inconvenient," Kai said. "If not entirely unexpected."

Amryssa. Oh, goddess. I had to get to the holy tree, *now*, by any means necessary. End the nightmares, because she wouldn't make it through another one on her own.

I pushed off the bed and pulled Kai to standing. "I came up here for my manacles, but maybe if I have you, I won't need them?"

His expression tightened. "If the storm overwhelms you—"

"Can't you just hold me down?"

He shook his head. "Even I can't pin a hellcat. Not for long. You'll need something."

"Okay." I whirled, pawing through the drawer until I came up with my shackles. If nothing else, Ky could use them on Amryssa while I slipped away and offered my blood to Zephyrine. "Here."

Kai took the restraints. "How long do we have?"

"Thirty minutes until Vick reaches the tree, probably. Maybe twenty-five, by now."

"Not much time, then. Let's go."

I nodded and put my hand in his. We bolted from the room. Down in the great hall, the front doors stood open. Outside, the night hissed and heaved. Merron stood just inside, sweat-soaked and panting. He babbled to Olivian, who looked like he wanted to murder the first person who dared to come within reach.

The seneschal's eyes blazed at our approach. "You had one job! *One fucking job.*"

"I know!" I launched straight into a shout. "And I'm going to go do it, right now. I'm going to get Amryssa back. With Kai's help."

The seneschal's gaze skipped past me. He was practically frothing at the mouth, fury churning off him in waves, but he wasted no time on surprise. "You two are going out into the nightmare?"

"Yes."

He growled. "You'll die. Which won't help a goddess-damned thing. Amryssa will be out there trying to get to Zephyrine, and you'll be busy tearing your own eyeballs out."

"No." I gestured to the manacles. "I have these. And Kai can resist the nightmares."

Olivian's face contorted. "That's impossible."

"It's not. I've seen him do it. More than once."

Olivian and Merron surveyed my husband with palpable shock. Kai only shrugged, as if to say, *What? I'm exceptional.*

Outside, thunder cracked over the swamp. The floor trembled, the scent of char sharpening the air. Olivian and Merron grimaced as my knees wobbled.

But Kai just stood there, looking ready for a stroll in the park. Or maybe a restorative nap.

When everything stilled, Olivian raked his gaze over my husband with renewed interest. "You intend to save her?"

"I do."

"Then I'm coming with you."

"No," I cut in. "You won't get more than a half a mile before the storm crushes you. Amryssa already lost her mother that way. She can't lose you, too. She needs you alive."

"I can't do *nothing.*" Olivian's shoulders strained, threatening to rupture his shirt at the seams.

"You won't be," Kai said smoothly. "You'll be ensuring your

survival, for the sake of your daughter. Go. Chain yourself. The moment the storm passes, come find us. We'll have her. We'll be waiting."

Olivian's mouth twisted, but Kai's words seemed to compel him in a way mine couldn't.

The power of bald-faced confidence, I supposed. Or maybe it was just a man thing.

"We're wasting time," Kai warned.

The seneschal swore. "Fine. Go get her. I'll come the second I'm able."

"Of course."

Olivian found my gaze and held it. So many things simmered in his eyes—terror, fury, agonized helplessness—and I tried to communicate my intent with a look. To assure him I'd give my life for Amryssa's. Maybe I was successful, because he gave me a bare nod.

"Please, Harlowe." His plea was soft. Gentle, even.

"I'll save her," I said.

Kai made for the door. I hesitated, then bade Olivian and Merron goodbye. I tried not to make it sound like the permanent kind, even though it was.

Merron looked stricken, but I stepped into the angry night and shut the doors.

Out in the drive, clouds piled above the trees, staining the sky purple. Kai scanned the swamp. "Which way?"

I flung out a finger. "There." In the far distance, below the storm's epicenter, the overgrown oak swayed in the wind.

My skin tightened. I'd try my best not to fall apart out there, but I couldn't be sure I'd succeed. "Whatever happens"—I caught at Ky's wrist—"just...know that I love you, all right?"

He froze, his eyes wide, his nostrils flared.

Despite everything, I grinned. At long last, I'd gotten the upper hand, if only for one brief and shining moment.

"Don't give me that look," I said. "You knew."

He recovered swiftly, his mouth curving. "Of course I *knew*. I just didn't think you'd ever say it. And I love you, too. Every ferocious, stubborn inch of you. Which you also knew."

I bundled the words up tight, tucking them against my heart, the most priceless treasures in my possession.

Seven hells, it was going to kill me to leave a world in which he could have been mine. Literally kill me.

But I had to. For Amryssa.

I held out my hand, and Kai caught my fingers in his. I savored the feel. "Come on. Let's go thwart a hero. And a goddess."

His nod was swift, full of intent. "Let's."

We ran.

The cypresses and tupelos thrashed, their glow taking on a frenzied quality. The nightmare's light illuminated Kai's face in one moment, then abandoned him to shadow the next.

I pushed my body to its limit. I dodged branches and dashed through puddles, my lungs snatching at the same wind I was displacing. The only thing that felt solid was Kai's hand. Everything else wavered, as if the veil draped over reality might rupture at any moment.

The forest was familiar, but not. It was the same swamp I'd grown up in, but changed by the rot, and I seemed to be barreling toward both my future and my past, toward some catastrophic epicenter where the two intersected.

The storm boomed overhead. My steps faltered, then recovered. I was yesterday's Harlowe—the orphan, unwanted—but also today's—a wife, and beloved. And despairing. And desperate, desperate, desperate.

Curtains of moss whipped past. Glowing mud splattered my skirts. Insects chattered in the underbrush, the sound invading my skull in a way that told me they weren't actually there. Neither were the things rising from the dark. They belonged to Zephyrine, to a mother's loss given hellish life.

Ahead, a deer stumbled from the underbrush, a misshapen creature with backward-jointed legs and too many teeth to count. Its head was upside-down.

Not real. I squeezed my eyes shut and angled a shoulder into it without slowing. The thing burst into purple mist as I passed through.

Around me, the nightmare screamed. *You are nothing. Worthless.*

No, I told it. *I matter.*

Its garbled voice faded. Moments later, Kai and I reached a clearing. In the middle, a majestic oak rose toward the raging sky, haloed by a moat of firm ground.

The holy tree.

But not just that. Something was here—something vast and dimensionless that threw my bodily functions into turmoil and made my teeth buzz in their sockets.

Kai's grip tightened, but I shook free. Wind scoured the grass, pressing the blades flat. Bursts of purple lightning zigzagged around us. Overhead, the storm brewed like a livid, inverted whirlpool.

"Harlowe," Kai shouted. "We should wait here. We have to stop Vick before he gets Amryssa near the tree."

I studied the empty clearing. We'd beaten Vick, but Amryssa wouldn't be safe until Zephyrine accepted my sacrifice. Then my friend would become a useless hostage. Vick would have no choice but to let her go, his mission to stop the nightmares fulfilled.

Amryssa and Kai would be safe. So would everyone else. I only had to buy their futures with mine.

"You stay here." I smiled, trying to ease the sting. "Keep Vick away. I need to talk to Zephyrine."

Kai's brow creased, but he had no way to know there was another way. One I meant to take.

"Please." I shouted over the ear-splitting shriek of the storm. "Just trust me."

His gaze clouded with doubt.

A knot gathered under my sternum, so constricting I could barely breathe. This was cruel. *I* was cruel, weaponizing his love for me like this. Somewhere inside me, those wings began to beat, heavy and thrashing. Part of me was trying to break away, to stay with him.

For a moment, I actually considered it. He stood so still amid the storm, just like when I'd first laid eyes on him. Only now he didn't look like a monster. Not even like a prince—not in those plain clothes, with his hair frothing on the wind. He looked like...

Just a man. A shepherd's son. One I'd married. One I loved.

"Are you sure?" he shouted.

I nodded. Even though I absolutely fucking wasn't sure. But the need to save Amryssa beat steadily inside me, a guiding star.

I couldn't look at Kai another moment without collapsing, so I turned to face the fevered storm. The tree loomed, stealing my attention.

The buzz in my teeth spread into my skull.

The strangest part was, it was familiar. It felt like the dagger's inhabitant, multiplied by a billion.

I took a step, then another. I glanced back once, but now Kai had his back to me. Vick stood at the clearing's edge, Amryssa anchored at his side.

My breath hitched, but Kai would handle them. Already, Vick trembled in the face of the nightmare's fury. Meanwhile, Amryssa strained toward the tree, soundless pleas coming from her mouth.

Kai set off toward them, straight-backed.

"I love you," I murmured. The wind snatched the words, and I dared to imagine it would deliver them. Whirl them around, polish them to shining, then plant them in Kai's ear, once I was gone.

Come, Zephyrine commanded, inside my head.

I turned to the tree and did as the goddess bade. One foot in front of the other.

Above me, the nightmare raged. *You are nothing.*

You're wrong, I answered.

You are worthless.

Fuck you, went my reply.

I erected a wall inside my mind, piled the bricks of my love for Kai and Amryssa atop it, then mortared it over with curses and refusals. The nightmare couldn't have me. Not right now.

When I reached the tree, I passed through some invisible barrier. All at once, the wind's grip loosened and died.

Apparently, the storm had an eye, and I'd found it.

I pushed my tangled hair from my face and ran my fingers down the oak's rough bark. Its trunk was massive, wider than my arms could span, and a jagged split ran down the middle. Purple light emanated from within.

It looked like the seam between closed doors. But...how to open it?

An offering, probably. Just like the Lady Marche had given.

Blood.

I plucked the magicless dagger Olivian had given me from my belt. The blade gleamed, reflecting the storm. I guided it across my palm.

Hot red agony raced up my arm. I gritted my teeth, then pressed my hand to the trunk's crack, wincing at the sting.

Blood coursed into the seam, muddying its glow. The buzz in my head intensified, like a swarm of wasps trapped inside a box. The crack widened, the tree peeling apart, the curtain of wood parting to reveal...

I staggered. A woman slept inside, suspended in a translucent amethyst cocoon, like a butterfly awaiting transformation. Only she was more magnificent than any butterfly in existence. Brown-skinned and black-haired, wrapped in a delicate shroud of palmetto leaves, Zephyrine was awe-inspiring, her beauty almost violent.

I threw up a hand to shield my eyes. Looking at her was like staring into the sun.

You have something to offer me.

The goddess's lips moved, though her eyes didn't open. Her words flowed straight to my mind, bypassing my ears.

"Yes," I said. "I came to complete the bargain. I'll give you my blood, all of it. And in exchange, you'll stop trying to bring back your daughter. Stop dreaming. Leave Oceansgate in peace. Let Amryssa return to you when she's an old woman."

The goddess's lips twitched—a smile, or a grimace, I couldn't tell. Her teeth crested to points at the tips. *You'd offer your life?*

"I would."

Very well. I accept. All your blood, for fifty years.

I paused. Fifty years. That should be enough. Amryssa would be seventy-seven, by then. I raised the blade again, set it against my wrist. Pain bit at me with bright teeth as I hesitated.

I chanced a look behind me. Kai, my sweet Kai, tussled with Vick, whose sword lay on the ground, now.

A spear of pure love pierced my chest. Despite Kai's lack of training, he would win, that much was plain. Vick was writhing, throwing sloppy punches, then pulling at his hair and screaming. In contrast, my husband moved with surety, landing blows and darting away again. Vick pinwheeled his arms, then turned on himself.

He was melting. Falling apart.

And Amryssa...

Wait. Where the hell was Amryssa?

When I turned back, there stood my best friend. She'd gotten past me, somehow, or maybe come from the opposite direction. She gazed up at her mother. The goddess had opened her eyes and pressed one hand against the wall of her cocoon.

Amryssa reached out.

"No!" I shrieked.

Fire lit my muscles. I snatched at Amryssa's hand and dragged her to the ground. Pebbles slammed into my kneecaps, but I ignored them. I hugged Amryssa tight, my knife angled so as not to hurt her.

"Not you," I babbled into her hair. "Let her have me, instead."

"Harlowe."

Every nerve heated to a live wire. There was something in her voice, a hum I'd never heard before. A command. I eased back, hating to let her go, but needing to see her face.

Amryssa took me by the shoulders. "Harlowe, it's all right. It's going to be all right."

"I know." Desperation coated my words. "Because I'm going to *make* it all right. Zephyrine can have me, and you'll stay here. Oceansgate'll be safe. No more nightmares. You'll help Olivian rebuild, and you can come back here when you're ancient. When you're done making the world better. When you're ready. Just like your mother said."

She smiled, sad but indulgent, like I'd offered her a dead bird and tried to call it a pet. "But I'm ready *now*."

My throat closed. "No. No, Am. You can't go. You're the best person in this goddess-forsaken place. Everyone needs you."

Her grip tightened. "No, I'm needed here, in the swamp. What's more, I won't let you sacrifice for me. Not anymore."

"But I want to."

"No. You're scared."

I reared back. Scared? This was the opposite of scared. I was offering up my life for hers. "No. Everyone dies. At least this way, my existence is worth something." I tried to pull away, but she held me in an iron grip. Goddess, when had she gotten so strong? And so...

I squinted. She looked different. Her eyes shone, but they'd also darkened, as if her proximity to Zephyrine had granted her new life. Brown ringed her irises, some ancient forest spirit peering out through her eyes. Even her hair shimmered with a suggestion of actual color. And I swore she'd gained weight in the last five minutes.

A smile curved her mouth. "My sweet friend. My *best* friend. My sister. I don't mean you're scared of dying. I mean you're scared of living."

I startled. How ridiculous. "What're you talking about?"

"Look at him." She gestured toward the clearing.

I did. Now Kai had Vick on the ground, holding him down as Vick thrashed. Kai's whole body strained, muscles bulging everywhere, and I saw what he'd meant about trying to pin a hellcat. He groped for the manacles, getting Vick halfway shackled. Kai dragged his screaming captive toward the forest, clearly aiming for a tree to anchor him to. The nightmare raged around them, shadows and lightning and violence.

But in here, we were safe. I turned back to Amryssa. "What about him?"

"You love him."

I swallowed. "So?"

"But you're afraid to let him love you. To let him choose you. You're afraid to choose *yourself*."

My voice deserted me. Well, fuck me sideways. Maybe she had a point. All this desperate maneuvering *did* feel easier than the alternative. I wanted so badly to give myself up, because then I wouldn't have to muster the courage to let her go. To march back out there and trust myself to matter enough to anchor my life around.

All this time, I'd made it about her, because that had been easier than making it about me.

"You know I'm right," she said gently.

Tears threatened. I squeezed the knife, then opened my hand. It landed in the grass with a thud. When I glanced up, Zephyrine smiled knowingly. As if she'd orchestrated all this. Dreamed us all together here, just to lay this choice at our feet.

"I…" My voice broke. "But I love you, Am. I can't lose you."

"I love you, too." Amryssa's eyes seemed to darken by the moment, glowing with some new vitality. Even her skin looked healthier, her pallor fading as pigment blossomed in her cheeks. "But you won't lose me. I'll be right here. Zephyrine gifted my mother with our years together, but I never belonged out there. I'm part of this place. I…can't explain it. I just know. I think I always knew, because that's what the storms have always told me. And as much as you've neglected to put yourself first, so have I. I tried so hard to belong. To be what you wanted, what my father wanted. But I should've told you. I should've asked you to let me go."

Tears spilled over, painting warmth down my cheeks. "You did, though. You asked me a thousand times, and I didn't listen."

Tenderness softened her face. "Will you listen now?"

The question filtered into my consciousness and settled, opening a wide, glossy expanse within me. Kai had finished with Vick and stood in the meadow, watching. Waiting, his expression taut, as if he understood exactly what was happening.

I studied Amryssa, tracing the familiar face of a friend I would gladly have gone to the ends of the earth for. My loyalty to her burned like a torch in my chest. Still. And following it had always been so easy. But maybe it was time to claim some of that light for myself.

"That's what you want?" I said.

"It is."

"But...Olivian'll kill me. He'll take my head off."

"He'll understand. Once you explain."

Fear filled me, a familiar weight in my chest, so old and primal that it slotted into the base of my lungs as neatly as a drawn breath. But that fear had never gotten me anywhere. Nowhere I wanted to be, anyway.

My first instinct was to do violence, to rip it from my skeleton by force. But I let it settle. Let it find a home between my heartbeats. Then I whispered to it. I ran my fingers along its careworn hide and crooned.

I don't need you anymore.

I let fear go. Let it fade into the mists of my past, where it could stay.

"I'll miss you," I told Amryssa. "Forever. I'll love you forever, too."

Tears welled in her eyes, and in mine, and then we were hugging, crying, hanging on to each other for dear life.

My heart fractured, but I papered over the cracks with the warmth of a friendship that had changed me.

That friendship wouldn't die, I hoped. Only change shape.

I let go, then climbed to my feet and pulled Amryssa with me. "Just...don't make me say goodbye, okay? Not out loud. I'm terrible at that kind of thing."

"You don't have to, though. I'm not actually *going* anywhere."

My attention slid to Zephyrine. Mother and daughter—I could see it, plain as day.

The goddess reached out. So did Amryssa. Their palms connected across the thin membrane of Zephyrine's cocoon.

I lifted my chin. Brave. Be brave. Zephyrine's hand burst through, and Amryssa pulled, hauling her mother from the heart of the oak.

The goddess stepped free. The chasm sealed behind her, still reddened by traces of my blood.

Amryssa and Zephyrine smiled, in eerie concert, like two facets of a unified whole.

I probably would never figure out how that worked, but then again, I didn't need to. I just needed to know they were happy.

"Thank you." Amryssa looked more peaceful than she ever had. She turned away, taking her mother with her.

They walked off into the thrashing forest, and I raised my eyes. I couldn't watch them disappear—it was too much like the last two times. And while my newfound resolve bolstered me, it felt tender, only freshly hatched, and could only extend so far.

Overhead, the nightmare churned. With Zephyrine awake, I knew this would be our last divine storm, but since this one had already been dreamed up, apparently it still needed to burn itself out.

When I lowered my gaze again, the forest was empty. Amryssa and Zephyrine were gone.

I turned. Across the clearing, Kai smiled, one hand outstretched.

I hesitated. I could stay here, in the tree's protective bubble. I could hide. Avoid the terrors the storm dredged up. Just close my eyes and wait for it to be over. Vick had my manacles, after all.

But my life was out there.

So I took a deep breath, threw back my shoulders, and stepped into the storm.

33·

When I got close to Kai, his cheeks were wet.

I stopped a foot away, cradling my bloodied hand and gazing up into his face. "Are you crying?" I said, with wonder.

He gave me a cocksure smile. "Of course not. This is just...liquid relief. Inconveniently leaking out through my eyes, for some reason. Very strange. Nothing like this has ever happened to me before."

I searched his gaze. Behind him, the forest heaved with things both inhuman and grotesque. The nightmare scrabbled at my mind, trying to find purchase. *You are meaningless. You are nothing.*

I'm not, I told it. *I mean something because I say I do.*

I lifted my good hand to Kai's face. "Did you know? About the blood-price? You knew what I was trying to do?"

His smile wavered. "Yes, well. I may have snooped in Vick's hut, back at the liberators' camp. Reread that damned book when he wasn't around, trying to figure out what he intended. And I may have discovered we hadn't uncovered *all* the Lady Marche's secrets, that night in our room."

Our room. The thought warmed me. "So you knew, and you let me go anyway?"

He swallowed. "You're my wife. And if you've taught me anything about loyalty, it's that sometimes it requires you to let people decide for themselves. Even if their choice might destroy you."

The enormity of that stunned me into silence. I didn't know how I could possibly have taught him that. I hadn't realized it myself until just five minutes ago.

But maybe that was the power of loving someone. It made you see them as more than they were, as whatever grander thing they would grow into.

I ran my fingers along the line of his jaw. "Did you also know I'd change my mind?"

"I *believed* it," he said. "And I know it might not have looked like it, but that was me fighting for you, just now. I may have had to kick Vick in the face just to get Amryssa away from him. Get her to you."

My throat worked. "You wanted me to have those minutes with her?"

"I wanted you to have a choice. Call it one last toss of the ring. An incredibly desperate one, but a toss, nonetheless."

I lost my voice, then found it again. "Then...I think you may have caught me, this time."

His eyes heated. "Did I?"

"Yes. And now I want...you. I want to stay with you. I want you to stay with me."

Emotion swirled in his face. He blinked hard. "Well, lucky for you, we're married. Which means you're stuck with me, whether you like it or not."

I laughed. "Honestly, how are you so perfect? Just *how*?"

He gave me a saucy smile. "I was born this way. Well, no. That's a lie. I worked very hard at it. But my raw charisma didn't hurt. Or my overwhelming good looks."

A scuffed chuckle warmed my chest. This man. I would never tire of his arrogance.

He cupped my face, and I tilted my cheek into his touch.

"How are you?" he said.

I knew what he was asking—whether the nightmare was about to crack my defenses and carry me away on its bitter flood. But the distorted shadows, for all that they scrabbled at my skirts, seemed distant.

"I'm...quiet, I think," I said. "Safe. Inside myself."

His half-smile bled into something wide and deep. "Gods above. How are *you* so perfect?"

I shrugged. "Just pure, dumb luck, I'm pretty sure."

He chuckled. His thumb smoothed across my cheekbone. "So now what?"

"Now, you should take me somewhere and make love to me. As soon as possible."

Brightness flared in his eyes. "That can be arranged." His gaze fell to the wounded hand clutched against my chest. "Let's just take care of that, first."

Before I could ask what he intended, he stalked toward Vick, who lay chained between two trees. His voice had gone. He writhed and thrashed, his mouth open in a never-ending scream. But only hoarse silence emerged.

Kai fiddled with Vick's belt. I frowned, but when he straightened, he held the dagger. *My* dagger.

My conduit to Zephyrine.

Hope—that horrible, treacherous, wonderful thing, fluttered into my throat. Would the blade still work? Allow me to talk to the goddess? Maybe to Amryssa? Were they even different entities, anymore?

Kai came and handed it over. I took the knife with my good hand, relishing the feel of the familiar antler handle.

It hummed, no different than before.

A star kindled beneath my ribs. *Hello?*

Harlowe. Amryssa's voice slid into my mind, wider and deeper and more...*more*, somehow. *My sweet friend, my forever-sister. I'm here.*

A joyous sob throbbed in my chest. "It's her," I cried. "I can hear her."

Kai grinned.

I breathed my way through a spiky riot of emotion. First relief, then a pang of love so fierce I had to steady myself with a heaping dose of husbandly eye contact.

What do you need? Amryssa asked.

Nothing, I told her, still looking at Kai. *I have everything I've ever wanted. But...I wouldn't exactly hate it if you could stitch up this cut on my hand. It does hurt like a bitch.*

Amryssa laughed. A moment later, warmth coursed into me. The line of fire on my palm faded to an ache, then a memory.

I marveled at my perfect, unharmed skin. The dagger went quiet, and I tucked it into the empty sheath at my belt.

"She's not gone," I said.

"I'm glad." He pulled me close, tucking my head beneath his chin. "Now, where to? I'd take you to the liberators' camp, but everyone there will be screaming. And not the sort of screaming that puts me in the mood."

A breathy laugh gusted from my lips. "No, I have somewhere else. A place I'd like to show you."

I offered him my hand, then looked around. Everything looked so different than when I'd been here as a child—the infected leaves pulsed purple while squiggles of shadow twined in the darkness. But I could superimpose the old onto the new. I still knew the way.

"Over here." I tugged.

Kai followed. We floated through the night like ghosts, threading between glowing sheets of moss. Shadows groped for us, including one that looked like a squirrel with spider legs and a human mouth, but I kept my eyes up, and eventually, they retreated.

Fifteen minutes later, we reached a place I hadn't set foot in for a decade.

It wasn't a clearing, anymore, really. Moss and gnarled vines had taken over, dotted with glowing amethyst swamp lilies.

Amid it all, my old shack still stood, its woven-branch roof caved in one side, the other choked by climbing vines.

"Your old home," Kai said softly.

"Yes."

He released my hand and tried the warped plank door, getting it open after a few stiff shoves. He waited on the darkened threshold.

I paused. It was strange seeing him here, in this place that had given my loneliness life. And yet it felt like the last stitch knitting together my past and my present.

Inside lay my stool and table, now heaped with the detritus of the caved-in roof. There was the spindly rack I'd once dried plants on, half-collapsed. And the bed. Its horsehair mattress had retained a miraculous amount of volume, though the sheet had crumbled to rags.

Kai ran his hands down my arms. "Here?"

I nodded, and shivered, desire already peeling open inside me like a flower.

Violet light from the window shimmered along his cheek. I reached for him, but he returned my hands gently to my sides. "No. Let me."

My breath turned hot and liquid. The nightmare screamed outside, but somehow that only added to the hungry chasm inside me, spiking my heartrate, sharpening the burn that followed his touch.

He brushed my hair back and fastened his mouth against my neck, doing that thing with his tongue again. Oh goddess, my favorite thing.

I closed my eyes. Heat flickered at my core, sparking an ache between my thighs. And somehow, the nightmare made everything burn hotter.

Kai kissed a path down my neck, then up to my mouth. His tongue parted the seam of my lips, so tender I felt the echo of it in the base of my spine. He kissed me, unhurried, while he unhooked my dress and unlaced my corset. He pulled everything off, then lifted my chemise over my head and laid it on the mattress as impromptu bedding.

He peeled away my underthings and stepped back. His attention raked over me, carving a smoldering path down my naked body. "My beautiful wife."

Goddess, I needed to touch him. "Take off your clothes."

He did—shirt first, then breeches. When it all lay on the floor, I drank him in, every line of him like nourishment. "My beautiful husband. You are one unbelievably gorgeous work of art."

His grin made my skin pull taut over my throbbing bones. He took me in his arms and eased me onto the bed. He anchored his elbows to either side of my neck, palming the back of my head, kissing me again. My legs curled around his hips.

He wasn't in any hurry. But the slower he went, the higher the flames inside me danced. He traced my curves with rough hands, then explored me with his mouth, his fingers. His tongue circled each nipple. He trailed touches up the inside of my thighs, teasing me until I whimpered and writhed. Until I had to press my fists into the mattress in order to keep from reaching for him.

Finally, I could stand it no longer, and I grabbed at his shoulders, hauling his face toward mine. "If you don't fuck me right this second, I'm going to scream."

His smile was full and white in the darkness. "I thought you wanted me to make love to you."

"Yes. Whatever. Just...do it now. Please." My words all piled atop one another. I sounded desperate, like some crazed addict.

"You greedy little thing." Kai hooked a hand behind my knee, pushing my leg up and outward, spreading me open and settling his hips against mine. "I like it when you beg."

I reached down and took him in my hand, earning myself a long, low sweep of his lashes. I guided him toward my entrance, but he held back, hovering on the brink of giving me what I needed, but refusing to cross that last distance.

A needy whine gathered in my throat. "What're you doing?"

"Trying to remember," he said, eyes still closed.

"Remember? Remember what?"

"Just give me a second, will you? Use it to beg some more, if you like."

"Please," I whispered. When he still didn't move, I raised my head and lapped at his birthmark, trying to coax him into continuing. He shuddered at the contact, then opened his eyes, flooding me with the heat of his regard. The hand behind my knee tightened, his body nudging at mine.

"Harlowe Hollander," he said.

My head thunked back down against the bed. "What?"

"Your name. Not 'just Harlowe.' Not anymore. You're Harlowe Hollander."

A sting stabbed my eyes, even while my body cried out for him. "That's my last name?"

"Yes."

"You were trying to remember your own last name?"

He chuckled. "No. I was trying to remember what I told you. Before. So I can tell you again. Because this time, the words are mine."

I lost myself in his eyes. I had no idea what he was talking about, but I would let him say anything he wanted, as long as it convinced him to get inside me already. "So say it."

"I will. But don't worry. You needn't say it back." He tilted his hips, sinking into me, inch by torturous inch.

Oh, thank goddess. I ran my hands up his back as pleasure thrummed along every nerve.

A tormented sigh bled out of me as he seated himself. Gods among us, but the fit was exquisite. He found a slow rhythm, one that saturated me with sensation.

"In the sacred embrace of the swamp," he said, "here under the watchful eyes of Zephyrine, I pledge my heart and soul."

My eyes snapped open, and...wait, when had they closed?

His starry gaze locked on mine, as if he were mapping every reaction sparked by the joining of our bodies. Molten pleasure pooled along my spine.

"I vow to forsake all others and seek refuge in your arms."

"What?" I whispered, although I'd heard him clearly. I just didn't understand.

He kissed me, soft and deep, never altering his rhythm. "Like goddess-blessed oaks, we grow alongside each other, our roots entwined, reaching for the same sunlit heavens."

Wait. Those words. I'd heard them before. *Said* them before.

The world's heartbeat faltered, plunging the moment into stillness. Sweet Zephyrine. Our wedding vows. He was saying our wedding vows.

"We remain as individuals." Every slide of his body ignited a constellation of pleasure, one star after another bursting into existence, lighting up a whole sky. "But together, we stand against the winds of adversity. United, we weather life's storms."

A soft cry rolled out of me. They were beautiful, these words. Dense and lush and graven with meaning. I couldn't believe I hadn't listened the first time.

"When you need shelter, I offer you my shade. When you need uplifting, I share my dappled light."

"Kai." My voice cracked. Wonder rushed in to seal up the break.

"Shh." Stroke. Slide. Quiet ecstasy. "Let me finish."

My hands drifted to the small of his back, which flexed and dipped. Every surge stoked the rising glow within me. "Yes. Please. Please finish."

"I offer you my years." His voice thickened. Roughened. "My heart and my body, and a place at my side. I vow never to leave yours, until darkness takes me."

I struggled to keep my gaze pinned to his. My lashes fluttered, trying to close, yet I was captive to the way he moved. To the searing pressure that pulled every piece of me toward a flame-lit center. "Oh, gods. You're going to make me—"

"By the whisper of the wind," he rushed out. "By the beating of our entwined hearts, I pledge myself to you, now and forever."

He made a sound that let me know I could finish.

My eyes closed. Bliss arrowed through me, silver-tipped, lighting a blaze along every nerve. It spread and consumed me, *became* me, until I could taste the cypress-smoke heat of him, see the molten glow of his touch as it pulsed behind my eyes.

I was crying out. Keening louder than the nightmare. Losing control of my body as it detonated, transforming me into a shower of white-hot satisfaction.

Holy.

Shit.

It peaked and lasted and finally faded to a sparkling afterglow. By the time I could feel my body again, Kai lay limp atop me. I almost regretted having missed the particulars—the tense of his body, the quiver of his muscles—but I had gone somewhere else. Ascended to some stratospheric pinnacle I'd never reached before.

"It can't *possibly* get worse than that," he mumbled into my shoulder.

I laughed, but there was hardly any life in it. It sounded weak and wrung-out, just like me.

"Don't be unimaginative," I said. "It can definitely get worse."

He raised his head. "Oh? I'd like to see *you* try."

I slanted a brow upward. "Is that a challenge?"

"Do you want it be?"

"Maybe."

A smile tugged at his mouth. "Then yes."

I smiled back. "Then challenge accepted."

He raised expectant brows, and I wriggled, managing to roll him onto his back without sundering our connection. He stretched out beneath me, propping his hands behind his head, his biceps bulging in a way that probably should have been illegal.

"Well?" His smile was nothing short of provocative. "I'm waiting. Hurry up and devastate me, my sweet wife."

I leaned down, taking my time, turning all the honeyed torture he'd subjected me to back on him. I tongued his birthmark, scraped featherlight fingernails down the insides of his arms, swallowed the purring groan I wrested from his throat.

He soon stirred inside me again, and I began a slow circle of my hips.

"Gods among us." He made the words into a labored exhale. "Yes, like that."

A devilish smile lit my face. I could do worse. Much worse. I locked my hips into a drawn-out rhythm and curled over him, as if to nip at his neck. He craned his head, exposing his throat, but I whispered in his ear, instead.

"In the sacred embrace of the swamp, here under the watchful eyes of Zephyrine, I pledge my heart and soul."

A breath sped in through his lips. His hands splayed against my thighs. "Lioness? You don't have to."

"I know. I want to. I vow to forsake all others and seek refuge in your arms."

His body stiffened—in anticipation, or surprise, or pleasure, or...all of the above, hopefully.

My hips rolled as I said the vows back to him, each and every word, though a few times, I had to take a moment and hunt for the next piece. I wasn't an actor, who could memorize lines with no apparent effort.

But I got through it, working him into a tense knot of heavy breathing and glazed eyes along the way. Warmth spun through me with every arc of my pelvis, but I held myself back from the edge. I wanted to watch him, this time.

And I did. His eyes turned up beneath falling lids. I savored the exquisite, shivering line of his throat as he rasped my name. The pull of taut muscle beneath hot skin, the clench of his abdomen as he spilled his pleasure into me.

I kept going, until he clamped his hands around my hips and held me still, panting and wide-eyed. I leaned down to kiss him. When I pulled back, a fresh shine had gathered along his lashes.

"Gods, you were right." He blinked hard. "That was definitely worse. Consider me defeated. Absolutely ruined."

"Mmm." I hummed, gloating. "Weird that your defeat looks a whole lot like an excess of emotion."

"Emotion? No. Of course not."

"Uh huh."

"Haven't I told you I don't have feelings?" He cleared his throat. "You've just caught me in a moment of extreme eye hydration. That's all."

"Oh, right. And let me guess. Nothing like this has ever happened to you before?"

"Never," he said, all solemnity.

I laughed, and kissed him again, and his hands found a place in my hair. He kissed me back, with feeling, until everything went quiet within me.

I finally eased off him and nestled into the crook of his arm, letting him tuck me against his side. "Harlowe Hollander," I whispered. "I do like that."

"Not nearly as much as I do."

I smiled into his chest. Beyond the window, the nightmare wailed, and for a hairsbreadth of a moment, I almost felt...sorry for it. It sounded like a child, throwing a tantrum because it couldn't have its way.

I lay there. This would be the last time I ever heard these sounds, and some part of me felt compelled to commemorate them, somehow. To listen and remember, even though the storm had all but given up trying to break me.

A few minutes later, the wailing changed. Fat raindrops slapped against broad leaves. The plip-plop swelled to a muted roar.

I blinked. Huh. That was new. Nightmares never ended with rain. But I guessed this one was different.

I nuzzled against Kai's side. "What do you think that's about?"

He didn't answer. And when I looked up, I laughed.

He was asleep. Of course.

I studied his face—the broad sweep of his brows, the taper his nose, the arrogant line of his jaw.

The wings in my chest rustled, because this was my husband. In the truest sense, now. And what a husband he was. If I'd fortified my defenses with high gates, he'd scaled the walls singing. If my heart had been a cold, black stone, he'd polished it to onyx, and now it gleamed when held up to his unfailing light. If I'd done my best to lock him out, he'd banged on the door so loudly and for so long that I'd finally opened it, exasperated, only for him to steal inside and declare himself on the front end of an indefinite stay.

Now all I had to do was let him.

I scooted closer, smiling. The last thought I had before falling asleep was that maybe being married felt different, after all.

34.

Kai woke me at sunrise.

The rain had subsided to a murmur. We dressed in the half-light from the window, but something about the dawn looked different. Wrong.

When we emerged from the shack, I realized why.

The rot had gone, its purple glow vanquished by the rain, which still fell in spears from a steel-gray sky.

The swamp glistened, olive and navy and silver. No purple to speak of. The rain soaked us in moments and stuck Kai's hair to his forehead, but being drenched felt right, somehow. Like a rite of passage that cleansed us, too.

"Ready?" he said.

A knot tightened in my throat. Olivian. He was definitely going to kill me.

But there was no help for it, so I took Kai's hand and nodded, pointing my feet toward home.

~

The seneschal met us in the drive.

His face crumpled when Kai and I emerged from the marsh, but I could tell by the defeated set of his shoulders that he already knew. Of course he did. Nothing else could have cured the rot overnight except the one thing he'd feared above all else.

I raised my chin and headed for him, leaving Kai behind. By the time I reached Olivian, he was on his knees in the gravel, his throat convulsing. I couldn't tell if he was crying. Rain coursed down his cheeks, soaking his beard, plastering his hair to his head.

"You promised," he gasped. A dark abyss lay beneath the accusation. "You *promised* me."

"I know." I got on my knees, too, ignoring the bite of gravel. "I'm so sorry."

He looked wild, his face a tangled mess of grief.

I reached for his hand, then thought better of it. "But she asked me, Olivian. She *wanted* to go. And I couldn't keep her here anymore. I just...couldn't. It wasn't right. I loved her too much to make her stay."

A sob tore from his chest. "I should kill you."

I waited, but he didn't move, and I could tell he didn't really mean it. He just needed to vent his anguish, by any means necessary.

"I brought *something* back, though," I said. "For you."

He just sat there. The light had left his eyes.

I glanced back at Kai, who nodded his encouragement. I eased the dagger from its sheath and offered Olivian the hilt. Rain collected in the channel that ran down the blade.

The seneschal stared, seemingly devoid of even the will to take the knife and bury it in my chest.

Not that I would've let him. "Hold it," I said. "And you can talk to her. Inside your mind."

A glimmer stirred in his life-starved eyes. He palmed the dagger with one massive hand.

His gaze unfocused. Then his body jolted and his eyes slammed shut and he was weeping, truly weeping—great, wrenching sobs that wracked his frame. He curled forward until his forehead hit the ground.

"My sweet girl," he babbled, between heaves. "My baby. My precious daughter."

I knelt there, a wealth of feeling stoppering my breath. I had never seen anyone fall apart so spectacularly, and I couldn't decide what to do. Eventually, I settled for an awkward pat of his back.

"Leave me," he growled. "Leave me with her."

I did.

I went to Kai, who brought me inside. We told the closest steward where to find Vick, then gave the man the keys to free him. Then my husband took me upstairs and undressed me in our room. We drew a steaming bath and washed each other with worshipful intention, which concluded with us making love on the bathroom floor amid a wonderland of reflections. I gazed into the mirrors the entire time. They showed me our joining from a thousand different angles, and it felt like glimpsing the future, like a promise that we would celebrate this way a thousand more times.

When it was over, Kai kissed me and said, "Hideous. Downright painful."

"Awful," I agreed. "It's like you get worse every time."

"Likewise. It beggars belief, honestly."

I laughed. What a stupid joke, and yet I couldn't imagine ever tiring of it. "I guess we'll have to try again."

His eyes glinted. "Poor us. Will the torture never cease?"

We stayed in Oceansgate until after Lunk and Miss Quist's wedding.

They held their ceremony in the library, and this time, the whole household attended. Everyone except Olivian. The seneschal had kept to himself for weeks, haunting the halls with the dagger clutched close, a husk of a man who spent every waking moment conversing with his lost daughter.

I wondered why he hadn't spent this much time talking to Amryssa when she'd been here under his roof, but I couldn't judge him too harshly. Olivian was broken. Beaten down by the brutality of loss in ways I couldn't comprehend and hoped I'd never have to.

But I dared to hope he'd come out of it, someday. That maybe he'd recover, and rebuild Oceansgate. Maybe even sire a new heir, instead of letting his line end in disgrace and ignominy.

On the night of Lunk's wedding, at the nuptial feast, I pulled the big man aside. Someone had hired a musical quartet, and fiddles dueled with one another while the stewards and housemaids danced. This song sounded familiar, and then I realized—it was the one Kai and I had danced to that night in town.

No wonder he'd seemed to know it—he actually *had*. At that point, he'd been here nearly a year.

Behind Lunk, streamers of orange leaves ran along the ceiling. Miss Quist hovered just out of earshot—she couldn't go far, considering the cypress vine that tethered her to her new husband.

Lunk grinned his beautiful, broken-toothed smile at me. "Keymistress."

"Lunk." I smiled back. "Or...Henry, is it? Your real name?"

He bobbed his head. "That's the one my mother gave me, yes. Lunk was the liberators' name for me. All of us had nicknames, there."

"Right. Well, Henry." I rolled the name around in my mouth, testing out the friendly letters. Lunk had never suited him, anyway. He was so much more than that. "I couldn't be happier for you. Can I hug you?"

His eyes crinkled. "Of course."

I squeezed him hard. It was mildly awkward, considering he had one arm leashed to his wife's, but we managed.

"I'm sorry I gave the dagger to Olivian," I said. "Before you could decide about changing anything, I mean."

He shrugged good-naturedly. "Oh, it's all right. I don't think I would've done it, anyway."

"If you ever change your mind, you could always ask him."

He chuckled. "I think he's just as liable to stab me as grant wishes."

"Good point." I grinned. "Probably better not to chance it. At any rate, I wish you two all the happiness in the world."

"And you as well."

We hugged again, and I turned away, intending to go find my husband and spend some time enjoying his gift for rhythm down here before I got to enjoy it again later, in a different way, upstairs. But then a thought struck me and I turned back.

"Henry?"

He paused. "Yes?"

"What was Kai's nickname? When he was with the liberators?"

"The prince," he said easily. "We always called him the prince."

I snickered. "Right. Of course you did."

Because really, what else?

35.

Kai and I left the day after the equinox.

The air carried a crisp edge as we hugged everyone goodbye in the drive. Even the marsh seemed to be seeing us off, the trees undulating in a russet-and-amber farewell.

Henry wept. So did Miss Quist. But I hugged them and promised we'd see them again. That I'd be back to speak with Amryssa from time to time, assuming anyone could pry the dagger from Olivian's hand.

The seneschal didn't attend our send-off. But I caught sight of his bulk filling a second-floor window. When I raised a hand, he only melted backward, into the shadows.

Merron accompanied me and Kai, at least along the Oceansgate road, which my husband insisted we travel on at night, in order to avoid the liberators, who were apparently alive and well under Vick's leadership.

Since the demise of the nightmares, a trickle of curious travelers had ventured into Oceansgate. More than a few had lost their belongings at swordpoint, courtesy of a certain orange-haired asshole.

"What a dick," I told Kai as we lay in our tent one night. "You'd think he would've learned his lesson, after you spared his life."

"He's a ginger." Kai slid one hand behind his head, probably because it made his chest flex in a way that made me breathless. As if he wasn't already guaranteed to be pounced on in about five minutes. "Does it really surprise you that he's also an unrepentant criminal?"

I lay on my side, my head on a hand, and cast a pointed look at his hair.

"Oh, no," he said. "Absolutely not. My hair is *not* red."

"It is. Brown, first, but definitely red, too."

"Don't you dare accuse me of the g-word," he said, haughty. "My hair has *vaguely reddish undertones*. Nothing more."

"Hmm. You look like a ginger to me."

Frosty eyes narrowed. "Say that one more time, and I'll be forced to punish you."

I squished my thighs together. I loved it when he threatened me. So I leaned in, pretended to kiss him, then spoke against his mouth, instead. "Ginger."

He growled, then tackled me, and indeed punished me, swiftly and decisively, in the most gratifying way possible.

We said goodbye to Merron at the crossroads, where the Oceansgate road intersected with the one that led to Hightower.

The bright autumn chill bit at my nape. Merron hugged me, long and heartfelt, then reluctantly shook Kai's hand. A scowl marred his handsome mouth, proof that he'd never warmed to my husband. But I supposed I couldn't blame him.

When Merron backed away, tears burned a path up my throat.

"Oh, don't cry," he said good-naturedly. "You had your chance."

I laughed through a sob. "I absolutely did. And I ruined it, didn't I?"

"You did. Can't win 'em all, I guess." He grinned, but it was edged with sadness. Still, he put on a brave face and took a page from Kai's playbook, winking at me before turning down the road toward Crystal Hollow.

"Birthing hips," I called as his figure shrank. "Remember that."

"How could I forget?" he called back. Then he was gone, just a speck in the scarlet distance.

The wind pushed fallen leaves past my boots as Kai skewed an eyebrow upward. "What was that about? Birthing hips?"

"It's a long story."

"Really." His regard thinned. "Wait. Don't tell me you two used to—"

"*Used* to," I said, stressing the past tense. I probably didn't need to tell him that my history with Merron extended right up until our wedding day.

"Hmm."

"Oh, don't go getting jealous on me, now."

"Jealous? I would never." The breeze ruffled his hair across his forehead in a way that made me itch to smooth it back. "Because in the end, you're mine, fair and square. *He* might not be able to win them all, but I certainly can."

I snorted. "Wow. Arrogant, much?"

"You love it," he said.

"I do, actually. I love *you*."

His half-smile shone. "And I love you, my dark lioness. So, where to?"

I raised my brows. "I get to decide?"

"Of course."

"Fairmont." I didn't even have to think about it. "Your last territory. Your last accent."

He caught my face in his hands and kissed me. "Excellent choice. And after that?"

"Hmm... Hightower, I think. I want to find Amryssa's old tutor. Eliana deserves to know what happened here."

He nodded. "And then?"

I shrugged. "Wherever you want."

"Anywhere?"

"Anywhere."

His brows burrowed together as he thought. "Gray's Reach,

perhaps? We could go to the theatre. We could go out drinking. We could do whatever we want."

I gazed up into the infinite blue of his eyes, into the promise of endless possibility. "I'd like that," I said.

Because this time, the offer sounded perfect.

Thank you for reading! For character art and a deleted (spicy!) bonus scene in which Harlowe gets jealous before Kai's marriage to Amryssa and he…ahem, *reassures* her…please visit **shaylingandhi.com/bonus**.

ALSO BY SHAYLIN GANDHI

Contemporary Romance

When We Had Forever

Love Letters for Other People

Fantasy Romance

Once Charmed, Twice Cursed

Song of the Hundred-Year Summer

ABOUT THE AUTHOR

SHAYLIN GANDHI is a traveler, scuba diver, and pianist. She lives in Denver, Colorado, with her husband, their identical twin daughters, and two rescue dogs. When not finagling words onto paper, Shaylin can be found hiking, biking, scheming up ways to add another stamp to her passport, or ingesting enough coffee to power a small city. Shaylin once spent forty-six days riding her bicycle from the Pacific Ocean to the Atlantic.

She can be found on Instagram or at shaylingandhi.com.

www.ingramcontent.com/pod-product-compliance
Lightning Source LLC
Chambersburg PA
CBHW030524190726
48283CB00006B/1758